Praise for
and her Emma Lord mysteries

THE ALPINE ADVOCATE
"An intriguing mystery novel."
—M. K. WREN

THE ALPINE BETRAYAL
"Editor-publisher Emma Lord finds out that running a small-town newspaper is worse than nutty—it's downright dangerous. Readers will take great pleasure in Mary Daheim's new mystery."
—CAROLYN G. HART

THE ALPINE CHRISTMAS
"If you like cozy mysteries, you need to try Daheim's Alpine series. . . . Recommended."
—*The Snooper*

THE ALPINE DECOY
"[A] fabulous series . . . Fine examples of the traditional, domestic mystery."
—*Mystery Lovers Bookshop News*

THE ALPINE FURY
"An excellent small-town background, a smoothly readable style, a sufficiently complex plot involving a local family bank, and some well-realized characters."
—*Ellery Queen's Mystery Magazine*

THE ALPINE GAMBLE
"Scintillating . . . If you haven't visited Alpine yet, it would be a good gamble to give this a try."
—*The Armchair Detective*

By Mary Daheim
Published by Ballantine Books:

THE ALPINE ADVOCATE
THE ALPINE BETRAYAL
THE ALPINE CHRISTMAS
THE ALPINE DECOY
THE ALPINE ESCAPE
THE ALPINE FURY
THE ALPINE GAMBLE
THE ALPINE HERO
THE ALPINE ICON
THE ALPINE JOURNEY

THE
ALPINE
JOURNEY

Mary Daheim

BALLANTINE BOOKS • NEW YORK

A Ballantine Book
Published by The Ballantine Publishing Group
Copyright © 1998 by Mary Daheim

All rights reserved under International and Pan-American Copyright Conventions. Published in the United States by The Ballantine Publishing Group, a division of Random House, Inc., New York, and simultaneously in Canada by Random House of Canada Limited, Toronto.

http://www.randomhouse.com

Library of Congress Catalog Card Number: 97-97175

ISBN 0-345-39644-8

Manufactured in the United States of America

First Edition: April 1998

10 9 8 7 6 5 4 3 2 1

Chapter One

"VIDA LEFT HER hat." Leo Walsh twirled the maroon pillbox on his fingers and eyed me with wonder.

I stared. "Vida went out?"

My ad manager nodded.

"Without her hat," I said, equally awestruck. Vida Runkel never went anywhere, except perhaps to bed, without one of her eclectic pieces of headgear.

"What gives?" Leo asked, placing the hat on his lap and sitting down in one of the two visitor's chairs in my tiny editorial office. "She's been kind of strange lately, don't you think?"

In the concentrated energy required by *The Alpine Advocate*'s special edition to celebrate the opening of Skykomish Community College, I hadn't had much time to observe my staff's vagaries. But Leo was right. Our House & Home editor definitely had not been herself for the last few weeks.

"Is it that retired air-force guy?" Leo asked when I didn't have a ready answer. "You know"—he made kissing sounds—"heart trouble?"

I shook my head. Vida had been seeing Buck Bardeen for over a year. It appeared to be a comfortable, companionable relationship based on shared interests. Since Vida and Buck were both in their sixties, I had assumed that unbridled passion played no part. But of course I could be wrong.

"She doesn't complain about him," I remarked. "She hasn't been to see Doc Dewey lately, so I don't think it's her health."

"It can't be," Leo said with an off-center grin that made his weathered face almost attractive. Our ad manager is a few years older than I am, and is from Los Angeles, a designation that carries with it a patina of sophistication for rural Pacific Northwestern natives. Leo has known the mean streets of alcoholism and the lean years of small newspapers. He appears to have come to rest in Alpine, settling in among the mountains and evergreens and gray days like an old dog hiding behind the stove. "The Duchess is invincible," Leo added, using the nickname that Vida despised.

Vida *seemed* invincible. She is a big woman, with unlimited energy and boundless curiosity. "If it were family," I mused, "she would have said something."

"God, yes." Balancing the hat in his lap, Leo lighted a cigarette. The match flared dangerously close to the pillbox. "All those damned relatives would drive me nuts. But then I'm not exactly a family man, am I?"

Leo had more or less surrendered his role as husband and father a few years back when his wife left him and his three grown children stopped speaking to him. In recent months, relations with the kids had warmed; it also sounded as if he and his ex could speak via long distance without blistering the telephone wires.

But it wasn't my ad manager's behavior that puzzled me. "Vida is usually so outspoken," I said, trying not to inhale secondhand, lest I create an urge to try smoking firsthand. Again. "I suppose I could ask."

"You could," Leo said, getting up. "I wouldn't. She'd take my head off."

Vida might. While she was quick with opinions, Vida retained a private core that I was reluctant to probe even after seven years as her employer and friend. If she had something on her mind, she'd tell us eventually.

The same thing apparently occurred to Leo. "It'll come out. Vida can't keep anything under wraps forever. That big bazoom of hers would burst." With a chuckle and another twirl for the pillbox, he left my cubbyhole.

I sat back in my chair, pondering the morning mail. Most of the letters addressed to Emma Lord, Editor and Publisher, were junk that could be thrown out without opening. But on this Wednesday in October, I found a letter I'd been waiting for: Mavis Marley Fulkerston, my old friend and former colleague on *The Oregonian*, had sent me directions on how to get to her new home in Portland.

I had been to Mavis's house in suburban Tigard many times when I lived in Portland, but she and her husband had recently bought a condo on the Willamette River. While I knew the city like the back of my hand, it seemed that there were always changes in street directions and new traffic islands and other innovative sources of confusion in my old stomping ground. Studying the hand-drawn map, I smiled. *If you get lost*—get lost! *My instructions are flawless!* Mavis's big scrawl careened across the bottom of the map, almost obliterating one of the street numbers.

I was tucking the map into my handbag when Vida came into the newsroom and headed straight for my office. She was hatless, breathless, and scowling.

"Carla is not to be the only person who has access to the college faculty," my House & Home editor declared. "How dare they!"

"How dare they what?" I inquired, blinking rather fast.

Looming over my desk, Vida didn't deign to sit. "The president, Ignatz whatever his name may be, and that dean of students—he also has a peculiar name. Tailfeathers, or some such. Really, Emma, can't these people call themselves something normal, like Holmgren or Skylstad?"

It wasn't like Vida to be so picky about non-Alpine— which translated as non–Northern European—surnames. "The president is Ignacio Cardenas," I said calmly. "He prefers to be called Nat. And the dean of students is Ryan Talliaferro. We've certainly run enough stories about both of them lately."

Vida snorted. "Carla's stories have run, you mean. She's hogged the entire college coverage from the day construction began. Now that classes have finally started, all I wanted to do was a story on Mrs. Cardenas and Mrs. Talliaferro. It turns out there is no Mrs. Talliaferro, and President Cardenas's secretary—who is Siamese and chews gum—informs me that Mrs. Cardenas doesn't care to be interviewed." With an emphatic gesture, Vida folded her arms across her impressive bust.

"Maybe Mrs. Cardenas is shy," I suggested. I'd met her only once, at an open house the week before fall quarter began. Justine Cardenas was pretty in a faded sort of middle-aged way, a too-thin blonde with nervous mannerisms. "Carla isn't trying to freeze you out of the new campus, Vida. Is that what's been bothering you?"

Vida drew herself up to even more imposing heights. "Bothering me? No, of course not. It doesn't *bother me* in that sense. It annoys me. Alpine has an important new enterprise for the first time in years, and that newcomer hogs it all. Why shouldn't I be vexed?"

Carla Steinmetz had worked on the paper for almost six years, but to Vida, she was still a newcomer. So, no doubt, was I. To a small-town native such as Vida, anyone who wasn't born and bred on local soil would remain an interloper until he or she was buried under it.

"Believe me," I said with feeling, "there'll be plenty of stories coming out of the college in the months to come. Except for the dedication ceremony and my editorials, I haven't written much about it, either. Don't worry about Mrs. Cardenas. By the way, President Cardenas's secretary's name is Cynthia Kittikachorn. And I think Siam has been Thailand for quite a long time now."

"You see?" Vida shot out an accusing finger, as if I alone were responsible for political change in Southeast Asia. "More ridiculous names! Why must countries keep calling themselves something else? Once you name a place, it ought to stay the same."

"Alpine used to be Nippon," I pointed out with what I hoped was an innocent expression. "Carl Clemans changed it on a whim."

"It was no whim," Vida declared, now hotly defending the man who had turned what was once a mere semaphore crossing on the old Great Northern line into a bustling mill town. "The Japanese miners and railroad workers had been gone for years. Alpine was a much more appropriate name for a forest-industry stronghold."

The description was a bit grandiose for the little spot on the map where, even in their heyday, mills could be counted on one hand, and only the inauguration of a ski resort had saved the town from going under after the crash of '29. Alpine's history was as rocky as the crags on which it had been built, its legacy an uncertain, imponderable future.

I shrugged. "That was then, this is now. Maybe we should call ourselves College Place. Given the state of the logging business, Skykomish CC employs more people than the woods do."

The comment rankled Vida as I knew it would. But even in her state of high dudgeon, she wouldn't excoriate the coming of the college. "It's been a godsend," she admitted, simmering down. "But I still want my fair share of stories."

"Granted," I said. "Where's your hat?"

"My . . . ?" Vida's hand flew to her unruly gray curls. "Oh! Wherever is it? I must have taken it off when I was . . . thinking."

I pounced. "About what?"

Vida assumed an uncharacteristically vague air. "Oh . . . next week's page. Now that Mrs. Cardenas has declined to be interviewed," she continued in a firmer voice, "I shall have to come up with some original ideas. Mid-October is always difficult. Too late for back-to-school, too soon for Halloween."

"Health care," I said suddenly. "I was going to do it myself, but since I'll be gone for a long weekend, why don't you write a piece on the difficulty of placing doctors in isolated communities?"

It was the wrong thing to say. Vida bristled: "Isolated? How can you say that when Alpine is situated on one of the major state routes in Washington? We're a virtual crossroads!"

"If you want to drive a mile off Stevens Pass to get here," I said in a more sardonic tone than I'd intended. Noting Vida's irate expression, I held up my hands. "I know, I know. The local economy is my bread and butter. I'm not knocking it. I just think I need . . . to . . . get away."

Vida's strong features hardened. "Perhaps you do. Portland, is it?"

"Yes. Right downtown by the train depot." I heard the apologetic note creep into my voice. Alpine had a downtown and it had a depot, but I knew that Vida was making mental comparisons. Portland was home to half a million people; Alpine could barely count four thousand residents. Vida Runkel didn't like it when Alpine came up short.

"Terrible traffic, I suppose. Crime. Expensive real estate. Drugs. Gangs. Tsk, tsk." Vida pursed her lips. "Your dear friend Mavis," she continued, exhibiting her inexplicable jealousy of my other female friends. "She must be a fascinating person."

"Yes," I agreed, "she's very sharp and a lot of fun. I haven't seen her for two years."

"Mmmm." Vida was gazing not at me, but at the clutter on my desk. "You leave Thursday night?"

"Right after work," I replied. "I'll be back Sunday."

Her head shot up. "I'll go with you."

"What?" Vida possessed her share of brass, but I couldn't imagine her horning in on my weekend with Mavis. "But . . . I don't know if Mavis and her husband have an extra . . ."

Shaking her head, Vida tapped one of the few bare spots on my desk. "I'm not intruding on your visit. I'll drive. I can drop you off in Portland and go on to my destination. I'll pick you up on the way back Sunday afternoon."

I was flabbergasted. "Where are you going?"

But Vida's response was interrupted by Kip MacDuff, our back-shop wizard and county-wide deliveryman, who was dropping off the first editions of this week's *Advocate*. As he handed Vida a copy and dumped a dozen or so on my desk, my House & Home editor made her exit.

"Looking good," the young man said as he always did except upon the occasion when half the paper had been printed upside down. "Carla's pictures of the new campus came out real well, don't you agree, Ms. Lord?"

With a critical eye, I surveyed the tabloid-size front page. The photos in this week's issue were left over from the special edition, but were still worthy of publication. Carla may not know an inverted pyramid from the Sphinx, but she has a gift with the camera.

"Nice," I said, nodding at the administration building and the lineup of students at the bookstore. "The college certainly helps offset the lousy timber business."

Kip agreed wholeheartedly. At twenty-one, he had come of age in the shadow of the decimated logging industry. "I really like my sociology class," he said, grinning at me from a face full of freckles. "Maybe next quarter I'll have time to take more than five credits."

"Maybe you can," I said in a noncommittal fashion. Between putting together the paper, the in-house job printing, and the Wednesday deliveries, Kip logged about thirty hours a week. At forty-six, I find myself increasingly amazed at the younger generation's lack of endurance—and ambition.

I could not, however, criticize my office manager, Ginny Erlandson, who is in her mid-twenties, and recently became the proud mother of a chubby, dour son. The baby, named Brad, was six months old, and Ginny had returned to work right after Labor Day. She had been gone five months, and during her absence we had made do with a series of temporary help that had included an alcoholic CPA from Snohomish, a scatterbrained former schoolteacher from Monroe, a disbarred attorney from

Wenatchee, and a local unemployed logger who had been arrested for making sexual advances to three of our paperboys. While Ginny was entitled to another month, I had begged her to come back early: she could bring little Brad with her, I would amuse him, change him, worship and glorify him—whatever was necessary to get his responsible, efficient mother back on *The Advocate*'s premises.

"Mr. Bronsky's been trying to reach you again," Ginny said in hushed tones, as if our former ad manager might waddle up behind her at any moment. "You told me not to put him through."

"That was yesterday"—I sighed—"when we were up against deadline. I could talk to him today. I guess." My tone suggested that I would just as soon put slivers under my fingernails.

Dutifully, I dialed Ed's number. He and his wife, Shirley, had recently moved into their new mansion, a pseudo-Mediterranean villa set in the woods above Railroad Avenue. They were still furnishing the place, but had disdained the advice of an interior decorator. It had finally dawned on Ed that the inheritance he'd received from an aunt in Cedar Falls, Iowa, wasn't going to last forever.

"We've got to take a meeting," Ed declared after answering on the first ring. "How's this afternoon?"

With Wednesday as our publication day, we usually had a slight lull. Having worked for *The Advocate*, Ed knew the drill. I suggested four o'clock, which should mean that Ed wouldn't want to stay too late, lest he miss a meal.

"What about lunch?" Ed said, and I sensed the anxiety in his voice. "I'll treat."

It was not quite eleven-thirty. His millionaire status notwithstanding, the fact that Ed had offered to pay was so unusual that I agreed.

"See you at the Burger Barn in half an hour," Ed said. "I'll make reservations."

No one has ever made a reservation at the Burger Barn, which, next to the local food bank, is the cheapest source of sustenance in town. With a shake of my head, I hung up the phone and considered my options for next week's editorial. The general election was coming up in November, and I'd been pushing an amendment to the county charter that would allow the sheriff to be appointed, rather than elected. I'd run one more hard-hitting editorial before we went to the polls, but preferred holding off until the last Wednesday in October. For the coming week I'd concentrate on the state legislature's failure to continue programs designed to help depressed logging communities. While the two-year college was intended to reeducate disabled and out-of-work loggers, the tax break intended to encourage new businesses in timber towns had been extended to most of the state. Towns like Alpine and Hoquiam and Darrington and a host of others now had no advantage over their less economically distressed cousins. Future graduates of Skykomish Community College would have new skills and trades, but might have to move elsewhere to apply them.

I had barely dug into my file when Vida returned to my office. She now wore her pillbox, though at a precarious angle.

"I'd like to borrow a map of Oregon," she said, one hand on hip, the other leaning on the doorjamb. "You have a current one in your desk, I believe."

I wasn't sure how Vida knew that. Only the previous

day I'd taken the map out of my aging Jaguar's glove compartment. But if Vida was omniscient, she was also not above peeking in my drawers.

I gave her the map. "Where did you say you were going?" I asked.

"I didn't." She turned on her heel and walked out in her typical splayfooted manner.

Twenty minutes later I was sitting across from Ed Bronsky in a booth at the Burger Barn. He twitched, he fidgeted, he scooted around on the plastic-encased seat until I thought he'd slip off and fall under the table.

"What's wrong, Ed?" I asked after we'd put in our orders. "You seem upset."

"It's *Mr. Ed*," he replied, not looking at me. "I haven't had one nibble from a publisher."

Mr. Ed was his autobiography, which, amid high hopes and unrealistic expectations, he'd started sending to major publishing houses the previous autumn. I'd tried to warn him not to expect too much too soon, but as usual, Ed hadn't listened. Nor had he taken my suggestion that he should try to obtain an agent first.

"I don't get it," Ed said, finally raising his fleshy beagle's face to meet my gaze. "All these so-called celebrities get big bucks for their life stories. What have they ever done that we don't know already? Blab-blab-blab—they're on TV all the time, shooting off their faces. But my story is different—it could be anybody's story—a small-town guy who suddenly finds himself rich. Now that's human interest. Can't those bigshot New York publishers see that? Or are they so caught up in city life that they've lost touch with the real world?"

"I take it you got another rejection," I said, trying not to look like I-told-you-so.

"Knopf." Ed hung his head. "That makes three. I'm at the end of my rope."

"But not the end of the publishers' listings," I pointed out, trying to be kind.

"That's not the point," he asserted, settling his jowls onto his hands. "It's the way these East Coast bozos have dealt with me. All three of them have sent letters saying the same thing, and I have a sneaky feeling they're some kind of form. Nothing personal, nothing to show they like the writing or the idea or that they even read the manuscript."

"I don't think you need to give up so soon," I said as our waitress approached with Ed's double cheeseburger and my standard burger basket. I was lying, of course; in my opinion, Ed should have given up before he started. But then I *had* read the manuscript.

Ed waited until we had been served before he responded. "No, I'm taking a new tack. You've got the back shop up and running. I want you to publish the book."

I'd been afraid of that. "We're not set up for big runs like that," I said, a bit too quickly. "You know what we do—wedding invitations, posters, brochures, handouts. A book—a four-hundred-and-fifty-seven-page book—is way beyond our capabilities."

But Ed shook his head, somehow managing to dislodge mustard from his chin in the process. "You could do it. It's just a matter of gearing up. I'll talk to Kip. We'll go fifty-fifty on the profits."

"Whoa." I practically choked on a french fry. "It doesn't work that way. From what I've heard in talking to some of my former colleagues who've had books published, authors get ten percent at most. We couldn't do a hardcover, we don't have a bindery. You'd have to pay us to print the book and absorb the other out-of-pocket costs."

"Such as?" Ed interrupted.

"Cover design, copy editing, photos—whatever." I was speaking off the top of my head. I really didn't know what was involved except that I wished it wouldn't be me. "Then you'd have to figure out how to distribute it. Your profit would come out of the actual copies sold. Once we printed *Mr. Ed*, we'd be out of it."

Ed chewed on his pudgy thumb. "How much?"

I shrugged. "Ask Kip. As I said, I'm not sure we could do it at all. He'd have to figure our cost and then calculate a reasonable profit. It'd get pretty complicated," I added in a dark tone. I was well aware that Ed had problems with complications.

"Hunh." Ed took a big bite of cheeseburger and chewed noisily. "Is Kip around this afternoon?"

"No. He's delivering the papers. Once he's done, he usually doesn't come back on Wednesdays."

Ed chewed some more. "Okay, I'll drop by tomorrow, around ten. Be sure and tell him that."

"I will." Suddenly I felt for Kip, who was young, naive, and probably putty in Ed's beefy hands.

But most of all, I felt for me. Disaster lurked around the corner, and its name was *Mr. Ed*.

At four-thirty on Thursday I was ready to leave. Just as I was about to tell Vida, the phone rang. It was Sheriff Milo Dodge, my longtime friend and current lover.

"Did you say you were going out of town this weekend?" Milo asked in his laconic voice.

"Yes, about six times," I replied a trifle testily. "I'm leaving immediately."

"Oh." Milo sounded disappointed. Worse yet, from my

perspective, he sounded surprised. "I was going to come over tonight. I guess not, huh?"

"Not." I tried to keep the annoyance out of my voice. "I'll be back Sunday night."

"That's not good for me," Milo said, and I could see him shaking his head and stretching his long legs out on his desk and cradling his coffee mug in his big hands. "I've got to go to Bellevue to see my son. I might be late getting back."

When Milo and his wife had divorced several years ago, Old Mulehide, as he called his ex, had been granted custody of their three children. All were now grown, and Old Mulehide was remarried. One of the two daughters had also married, but the other girl and her brother were still in college, if on an irregular, desultory basis.

"I might be late, too," I said. "Call me Monday."

"Why do you have to leave so early?" Milo asked in a slightly irked tone. "You'll get into rush-hour traffic on I-5."

I knew what Milo was thinking, and it annoyed me: our physical relationship, which had begun some eighteen months earlier, was predicated on Milo's masculine whims. When he felt like making love, I was supposed to be available. When I felt like making love, he went fishing. Or so it seemed to me. Our friendship, which had been deep and true and real, seemed to have deteriorated from the moment we had fallen into each other's arms.

"It's a long drive, and we'll be going against traffic," I countered.

"*We'll?*" The word sounded strained. "I thought you were going by yourself."

At least Milo had remembered that much, if not the departure time. "Vida's driving. She has to go to Oregon, too, and she's dropping me off in Portland."

"Vida's going to Oregon?" Milo sounded flabber-gasted, for which I didn't quite blame him. "Why?"

"I don't know," I answered truthfully. "She hasn't said. Look, she's waiting for me. We have to stop at my house so I can drop off the Jag and grab my luggage. I'll talk to you Monday."

"Okay." There was a heavy sigh. "Have fun." The sheriff sounded as if he were wishing I'd catch plague.

Vida and I were on the road in her big Buick by five o'clock. We planned to stop for dinner at the Country Cousin in Centralia. I had made up my mind not to ask any more questions until we were seated in the restaurant. Thus we engaged in chitchat for the first leg of the trip, mostly about Ed and his awful book. Kip was supposed to spend part of his weekend figuring out if the project was feasible. Vida provided dire warnings, all of which I already understood.

When at last we pulled off I-5 around seven-thirty, I waited until we were served before I delicately probed into the reason for her journey. Vida, who was wearing the most god-awful green felt hat with what looked like turkey feathers, gave me her gimlet eye.

"Ernest has family in Cannon Beach," she said after a long pause.

Ernest was her husband who had been dead for almost twenty years. There were many Runkels in Alpine, as well as Blatts, who were Vida's own blood kin. My House & Home editor discussed them freely and often. Indeed, I knew most of them by now, though I was still occasionally surprised when a shirttail relation surfaced.

"I didn't realize that," I said in what I hoped was an innocent tone. "Have I heard you speak of them before?"

"No," Vida said, and speared a leaf of iceberg lettuce from her salad.

"Are they close?" I inquired.

"No." Vida nibbled on a bread stick.

I tried a slightly different approach. "Cannon Beach is a lovely little resort town."

"Is it?" Vida seemed disinterested. "Do you think," she continued after an awkward pause, "that Carla is seeing that Talliaferro person from the college?"

I didn't know and, for the moment, didn't care. But for the rest of the journey, I got absolutely nothing more out of Vida about the Runkels who dwelled in Cannon Beach. It was unlike her, and I was worried.

Chapter Two

MAVIS'S WELCOME WAS warm if flippant, typical of her exuberant, irreverent personality. She was almost ten years older than I, and her husband, Ray, had recently retired from the advertising department at Jantzen. Their newly acquired condo was situated on the Willamette River, with the Broadway and Steel bridges on either side, rather like bookends. With their three children grown and on their own, the Fulkerstons had shed themselves of all but their most cherished furnishings from the old split-level, and acquired some tasteful antiques.

"Our original stuff was almost antique," Mavis said as we sipped cognac in the comfortable living room with its splendid view of the river traffic. "Officially, that is. But who needs a bunch of Sixties crap that looks like it came off a bad mushroom trip?"

I admired a rewoven Turkish carpet, a Queen Anne breakfront, a Japanese screen, and a small but enchanting Etruscan carving of a stag. "I envy you. I'm lucky to have the basics. Weekly newspapering is no way to get rich."

"It is if you own a string of them," Mavis said. "I'll bet Tom Cavanaugh isn't complaining. How is he, anyway?"

The mention of my onetime lover and the father of my son made me flinch. I hadn't spoken to Tom in almost

17

two years. The brief resumption of our affair had come to a dead end when he reneged on his promise to divorce his rich but nutty wife, Sandra.

"I don't know," I said, trying to sound casual, and failing. "I suppose he suffers losses like anybody else in the business these days. But at least he has Sandra's family fortune to keep him in Brooks Brothers suits and Beluga caviar."

"Well." Unlike some people, Mavis wasn't embarrassed by her question or my response. "It sounds like you two aren't an item anymore. But then you never were when we worked together at *The Oregonian*." She laughed, and turned to her husband, who was looking bemused. "Emma kept Mr. Cavanaugh a deep, dark secret until one night after work I got her gassed at Trader Vic's."

"Devious," Ray remarked with good humor. He's a man of few but measured words who prefers to let his wife do most of the talking. Or maybe he has no choice. "I always figured that was how you got your interviews for the paper."

"Sometimes." Mavis shrugged. She is a small, athletic brunette with gold highlights in her shoulder-length hair. "I wasn't devious enough to get a deal on this condo, though. Last winter when the river rose as high as we'd ever seen it, some of these places were flooded. We'd already had our eye on them, so Ray and I figured the prices might come down. They didn't."

Ray's lean, homely face wore an ironic expression. "In some cases, the prices went up. But that was mostly the rentals. These units aren't all condos."

"But what a great setting," I said enthusiastically, grateful that the conversation had veered away from Tom. "You're close to everything, and the view is terrific."

Mavis nodded, one hand gesturing toward the window, where we could see the lights of a small freighter moving against the backdrop of the new Rose Garden sports arena and the older Portland Coliseum, which had been dubbed the Glass Palace. "It constantly changes. We watch the ebb and flow of the city. And then there are the trains behind us and all the traffic that goes over the bridges."

"In Alpine, I see trees and an RV parked across the street," I said in mock self-pity. It wasn't quite true. On a clear day, I could also see Mount Baldy and the surrounding foothills from my cozy log house.

"Alpine must be pretty," Ray put in.

"It's a pretty setting," I admitted. The town itself was another matter. There were too many storefronts boarded up in the small commercial district, too many ramshackle frame houses with tin roofs, too much junk left lying on overgrown lawns, too much rural blight, which shriveled the souls of local residents and made hope as elusive as the spotted owl that had helped bring about Alpine's hard times.

Mavis was offering the brandy bottle, but Ray and I both refused. "I wanted to meet Veda—or is it Vida?" She paused for the correction before continuing. "You should have brought her in for a drink."

"Vida still had that long drive out to Cannon Beach," I said, avoiding Mavis's cat's eyes gaze. "She was anxious to get going." It wouldn't do to mention that Vida had practically thrown me out of the Buick in her haste to head for the coast.

Ray was on his feet, stretching and yawning. "Golf tomorrow. I'm heading to bed. Good to see you again, Emma." He gave me a friendly pat on the shoulder and kissed Mavis. "Don't talk all night."

After he had left the room, Mavis laughed in her throaty manner. "He's the world's worst golfer. In thirty-five years he hasn't broken ninety. But he likes to pretend." The green-and-gold-and-brown cat's eyes glimmered at me. "So do you. What's up with Cavanaugh? I thought you'd gotten back together, if briefly."

"We did, but it's been a while." Mavis knew all about how I'd excised Tom from my life when I discovered I was pregnant with Adam some twenty-four years ago. Tom had resurfaced a year or so after I bought *The Advocate*, and finally met our son. Despite Tom's avowals of unceasing love for me, he couldn't quite cut the deformed bonds that tied him to Sandra. He called it honor, I called it cowardice, and the truth was probably somewhere in between. I knew Tom and Adam kept in touch, which was a good thing. I'd been wrong to turn father and son into strangers. But after a quarter of a century I'd finally stopped loving Tom. I had, I really had. I'd said it so often that it must be true.

I said it again to Mavis, who, typically, did not comment. My old friend is quick to speak her mind, unless the matter at hand is serious. Then she mulls and waits and eventually pounces. "So how's Adam?" she inquired. "Is he still thinking of becoming a priest?"

"Yes, he is," I answered, trying not to notice the skepticism on Mavis's face. "He's finally finishing his degree at Arizona State. After the first of the year he expects to enroll in a seminary somewhere in California. He and Ben are working on it."

"And you resent that," Mavis said with her usual acuity. "Your brother has confiscated your son."

"I don't know squat about seminaries," I retorted. "Ben does. He's a priest."

"It's too bad he's a Catholic priest." The cat's eyes

danced. "Now, if you were all sensible Episcopalians like us, Adam could be a priest and still get married."

Over the years Mavis and I had engaged in good-natured banter about each other's religious preferences. But when it came to Adam's decision to enter the priesthood, I seemed to have lost my sense of humor.

"It could still happen," I said defensively. "A married Catholic priesthood may be down the road."

"A long, bumpy road," said Mavis, polishing off her brandy. "You should live so long. So should Adam."

"I just hope he's sure," I said. "He's changed majors and colleges so often that I can't really believe he's got a vocation."

"Once he's in the seminary, he'll find out." Mavis uttered a small laugh. "We never think our children know what they're doing. Look at our three—just because Jeff liked to scuba dive, he decided to become an oceanographer. Ray and I thought he was nuts. But he's down there in San Diego, loving it. And Brent wanted to make movies, which really struck us as harebrained. He'll never get to Hollywood, but he's happy as a clam producing films for the City of Portland."

I smiled, recalling the Fulkerston boys as little kids who couldn't have been more different: Jeff was an obstreperous, fidgety child who, if the condition had had a name in the Seventies, probably suffered from Attention Deficit Syndrome. Brent was shy, withdrawn, almost introverted, yet gifted with tremendous imagination. But it was Mavis and Ray's daughter, Jackie, who I knew best. I had stayed with her and her husband, Paul Melcher, in Port Angeles three years ago. The baby that Jackie had been carrying that summer was now working his way through the Terrible Twos.

"They're all fine," Mavis responded in answer to my

question about the Melcher ménage. "Little Rowley is a terror, but he'll get over it. Maybe. It's a good thing Jackie has so much energy. When she isn't down in the dumps, that is." Mavis made a face.

Jackie was a combination of her brothers, exuberant one minute, morose the next. I'd hoped that motherhood would put her on a more even keel, but apparently it hadn't. "I'm sorry they may have to move," I remarked. "They had such wonderful plans for that old house Paul inherited in Port Angeles."

Mavis shrugged. "You know all about timber towns. ITT Rayonier is closing the pulp mill, and Paul's probably out of a job, along with three hundred and sixty-five other people. He's hoping that with his engineering degree, he can find something else in the area, especially if the site is converted into some kind of similar, downsized operation. But right now everything's up in the air."

"That's rough," I said with feeling, and leaned back against the peach-and-plum-striped sofa. "We never stop worrying about our kids, do we?"

"Nope." Mavis stared out through the big picture window, where a sleek pleasure craft passed close to the riverbank. The city sparkled around us, lights like fireflies dancing among the gentle hills. Even after dark, Portland seemed alive. In Alpine, the clouds come down over the mountains, and sometimes the only sound is the lonely whistle of a freight train, crying like an abandoned child. The lights of logging towns are going out in many ways.

"So," Mavis said after a long pause, "tomorrow we'll head downtown and you can see all the changes since you lived here. We'll drive by the Rose Garden where the Blazers play and maybe stop at Lloyd Center. Then, if we have time, we can go to a special place made for middle-aged mamas like us."

"Which of the bars on Burnside do you mean?" I asked with a smirk.

Mavis smirked right back. "Actually, I was thinking of the Shrine of Our Sorrowful Mother. But come to think of it, I like your idea better."

On Saturday, we did everything we'd intended to do except the shrine and the bars. By five o'clock we were still at Lloyd Center, trying on shoes. We were supposed to meet Ray for dinner at six.

"We're going to be late," Mavis announced, staring at her feet, which were presently shod in expensive brown suede pumps. "If I buy these—and I don't think I can help doing it—I'll need a purse to go with them, and I have to have it now."

"But don't we have a reservation for six at Jake's?" I asked, wiggling my toes around in semisensible navy flats that were reasonably suited to my informal Alpine lifestyle.

"Jake's is so jammed on weekends that you never get seated on time. I'll call Ray from here and tell him to hold down the fort for half an hour. Besides," she added with a faint leer, "we still haven't discussed your love life."

"Whatever that may be," I murmured, thinking of Milo half-asleep on my sofa after a ten-hour day chasing speeders and breaking up domestic brawls.

Our salesman returned, bearing yet another half-dozen enticing boxes. Mavis, who has the usual brass of a long-time journalist, waved away the new arrivals and asked to use the phone at the sales desk.

"I'm taking these," she said, tapping her toes. "The black lizardy ones, too."

I hemmed and hawed. The salesman, who was very young and earnest, trotted out two more pairs in my size. "You might think green this fall," he said. "Lime is the new neutral."

I started to protest, but upon closer inspection, lime looked rather nice. There was no doubt in my mind that I'd be the first woman in Skykomish County with lime shoes.

If Mavis could buy two pairs of shoes, so could I. "Let's try them," I said.

They fitted as well as the navy pair. But where were my basics? "Maybe," I temporized, "I should try on the black ones with the patent toe again."

I was parading around in front of the mirror when Mavis returned, looking worried. "Ray says there's a message on our machine from your friend Vida. She won't be coming back to Alpine Sunday, and wants you to call her and let her know if you can make other arrangements. Here's where you can reach her, at least until six." Mavis handed me a Nordstrom sales-associate card on which she'd scrawled the number.

I lacked the brass to use the desk phone. Besides, it was long distance, and given Vida's message, I sensed that privacy was required. Flustered, I told our salesman I'd take all three pairs of flats, handed him my credit card, and rushed off to find a pay phone.

I was so flustered by Vida's message that it took me three tries to get through. When I finally heard the phone ringing at the other end, a charming voice informed me that I had reached the Ecola Creek Lodge. After asking for Vida, I heard another three rings before she answered.

"What's wrong?" I demanded in an anxious voice.

"It's a family emergency." Vida sounded like an automaton.

"What kind?"

"The worst kind."

I sucked in my breath. "You mean . . . ?"

"Can you take a train to Seattle and find a ride to Alpine?" The brittle tone in Vida's voice was unfamiliar.

"I could rent a car," I said doubtfully. "I could rent it here, for that matter, and drive. . . . Vida, what's the matter? Can I help?"

There was such a long silence that I thought we'd been disconnected. "No." Her voice was now hushed. "No," she said more firmly. Then, added on a rollercoaster of emotions: "I don't think so."

"Vida, I'm coming to Cannon Beach. Tonight. Where is this place you're staying?"

"No, no, no." The last *no* was almost inaudible; I could picture Vida propping the phone against her shoulder, whipping off her glasses, and frantically rubbing at her eyes. "I couldn't ruin your weekend with Mavis."

"We've already talked our heads off," I asserted. "If you've got problems, I want to help. Just give me directions. I'll have dinner with Mavis and Ray, pick up my stuff at their place, and rent a car. They must have a drop-off in Cannon Beach—it's a tourist town."

"Really, Emma, I don't think . . ." Vida sounded fretful.

"Directions, please."

Reluctantly, Vida gave them. They were easy, since the Ecola Creek Lodge was right on the first turnoff into Cannon Beach. She warned me, however, that she was going out for a while and wouldn't be back until ten.

"That's okay," I assured her. "By the time I eat and get the car, it'll be about that time before I get to Cannon

Beach. See you soon." I rang off before Vida could change her mind.

Mavis was disappointed, but understanding. "You're sure she's not exaggerating whatever's going on?"

"No," I answered. "Vida's not like that. Besides, this whole trip of hers has been very mysterious. There's something amiss, no doubt about it."

"Cannon Beach," Mavis said in a thoughtful voice. "In the off-season, it's a very small community; maybe twelve, fifteen hundred people. It seems to me there was something in the news lately, but I can't quite . . ." She stopped at a traffic light and rested her elbows on the steering wheel. Having purchased five pairs of shoes and one handbag between us, we were now headed for downtown and Jake's venerable seafood restaurant. "I don't remember," Mavis admitted. "It's a funny thing—once I got out of the business, I sort of stopped being engrossed in the news. Otherwise, I found myself getting so caught up that I wanted to rush out and interview people and make a dozen phone calls and kick the living crap out of whoever was covering the story I was following."

I nodded. "An occupational hazard. I still feel that way about stories in the met dailies. I'm stuck with reduced timber sales and Highway 2 closures and the high-school football team's latest losing season."

"You've had at least a couple of juicy homicides, though," Mavis pointed out as we crossed yet another of Portland's many bridges.

"More than a couple. Too many for Alpine." The big black headlines were no solace when I knew the victims personally. "Luckily, we've gone for over a year without a murder."

Luckily for Alpine. But, as it turned out, my own luck wouldn't hold.

* * *

I arrived in Cannon Beach at ten-thirty, snaking down the exit off Highway 101 on a narrow, dark road that wound among dense trees. The green Ford Taurus I'd rented in Portland had handled nicely during the ninety-minute drive to the coast. The first sign of civilization was the Ecola Creek Lodge, tucked in between a three-way fork. I spotted Vida's big white Buick at once and pulled into the adjacent spot. Most of the complex was old, but well maintained, with the contiguous brick-and-wood-frame units facing either the parking lot or the street. I figured that Vida was staying on the neatly land-scaped street side where I could see the Pacific Ocean beyond what appeared to be a park.

During this off-season only half the lights were on in the motel. Most of the units, including Vida's, had the drapes pulled, though I could see into one of them where a senior-citizen foursome played cards. The fog was coming in, and I felt a damp chill in my bones as I went up the short walkway to number 11. Vida responded to my knock so quickly that I thought she'd probably been standing by the door.

"Emma!" she exclaimed, as if she hadn't expected to see me. "Come in, come in. I really wish you weren't here."

I didn't know whether to believe her or not. "So what's up?" I asked, setting down my suitcase and getting out of my duffel coat.

Vida didn't answer directly. The room smelled of salt air and I could just make out the sound of the surf in the distance. "I'll make tea," Vida said, not looking at me but in the vicinity of an older-model television set with rabbit ears. "There's a kitchen, so I bought some provisions."

Ordinarily, when I'm at Vida's home in Alpine, I

follow her into the kitchen and we drink our tea there. But I sensed that she didn't want me to join her—yet. There was a small mirror next to a door that led into a hall where I could see the bathroom. I glanced at my image, saw my disheveled chestnut hair, bleary brown eyes, and slightly drawn round face. It had been a long day.

I settled into an armchair, shedding my shoes and working out the kinks caused by the long drive. The unit appeared to be a small suite, its living room outfitted with well-worn but comfortable furniture and a fireplace. A painting above the brown tweed sofa showed, predictably, large waves crashing against the shore. The room was warm, almost too warm, and I wondered if the sofa turned into a bed, or if I would have to sleep with Vida. We'd never traveled together before, and it occurred to me that she might snore.

I occupied my brain in this unproductive manner for at least five minutes. An occasional sound emanated from the kitchen, where Vida apparently was waiting for the water to boil. When I was considering unpacking my one small suitcase, she finally came back into the living room bearing two mugs.

"I'll fetch sugar and milk," she said, still avoiding eye contact.

I waited. Just as Vida reappeared the phone rang. It was sitting on a table between my chair and the sofa. "Shall I?" I inquired.

"I'll get it." Vida set the milk pitcher and a bowl of sugar cubes on the coffee table, then flung herself across the sofa and picked up the receiver. "Yes? . . . Yes, she did . . . No, Stacie, I really don't think I should do that now . . . You already have a houseful . . . Yes, of course . . . I'll be there early . . . Please don't fuss . . .

We'll work this out ... And do tell Molly to stop crying ... Very well, dear. Good night."

In a somewhat ungainly fashion, Vida sat down on the sofa. "Well." She continued to stare straight ahead.

There was no point in prodding her. I stirred my tea and kept quiet. At last Vida turned to me, her gray eyes troubled behind the big glasses with the tortoiseshell frames.

"Have you ever heard me mention Ernest's brother, Everett?" she asked in a tight voice.

I tried to remember. Vida talked about so many of her relatives, both shirttail and otherwise. "I don't think so," I finally said. "I've heard you speak of an Elmo and an Edward, but maybe not Everett."

Vida gave a brief nod. "If I didn't speak of him, it was because he no longer existed in Ernest's family. Everett, you see, was the black sheep." She nodded again, as if to underscore Everett's unworthiness.

"But he exists?" I asked, trying hard not to smile. To my knowledge, Ernest Runkel's family had always been pillars of the community. Ernest's father, Rufus, had been one of the risk takers who'd built the ski lodge that had helped save Alpine.

"Oh, yes. He exists." Vida sipped her tea, then heaved a deep sigh. "Everett—he was called Ev by the family, but insisted on calling himself Rett, which explains quite a bit, if you ask me—was the youngest of the six children. When he was seventeen, he quit school and ran off to join the coast guard. That was 1949, and he ended up serving in the Korean War. After he was discharged, Ev—or Rett, if I must call him that—married a woman named Rosalie and settled in Cannon Beach. Ev—Rett—never returned to Alpine." Vida uttered the words as if

she'd announced that her brother-in-law had turned his
back on the Pearly Gates.

"So he lives here?"

"Yes. He and Rosalie were divorced some years later.
There was a brief period before Ernest died when ...
Rett—or perhaps it was Rosalie—sent Christmas cards. But
after my husband met his unfortunate end, I stopped hearing from them, and so did the rest of the family. I suspect
it was about then that Rosalie left Rett."

I was well acquainted with the demise of Ernest
Runkel, which had involved an ill-fated attempt to go
over Deception Falls in a barrel. "So you've come to
Cannon Beach because of Rett?" I asked, wondering
when Vida would get to the point.

"Not exactly." Vida stroked her upper lip. "Rett and
Rosalie had two children, Marlin and Audrey. Marlin is a
bit peculiar, I'm told, and lives alone up in the hills above
the town. Audrey married a man named Gordon Imhoff
twenty years ago, and lived in San Francisco for a time.
Then she and Gordon moved back here with their three
children—Derek, Stacie, and Molly."

I finally heard a name that rang a bell. "That was
Stacie who called just now?"

"Yes. She's a high-school senior, a pretty thing, but
lacking in self-discipline. They live at the other end of
the town, almost to Tolovana."

I recalled how the spur from Highway 101 cut through
Cannon Beach, then rose to zigzag above the ocean until
it dropped almost to sea level. Houses were built in the
pockets of rock and along the steep hillsides and, in
some cases, jutted out on stilts. The perches had always
struck me as precarious, but the views must have been
spectacular.

"It must be lovely," I remarked. "Do they all enjoy living in a beach town?"

Vida's face had turned grim. "That's the problem, you see. They're not all living."

I must have looked stupid; certainly I felt that way. "What do you mean?"

The rumble of a stereo's bass throbbed as a car passed outside. "Really, I don't know. . . ." Vida bit her lip.

While I was accustomed to my House & Home editor's long-winded family histories, her sudden reticence was uncharacteristic.

"Vida," I began in a reproachful tone, "I interrupt my vacation and drive all this way so that you could turn into a clam?"

The gray eyes fixed on my face, though the light struck the tortoise-framed glasses in such a way that all I could see was glare. "Audrey was murdered last month, and her husband, Gordon, has disappeared," Vida said in a flat, emotionless voice. "That's why I came to Cannon Beach."

Chapter Three

Vida explained that she had seen the story on our wire service. She hadn't recognized Audrey's married name, but knew how small Cannon Beach was, and that there couldn't be too many Audreys who were forty-three years old. She had made some phone calls and discovered that Audrey's maiden name was indeed Runkel.

"I waited a few days before I called the house," Vida recounted. "I could have telephoned Rett, but I didn't know if he still lived here, or even if he was alive. There was no listing for him, you see. So about three weeks ago, I called the Imhoff residence and asked for Gordon. It didn't seem right that no one from Ernest's family had inquired or offered condolences."

It also didn't seem like Vida to ignore anything as intriguing as murder. Her curiosity must have been at detonation level. No wonder she had been acting oddly at work.

"Did you consult with any of the other Runkels?" I asked innocently.

"Well . . ." Vida's mouth twisted. "No. The surviving members of Ernest's generation are either gaga or have no sense. My sister-in-law Evelyn—she's a Gustavson, you may recall—is the best of the bunch, and she talks so

32

much that I can't ever get a word in edgewise. Evie simply tires me out."

I couldn't imagine such a thing. But of course I didn't say so, and thanked my lucky stars that my encounters with Evelyn Gustavson Runkel had been few and brief.

"Did Gordon tell you what had happened to Audrey when you finally called?"

"No. He'd already disappeared. I spoke first to Derek, who is—what? nineteen, twenty?—and somewhat surly." Vida's mouth turned down in disapproval. "I got very little information from him, but Stacie was more forthcoming. The wire-service story said only that the body of a forty-three-year-old Cannon Beach woman named Audrey Imhoff had been found at the beach near her home. Foul play was suspected, local authorities investigating. There were no details, and there was never a follow-up story.

"Stacie—who really had no idea who I was—told me her mother had been hit over the head. It seems that Audrey was given to nude swims in the middle of the night, after everyone else had left the beach. Naturally, Stacie thought it was a sex maniac, and perhaps it was. But the day after the funeral service, Gordon disappeared. At that point Stacie broke down, and said that she knew that if the police didn't suspect her father before, they must now. I offered to come down then, but she hung up. I waited until the next day to call back, and got Molly instead. She's only fourteen, but seems more sensitive and sensible than either Stacie or Derek. I asked how the three of them were getting along, and she said they were all right. Their grandmother, Rosalie, had remarried some years ago and moved a few miles down the cost to Manzanita, but she's been staying with the children off and on. Molly said that she and Stacie were going to school and getting their homework done and doing as well as could be expected. Derek, unfortunately, has brought his girlfriend to live with him. Her name, I believe, is Dolores."

Vida paused for breath. In the silence, I could hear the thrum of the ocean and the moan of a foghorn. "What about Rett?"

"He's here." Vida grimaced. "I went to see him this afternoon. He wouldn't let me in."

"And his son, Marlin?"

Vida shook her head. "Uncle Mar—as the children call him—is even stranger than his father."

"Have you spoken with the law-enforcement officials?"

"No. It's county, the same as Alpine, but the seat is in Astoria. That's one reason I'm staying on—I want to drive up there Monday and speak with the sheriff or whoever is in charge of the case."

Off the top of my head, I calculated that Astoria was about thirty minutes away. Located at the most northwestern tip of Oregon on the mouth of the Columbia River, it was the seat of Clatsop County. I had once had a contact there in my days on *The Oregonian*.

"I used to know Bill Wigert," I said. "He was in charge of their forensics division."

"Really?" Vida brightened. "Is he still there?"

"I don't know. That was seven years ago." I leaned back in the chair, considering my options. Tomorrow was Sunday, and if memory served from the last time I was in Cannon Beach a decade ago, I'd have to attend Mass in Seaside at Our Lady of Victory. Seaside was ten minutes away, which would cut some time off the trip to Astoria. Bill was an easygoing kind of guy, and might—just might—let Vida and me intrude on his Sunday.

The local phone book included Astoria listings. Wigert,

W. L., was still there. "I'll call him in the morning," I said, and suddenly yawned.

"Your friend Mavis must have tired you out," Vida said in a prim tone. "No doubt she's a bundle of fun."

"She is, actually. We went shopping." I yawned again.

Vida took another sip of tea, which, like mine, must have grown cold. "You shouldn't have come. I've ruined your visit."

It occurred to me that I should insist that Vida meant more to me than Mavis did, but that wasn't true. I was fond of them in equal measure. Or I should say that if Vida had troubles, I would never leave her in the lurch. That was more honest, yet it wasn't the real reason I'd come to Cannon Beach. I could even say that with the Runkel connection to Alpine, there was a story here for *The Advocate*. If we stretched it, we could run it—depending on what happened next.

"Vida," I finally said, "haven't we been through a lot over the past seven years, murder included?"

"Well, certainly." Behind her glasses, Vida blinked several times. "That happens on a newspaper. And when you live in the same smallish town."

I nodded. "I wouldn't miss this for the world. And I'm not leaving until you do."

For the first time since I arrived, Vida smiled.

The Catholic church in Cannon Beach is made of wood, painted white, and not unlike St. Mildred's in Alpine. It was about two-thirds full on this foggy Sunday morning in October, and I assumed that the attendees were mostly year-round residents.

Vida had gone off in search of a Presbyterian house of worship, warning me that she might take longer, since members of her faith "didn't whisk through their service" in the manner of Roman Catholics.

We had agreed to meet at the Shilo Inn, which is located on the promenade that extends the length of the downtown area. I had dropped off the Ford Taurus before Mass, since, as it turned out, there was no car-rental office in Cannon Beach. Being the larger by far of the two resort towns, Seaside provides many more services and accommodations.

But in autumn, the town takes on a desolate air. There are no kites flying above the beach, the sidewalk bazaars are gone, the pedal carriages no longer clog the narrow streets. In summer, Seaside swarms with pedestrian traffic, T-shirted, shorts-wearing, thong-shod men, women, and children who drift from one souvenir shop to the next, consuming bowls of clam chowder and baskets of fish and chips and sugar and cinnamon-covered pastries called elephant ears. The carousel in the mini-mall never stops, nor does the stream of out-of-state cars, RVs, and campers.

By the time I got out of church and walked the two blocks to the Shilo Inn, the fog had dispersed and the sun was out. Having expected a cool, damp morning, Vida and I were to rendezvous inside the motel's main entrance. I was standing in the wide corridor near the pay phones when a bearded man about my age hurried through the doors and dropped something. He looked like a vagrant, and I wondered if he'd literally get the bum's rush. While the homeless seem always with us, even in Alpine, I suspected that resort towns tended to discourage their presence.

Apparently, the man had lost a quarter, which had rolled behind a terra-cotta planter. Scrambling around on the deep blue carpet, he picked up the coin and went to one of the pay phones.

Vida was the next person to enter the motel. "The

early service at the local Presbyterian church is rather short," she said almost in apology, then spotted the row of phones. "Oh, good. Have you called your friend Bill yet?"

"No. I was waiting for you."

Vida made a beeline for the pay phones, where the man with the heavy beard and longish hair was huddled over the receiver in the last stall. "Let's hope Mr. Wigert is in," said Vida, standing very straight and looking slightly out of place in her Sunday best, which included an off-the-face black straw hat with big black roses.

Bill Wigert was home in Astoria. He remembered me, which was flattering, and expressed surprise that I was in Seaside at this time of year.

"It's Indian summer, all right," he said in that faint drawl that betrayed his Alabama origins. "Can't you leave your woodsy outpost in the summertime when all the other tourists are jammed up along the coast?"

"It's not all pleasure, Bill," I said, trying to position the phone so that Vida could catch some of his half of the conversation. I explained about the alleged Imhoff homicide, and my House & Home editor's family connection. "So what I'm wondering is, could we drive up and talk to you about it? Or were you involved?"

"I was, as a matter of fact," Bill replied. "Sure, come ahead. The wife's gone into Portland for the day to see her sister, and the kids are both away at college. I was going to give the lawn one last mow, but my, my—it can wait until April. Here's how to get to our house. . . . You got a pen or is that a dumb question to put to a newspaper lady?"

It was, of course, though I had to fumble in my purse for a few seconds. An hour later we were inside the Wigert residence, which was a bright blue late Victorian house built against the side of the steep hills that make up most of Astoria. Many of the buildings, both residential and commercial, are painted vivid colors, the result of a movie crew's visit some years ago. Having once suffered through a production company's insistence on several coats of canary yellow for *The Advocate*, I understood the surrender of personal taste.

In 1805, Lewis and Clark had built a log fort nearby, and shortly thereafter, John Jacob Astor set up a key fur-trading post. What was known then as Fort Astoria later became the last stop for weary pioneers on the Oregon Trail. Now it was primarily a fishing port at the mouth of the Columbia River, and home to Clatsop Community College. Many of its ten thousand residents lived a vertical existence on the granite slopes that rose above the river within view of the great bridge that crossed over into Washington state.

"I made coffee," Bill announced after introductions were completed. "It's kind of early for lunch, but I could put some sandwiches together."

Vida and I declined the offer of food. Though I had spoken to Bill many times over the phone, we had never met. My mental picture of him was all wrong—the slightly chubby, balding man I'd imagined gave way to a muscular six-footer with thick iron-gray hair.

"I take it," Bill said after he'd delivered our coffee, "that you weren't close to your niece?" The question was directed at Vida.

"I didn't know her," Vida replied. "In any case, Audrey would have been my husband's niece."

"Okay." Bill folded his hands on his knees and seemed to collect his thoughts. "Then I can be candid—no personal, sensitive feelings involved."

"Certainly," said Vida, at her primmest.

"Audrey Imhoff was something of a free spirit," Bill began, the drawl diminishing as he got down to business. "She did this nude-swimming thing almost every night until about this time of year when the weather changes. The Imhoff house is right on the beach, with a wooden dock built on concrete pilings. According to family members, she'd dive off the dock and swim for about half an hour. Usually this was around one, two in the morning. In the summer, people walk the beach until pretty late." He paused and sipped from a mug that displayed the Astor Column, a tall, slim granite cylinder that crowned the city and commemorated its history. I'd climbed it once when I was a teenager, and had vowed never to do it again.

"On Friday, the thirteenth of September"—Bill paused again, this time to allow us to catch the irony of the date—"Audrey apparently walked out of the Imhoff house, naked as a jaybird. She swam, and came back to the dock. Someone must have been waiting for her, because it was there that she was killed by a blow to the head."

"You mean," Vida said through taut lips, "she was all wet?"

The opposite was true, according to Bill. "Even though she'd dried off by the time she was found, we could tell she'd been in the water. There were traces of kelp and other such residue indicating that she'd already had her swim."

"Who found her?" I asked, sensing the contrast between our grim conversation and the bright blues, greens, and yellows of the living room's cheerful decor.

"Her son, Derek," Bill answered. "He'd come home very late—I think he'd been visiting his girlfriend—and he'd gone to bed. But he didn't really sleep, and got up around eight so he could get to his part-time job at a local grocery store by ten. The kid's nineteen, and no whiz in the kitchen. He peeked into his mother's bedroom to see if she was awake and would make breakfast. Audrey wasn't there, so he started to look around. No sign of Mama. He went outside, and some early-morning walkers were standing around, pointing to the dock. Sure enough, there she was. Derek called the cops."

"Whoa," I said. "Where was Audrey's husband?"

"Good point," Bill said with a quirky smile of approval. "Gordon and Audrey had separated about a month ago. He was living in their shop, the Jaded Eye. It's one of those tourist-oriented places with lots of glass balls and seashells and agate jewelry."

Vida gave a little start. "No one told me," she said, and the words reeked of accusation.

"Told you . . . ?" Bill let the question dangle.

"That Audrey and Gordon were separated. The children presented a remarkably united front." Displeasure radiated from Vida. "It was like a conspiracy."

"Maybe," Bill suggested as the drawl resurfaced, "they had other things on their mind."

Vida shook her head, causing the black roses to bob. "The estrangement is crucial information. I should have been informed."

Bill's broad face appeared amused. "I don't think it was any secret, ma'am. According to half the town, the missus planned to file for divorce shortly."

"Divorce!" Vida cried, as if she'd never heard the word before. "Runkels don't divorce!".

I must have looked puzzled. Rett Runkel was divorced, and even in Alpine, a couple of other Runkels had been married at least twice. "Tell us about cause of death," I said, steering the conversation around to what I hoped might be a less volatile topic.

Bill again assumed his professional air. "It baffled me at first. Death resulted from a severe blow to the head, causing extensive damage to the lining of the brain. I won't go into the details, but there were three such blows in all, which indicates that they were dealt in rage. It's very likely that the first one didn't kill the victim, but we can't be sure. Our next problem was to identify the weapon." Bill's face turned ironic. "We couldn't. It was heavy and pointed and almost certainly made of metal. The closest we could come was something like a harpoon."

I shuddered. "Are you saying that Audrey Imhoff was killed by a blow—or was actually stabbed?"

"Both, in a way," Bill said slowly. "There was a deep puncture as well as fracturing of the skull. The killer either took the weapon with him—or her—or threw it into the ocean. If it had been the latter, we hoped it'd wash up on the tide. But it didn't, and we had to send for divers. So far, no luck. There's too much kelp in that area, for one thing. Whatever it was, it could have gotten tangled and swept away in just about any direction."

"Except the shore," Vida put in.

Bill shrugged. "We can't even be sure of that. If a tourist is walking the beach and finds an odd object, he—excuse me again—or *she* might pick it up. *Or* ignore it. We haven't given up on finding the weapon, but we're not optimistic."

"My, my." Vida was resting her chin on her hands. "It sounds rather vicious, doesn't it?"

"That, as well as premeditated," said Bill, passing the coffee carafe around. "Whatever was used probably wasn't the sort of thing you casually carry out to a dock in the middle of the night."

"You've established time of death?" I asked after thanking Bill for the coffee warm-up.

Bill gazed at me with a bemused expression. "This is one of those cases where, if we had to go by body temperature, rigor, and the usual scientific evidence, we'd come up with about a four-hour time frame. The victim had been swimming in the ocean, which isn't exactly warm; it was night, with the temperature down in the low fifties; she was outdoors. You get the picture." He looked up as a big, rather stiff-legged collie came into the room. "Sit, Spock," Bill commanded the dog. Spock continued to amble around the room.

"He's old and deaf," Bill said. "Ignore him when he starts sniffing your shoes. Where was I? Oh—but in this case, we learned the possible parameters from the victim's habits, and from Derek Imhoff's evidence. If his mother went swimming between one and two A.M., and he went out looking for her around eight-thirty, then she'd probably been killed between one-thirty and two-thirty A.M. That jibes with our conclusions, but it does narrow the window of opportunity."

Vida gave a short nod. "What you're saying is that once Audrey finished her half-hour swim, she wouldn't lie around the dock. Thus her killer was waiting for her."

"Probably," Bill agreed. "The family members said that as far as they knew, no one ever accompanied her on these moonlight swims."

Vida was quick to pick up on the telling phrase. " 'As far as they knew'? What does that mean?"

Bill registered surprise. "Well . . . it means just that. Gordon and the kids said she always went alone."

But Vida was shaking her head. "No, I'm afraid it doesn't mean that precisely. The implication is that

Audrey might have gone swimming with someone she wouldn't have mentioned to her family."

Bill chuckled richly. "Damn, ma'am, you're sharp! You've heard about the Damon kid?"

Now it was Vida who looked surprised. "Who?"

A disconcerted look crossed Bill's face, and he turned to me. "I'm not sure where I stand here, Emma. Is this official for a newspaper story, or is it just family?"

I recognized Bill's problem. He was about to repeat hearsay. "It's just family," I asserted. "Even with the Alpine connection, we wouldn't run more than a paragraph reporting Audrey's death. Next of kin, how related, that sort of thing."

Maybe it was my reassurance, or perhaps Bill remembered that in the past he'd been able to depend on my discretion. Whatever the case, he relaxed. "Okay. It seems that Audrey had been seeing a much younger man, which happens these days. She was a fine-looking woman, as you know."

"We don't know," I put in.

"I've seen photographs," said Vida.

"Oh—that's right, I forgot." Bill gave himself a little shake. "So she and this Damon kid—he's twenty-two or so—had something going this summer while he worked as a general handyman for one of the big motels along the beach. The investigating officers have sort of ruled him out as a suspect, because he's in law school at Willamette University in Salem and left Cannon Beach before the murder."

Adjusting her glasses and her hat, Vida asked if the sheriff's department was making progress.

"Define progress," Bill replied dryly. "You know about Gordon Imhoff leaving town?"

"Yes," Vida said in a worried tone. "It seems an odd

thing to do. You said he wasn't living at home at the time his wife was killed?"

"That's right," Bill said as the old collie settled next to me and began to nose around my shoes. "The shop that the Imhoffs owned has been closed. A part-timer tried to keep it going after Audrey died and Gordon took off, but she couldn't manage by herself, even when the place isn't real busy this time of year."

I reached down to stroke the dog's head. "Do we get the impression that Gordon is the main suspect?"

Bill lifted one shoulder. "You always have to look at the spouse in cases like this, especially when the marriage is in trouble. We put out an APB, but so far, no luck."

"Gordon could be anywhere," Vida murmured. "Or nowhere."

"What?" Bill leaned closer.

Vida regarded him with her most owlish expression. "I shouldn't have said that. But when one spouse has been killed and the other can't be found, it might mean—in certain cases—that they're both . . . dead."

Bill suddenly looked grim. "It might. Or maybe it just means that Gordon Imhoff wishes he were."

We had gotten the names of the investigating team from Bill Wigert, but neither officer was on duty until Monday. In an unusually quiet mood, Vida and I drove back to Seaside. It was well after noon, and we decided to stop for lunch. Vida, who is no cook under any circumstances, had served toast for breakfast. Five hours later I was famished.

"Oh, dear." Vida sighed after we had been shown to a table at a busy restaurant called Dooger's. "I don't think they know what they're doing."

"Who?" I asked in surprise. "The local sheriff?"

"Yes. Well, no." With great care, Vida repinned her hat. "I'm sure they're competent, and much better equipped than Milo and his staff. But these people are working at a disadvantage. Cannon Beach is some distance from Astoria. They can't know the town the way that . . ." Her voice trailed off.

I couldn't resist grinning at her. "The way we know Alpine?"

"I suppose that's it. These Astorians, or whatever they call themselves, couldn't be expected to know a town so far away. Goodness, it would be like someone from Monroe trying to understand Alpine. It's simply not possible." Vida looked as if she actually felt pity for the residents of Monroe, which, though it happened to be in another county, was the nearest town of any size along the Highway 2 corridor.

I also had an inkling of what was going on in Vida's brain. My initial reaction was that I didn't much like what she was thinking.

"I'm going to call Leo and tell him neither of us will be back tomorrow," I said, hoping to deter her. "But we'll have to be at work Tuesday to get out this week's edition."

Vida was looking not at me, but at a family of five preparing to leave. "My page is ready to go."

I was irritated. Never in all the years that I'd been the official editor and publisher of *The Advocate* had Vida required the slightest reprimand or even nudge. Indeed, her deep feelings for both the paper and the town had sometimes caused her to nag me when she felt I wasn't putting forth my greatest effort. But now she seemed to be balking.

"You may have last-minute items," I reminded her.

"You usually do, with stories that come in after the weekend."

"Oh, pooh!" Vida exclaimed. " 'Grace Grundle served one of her terrible pumpkin pies to three other dotty old ladies who didn't know the difference and are still picking seeds out of their dentures.' 'Norm and Georgia Carlson entertained the So-and-Sos from Startup Saturday night, despite the fact that both couples have never liked each other since an unfortunate incident involving a giant dahlia at the Skykomish County Fair.' 'The Dithers sisters sat up with a sick horse who probably got that way because they allowed him to watch too much television with them.' " Pausing, Vida glared at me. I cringed, taking in the depth of her concern for the Imhoff tragedy. It wasn't like Vida to speak disparagingly of her news items. "There are times when news can wait," she asserted. "Carla could handle those items, if she has room on my page. But I've always put family first, and I'm not changing this late in life. Have you—perchance— forgotten that I still have five days' vacation coming to me before the year is out?"

I had. Vida usually reserves those five days for Thanksgiving and Christmas. As usual, she had me beat.

"Okay," I said, picking up the menu. "But I'm leaving tomorrow."

"Tomorrow night," Vida put in, now looking smug.

"No. It's a long drive, I'll have to rent another car, and I don't want to pull in at midnight." My face set. "I'll leave around noon."

"As you please." Vida perused the menu. "I should think they'd have lovely clam chowder. That and a small shrimp salad." She set the menu down in front of her, lining it up perfectly between the pieces of her table setting. "You should have kept the other car. We're going to have to split up."

Caught in a dilemma between halibut and chips and a crab Louis, I slapped my menu down in exasperation. "What are you talking about?"

Vida gave a shrug of her wide shoulders. "We'll waste time working together. I'll make a list of people we should interview, and we'll divvy it up between us. Actually, we don't need a list. I'll take the family. You talk to the rest."

"The rest of what?" Now I was definitely cranky as well as hungry. "Vida, we aren't detectives. Anytime that we've been involved in a murder investigation, it's because we were working on the story. This is different, this is another state, another town. These people may be related to you in some tenuous way, but it's not our problem. Until now, you didn't even know that most of them existed."

Under the swooping brim of her hat, Vida's face was without expression. "If memory serves, you helped your friend Mavis's daughter solve a murder case in Port Angeles."

"It wasn't a case," I argued, recalling how Jackie and Paul Melcher and I had dug into the past to solve a family mystery. "The victim had been dead for almost ninety years."

"Since it was Mavis's daughter, it *would* be different." Vida's mouth was so pursed that her lips had practically disappeared.

So, I thought, *that's what this is all about?* Did Vida actually feel a rivalry between herself and Mavis?

I didn't dare mention my suspicion out loud. Nor did I have the opportunity. Vida had unpursed her lips and was speaking again.

"How would you feel if it were your family? Would you simply walk away if you thought your kin might be suspected of murder?"

In defeat, I sighed. "Okay, I'll do what I can while I'm still here. Who do I contact?"

Reaching into her purse, Vida pulled out a slip of paper she had torn from a pad at the Ecola Creek Lodge. Obviously, she had been thinking ahead. I wished I'd known that when I'd turned in the rental car.

"I jotted down a couple of names," she said, shoving the paper in my direction. "You should talk to the neighbors on the south side, the Skellys, John and Marie. The other house next door is vacant—the people who own it come down only in the summer. You might try getting this girlfriend of Derek's to be more forthcoming. Dolores Something-or-other. And now that we've learned more information from your old friend Bill, you should contact the Damon boy in Salem, and also try to find out how far along the divorce plans had gone. Oh, yes— don't forget the woman who worked part-time at the Jaded Eye. I'll get her name from the children."

My head was spinning so fast that I could hardly give my order to the waitress; I ended up asking for the same thing as Vida.

"We'll start by introducing you to the family, just so that you get some background," Vida declared, her strong features now animated.

"Fine," I said in a weak voice. My mind, or what was left of it, was elsewhere, wondering if I could work some kind of deal on the car rental. As it stood, I'd had to pay a drop-off charge.

"Excuse me, Vida," I said, interrupting what had started as another set of instructions, "I'm going to call the car place. I'll be right back."

The green Ford Taurus had already been rented. There was nothing the agency could do except give me their low, low weekend rate, which I suspected wasn't that low despite the fact that I was doing them a favor: the Plymouth Neon they gave me had Washington plates, and in effect, I was returning it for them. Despite their smiling reassurances, I felt I'd gotten screwed.

Our salads had been delivered during my absence. "This is excellent," Vida said, gesturing with her fork. "Don't dawdle. We haven't a minute to spare."

I was inclined to take my time. This was supposed to be a mini-vacation. But Vida had decided otherwise, and as usual, I obeyed.

For once, I should have rebelled, eaten a leisurely lunch, picked up the rental car, and driven home.

But of course I didn't.

Chapter Four

WHEN STUDYING THE current crop of teenagers, I always marvel that I was ever their age. Generally, they seem better looking, more sophisticated, and yet infinitely dopier than I remember being during my own adolescence. I'm aware that even in small towns such as Alpine and Cannon Beach, they face far greater and more complicated temptations than I experienced in a big city like Seattle. Still, I would love to endow them with a sprinkling of wisdom or, as Vida would put it, "good sense."

Derek Imhoff was a gawky six-footer with long sandy-brown hair and somewhat sly brown eyes who lounged on the sofa in such a sprawling, peremptory manner that there wasn't room for anyone else. Stacie, who had blonde hair cascading down her back and wide-set green eyes, most resembled a photograph of her mother that stood on a table made out of a barrel. At fourteen, Molly was still in that nebulous formative stage, not quite full-grown, with features that looked as if they'd been sketched in and shoulder-length auburn hair.

Vida had wasted no time interrogating the youngsters about their parents' estrangement. "You should have told your aunt Vida," she scolded as we sat in the Imhoff living room. The house was a one-story affair, probably a beach cottage that had been added onto over time. There was a good deal of clutter, not just from the absence of mother and father, but, I suspected, from the family's apparent avocation for collecting all manner of flora, fauna, objets d'art, and junk. Dozens of seashells, Japanese floats, rock-filled bottles, and pieces of driftwood mingled with copper etchings, metal sculptures, myrtle-wood bowls, novelty clocks, and various types of glassware, pottery, and knickknacks. A floor-to-ceiling bookcase was jammed with volumes, both old and new. Sand speckled the floor, and the entire house smelled like the sea.

"It's no big deal," Derek asserted, his chin resting on his chest. "I mean, it's not like they were divorced yet."

"Besides," Stacie chimed in, her voice defensive, almost hostile, "so what? Like it's so weird for parents to split up these days?"

"It *is* weird." The words, which were no more than a whisper and something like a sigh, came from Molly. She sat on a big satin pillow, entwining her auburn hair in her plump fingers.

"Oh," Derek said, aiming a kick in his youngest sister's direction, "what do you know? You're just a kid."

"I don't care," Molly retorted. "I think it's weird they'd get a divorce. They'd been married for a zillion years. I still think it was just a . . . you know, like a . . . um . . ."

Vida supplied the phrase. "Passing fancy?"

Molly didn't seem to recognize it. "Huh? You mean . . . ?" Her muffinlike face puckered in thought. "Yeah, right, maybe."

"That can happen," Vida said in a reasonable tone. "People reach a point in their lives where they feel frustrated or thwarted. Instead of going inside themselves to solve the problem, they strike out at their spouse." She winced, aware that the choice of words was unfortunate under the circumstances. "You always hurt the one you love," she added hurriedly, though the amendment was actually worse.

No one responded to the ill-phrased platitudes. Perhaps the Imhoff kids were as callous as they sounded. Maybe they were numb. As the youngest, Molly seemed the most sensitive, or perhaps she was merely more impressionable.

The silence dragged on. Through the big living-room window, I could see the ocean and the beach. The afternoon was bright and beautiful, bringing out off-season visitors and local residents. A steady stream, including people on horseback, passed over the sands. To my right, I could see the big outcropping known as Haystack Rock, a name that aptly described its bulky, conical appearance. Smaller rocks jutted up from the incoming tide, surrounding Haystack like attendants awaiting their master's whim.

"They fought a lot." Stacie volunteered the information, her lower lip fixed in what appeared to be a permanent pout. "Always."

"No, they didn't," Molly countered, stamping one bare foot. "It was just lately, like since Christmas."

"Since Mom wanted to move," Derek put in.

Stacie shrugged. "Whatever. Butt out, Molly."

Vida, who had assumed a seat in a straight-backed chair that might have been authentic Jacobean or early Levitz, leaned forward in a confidential manner. "Your mother wanted to leave Cannon Beach?"

"Right." Derek's response was almost snide.

"She never liked it here," Stacie added, picking up a

bottle of nail polish from a bookcase ledge. "Mom wanted to live in a big city again."

"Again?" I said, and then remembered that Vida had told me how Audrey had met Gordon in San Francisco. "Did she want to go back to the Bay Area?"

"No," Molly answered quickly. "Portland. Or Seattle."

"She didn't want to be redundant," Stacie said, finally sounding more like an adult than a sulky teen. "Mom told me she'd grown up in Cannon Beach, and once was enough. She wished she'd never come back. She wasn't going to make the same mistake twice by moving back to San Francisco."

"And your father?" Vida prodded. "Did he want to move, too?"

The Imhoff children exchanged wary glances. "No," Derek finally replied. "He liked it here. Dad hates cities."

"I see," Vida said as we heard the back door open. Everyone turned as a pretty, dark-haired young woman in a waitress's uniform came into the living room.

"Hey, Dolly," Derek said, brightening. "What's up?"

"Not much," the young woman responded, eyeing Vida and me with curiosity. "It's slow this afternoon. They let me off early."

"Cool," Derek said. "Want to chill on the beach?"

"Maybe." She started to leave the room, but Vida spoke up.

"I don't believe we've met," she said with unmistaken authority. "Is this Dolores?"

Derek looked pained, no doubt at the necessity of making introductions. "Yeah, right. Dolly, this is Aunt Vida, and Mrs. . . . Sorry, I didn't catch it."

"Lord," I said, getting off the love-seat to shake hands. "Emma Lord. Dolly, is it?"

The young woman had a steady gaze that was penetrating and yet detached. "Dolores Cerrillo. Derek calls me Dolly. Nobody else does."

The implication was that nobody else would dare. On closer inspection, Dolores was younger than I'd first guessed. Seventeen, eighteen at most, I decided. It was her eyes that were old. Wherever she'd been and whatever she'd seen in her short life lent her a haunted look beyond her years.

"I'm going to change," Dolores said, and left the room.

"So," Vida said, attempting to pick up the conversational thread, "your parents quarreled over the decision to move from Cannon Beach. Is that what caused the breakup?"

"I guess." Hands stuffed into his jeans, Derek looked belligerent. "Mom said she'd leave without him if she had to."

"Bull," said Stacie. "That wasn't all of it. Dad was being a prick about a lot of things."

"Shut up, butthead," Derek shouted, leaping to his feet. "You don't know dick!"

Stacie had also risen, standing chest to chest with Derek. "I know Dad was screwing that real-estate bitch! I saw them on the beach one night, going at it!"

Vida, who is usually appalled by vulgar language, appeared spellbound. I, however, felt awkward and embarrassed. I glanced at Vida, in the vain hope that she would consider this an appropriate point of departure. Naturally, she remained glued to her chair. Stacie and Derek continued hurling insults at each other.

"Why are you picking on Dad? You didn't want to leave Cannon Beach, either," Derek yelled.

"Neither do you!" Stacie snapped. "You wouldn't leave your precious girlfriend for ten minutes!"

"Guys!" Molly was now standing beside her brother and sister, small, plump hands waving. "Don't! Mom and Dad had a . . . a midlife crisis, that's all! It would have been okay! They just needed space."

Stacie, who was at least three inches taller than Molly, stared down at her little sister. "Moll, you must be on crack. Mom and Dad were a done deal, Mom was out of here, Dad didn't care. Wake up, bratfinger. They were getting a D-I-V-O-R-C-E."

Abruptly, Molly turned away. Her round face was blotchy and she looked as if she were going to cry. "No, they weren't," she said under her breath.

But Molly's interference had taken the steam out of Derek. "I'm gone," he said, and headed out of the room, following in the direction that Dolores had taken.

"Perhaps," Vida said delicately, "both your parents had found other loves. It can happen."

Neither Stacie nor Molly fell into the trap. "I've got to do my homework," Molly mumbled. With a nod, she went out the front door, which faced the ocean.

"So do I," Stacie said, avoiding our eyes. "I'm a senior this year," she added as if her class status gave weight to her excuse for leaving.

Vida deftly picked up on the cue. "Ah, yes." She turned to me. "The girls ride the school bus every day into Seaside. Cannon Beach has only an elementary school."

"Oh." I nodded gravely, as if informed of a major scientific discovery.

"It would be hard," Vida went on, now speaking again to Stacie, "to leave in your senior year, wouldn't it?"

"Yes," Stacie replied with an air of suspicion. "Yes, it would."

"Do you plan on going to college?" Vida inquired in a very auntlike manner.

"I don't know," Stacie answered a bit impatiently. "Maybe."

"I understand your mother made friends with a young man who's attending Willamette University. A law student, I believe. What was his name?" Vida's forehead furrowed in the apparent effort of recollection.

"His name was Asshole," Stacie retorted, and stomped outside to join her sister.

Vida and I were left alone in the living room.

"That," I declared as we drove up the dirt driveway to the main road, "was a dirty trick, Vida."

"Twaddle," Vida responded, braking at the arterial. "How else are we going to learn anything? Those children spend all their time wrangling with each other. I wish Rosalie had been there. She might exert some control over their filthy mouths."

It took me a moment to recall that Rosalie was their grandmother, and Rett Runkel's ex-wife. "Have you met her yet?" I asked.

"No," Vida answered, and took a right instead of a left back into town. "But we will. We're going to Manzanita."

Resignedly, I leaned back against the Buick's deep blue upholstery. "I thought we were splitting up. Why am I paying for a rental car that's parked back at the motel collecting seagull droppings?"

"You'll have your chance after this," Vida insisted. "It's a short drive to Manzanita."

That much was true. The town, which sits above the curve of Nehalem Bay, is even smaller than Cannon Beach, and doesn't boast the cachet of a well-known tourist spot. Rosalie and Walt Dobrinz lived in a small pink stucco house at the edge of town. They had no view of the ocean, but apparently tried to fill the visual void with garden statuary. Vida and I wound our way among deer, squirrels, leprechauns, bunnies, frogs, and a solitary giraffe before we reached the front door.

Rosalie wasn't expecting us, and she didn't seem pleased by our arrival. "So you're Vida," she said, not inviting us inside. "Rett had a picture of you and Ernest. I think it was taken on your honeymoon."

"I've changed," Vida declared. "That was in fifty-one. We spent four days in Victoria, B.C. Ernest came down with shingles."

"Men," Rosalie murmured. She was short and stout, her curly gray hair caught in a ponytail. "I'm afraid you've come at a bad time. Walt's taking a nap in the living room."

"What a shame!" Vida shifted her stance on the small front porch. "Is there somewhere else we could talk? A nearby café?"

Rosalie's blue eyes darted around, as if she expected someone to come up behind her and veto the outing. "Can we take your car?" she finally said.

"Of course." Vida's manner was gracious.

"Good," Rosalie responded. "Mine's broken. I'll get my purse." She went inside, closing the door behind her.

I was following Vida's gaze, which led to the carport at the side of the house. An aging sport utility van was parked there, and a new green Ford Taurus was behind it in the driveway.

"That car looks like the one I rented in Portland," I said in an idle tone.

"Cute," Vida remarked, tapping her foot. "Rosalie's not very welcoming."

"Maybe Walt's a pain," I suggested. "She may not have improved her lot the second time around."

"That's often the case," said Vida, frowning as she attempted to peer into the windows, which were all closed up. "It's poor judgment, which is seldom overcome by experience."

Rosalie emerged, wearing a white sweater over her flannel shirt and black slacks. "We don't have much in the way of eating places," she apologized, "but there's a spot a couple of blocks from here. Clean, anyway."

Clean, as well as old and small described the restaurant where we found ourselves five minutes later. Vida began by inquiring about the children. Rosalie hadn't seen them since Tuesday, though she'd talked to Molly Friday night.

"It was just before you came, I guess," Rosalie said. "You got in late."

"So I did." Vida's manner had become ingratiating. "You've been a very good grandmother to the young ones. It can't be easy at their age."

Rosalie laughed, a short bark that jarred my ear. "At my age, either. Luckily, Walt's kids and grandkids are grown and out of here. Stepchildren are no picnic."

"You've had your share of woe," Vida commiserated as a pigtailed waitress poured coffee for Rosalie and me. Vida was drinking tea. "I'm sure the children miss their mother. They must have been very close."

"Audrey wasn't your usual kind of mother," Rosalie said with a frown. "She wasn't your usual kind of daughter, either. She always listened to a different drummer. I wish ..." Grimacing, she pressed her fist against her cheek. "Audrey was Audrey."

"And of course you miss her all the same," Vida said in a comforting tone.

"Well," Rosalie began, taking a pack of cigarettes out of her purse, "I do. But you know, it was funny—we lived fifteen miles apart, and it might as well have been fifteen hundred. I don't think I saw her more than four, five times year."

"The shop, I suppose," Vida murmured. "It must have kept her and Gordon busy during the tourist season."

"Yep," Rosalie replied, lighting up. "That—and other things."

"Hobbies?" Vida was wearing her owlish expression.

The short bark again jolted my ear. "I guess you could call it that."

"Call it what?" Vida seemed genuinely perplexed.

Rosalie shot Vida a sly look. "Audrey was a sexy girl, even if she was my daughter. Hey," she went on, sitting back in her chair and showing off her stubby figure, "I used to be kind of sexy myself, though you wouldn't know it to look at me now. Anyways, men liked Audrey, especially young men. She had to beat them off with a bat—when she'd wanted to."

"Which, we're told, she usually didn't," I put in, feeling as if I'd been playing the stooge for Vida too long. "We hear the most recent was a college student, Something-or-Other Damon."

"Was that it?" Rosalie flicked ash into a clamshell. "I wouldn't know. I hadn't seen Audrey since the Fourth of July."

A group of leather-clad bikers came into the restaurant and sat down at the table next to ours. They were middle-aged couples, probably off on a weekend round of excitement, a break from the office routine. Vida, whose straw hat looked incongruous in this homely setting, glanced at the new arrivals before turning back to Rosalie.

"We understand that Gordon sought comfort else-where," she said, lowering her voice.

"Well, why not?" Rosalie retorted. "You couldn't blame him. What's a man going to do when his wife is playing around? Gordon's human."

"Where is Gordon?" I asked.

Rosalie bridled at the question. "How should I know? Looking for a job, maybe. The shop doesn't bring much money in during the off-season."

"I wouldn't think," I said in a musing voice, "that he'd leave the children for such a long time right after their mother's death."

"He wasn't living at home." Rosalie sounded defensive. "He'll show up."

Vida was ostensibly studying the bikers who had ordered pie and coffee. "So unusual," she murmured, then eyed Rosalie. "Your kindly feelings toward Gordon, that is. Mothers-in-law aren't generally so open-minded."

Rosalie shrugged. "Gordon's an okay guy. Nobody knows better than I do what he had to put up with in Audrey. At least the last few years. Maybe they should have stayed in San Francisco."

Vida and I both let that remark pass. "I would imagine," Vida said, "that Gordon's lady friend is wor-ried about him."

"Could be." Rosalie seemed indifferent.

"She's in real estate?" There was an edge in Vida's words as her deferential manner began to fray.

"Right," Rosalie concurred. "Stina, I think her name is. She and her husband have an office in Cannon Beach and one in Lincoln City."

There was a lull during which the bikers exchanged good-natured ribbing among themselves, a pair of teenage lovebirds came into the restaurant with their hands all over each other, and an older man in coveralls followed almost upon their heels. To our surprise, Rosalie let out a little gasp.

"Walt!" she exclaimed. "What are you doing here?"

Walt Dobrinz peered through thick glasses, then walked over to our table with a pigeon-toed step. "Rosie? Where you been? I just got—"

"Walt, meet Rett's sister-in-law, Vida, and her friend Emmy." Rosalie had risen to her feet in such a hasty fashion that she dropped her cigarette. "Damn! Now where'd that go?"

"Another Runkel, huh?" Walt put out a callused hand. "Nice to meet you. You, too, Emmy."

"It's Emma," I said, then noticed that Walt wore hearing aids in his glasses.

"Walt, honey," Rosalie said, stubbing out her cigarette and putting a hand on her husband's shoulder, "can you give me a lift home? These nice ladies want to be on their way."

Walt's weathered face clouded over. "Gee, Rosie, I was going to get a piece of that marionberry pie," he said, pointing to a display case that held several selections, from banana cream to pecan. "What's the rush? Can you wait ten minutes? Or is—"

"I can wait." Rosalie gave Walt a toothy smile, then shook our hands. "Thanks for the coffee, gals. I'll wait with Walt. He likes to sit at the counter."

Vida and I were dismissed. With a scowl, she picked up the check and stamped over to the register. "Nap indeed," she scoffed as we went out into the unpaved parking lot where the big, sleek motorcycles were parked two by two. "What's Rosalie hiding?"

"Maybe she's just a lousy housekeeper," I suggested, getting into the Buick.

"I don't doubt that," Vida said, giving the ignition key a vicious turn. "Her garden needed weeding in the worst way. You can't hide untended flower beds with ugly garden statuary. It doesn't work for Darla Puckett, either. Have you seen her ceramic Bo-Peep and the six walleyed sheep?"

I vaguely recalled Darla Puckett's residence, which was on the other side of Alpine from where I lived. "I think so," I said vaguely. "Stina, huh? She shouldn't be too hard to track down. Why don't I collect my rental car and start on my appointed rounds?"

It was after three o'clock. Vida didn't respond right away; she was concentrating on Highway 101's tricky curves.

"We should make one more stop together," she said as the primitive beauty of Cape Fallon rose before us. "You must meet Rett."

I grimaced. "Must I? What about Marlin?"

Vida shook her head. "Not Marlin. No one needs to meet Marlin."

Given my crowded schedule, I didn't argue. "Does Rett live right in Cannon Beach?"

"No. He has a trailer home just north of town. I stopped in on him yesterday," Vida said as the highway moved away from the ocean and cut through the forest, where the leaves of the beech and alder and cottonwood had turned to burnished gold and bronze. "He's definitely not much of a housekeeper."

Rett Runkel wasn't much of anything, as far as I could tell. While I'd only seen photographs of Ernest Runkel, I could find no resemblance, except that both had been big men. The muscle and sinew I'd perceived in Ernest at age forty had turned to fat in Rett at sixty-plus. He was a huge, shambling man with lank gray hair and a face I could only describe as blubbery: big lips, bulbous nose, heavy eyelids, triple chins. He held up his pants with one hand and shook my hand with the other while a large black dog that looked as if it were part jackal lurked behind its master.

"That's T-Bone," Rett said, giving the dog's head a pat. "He and Brownie are my security system."

T-Bone barked on cue. "Brownie?" Vida echoed. "I don't recall seeing another dog."

Rett grinned, displaying uneven, stained teeth. "Brownie's not a dog. It's my Browning high-power pistol. Let's sit out here," he said, clumsily unfolding two plastic-and-aluminum chairs that matched the one resting next to a pedestal ashtray and a wooden crate that held two cans of beer. "Indian summer, huh?" His tone was conversational, but abruptly changed. "Whaddaya want now, Vida?"

"Iced tea would be nice," Vida said with a sickly-sweet smile. Then she, too, switched gears. "Emma wanted to meet you. She's helping me sort out this mess with Audrey."

"Whaddaya mean, 'this mess with Audrey'?" Rett belched none too gently as T-Bone circled our chairs before settling down at his owner's feet. "The sheriff's sorting things out just fine."

"Nonsense." Vida sniffed. "He hasn't caught Audrey's killer."

"He won't." Rett seemed complacent about the idea. "It was some sex nut, mark my words. He's long gone, probably to California."

"That's possible," Vida admitted. "But aren't you

curious about your daughter's murder? What if it wasn't some . . . sex nut?"

"Then it was some guy trying to get into her pants," Rett responded. "For once, she told him to fuck off. Instead of fuck her. Get it? I made a joke." He rumbled with laughter.

"A very poor joke in shockingly bad taste," Vida declared with an icy stare. "You're speaking of your daughter."

"I'm speaking the truth," Rett retorted. "Audrey was easy, or so I hear. But then you missed the part about the abortions in San Francisco. They were legal and all, but they still cost me a couple of bucks. Being a flower child or whatever the hell they called themselves back then meant more birds 'n bees than I could count."

Vida appeared somewhat shaken by Rett's disclosure. "I didn't know about Audrey's youthful . . . promiscuity. I'm afraid I lost track of your side of the family after you and Rosalie divorced."

"Rosalie!" Rett grunted. "That hump—you been hangin' out with her?"

"We called on her, yes," Vida replied primly. "We also met Walt Dobrinz."

"I call him Walt Dough-Prick," Rett said, the laughter again rumbling out of his big belly. "What Rosie ever saw in that little toad beats the crap out of me. Want a beer?"

"I think not," Vida said, answering for both of us. "And I wish you'd watch your language, Everett. Ernest never used such vile words in my presence."

"Ernest was a namby-pamby," Rett declared. "How the hell did he ever get the nerve to go over them falls in a damned barrel anyway?"

Vida was sitting up very straight, exuding dignity and self-control. "He didn't. The truck belonging to the brewery that sponsored the event ran over him first."

Rett's laughter could have been heard all the way to Seaside. "You're shittin' me! I never heard that part! Good God Almighty!" The flimsy aluminum chair rocked beneath his weight. T-Bone tensed, his pointy ears standing straight up.

"You're vile," Vida asserted in an angry voice. "Callous, too. No wonder you don't care about what happened to Audrey."

Rett Runkel looked mildly shocked. "Hey, who said I didn't care?" He picked up a half-smoked cigar from the ashtray and attempted to relight it. "What I'm sayin' is that if the cops haven't collared the guy who killed Audrey by now, they won't. Not unless he's one of them serial killers roamin' up and down the coast, bumpin' off women."

"He's not," Vida said firmly. "There have been no reports of possible serial killers in this area. I know, I've been watching the wire. Besides, Stacie told me that her mother wasn't sexually assaulted. I should think that would eliminate a serial killer, as well as any perverts."

"So?" Rett was still trying to start the cigar. From the way he huffed and puffed, the task might have been the most arduous he'd tackled that day.

But Vida's face had again fallen. She sat there in the folding chair, now looking stricken.

I decided to rescue her, though under the circumstances, the phrase wasn't really apt. "What Vida means," I said, "is that the murder was personal. Audrey probably knew her killer."

"Yes," Vida said in a faint voice. "It could have been

one of the family." She leaned forward in the rickety chair and jabbed a finger at Rett. "It could have been *you*."

Chapter Five

RETT RUNKEL HAD guffawed at the accusation and, in the process, expelled the half-smoked cigar onto the ground next to Vida's foot. She had withdrawn her sensibly shod feet and continued to glare at her brother-in-law.

"We're leaving," she announced. "It was useless bringing Emma here. You don't know how to behave around civilized people. Goodbye, Rett. I hope I never see you again."

"Now, don't go away mad," Rett called after us.

His laughter followed us all the way to the car. Vida spent the next five minutes apologizing for her distant kin.

"Forget it, Vida," I finally said as we pulled into the Ecola Creek Lodge's parking lot. "You're not responsible for Ernest's family."

"The rest of them seem like jewels compared to Rett," she fumed. "I will never, never criticize any of them again."

"Let's not get carried away," I said as we headed under the archway between the parking area and our unit. "I'm going to check the local phone book and try to find a real-estate company owned by somebody named Stina."

"I don't know what to do," Vida asserted, struggling with the motel key. "We really aren't getting anywhere.

No wonder the sheriff's people haven't made any progress."

"Maybe it's too simple," I said as we entered our unit, which felt very warm and a trifle stuffy. "Wife gets murdered, husband disappears. He done it."

"He didn't disappear right away," Vida noted. "He stayed for the funeral."

"He panicked," I offered, flipping through the phone book to the Yellow Pages. "Maybe the police began asking some tough questions. Maybe his alibi didn't hold up. Maybe what he'd done didn't hit him until after the funeral."

Vida's expression was skeptical, but, for once, she said nothing. I found plenty of real-estate and vacation-rental listings for Cannon Beach, as well as in Seaside, Astoria, and Lincoln City. Several displayed the names of sales associates, but none was named Stina. Then I spotted Kane's Ocean View Properties: CALL CHRISTINA OR STUART KANE TO MAKE YOUR DREAMS COME TRUE ALONG THE OREGON COAST.

Figuring that Christina must be Stina, I dialed the local number. A man's recorded voice answered, telling me that Kane's Ocean View Properties, with convenient locations in Cannon Beach and Lincoln City, were open Monday through Friday from nine to five. I checked the residential listings; the Kanes had a home on Larch Street. This time I heard a woman's voice, full of girlish bubbles, informing me that Stina and Stu were out, but that they'd be delighted to return my call.

I didn't leave a message. Instead, I got out my calling card and dialed Leo's number in Alpine. His recorded message hadn't changed since he moved to Alpine. "This isn't really me. If you don't know what to do after the beep, try hanging up."

I'd asked Leo to change the recording, lest our advertisers call him at home and take offense. But Leo had responded that any advertisers who wanted to get hold of him after working hours were too damned dumb to stay in business. I, at least, knew what to do when I heard the beep: I left a message, telling Leo that I wouldn't return to Alpine until later tomorrow, that Vida was remaining in Oregon for an indefinite period of time, and that he and/or Carla should check our in-baskets and telephone messages for any late-breaking news.

"I'm stymied," I said to Vida, stretching my legs out on the wooden coffee table. "The Kanes are out, we don't know Damon's first name, and we didn't find out who worked part-time at the Jaded Eye. Can I go home now?"

Vida ignored my request, which was only semifacetious. "I'll call the children. They'll know who worked at the shop."

She managed to reach Stacie, who said the woman's name was Ruth Pickering, and that she lived on Hemlock, "the main drag, sort of across from the Cannon Beach Hotel." Stacie thought she'd be home because Mrs. Pickering spent all her spare time gardening.

"Okay, okay," I said as Vida replaced the phone and gave me her gimlet eye. "I'm going. What are your plans?"

"I intend to invite the children out to dinner," she said, looking pained. "It's a necessary expense, but I doubt that they'll turn me down. They can't be eating properly."

"Good luck," I said, grabbing my handbag and heading out the door. The sky was still virtually cloudless and the afternoon had grown so warm that I tossed my duffel coat into the backseat of the Neon. For the first time since arriving, I was on my own in Cannon Beach. I drove over

the bridge that spanned Ecola Creek, glimpsed the turnoff
to the horse-rental stables, and continued past the kite fac-
tory. Straight ahead was the city park, located on a small
bluff above the ocean. Rollerbladers and skateboarders
zipped around while picnickers enjoyed the sunshine.

Hemlock turned into a long, straight thoroughfare
flanked by commercial enterprises. Though there is con-
formity demanded by zoning laws, Cannon Beach seems
neither contrived nor self-conscious. The shake-covered
buildings and log structures that make up most of the
small downtown blend beautifully with the surroundings,
bridging the gap between the ocean on the west and the
foothills of the Coast Range to the east. The gentle slopes
rise almost directly above town, while the ocean is just
two blocks away, an endless vista of sky and sea. To pre-
serve an unobstructed view, nothing in what is known as
downtown is taller than three stories. Most exteriors have
been stained brown, or left in their natural state. Imagina-
tive architecture lends a grace note, and the heart of
Cannon Beach invites the eye and mind, along with the
tourist dollar.

During summer, Hemlock is clogged with pedestrian
and foot traffic, but on this Sunday in October, driving
was relatively hassle-free. Past the many art galleries,
restaurants, and specialty shops I went, until one store-
front in particular caught my attention: on my left, not far
from the post office and across from the live theatre,
stood the Jaded Eye. The carved wooden sign showed a
big green eye, and the windows appeared filled with
objects intended to seduce the tourist trade. There was a
"Closed" notice on the door, and the interior looked dark.
I kept driving, up a little hill and around a bend, then
onto the flat again, with Haystack Rock looming before
me. This was a more eclectic part of town, with bicycle

rentals and motels and restaurants sitting side by side with private residences. Most of the houses looked as if they had originally been summer homes, and their blue and gray and white exteriors reflected the ocean.

Ruth Pickering lived in a small pale green bungalow where a profusion of dahlias, chrysanthemums, marigolds, and several species I didn't recognize brightened the exterior. There were tubs of flowers, baskets of flowers, window boxes overflowing with flowers. Seashells provided edging for the flower beds, the drive, and the walkway. Instead of the plaster animals and gnomes that cluttered Rosalie and Walt Dobrinz's yard, a half-dozen metal sculptures were set into the lawn. A couple of them looked like birds; the rest didn't look like much of anything.

Upon hearing my car scrunch in the gravel drive, Ruth came around from the side of the house, looking much like a flower herself in a red-and-green-and-orange smock that reached to her knees.

"May I help you?" she inquired in a cautious voice.

"I hope so," I said, suddenly feeling embarrassed by my unannounced arrival. Hurriedly, I introduced myself, explaining that Stacie Imhoff had suggested I talk to Ruth about the Jaded Eye.

"I don't understand," Ruth said in her soft voice. "Are you interested in buying the shop? I'm not certain it's for sale."

"No, no," I answered hastily. "I'm here with Audrey's aunt, who is trying to learn what might have happened to her niece. Vida Runkel—Aunt Vida—isn't satisfied with the investigation so far."

"Oh. I see." But judging from Ruth's manner, she didn't. "I really can't be of much help. I've told the sheriff's people all I know."

"I'm sure you have," I said in my most agreeable

fashion. "That's the problem—we haven't been able to talk to the investigating officers."

Ruth Pickering gazed out toward the ocean, her fine blue eyes troubled. I guessed her to be in her early sixties, a thin woman of medium height with a prematurely wrinkled face and short silver hair.

"Murder is very unusual around these parts," she said at last. "I've lived here for thirty years, and I can't recall anything like this. I still think it was some sort of freakish accident."

"Why do you say that?" I moved to one side to avoid the sun, which was starting to dip down over the ocean.

"Because we don't have murders here," Ruth said doggedly. "Audrey must have fallen and hit her head. Or she ran into something while she was swimming and just managed to get back on the dock before she . . . expired."

"You liked her?" I asked, wishing that Ruth would invite me inside or kick my butt down the drive. The sun was giving me a headache.

Again, Ruth didn't respond immediately. "Yes, I think I did," she finally said. "She had a good heart."

"And Gordon? Did you like him as well?"

"Oh, yes." A faint smile played at Ruth's small mouth. "Gordon was—is—a good man. He genuinely loves Cannon Beach."

Echoes of Alpine flitted through my mind. In a small town, people who cared about their community, who openly expressed their loyalty and affection, could be forgiven a multitude of sins.

"Then why isn't he here?" I asked, shielding my eyes with my hand.

"Oh . . ." For the first time Ruth seemed to note my discomfort. "Would you care to come around to the back

of the house? I have a small patio where there's some
shade."

"Thanks, I'd like that."

The patio was flanked with more flower-filled pots and
tubs and barrels. Another neat row of seashells lined the
patio, and two more metal sculptures stood in the ad-
joining grass. Piles of hyacinth and tulip and daffodil
bulbs lay on an old newspaper. Apparently I'd interrupted Ruth in the middle of planting for spring.

We sat in wrought-iron lawn chairs under a striped
canvas awning. Ruth asked if I'd care for a glass of wine,
but I declined. The offer seemed somewhat grudging,
and in any event, I'm not much of a wine drinker.

"Was the shop still open when Audrey was killed?" I
inquired, deciding that factual questions were best.

"You mean . . . ?" The blue eyes blinked several times.
"Oh, you mean for the season. No, it stays open year-
round. We have much more than the spring kite festival
and the summer sandcastle competition and the arts-and-
sciences program. There's the Stormy Weather Festival
of the Arts in November and then all the Christmas
activities, including the lamplighting ceremony. Cannon
Beach does its best to be a complete vacation spot, never
mind what month of the year you choose to visit."

The woman was beginning to sound like the chamber
of commerce. Maybe she only opened up when pro-
moting her beloved community. It was no wonder that
she found murder hard to accept. It might scare away
business.

"So the shop was closed only after Audrey died and
Gordon disappeared?" I tried to phrase the question in
a matter-of-fact voice. Dealing with Ruth was like
handling a skittish mare.

"That's true," Ruth agreed, then sadly shook her head. "It was my fault, really. I simply couldn't handle the whole thing by myself. My nerves haven't been the same since Rupert died."

"Rupert?"

"My husband. He passed away two years ago. Cancer." Her head drooped and her hands clutched at the wrought-iron-and-glass-topped table.

"I'm sorry," I said in what I hoped was a sympathetic voice. "Did you and he own a business here?"

Ruth nodded. "He made kites. We had a shop next to the liquor store." Her left hand gestured feebly toward Hemlock Street. "We sold it. I still make my sculptures in the basement, but my heart's not in it."

"What kind of sculptures?" I asked, working hard at exuding interest.

"Metal. Beaten metal, mostly abstract. I sold them mainly through the Jaded Eye."

My gaze traveled to the pieces standing in the grass. One looked like the old hammer-and-sickle symbol of the Soviet Union; the other resembled a pancreas. I recalled seeing similar pieces at the Imhoff house that might have been crafted by Ruth. To my mind, they were all pretty ugly, but I'm no art expert. I was beginning to think I wasn't much of an investigative reporter, either.

"Intriguing," I said, for want of a better word. "I understand that Gordon had moved into the shop." Changing the subject was mandatory for more than one reason: if I didn't drag some helpful information out of Ruth, Vida would want to kill me. "Is there an apartment in the building? It looks rather small."

"It is. But there's an office at the back, and that's where Gordon stayed."

"It must have been cramped," I said, for lack of anything more brilliant.

"It was. But he had no choice, until Audrey moved out of the house."

I tried not to miss a beat; we finally seemed to be getting somewhere. "How soon did she plan to do that?"

"The middle of September was her deadline," Ruth responded, inspecting her short fingernails, which showed the dark earth from her garden. "She was moving to Portland. I can't think why."

No Alpiner could ever figure out why someone would desert their town for a big city. Moving out was considered a betrayal. "Did Audrey have a job lined up there?" I asked.

"No," Ruth said on a note of disapproval. "She had no qualifications, except in retail sales."

"She must have known something about art objects and antiques and collectibles," I pointed out.

"To some extent, yes," Ruth answered slowly. "But it was Gordon who had the knowledge. And the eye. That's most important."

"It costs much more to live in Portland than it does in a smaller town," I remarked, thinking of Mavis and Ray's expensive river condo. "I'd hate to think of moving to a big city without a job, at least after turning forty."

Ruth said nothing, which I found rather odd. The silence stretched out between us, a growing awkwardness that seemed to mingle with the salt air and the distant roar of the ocean.

"Your garden is magnificent," I said at last.

"Thank you." There was no hint of warmth in Ruth's manner; she accepted the compliment as deserved, rather than mere flattery. "The climate and soil here are conducive to plants. Cannon Beach is filled with beautiful flowers and shrubs, especially during the summer."

We were back strumming the chamber-of-commerce theme. I decided it was time to leave. Opening childproof aspirin bottles was a cinch compared with extracting information from Ruth Pickering.

"Don't get up," I urged. "I'll let you get back to planting your bulbs."

Ruth didn't insist on accompanying me to the car nor did she offer to shake hands. "Goodbye," she said, perhaps in relief. "Enjoy your stay in Cannon Beach."

Given the circumstances, it was a funny thing to say. But there was nothing funny about the note that was plastered on the windshield of my car. Printed in black marker pen on a piece of flimsy cardboard were the words GO HOME BITCH.

The message might have panicked someone less inured to letters and phone calls from irate readers threatening bodily harm on a weekly basis. Still, this wasn't Alpine, and my reputation as an editor hadn't preceded me. A chill crept up my spine that had nothing to do with the breeze coming off the ocean. I hurried out to the edge of the street and scanned both directions. A family of bicyclists were pedaling away from town, a pickup truck and an older-model sedan were driving in opposite directions, a young couple was strolling along hand in hand. No one else was in sight.

Putting the note facedown on the passenger seat, I drove back into the heart of Cannon Beach. It was just after four, and I scratched my brain for some productive way of filling the next few hours. It occurred to me that I was a moving target for whoever didn't care for my presence, but I refused to be intimidated. After all, in twenty-four hours I'd be almost back home.

Vida had indicated that I didn't need to meet Marlin Runkel. Rett, however, had passed muster, but after meeting the family patriarch, it was hard to imagine how much worse Marlin could be.

I pulled into the parking lot next to the Mariner Market. Two phone booths stood near the entrance. Searching through the local directory, I learned that Runkel, M.E., resided on Elk Creek Road. He had a phone, but I didn't try calling him. All I wanted was a look at Marlin's home.

According to the pocket map I'd picked up at the motel, the Elk Creek Road was on the other side of Highway 101. I drove back the way I had come, slowing as I passed Ruth Pickering's house. She was nowhere in sight. A moment later I was at the left-hand turn that would take me under the highway and, hopefully, to the Elk Creek Road.

A campground, surprisingly full for this time of year, lay on my right. A big RV park was on the left, and it, too, seemed busy. The road began to climb, weaving through the forest with its glorious golds of autumn. Shafts of sunlight filtered through the trees, and signs of civilization disappeared. The pavement ended, turning into gravel and then dirt. Maybe I'd passed Marlin's house; but the number was high, compared with the mailboxes I'd seen closer to the RV park.

The road dead-ended at a tin-roofed shack where an old brown Camaro with its wheels stripped sat in what might charitably be called the front yard. The space allowed for a turnaround was measly. Fortunately, the Neon was small, and it only took me three tries to get the car headed back in the right direction. By that time a man with a bow and arrow was blocking my way.

"You see the sign?" he yelled, jerking his head in the direction of a big maple tree.

I hadn't seen any sign, but now I saw the back of it, nailed about five feet from the ground.

"Sorry," I called through the open car window. Then, because I sometimes like to consider myself plucky as well as stupid, foolish, and prone to inviting disaster, I smiled broadly and started to ask if I had the pleasure of speaking to Marlin Runkel.

"It says 'No Trespassing,' " the man shouted, though he was only a few feet away. "That's what it means. Beat it."

Having just received an ugly message on the windshield of my rental car, and with nothing much else to do that afternoon, I continued on my road to ruin. "Come on, Marlin, put down the bow and arrow. I'm not the Sheriff of Nottingham."

Though he didn't exactly follow my instructions, the man I assumed was Marlin at least looked slightly curious. "Then who the hell are you?"

"I'm a friend of your aunt Vida's," I said, killing the engine. "She came to see you yesterday, right?"

"She tried," Marlin responded, then chuckled in an unpleasant manner. "I told her to get her big butt out of here."

"Did she?" I tried to picture the encounter between aunt and nephew. Maybe Vida only met her match when facing off with kinfolk.

"Eventually," Marlin replied, still smiling. "I don't need any relatives. I don't need any people hanging out at my pad."

Marlin didn't look particularly menacing, not even with the bow and arrow at the ready. He was over six feet tall, but had a pasty pallor and his fair hair was thinning. And any man in his forties who referred to his house as his *pad* had to be living in a time warp. Or, it dawned on me, as the smell of marijuana came floating into the car, maybe he was living on a pretty pink cloud.

"Vida told me not to come." I smirked and tossed my shaggy mane, hoping to convey a raffish air.

Marlin's sleepy eyes widened. "She did?"

I uttered a little snort. "You thought I was a spy?" More likely he thought I was a narc. "No way. Vida told me you shouldn't be seen." The phrase came out awkwardly, but I trusted that my meaning was clear.

"I don't want to be seen," Marlin retorted, lowering the bow and arrow. "That's different."

"Now that I've seen you, I'll be on my way. Maybe you ought to step aside. I'd hate to run you down." I gave Marlin a simpering little smile.

But Marlin didn't budge. "Who'd you say you were?"

"I didn't, exactly. I'm Emma Lord, and I'm a friend of your aunt's from Alpine."

Marlin studied me for a moment. "You don't look like a friend of hers."

Maybe he meant I was too young; maybe it was my informal garb; maybe Marlin hadn't experienced enough friendships to realize that external barriers were easily broken if people liked each other. Then again, maybe his brain had turned to fuzz.

"We work together," I said, thinking that being colleagues would better explain the relationship. "She's very upset about your sister's death."

"So am I," Marlin said, and looked as if he meant it. "Audrey was a great person."

I probably looked surprised. Marlin's comment was the first unqualified endorsement I'd heard of Audrey Runkel Imhoff.

"You were close?" I was getting a stiff neck from hanging out the window.

"You could say that." Marlin juggled the bow and arrow. "She's the only one I let come up here. We had some good times." His gaze, now melancholy, wandered to the ramshackle dwelling he called home. For the first time I noticed a couple of equally dilapidated sheds farther into the woods. Marlin's layout was more elaborate than I'd realized.

"Who do you think killed her?" I asked. The query was worth a try.

Marlin rested the bow and arrow against his leg. The weaponry toppled to the ground, but he didn't seem to notice. "I wish I knew. I'd strangle the bastard."

"Did she have any . . . enemies?" The word seemed too strong.

"Hell, no." Marlin scratched at the front of his frayed T-shirt. "I told you, she was great, always knocking herself out for other people. She had the shop to run, three brats to raise, and Gordon was kind of a washout, if you ask me. She got taken advantage of because she had such a big heart."

This was definitely another side of Audrey. "Do you mean she was a volunteer in the community?"

"In a way. That is," Marlin went on, squinting up into the trees where an occasional leaf drifted downward, "she was always helping somebody, especially the old farts. They got so they relied on her. So," he asked with a faint sneer, "what are they going to do without her? The ones that are left, I mean."

"Left . . . where?" I asked. Marlin was beginning to lose me.

Apparently, he had lost himself. Without another word, he picked up the bow and arrow and walked slowly toward the house. I sat for a few moments, watching the front door, which he'd left open, half expecting him to

come back outside. But he didn't. With a sigh, I started
the car and drove back down the Elk Creek Road.

Vida was putting the finishing touches on her toilette
when I returned to the motel. "Are you coming with us?"
she asked, applying powder in her usual slapdash
manner. "I'm meeting the children at the Wayfarer at
five-thirty."

"I don't think so," I replied, holding up the sign I'd
found on the windshield. "I'm not very popular around
here."

Putting on her glasses, Vida peered at the piece of
cardboard. "Goodness! When did that show up?"

"While I was at Ruth Pickering's. Who else knew I
was going there besides Stacie?"

Vida was still staring at the crude message. "Oh, dear,"
she murmured. "The other children, I suppose. Perhaps,
Dolores . . . Cerrillo, is it? Or maybe it's the rental car."

I didn't understand. "What about the rental car?"

Vida waved a hand. "You know—rentals can be
detected because of the sticker the company puts on one
of the windows. This note may have been left by
someone who doesn't want outsiders in Cannon Beach."

"It's a tourist town," I said dryly. "Besides, whoever
did this knew the car was driven by a woman." I tapped
the word BITCH. "It's not that far from Ruth Pickering's
to the Imhoff house—less than a mile, I'd guess. And
anyone who's seen me since I got here could recognize
my duffel coat. I left it in the backseat."

"My, my." Vida removed her glasses and rubbed her
eyes, though not with her usual ferocity. "Have you
thought about taking the note to the police? The station is
a block off Hemlock, on Spruce."

"I've seen a couple of cops on bicycles," I said, putting

the sign on the coffee table. "No, I don't think I'll bother them. Have you asked the locals about the murder?"

"Yes," Vida answered. "They were the ones who referred me to the sheriff's office." She paced the living room for a moment, and then gave me a baleful look. "So you won't face the children at dinner? Assuming it was one of them who left the note?"

"I'm not afraid to face them," I said, fingering the cardboard. "Offhand, I'd say this was from a package of typing paper. It's the kind of thing that people use to protect photos when they mail them in to *The Advocate*."

"Yes, I can see that," Vida said rather testily. "It tells us nothing. Are you coming or not?"

It was true that I was getting hungry. But I didn't relish spending an hour or so with the Imhoff offspring, who struck me as both callous and contentious. On the other hand, I sensed that Vida wanted moral support. Or at least a second set of ears and eyes.

"Okay, I'll go. But I've got to change first." I reached for my suitcase, which was under the coffee table. The sofa had indeed turned into a bed, and I'd spent the night in the living room.

"Tell me about Ruth Pickering," Vida requested, pulling the drapes.

I told her what little I'd learned. She wasn't pleased with the results. Then I argued with myself about relating the visit to Marlin. Vida hadn't wanted me to meet her nephew-in-law. If I revealed that after his initial hostility, Marlin had become almost chatty, Vida might take umbrage. I decided to keep my own counsel for the time being.

"I have some news, too," Vida said in a tone that indicated her sleuthing had been more effective than mine. "I spent some time with the children this afternoon. With

Molly, actually. Derek and Dolores had gone out, and Stacie was on the phone with a chum."

"And?" I said, exchanging my rumpled teal pants and Mariners T-shirt for black silk slacks and a butter-colored cotton top.

"Those youngsters had let the mail pile up. Condolences, bills, letters pertaining to their mother's death—they'd hardly touched any of them. I told Molly we should go through everything. She didn't seem to realize that there are a great many matters to attend to after a person has died."

While Vida spoke in a brisk, matter-of-fact manner, I could picture her practically salivating over the unopened correspondence. "Well? What did you find? Salacious love letters? Blackmail threats? A signed confession by the killer?"

"Of course not." Vida huffed. "Most of it was perfectly ordinary, like the PUD and phone and funeral bills. Even the sympathy notes and cards didn't suggest anything unusual." She paused, the gray eyes sparking. "It was the bank statements. Gordon and Audrey had two accounts with the local branch of the Bank of Astoria, one personal, one commercial. Between the two, they had about five thousand dollars in savings and checking. But Audrey had another account under just her name at US Bank in Seaside. She had a balance of more than a hundred thousand dollars."

"Wow!" I cried, poking my head through the cotton top. "That's a pretty big bundle for somebody running a risky business."

"Indeed it is," Vida agreed. "And why in Seaside? There's a US Bank here in Cannon Beach, just before you get to those shops in Ecola Square."

"Privacy, maybe," I mused. "Audrey didn't want Gordon to know how much money she'd socked away. She probably opened all the mail. I'll bet that was her stash for the move to Portland."

"Hmmm." Vida was standing by the fireplace, looking thoughtful. "This Ruth person said the move was imminent?"

"Within days," I replied, going to the mirror by the hall door and contemplating what I could do with my makeup without starting from scratch. " 'Mid-September' was what Ruth said. Audrey was killed in the wee small hours of Friday, September thirteenth. I'd guess she was planning to take off Sunday or Monday."

"Audrey didn't go." Vida's mouth set in a grim line.

I wielded my mascara wand, with dubious results. "No, she sure didn't."

"Is that why?" Vida asked in a pensive tone.

"Why what?"

"Why she was killed." Vida picked up her purse from the mantel. "Someone didn't want her to leave Cannon Beach. Who was it?"

Chapter Six

THE IMHOFF KIDS and Dolores Cerrillo looked about as happy to see us as I was to see them. Only Molly made an effort to smile as the foursome trooped into the restaurant where Vida and I had been waiting for ten minutes.

"Well now," Vida said with exaggerated enthusiasm after we were seated at a window table, "I hear the clam chowder here is especially delicious. Would anyone care for a soda first?"

"I just had a couple of beers at home," Derek said from behind the menu. "I want a big steak."

"Red meat isn't good for you," Stacie declared. "I'm having prawns."

"So am I," said Dolores. "With a Caesar salad on the side."

"Could I get spaghetti?" Molly asked, chewing on a fingernail. "It's my favorite."

"Of course," Vida replied stiltedly. She was scanning the prices of the other entrées, which weren't cheap, at least not by Alpine standards. "A salad and chowder sound very good to me. What about you, Emma?"

"I'm the other hostess," I said on impulse. "Thus I'll take the plunge for the salmon." If the family's recent tragedies hadn't dimmed the Imhoffs' appetite, I wasn't going to let the prices dampen mine.

"Really, Emma, that's not necessary," Vida began, but I kicked her under the table. "If you insist."

We gave our orders, and I had the temerity to ask for a Rob Roy, straight up. It had been a long day. Tomorrow, with the drive home, would be even longer.

"So," Vida said smoothly, "it seems your mother had quite a large savings account. How was she able to save so wisely?"

Derek and Stacie looked blank. Dolores simply stared through the window at the outgoing tide. Apparently, only Molly had been privy to Vida's discovery.

"She used to make her own clothes," Molly volunteered. "But the sewing machine broke."

"Very economical," Vida said. "But it doesn't quite explain such a goodly amount. Perhaps she'd made some big sales at the shop?"

Derek's laugh was harsh. "Like fifty bucks for one of Mrs. Pickering's butt-uglies? No way—Mom and Dad nickel-and-dimed it." At last the meaning of Vida's question seemed to sink in. "What do you mean by big savings?"

"A hundred thousand dollars," Vida responded calmly. "That's not a fortune by any means, but it's a comfortable figure."

"Sheesh!" For once, Derek lost his complacency.

"That's impossible!" Stacie asserted. "Mom couldn't have put away that much money!"

Even Dolores had turned away from the window. "Did she inherit from someone? Or win a prize in the state lottery?"

Molly set her elbows on the table and rested her face on her hands. "It must have been the lottery. We don't have any relatives."

Vida raised her eyebrows. "You mean you have no

relatives with whom you've kept in touch. In fact, you have many relatives in Alpine, including me."

"But you haven't given Mom any money," Stacie said with a touch of resentment.

"That's quite true," Vida agreed. "Have your parents kept up with your father's side of the family?"

"Dad left home when he was eighteen," Derek said, sounding as if he thought his father had had a good idea. "He went to San Francisco to find himself."

"If he did," Vida said archly, "he's managed to lose himself again. Perhaps he returned there after all these years."

"Could be," Derek said. "It's still a happening place."

"The lottery," Stacie was saying, more to herself than to the rest of us. "It's got to be the lottery."

"Then why didn't she tell us?" Molly asked in a sullen voice. "We'd have been all thrilled."

The three Imhoffs exchanged glances, as if each thought the other might have known but hadn't told. Dolores toyed with her silverware before she spoke up in her soft, detached voice.

"She would have said if she had won. Your family was not like mine, where no one talked, except in anger."

Derek put an arm around Dolores, who obviously brought out his softer side. "That's because your folks were always wasted, Dolly. It's not because they didn't love you."

With one sweep of her arm, Dolores knocked over her water glass. "Stupid! You don't know what you say! My family never loved any of us! I hate my parents! I hate them so much!" She burst into tears.

Derek had suffered the brunt of the spilled water, which soaked his red Henley shirt. He ignored his girlfriend's ranting and tried to mop himself up with his linen napkin. Dolores wound down, but continued to sob.

Stacie reached across the table and righted the glass. "It's okay, Dolores. Alcoholics don't know what they're doing. They're not really who they seem."

Dolores flung herself on Derek. "Take me home! I want to leave. I feel sick!"

Derek was still dabbing at his jeans. "Hold on, Dolly," he said in what wasn't an unreasonable tone, considering his own nature as well as the circumstances. "I'm kind of hungry."

Dolores began pummeling Derek with her fists. By now, most of the other diners in the half-filled room had turned to stare. "Now! We must go! Now!"

His cheeks darkening with embarrassment, Derek awkwardly got to his feet, hauling Dolores with him. "Sorry," he mumbled, "I guess we gotta go."

Under her green turban, Vida's face was inscrutable. "Then please do. Your young lady is upsetting everyone. Including me."

Derek and Dolores left. She was still sobbing and had to lean on her companion. Every eye followed them out of the restaurant. I gulped at my Rob Roy, which, happily, had arrived just before all hell had broken loose.

There was a long pause before anyone spoke. It was Stacie who broke the silence.

"Dolores's parents are drunks. She has three brothers and sisters, and at least one other's left home besides her. She dropped out of high school last spring and got a job. I don't think she's had a very happy life."

Vida was still gazing at the entrance through which Derek and Dolores had just passed. "Your brother appears to treat her kindly. I'm rather surprised."

Stacie and Molly exchanged knowing glances. "You

mean," Stacie said, "because Derek usually acts like a jerk? He's really not, at least not all the time. And he's crazy about Dolores. They're going to get married as soon as she turns eighteen in November."

"Ah." Vida nodded once. "Did your parents approve?"

Stacie flinched and Molly ducked her head. "Not really," Stacie finally said. "Dad thought they were too young, and Mom felt that Derek should at least give community college a try."

"Very sensible," Vida said. "People who live in small towns tend to marry early. Often the marriages don't work out. Not," she added hastily, "that it's the fault of the town itself. The couples are just too immature."

"Maybe Mom and Dad were too young," Stacie said as the waiter approached with our salads. "Mom always said that people who got married before they knew themselves usually broke up sooner or later."

"But they stayed married for twenty years," I pointed out. "Most youthful marriages break up before the fifth year. Or so I've heard."

The romaine salads were delivered to Vida and me. The Caesar, however, had been intended for Dolores.

"I'm afraid," Vida said in apology, "that we must send it back. Oh, we meant to cancel the steak and one order of prawns as well."

The waiter, who had been the soul of bonhomie, now frowned. "I'm sorry, but the orders already went in. There's nothing we can do. Would you like to have us put them and the Caesar in a carryout box for later?"

"I'll eat Dolores's salad," Molly volunteered. "We could take the steak and prawns home to her and Derek."

Vida tried not to look miffed. "Very well." The smile she gave the waiter was strained. "By all means, put everything in a doggy bag." Seeing Molly's puppylike eyes, Vida relinquished the Caesar.

"I'll share with you, Stacie," Molly offered. "It's really big."

Stacie began to fork some of the salad off her sister's plate. "I'm never getting married," she said. "I might live with somebody, but I wouldn't want to be tied down. I think that's what bothered Mom."

"No, it wasn't," Molly asserted. "She just didn't like living here anymore. It had nothing to do with Dad."

"I didn't say it did." Stacie gave her sister a superior look. "Mom was a free spirit. It wouldn't matter who she married, she'd still want to move around."

"But," Vida remarked, "your mother was the only member of the family who wanted to move. Isn't that so?"

"I guess." Molly let out a big sigh. "Stacie and I wanted to stay in school here, Derek wouldn't leave Dolores, and Dad likes it here a lot."

"So," Vida said smoothly, "the only way your mother could leave was to go alone."

Again, the sisters exchanged glances. "I guess," Molly said again. "But that didn't mean she was going to get a divorce. Portland's not that far away. Mom and Dad could have . . . commuted."

"They wouldn't," Stacie said flatly. "Molly, can't you get it through your thick head? Mom and Dad were finished with each other. They both had found other people. They didn't love each other anymore and they weren't going to stay married. Why do you have a problem with that?"

Molly clamped her mouth shut and glared at Stacie. "I don't believe it," she finally said, her face flushing. "They wouldn't get a divorce. Not after all this time. Divorce sucks."

Stacie rolled her eyes. "Look, bratfinger, how many of the kids in your class have parents who're divorced? Half of our senior class have stepmothers or stepfathers or single parents. Wake up, it's almost the twenty-first century."

"It's not right." Molly turned mulish.

"Are your classmates happy with their situations?" Vida inquired of Stacie.

It was a question that Stacie obviously had considered, but answering it weakened her argument with Molly. "Oh—some of them are okay with it. But until they're eighteen, they have to do all this switching back and forth on weekends and holidays and during the summer. That can be a pain, especially when one of the parents moves somewhere else. And then there are kids who don't get along with their stepparents. That's a bummer."

"See?" Molly said, her pudgy chin jutting. "You're right, lots of kids in my class come from broken families. Half the time their parents don't know where they are or what they're doing because their families are all screwed up. That's why kids get into so much trouble. Last year Kelly Stafford tried to commit suicide when her mom and dad broke up because she thought it was her fault. Two years ago Kevin Nerstad broke a bunch of windows in Seaside because he was so mad when his parents split. And ever since school started this fall, Jason Claypool gets high on catnip between classes."

Stacie bestowed a patronizing look on her sister. "You can't get high on catnip unless you're a cat, dummy."

"Jason can," Molly replied, on the defensive. "He just sort of rolls around the halls."

"And purrs," I muttered under my breath. Aloud, I ventured an opinion. "I don't think anyone can argue that divorce is good for children except in extreme cases where a parent is abusive. Too many people fail to work at staying together because they're just plain selfish. They're thinking about themselves, not about the family unit."

It was the wrong thing to say, and I should have known that. Stacie bridled and Molly looked as if she were going to cry again.

"You have to live your own life," Stacie asserted. "If you're not happy, you're not going to make anybody else happy, either."

"Define happy," I retorted. My perverse nature had gotten the better of me; I wasn't backing down.

"That depends," Stacie responded. "I mean, what might make me happy might not make somebody else happy. Take Mom—she wasn't happy in Cannon Beach."

"There's always compromise," Vida remarked as the waiter removed our salad plates. "Your parents could have moved closer to Portland, but stayed in a small town. Did they ever discuss that?"

"I don't know." Stacie folded and refolded her napkin, then spread it out again in her lap. "I doubt it. Dad was determined to stay here. He loved—loves—the ocean."

"That's my point," I said, trying to sound reasonable. "Maybe they could have considered moving to Puget Sound, to one of the smaller communities on the water but within a ferryboat ride of Seattle."

Stacie picked up the napkin, crumpled it, and tossed it onto the table. "What difference does it make if they didn't love each other?" Her eyes flashed with anger, but her overall expression was miserable.

"Define love," I said, still perverse.

"You define it," Stacie snapped. "How long have you been married?"

I was taken aback, deservedly so. "I'm single," I said. "I've never married."

"See?" said Stacie, almost gleeful. "You don't know what you're talking about."

She was right. I didn't.

But neither did Stacie and Molly.

"I've done my duty by the children," Vida said after we'd returned to the motel. "At least as far as treating them goes. Thank you for helping. You didn't have to."

"I know," I said. "But I wanted to. Besides," I went on, with a sheepish look for Vida, "maybe it makes up for my visit with Marlin."

"Marlin!" Vida whirled on me. "You didn't! I told you . . ."

I held up my hands. "I know, I know. But it didn't seem right that he'd be the only family member I hadn't met. How do you expect me to get any perspective on these people if I don't meet all of them?"

To my surprise, Vida was only mildly outraged. "Marlin is a disgrace. He's done nothing with his life, except to sit up there in his awful house and smoke marijuana. I suspect that he grows it, too. I hate to admit he's a Runkel."

I hated to admit that I preferred Marlin to his father, Rett. Instead I related how Marlin had extolled his sister's virtues.

"You're right," Vida conceded. "Marlin presents a more favorable portrait of Audrey. A regular do-gooder, if he can be believed."

"I don't see why he'd lie," I said, opening the drapes so that we could watch the sunset. "Unfortunately, his information doesn't help us figure out who killed her."

"No," Vida agreed, carefully removing her turban. "Quite the opposite. It sounds as if some people were dependent on her."

"Motive," I said, settling into one of the room's two armchairs. "If we're playing detective, we ought to discuss motive."

"True." Vida sat down in the other armchair. "Jealously comes to mind. Alas, that points to Gordon."

"It could also be the young man, Damon Whoever," I noted. "Or Stina Kane, Gordon's alleged lover."

"It could be a rejected suitor," Vida mused. "Someone we know nothing about."

"That's the problem," I admitted. "We don't know much."

"Jealously often results in crimes of passion," Vida said. "I sense that's what this was."

The sky was turning gold. A trawler moved south, bobbing gently on the big waves. "That narrows the field a bit," I said. "How about gain? Now that we know Audrey had a sizable savings account, who gets it?"

"I believe," Vida said slowly, "that Oregon, like Washington, is a community-property state. Dear me." She grimaced. "That brings us back to Gordon."

"But Gordon may not have known about the stash," I pointed out. "Why else would Audrey keep it at a separate bank in a different town under just her name?"

"A point well taken," Vida allowed. "And the children didn't snoop. Goodness, they didn't even open mail addressed to the family!"

"Revenge," I said, going down the list of possible motives. "But who for what?"

Vida shook her head. "I've no idea." Then a sly look crept into her eyes. "Blackmail—now that's a possibility. It might be how Audrey accumulated her savings."

"That's good," I agreed with a sudden enthusiasm that swiftly dimmed. "But again—who for what?"

Vida didn't answer. She sat with her hands resting on the chair's arms, her head tipped back. "It's all so difficult." She sighed. "Maybe we should concentrate on the crime scene." Abruptly, she sat straight up. "Good grief! I forgot about 'Scene'! What shall I do?"

"Scene Around Town" was Vida's weekly gossip column, which included such tantalizing tidbits as Cal Vickers's new gas pumps at the local Texaco station, Darlene Adcock losing control of her grocery cart at Safeway, Sunny Rhodes conducting her Avon-lady route on a new ten-speed bicycle, and the Reverend Minton Phelps singing verse two instead of verse three of "Throw Out the Anchor, Someone's Floating Away." As trivial as these items might seem by big-city standards, they were hot news in Alpine. "Scene" was the best-read part of the paper, narrowly edging out the obituaries. When we had any.

"Think back," I urged Vida. "What did you notice before we left for Oregon?"

Vida looked abashed. "Dear me, I don't recall. I was so distressed about Audrey. I . . . just . . . wasn't . . . paying attention."

The admission was tantamount to the Pope revealing that he'd scarfed down a couple of eight-ounce T-bones on Good Friday. Maybe that was the moment when I fully realized how concerned Vida was with the murder of her niece-by-marriage. This was no whim of curiosity, no desire to poke her nose where it wasn't wanted. My House & Home editor was on a mission, and I realized that she wouldn't come back to Alpine until she'd unraveled the family mystery.

"Oh, boy," I said under my breath.

"Beg pardon?" said Vida.

"We can't leave out 'Scene.' I'm going to call Leo and see if he and Carla can fill the space." I got up and went to the phone.

"Wait!" Vida exclaimed. "Call Milo first. We need his help. He can get information out of Clatsop County that they won't give to us."

"Milo's in Bellevue," I replied. "He won't get home until late."

"Oh." Vida's face sagged. "Does he expect you back tonight?"

It dawned on me that I hadn't thought much about Milo since leaving Alpine. Except for the brief discussion with Mavis about our so-called romance, the sheriff hadn't crossed my mind. I not only didn't miss him, I realized he was becoming a peripheral figure in my life. The insight was upsetting.

"Yes, I think I told him I'd be in late," I replied, rubbing at my forehead with both hands. "But he'd be late, too. So he won't know I'm not there. Damn."

"What?" Vida seemed put off by my comment.

"It's nothing. But we can't call him until tomorrow." I picked up the receiver. "It's almost seven. Maybe Leo's home by now."

Leo answered on the second ring. "You never call me at home, babe," he said, using the nickname I loathed. "Miss me?"

"Like blisters," I replied. "You got my first message?"

"You mean the one where I teach Carla the difference between a subject and a predicate, and that the lead shouldn't go at the end of the story? Yeah, I got it. What now?"

Leo's breezy manner irked me, though it wasn't his fault. It was mine, for still being in Cannon Beach. "Vida didn't get a chance to finish 'Scene,' " I said, avoiding my House & Home editor's anxious gaze. "Can you and Carla and maybe Ginny and Kip come up with some items?"

"Vida never started 'Scene,' and you know it," Leo said. "After I got back from Seattle this afternoon I stopped by the office to check page layouts. Alpine Appliance has to get rid of a bunch of used stoves and refrigerators they got as trade-ins to make room for the new models. They're taking out a half page, which means—in case you've forgotten while you're beachcombing or surfboarding or whatever the hell you're doing down there—that I have to virtually redo the whole damned paper. One of the missing links was 'Scene.' "

"Right. Have you got anything?" I kept my voice calm so as not to further agitate Vida.

"Grace Grundle walked into a phone pole at Front and Fourth. She broke her glasses. How's this: 'Retired Grade-School Teacher Makes Spectacle of Herself, Wrecks Spectacles, Former Students Speculate If Two Plus Two Doubles Equals One Drunken Old Broad'?"

"Grace has an inner-ear problem, as you very well know," I said testily. "I doubt that she's ever had a double anything in her life."

"How about Clancy Barton crawling out of the Elks Club on his hands and knees Friday night? He had a G-string in his teeth."

"Stop it, Leo." I didn't know if my ad manager was kidding or not. "You and the rest of the staff have two days to fill that column. Do it."

A heavy sigh emanated from the other end of the phone line. In my mind's eye, I saw Leo stretched out in his La-Z-Boy chair, the phone in one hand, a cigarette in the other, an adult beverage on the side table. He would be rumpled but comfortable, at ease in his small apartment on Cedar Street across from St. Mildred's Catholic Church and flanked by the Alpine Medical Clinic on one side and the Baptist church on the other. Leo should have benefited from his neighbors, both spiritual and temporal, but he seemed to prefer the occasional fifth of Jack Daniel's instead.

"We'll do it," he said at last, sounding as if he'd prefer walking down Railroad Avenue wearing buttless chaps and a sign that read TWEAK ME, I'M YOURS. "Ginny's good at that stuff. Unlike the rest of the younger generation, she notices what's going on around her."

"Thanks, Leo. I'll try to come up with something after I get back Monday afternoon. I should be in around three." I started to sign off, then thought to politely inquire if he'd had a good time in Seattle.

"You bet," Leo replied. "It was kind of off-the-wall. I got a phone call Friday night from an old pal in the Bay Area. He was in Seattle on business and wanted to see how I was doing. I used to work for the guy in Southern California, and I guess he wondered if I was still seeing little purple people doing the macarena at the foot of my bed. I told him I'd gotten a grip on my life—more or less—so he asked if I'd like to come into town and have lunch or brunch or whatever with him this morning. I said sure; he's a helluva guy, and it'd been a while since we'd gotten together, at least when I was sober enough to remember the occasion. By the way, he asked about you."

My heart sank. "Who was it?" I queried through taut lips.

"The guy who gave you the recommendation to hire me. You remember—Tom Cavanaugh."

I remembered. Too well.

Chapter Seven

I WANTED TO ask Leo a zillion questions about Tom, but through a monstrous act of will, I refrained. Though Leo had worked for one of the Cavanaugh weeklies years ago, and Tom had written to give him a recommendation, neither of us had ever enlightened my ad manager about our relationship. That was three years ago, during the rejuvenated halcyon days of intimacy when we shared a frayed thread of hope.

But that thread had snapped along with Sandra Cavanaugh's mind. Since hiring Leo, I'd half expected him to notice a resemblance between my son and Tom, but so far he had never mentioned it.

Vida had taken in my startled expression, and pounced as soon as I finished giving Leo instructions.

"Well? Has something happened in Alpine?"

"No," I answered, but knew that trying to deceive Vida was useless. I told her that Leo had seen Tom in Seattle.

A slight smile touched her lips. "Well now. That's very nice. Have you no reaction other than your slightly shaking hands and flushed complexion?"

"Shut up, Vida." I suddenly wished I had a cigarette. And another Rob Roy. "Why do you persist in romanticizing my relationship with Tom? It's over."

"So you say." Vida didn't sound as if she believed me.

"Then I shouldn't think news of Tommy would upset you."

"I'm not upset," I asserted, irked at Vida's insistence on calling Tom "Tommy." It made him sound about twelve. "I was startled, that's all. What *is* upsetting is how you encourage me to hold on to some tattered memory of a love affair that should have ended twenty-five years ago. It did, really. The brief resumption was folly, an epilogue that didn't need to be written."

"How poetic," Vida remarked, picking up the telephone directory. "You surprise me. I'd come to believe that you had no poetry—or romance—in your soul."

"I don't," I retorted, and then realized that Vida did. The insight amazed me. Vida was so down-to-earth, so practical, so suffused with her favorite attribute: good sense. That somewhere deep down was a hankering for romance, even of the vicarious sort, gave me pause.

"You believe in happy endings," I said in an awe-struck tone.

The gray eyes narrowed slightly. "No. Not that. They occur so seldom. But I believe in love. It comes in many forms, and it can change over time. Love is precious, even rare, especially the kind that you and Tommy . . . had."

She had started to say "have"—I was sure of it. "Long ago, you told me to forget him and move on with my life. What made you change your mind?"

Vida sighed and pushed her glasses up on her nose. "Ordinarily, it would be good advice. But as time went on I sensed the depth of your feelings for each other. It struck me as foolish at first because I felt you'd built barriers to prevent being hurt again. If you told yourself you still loved Tommy, you couldn't fall in love with anybody else. You were safe. Then you decided you didn't love him anymore—which is impossible to do. Love can't be ordered around like a servant. You've tried to fall in love with Milo, but I don't believe you can. You should have remained friends, which is very pleasant. Besides, it became clear that Tommy, though ambivalent about his responsibilities, still loved you. Such powerful emotions can't be dismissed or ignored. Surely you must see that."

If I did, I wouldn't admit it. But what had become clear, even as Vida spoke, was that she had never known passion. The word, along with sex, had been avoided. As outspoken as she was, perhaps Vida would not personally confront either passion or sex. Not verbally, not physically, not emotionally. I'd never sensed that Vida's marriage had been loveless, but maybe it had lacked fire. My mental picture of Ernest Runkel evoked a stolid man of even temperament who might have been overwhelmed by his wife and three daughters. He had been the assistant superintendent at the old Cascade & Pacific Mill, a hardworking, diligent man. Yet he'd possessed a streak of daring that had led to his demise at Deception Falls. Maybe I didn't have the complete portrait of Ernest—or of Vida. Maybe nobody ever does know another person through and through. It's tough enough to know oneself.

"Vida," I finally said, "it's pointless to talk about Tom and me. He's never going to leave Sandra. Even if he did, what kind of future would we have? Can you picture Tom moving to Alpine? He's a city person. Most of his business interests are in California. And I can't see myself packing up and heading south. I'd dry up and blow away from lack of rain."

"Compromise," Vida murmured. "Just what Audrey and Gordon should have tried."

"Maybe. Let's talk about them instead. Shall I try the Kanes again?"

"You won't face facts," Vida said flatly.

"I just did. I've been doing it for a long time." We were staring at each other, neither of us willing to give in. "The subject is closed. I'm here to help you with your family tragedy."

Maybe I'd made a dent in Vida's thinking; maybe it was the Runkel catastrophe that brought her around. Whatever the reason, she handed me the phone book. "I was going to look up the number for Willamette University, but Salem's not in here," Vida said, her manner uncharacteristically stiff. "I suppose you'll have to take a small detour on your way home tomorrow in order to track down Damon."

I gaped at Vida. "Salem isn't a small detour from Cannon Beach. It's at least a hundred and fifty miles from here. I'm not going."

"But he's on your list of people to be interviewed," Vida protested, no longer rigid but clearly vexed.

"No, he's not," I shot back. "He was nowhere near Cannon Beach when Audrey was killed. He was already back on campus."

"We don't know that for certain." Vida was looking adamant.

"Then you go to Salem," I said. "I will not—cannot—drive all the way to Salem, then back up to Portland, and on to Alpine. It'd take the entire day."

Vida gave a small, piqued shrug. "Very well. I thought you just said you were here to help me with this unfortunate situation."

I wanted to placate Vida, to be reasonable. "Call Damon. Or I will. He can probably provide an alibi for

September thirteenth. Then we can drop him from the suspect list."

Vida regarded me as if I were the class dunce. "For the middle of the night? Unless he was sleeping with a young woman, which is possible, he can't have much of an alibi for the time between, say, midnight and four A.M."

"Give it a try," I said dryly. "I'm calling the Kanes."

This time the bubbly voice belonged to a real person. Stina Kane was somewhat confused by my call, which was understandable.

"You're a friend of Audrey's?" she asked after I'd gone through a rather circumlocutory explanation.

It was easier to say yes than to explain. "Is there any chance you'd be able to meet me for a drink?"

Stina hesitated. I had the feeling that she was either consulting her husband, or checking to see if he was comatose in front of the TV. "Okay, fine. Do you know the Driftwood Inn? It's right across from Sandpiper Square."

I recalled Sandpiper Square, a collection of shops in a barn-inspired building on the ocean side of Hemlock. Stina said she could meet me in ten minutes. "I'm short, blonde, and fifteen pounds overweight," she declared, and the bubbles threatened to erupt in my ear.

The Driftwood didn't conform to most of the other buildings in the downtown area, and I suspected it had been built before the code was enforced. The exterior was Olde English, with lace curtains at the windows. There was a waiting list for the snug, beamed dining room, and the small bar was jammed.

Stina, however, knew the ropes. With friendly greetings all around, she cleared a path for us and put in our orders. Two thirtysomething men wearing Seahawks and

Trail Blazers shirts respectively stepped aside at the end of the bar to make room.

"We'll get a table as soon as some of these people are moved into the dining room," Stina said, glancing at her diamond-studded watch. "It's after seven-thirty. The rush ought to be just about over."

The room was noisy, and no one seemed to be paying attention to us, but I didn't like asking indiscreet questions in a raised voice. Thus I opted for a general query.

"What do you think happened to Audrey?"

Stina looked puzzled. "How do you mean? Somebody conked her over the head, as far as I know."

"I put that badly," I admitted, my concentration derailed by the crowded surroundings and the constant chatter. "I should have asked why you thought she was killed."

Stina set her martini glass down on the bar. She was pretty in an artificial way, with platinum hair that couldn't have been natural, a pouting lower lip that might have been the result of implants, and a voluptuous figure that carried the alleged extra poundage quite capably. "How well did you know Audrey?" she asked, her voice so low that I had to strain to hear her.

Should I lie? Truth had a way of coming out quickly in small towns. "I knew her only through her aunt, who works for me in Alpine," I said, and noticed that Stina continued to look puzzled. "Alpine, Washington," I specified. Sometimes I forget that most of the world has never heard of our little mountain aerie.

Stina's brow cleared. "Audrey was a real piece of work, in my opinion. She'd dropped out years ago, took off for San Francisco, did the whole scene, got in a lot of trouble, and somehow ended up married to Gordon Imhoff. They moved back here—what? seven, eight years ago?—and opened their shop. Stu and I'd come to Cannon Beach from Eugene not long before that, so what I know of Audrey's previous history is hearsay, but it's consensus." Stina paused to sip from her drink. She talked with her hands, no mean feat given the crowded confines at the bar. Her long nails were polished a glossy pearl, and diamond studs flashed in each pierced ear.

"Stu was in property management, vacation rentals mostly, but we decided to open our own real-estate office about five years ago," Stina continued, hardly missing a beat. "We added Lincoln City a year later. Gordon worked part-time for us for a while, mostly handling the seasonal stuff. With three kids, he and Audrey needed the extra money. But last fall he quit. Gordon said Audrey felt he should spend more time with the shop—she couldn't handle it by herself."

Stina's hazel eyes had been darting in every direction even as she talked nonstop in her bubbly voice. The vigilance paid off: a middle-aged couple was getting up from a corner table. With an outstretched hand intended to waylay anyone who dared encroach on her designated territory, Stina swiveled her hips between the other customers and claimed the table as our own.

"Ah," she said with satisfaction, "now we can be comfortable. Where was I?"

"Audrey was overwhelmed," I prompted. "Why?"

"Good question. The woman didn't do anything. Oh, she puttered around the shop and went looking for collectibles and every once in a while she'd take up with some new passion. But they never lasted."

"You mean . . . ?" Tactfully, I let the sentence dangle.

"Watercolors. Quilting. Soapstone carving. Glassblowing. Audrey thought she was an artist, or at least a craftsman. But she had all the talent of a clamshell." Stina looked disgusted.

Having thought that Stina was referring to Audrey's love life, I tried to hide my embarrassment. "She had a husband and three kids. They certainly required time and energy."

Stina sniffed indignantly. "What they required and what they got were two different things. As far as I could tell, the kids were pretty much on their own. And Gordon might as well not have been there. In fact—as you may have heard—he wasn't. Not lately. He'd moved out."

Something didn't jibe. While the noise level was beginning to ebb, I was still having trouble keeping focused. "You felt sorry for Gordon, I gather." The words were intended to sound innocent.

"You bet," Stina said with feeling. "He was a solid kind of guy who really cared about his family. He cared about Audrey, too. But she got this wild hair to move. She wanted a flower cart."

"What?" Now I was sure that my ears, as well as my brain, were playing tricks on me.

"You know—one of those carts they have outside of buildings or in the lobby with fresh flowers and maybe espresso." Stina lifted her head and her empty glass, signaling to the bartender. "That was her dream. She'd move to Portland and set up shop—or cart, if you will—in the downtown core. Gordon thought she was nuts. I agreed."

A second martini and another bourbon and water arrived. My companion exchanged slick banter with the bartender, nodded at a trio of newcomers, and turned back to me. Despite Stina's persistent eyeballing of the bar, she managed to convey a sense of empathy. It was a trick of her real-estate trade, but it worked. I found myself liking Stina Kane.

"Audrey wanted to put the house up for sale," she went on, placing the olive from her martini in an empty ashtray. "Gordon fought it. Not that it mattered to Stu and me—Audrey wouldn't list it with us in any event."

"She didn't like you and your husband?" I ventured.

Stina gave a slight shake of her head. "I don't know and I don't really care. I think she had a buyer in mind, and wanted to sell the place without paying a commission. But as I said, Gordon refused to go along with it."

"But he moved out," I noted. "And now he's gone. Do you have any idea where he could be?"

"He's scared." Stina chewed on her full lower lip. "He thinks the police figure he killed Audrey."

"Did he?"

This time she not only shook her head with vehemence but laughed. "Heck, no! Gordon wouldn't hurt a sand flea. He's out wandering the beach somewhere, or holed up in the mountains. There's plenty of empty space in Oregon where a person can get lost. I imagine Gordon's waiting for the sheriff to find the real murderer."

I tipped my glass toward my mouth. "And that would be . . . ?"

"Some drifter. Let's face it, this is the coast. People running away from their troubles and from themselves wander across the country and end up here. The next stop is Asia, or putting a bullet in your head." The concept didn't seem to perturb Stina; drifters weren't prospective clients.

"When did you last see Gordon?" I winced; the query smacked of official interrogation.

Stina didn't seem to notice. "At the funeral, I think.

No, I saw him that evening outside the Jaded Eye. He was in his van."

"Which the police have never found?"

Stina shrugged. "I guess not. If they have, the rumor mill didn't grind down this far from Astoria. Heck, it's a big state. Gordon could be anywhere. But I'll bet he's not far."

Stina was right. But the way I found out was all wrong—for Gordon, and for me.

"Well?" Vida demanded, fists on hips. She was in her blue chenille bathrobe, with cream smeared all over her face and her hair done up in big curlers. "Is she or isn't she?"

The question referred to Stina Kane's relationship with Gordon Imhoff. "I couldn't tell. She seemed very candid in her responses, but didn't give anything away."

"Typical." Vida huffed. "A real-estate agent. They seem so friendly and outgoing, but of course they're hiding all sorts of things, like termites and bedpost beetles and dry rot. You never knew Neeny Doukas when he first started selling real estate in Alpine. Such a glad-hander, and always extolling the virtues of a property while hiding the defects. The first house that Ernest and I looked at had no kitchen, which Neeny had forgotten to mention. Neeny called it the Love Nest. When we asked why there was no place to cook, he said it was because newlyweds should always eat out. It was more romantic."

I laughed, though secretly wondered if Neeny knew that cooking had never been Vida's strong suit. "Stina wasn't trying to sell me anything," I said, carefully removing my shoes and emptying the ever-present sand out onto the hearth.

"Nonsense. Real-estate agents are always selling

something, even if it's only themselves." Her tongue was sharp, but Vida's earlier annoyance with me seemed to have faded. It usually did, given an hour or two.

"There *was* something," I confessed. "It was Stina's general attitude toward Audrey, as if she could do no right. But we've seen the house, and while there's clutter and disarray, the basics looked well tended. None of the kids are in jail, and if they're using drugs, I can't detect it. They've stayed in school, and in fact, Stacie and Molly obviously want to continue here and graduate. Those things speak well for Audrey. And Gordon."

Beneath the gooey cream, Vida appeared thoughtful. "Their grief is under wraps, except perhaps for Molly. Or else they've done all their mourning, and their concern now is for their father. I wish the sense of loss showed more. Sometimes they seem quite unaffected, as if their lives had never been so brutally disrupted."

"Denial, maybe," I said.

"Resentment," Vida murmured. "I feel they resent both their parents."

"Because they were separated?"

"Because they're gone." Vida, who wasn't wearing her glasses, gazed at me with eyes that looked as if they were sunken in meringue. "They feel abandoned. As indeed they are."

"True," I allowed as my gaze now wandered toward the hall that led to the kitchen. It was after nine, and we'd eaten dinner early. I was vaguely hungry, but knew that Vida's rations were meager. I started to ask if she'd bought eggs when something clicked in my brain. "Breakfast! That's what I was trying to remember— Derek expected his mother to make breakfast for him before he went to work. Does that suggest a derelict parent?"

"No," Vida agreed, "it doesn't. Stina must have a grudge against Audrey. I suspect it has to do with Gordon."

I was changing into my robe. "Stacie implied that Gordon and Stina were making love on the beach."

"Again"—Vida sighed—"we have to consider our informant's agenda. Did Stacie say that so Stina might become a suspect instead of Gordon?"

"Probably." I began wrestling with the sofa, converting it into a bed. "I should probably get under way by nine tomorrow morning."

Vida was standing in front of the small mirror, her back to me. "I'll set the alarm for five." She redid one of the big curlers, but I couldn't detect any improvement. Wisps of hair still stuck out at various angles.

"Five? Why so early?"

"We haven't visited the crime scene," Vida responded, turning to face me. "It would be best to do so before the children get up."

I groaned, but didn't argue. After a month it seemed futile for us to inspect the crime scene. But the least I could do was humor Vida for a few more hours. Tomorrow night I'd be home.

Dawn was just beginning to break behind the hills when Vida and I drove to the Imhoff house. We parked halfway up the drive so as not to wake the family. I'd brought the small flashlight from my rental car and Vida was carrying the high-powered lantern she kept stored in the Buick's trunk. The morning was cool and damp, though only a low line of fog lay across the horizon.

The tide was out, which made walking the beach easy. The dock, which I had glimpsed from the Imhoff living room the previous day, was old but sturdy. It began at the edge of a short, sloping dune where the grasses grew in tufts and remnants of old campfires could be seen in the dry sand. The dock's weathered boards were only about a yard wide, though they stretched some two hundred feet out into the water. I suspected that they had to be replaced every few years. The pilings, however, were concrete, sunken deep enough to withstand winter storms.

Vida and I virtually tiptoed single file. Gulls swooped and dived, shrieking their wake-up call to the silent beach. As the sky began to lighten I could see the bulk of Haystack Rock on my right.

"Nothing," Vida said as we reached the end of the dock. "Oh, well."

"What did you expect? A note from the killer?"

Vida didn't answer. She was standing on the edge of the dock, staring down into the murky waters. "Why wasn't she drowned?" In the morning calm, the question seemed to come from nowhere.

I moved closer to Vida, tasting the salt air. "What do you mean?"

Expelling a deep breath, Vida sank her hands into the pockets of her brown tweed coat. "I misspoke. What I meant was, why didn't the killer throw her in the water? Even now, at low tide, it's fairly deep at the end of the dock. A push, a nudge—that's all it would have taken." She tapped the aged boards with her foot.

"The body would have washed up eventually," I reminded Vida.

"Not necessarily," she replied. "Even so, it would still have given the killer time, or confused the issue. Didn't your friend Bill say this was probably a premeditated murder?"

"That's because the weapon appears to have been something that wouldn't ordinarily be carried out to the dock," I said, watching the waves crest and disperse, then reappear in the sea's relentless, fascinating ebb and flow. "But Bill could be wrong. The real question is why was anyone else out here with Audrey in the middle of the night? Did she bring someone with her? Was she followed? Had she gotten a cramp and called for help?"

"The children heard nothing," Vida said. "I asked them."

"Derek wasn't home. He was with Dolores that night. Gordon was living at the Jaded Eye. Stacie and Molly would have been alone."

Again, Vida fell silent. When she spoke again, she turned around to look at the house. Only its outline was visible as it lay in the shadow of the foothills.

"Stacie and Molly were used to having their mother leave during the night," Vida said slowly. "Her comings and goings wouldn't disturb them. I assume they'd sleep through other noises as well. They were conditioned."

I had to agree with Vida. We remained on the dock for a few more minutes, both lost in our own thoughts. The bare boards, the murmur of the sea, the swooping of the gulls all lent a peaceful, timeless air. Yet a woman had died here, probably where we were standing. I shivered, and started back to the beach. Vida followed, but her steps sounded heavy behind me.

We ate breakfast at the Lazy Susan Café in Coaster Square. When we got back to the motel, I kept my word and called Willamette University. It was just after eight, but someone was on duty. There was no one named Damon listed in the student housing directory.

"Maybe," I said on impulse, "it's a first name. He's supposedly a law student."

"Oh," said the voice, which was young and female.

"You must mean Jesse Damon. I know him. He lives off campus. Would you like his number?"

Jesse Damon didn't answer and there was no recording machine. After a dozen rings I hung up. "He's probably off to class or in the library or wherever law students go at the crack of dawn," I told Vida. "Here's the number if you want to try him later."

Vida frowned. "Yes, I'll call this afternoon. I feel he's an important piece of our puzzle."

It didn't take me long to pack. But when the moment came to leave Vida, I felt guilty. "We've made some progress," I said, trying to sound optimistic.

"No, we haven't." Vida shot back. "We're completely muddled. I'm going to call Milo as soon as you leave and see if he can get more information out of Clatsop County."

"That might help," I said, and then did something I rarely do because Vida and I aren't casually affectionate: I put my arms around her and gave her a big hug. "Call me as soon as you learn anything important. I honestly do care. But I've got a paper to put out, and you know better than anyone what that means."

"Of course." Vida had gone rigid in my embrace, and when I stepped back, I saw that her face was devoid of expression. "Drive safely," she added in what sounded like an afterthought.

I said I would. Vida didn't follow me to the car, but closed the door as soon as I got outside. With a sigh, I trudged down the walk and under the archway that led to the parking lot. The Neon was covered with mist, and I had to dig into my laundry bag to find something I could use as a rag.

The dashboard digital clock showed eight forty-one. I

was ahead of schedule, which pleased me. I might be able to stop in Seattle for a late lunch.

Patches of morning fog filtered across the road as I wound my way to Highway 101. Hopefully, the fog would disappear as soon as I left the coast. I slowed down as I neared the arterial; visibility was so poor that I couldn't see the sign.

But I felt the crash. The Neon seemed to buckle, and I was thrown forward so hard that I felt the seat belt dig into my waist and chest. Wrestling with the wheel, I tried to keep the car on the road. But the moisture on the asphalt sent me into a skid—and a ditch.

Vaguely, I could hear brakes squeal, car doors slam, and someone shouting. With enormous effort, I flexed my feet, my legs, my hands, my arms. They were all still attached and seemed to be in working order. Next, I turned my head, first to the right, then to the left. The car was on its side. All I could see through the front window was underbrush and leaves and wisps of fog.

It dawned on me that the engine was still running, so I shut it off with shaking fingers. That was what was wrong—I was shaking all over, and breathing in little gasps. I must have been in shock. Somebody should cover me with a blanket, I thought hazily. Or offer brandy. On the other hand, I was off the road; I could just lie there for a couple of days until my nerves recovered.

But there was a man peering through the passenger window. In my stunned state, I thought he looked familiar. Milo? No. I wasn't in Alpine. Where was I? Who was he? Why didn't he offer brandy?

"Are you all right?" the man asked in an anxious voice.

There is some atavistic quality in females that makes

them want to please. Or maybe it was my mother's insistence on good manners in all sorts of dire circumstances. Whatever the reason, I rallied sufficiently.

"I think I'm just shaken up," I said. "Can you open the door? I don't think I locked it."

But the door was jammed. The car had been hit broadside. "Is there any room for you to get out the other way?" the man asked.

On closer inspection, I saw that the front end of the Neon had come to rest against an old stump. There were at least six inches between the driver's door and the ground. If I writhed and wriggled, I might get out. But I dreaded making the effort.

Somehow, I managed. As soon as the damp salt air struck my face, I felt the world come into better focus. Using the car to steady myself, I moved clumsily to the edge of the road. By now a dozen other cars were backed up between the turnoff and the highway.

"Help's on the way," the man said, coming around to give me a hand. "The driver who came up behind you went back to call the police and an ambulance."

"I don't need an ambulance," I said, then finally looked more closely at my benefactor. He was about my age, maybe a bit younger, just under six feet tall, with a good head of brown hair and a well-trimmed beard that showed a few streaks of gray. He still looked familiar, but I figured I was hallucinating. "Are you okay?" I asked, remembering all those good manners.

"I think so," he replied. "I'm afraid you ran that arterial."

I let out a weary sigh. "I couldn't see it in the fog. I was going only about ten miles an hour."

"A good thing," he responded. "I wasn't breaking any speed limits myself."

I looked at his car, which was parked in the middle of the intersection. Some of the other vehicles were now making their way around it, creeping forward like chastened children who had just received a hard-learned lesson. Which, of course, they had.

The car that had struck me had a broken headlight and a badly dented front end, but appeared drivable. Yet what captured my attention was that it, too, looked familiar. The vehicle was a green Ford Taurus, just like the one I'd turned in at Seaside.

In the distance, I could hear sirens. "We'll need to exchange information," I said, desperately trying to collect my wits. "The Neon's a rental, but I have insurance. I'll give you my name and address, as well as where you can reach my agent."

"It's okay," the man said, and his voice had taken on a sudden urgency. "My car's not badly damaged. In fact, I'm going to move it now. My main concern was that you weren't hurt."

"I'll still need your name and address," I said as he started for the Taurus. "You do have insurance, don't you?"

But the man didn't seem to hear. The sirens came closer. I leaned against the Neon's trunk and watched the man get into his car. Then, instead of pulling over, he gunned the engine, made a U-turn, and drove back the way he had come. He hadn't learned his lesson, and I was dumbfounded.

Before I could try to sort out the man's odd behavior, everything seemed to happen at once. A sheriff's patrol car arrived along with an ambulance and a Medex van. Another car, some sort of Chev, pulled off the road a few feet from where I was standing, and a short, muscular blond man in his thirties got out.

"Wow!" he called to me. "You're okay! I was the one who sent for the emergency guys."

They were guys *and* gals, as it turned out, and suddenly the intersection seemed clogged with people and vehicles. A sheriff's deputy immediately began setting up flares while the Medex team, a man and a woman, hurried to my side.

Despite my demurrals, they insisted that I should be taken to Providence Hospital in Seaside for evaluation. I insisted that they take me back to the Ecola Creek Lodge. I lost the argument.

Just as they were asking if I could walk to the ambulance, the muscular blond man who had been gazing intently at the chaos turned to me. "Where's Gord?" he asked.

"Who?" I still wasn't in any shape for trick questions.

"The guy in the Taurus, the one who hit you." He paused, taking another look around as if car and driver might suddenly materialize, like a pookah. "Didn't you get his name? It's Gordon Imhoff."

Chapter Eight

ONE OF THE sheriff's deputies, a fine-featured young man with piercing blue eyes and a name tag that read RANDY NEAL, swung around to stare. "McConnell, is it? What did you say?"

"Jeff McConnell, Cannon Beach Charters," the muscular blond said with a nod. "I said that was Gordon Imhoff. Haven't you guys been looking for him?"

"Yes, we have," Neal replied gravely as his partner, a husky Native American, joined him. "Are you positive that Imhoff was driving the car that struck the Neon?"

"Sure," McConnell answered. "I've known Gord since he moved here. When I saw him just now, I was surprised. But then I figured you guys must have tracked him down and I hadn't heard about it. I've been taking charters out of Depoe Bay for the past few weeks."

Depoe Bay was approximately a hundred miles south of Cannon Beach, and about the same size. Outside of tourist season, it probably wouldn't provide a hiding place for a man on the run.

The deputies exchanged glances. "I'm calling in," the Native American said, and hurried to the squad car. I managed to glimpse his name tag; he was Charles St. James. I etched both deputies onto my brain; it seemed important to remember their names. Maybe that was because I wasn't sure I could remember my own.

"Which way did he go?" Randy Neal asked, looking first at McConnell, then at me.

I found my voice. "South on 101. He was coming from that direction when we collided."

Neal shouted the information back to St. James. Meanwhile, the Medex team hovered over me. The woman, who had curly brown hair and red-rimmed glasses, wore picture I.D. around her neck with MARY JEAN PRATT in big, bold letters. She regarded me with concern.

"You'd better come along with us now," Mary Jean Pratt said kindly. "The police can sort out this other matter. You need to be checked."

"Actually," I said in a surprisingly firm voice, "I don't." The identification of Gordon Imhoff had acted as a steadying influence. "I'm fine, really. I have a friend just down the road at the Ecola Creek Lodge. After I get my luggage out of the Neon, I'll walk back."

The two Medex people looked at me, then at each other. Mary Jean shrugged. "If you insist. We can't force you. But you're not walking back down this foggy road. If you have any symptoms later, please call this number." She gave me her card.

"I'll give her a lift," Jeff McConnell volunteered. "I ought to stick around anyway. I'm a witness. Do we fill out the reports now?"

Mary Jean's partner, a balding, lean man with a lantern jaw, turned toward the sheriff's men, who were now conferring in the squad car. "You'd better check with them," he said.

Charles St. James got out of the car and headed in our direction. I explained that I was returning to the motel with Jeff McConnell.

"Okay," said the deputy. "We'll come with you. A tow truck's on the way. Where do you want the car taken?"

I thought of the hassle that would ensue with the rental agency, and felt a headache coming on. If that was a symptom from the collision, I wasn't going to mention it.

"Find out where the rental agency has repairs done," I said. "I suppose they use someplace in Seaside."

"Okay," St. James replied. "Let's go."

I didn't budge. "What about Gordon Imhoff?"

The deputy frowned. "You mean his part of the report?"

"Ah . . . yes." I didn't think it would be wise to mention that I knew of Gordon in any other context than the accident.

"We've got another patrol car on his trail," St. James answered. "He can't have gone too far. This time," he added ominously.

Two minutes later I was back at the Ecola Creek Lodge. Vida was on the phone, talking to Milo. She had to put him on hold to answer the door, and her jaw dropped when she saw me accompanied by Jeff McConnell and the sheriff's deputies.

"Good grief!" she cried. "You look awful! What's all this?"

"I ran into Gordon Imhoff," I said. "Actually, it was the other way around. He ran into me."

"What?" Vida yelped. I could imagine Milo at the other end of the phone, hearing our voices and wondering what the hell was happening.

I sank into one of the armchairs while the three men stood in the middle of the room, watching Vida warily and looking as if they'd been called to the principal's office. It dawned on me that my revelation about Gordon had blown my cover; the deputies must have realized that

I knew who Gordon Imhoff was. Maybe my brain was scrambled after all.

Vida gave me one last hard look, as if to make sure I was all in one piece, and dashed back to the phone. "Milo," she said in a tense voice, "Emma's here. She's been in a wreck. The sheriff's men are with her and so is . . ." She frowned at Jeff McConnell. "So is some other man I don't know. I must go. Please call back when you hear something from Astoria." She hung up.

It took over half an hour just to fill out the proper forms. They weren't particularly complicated, but Vida kept interrupting. She fired questions at the officers as well as at me, sending my brain ricocheting off the walls and causing the sheriff's men to acquire a dazed expression. As usual, when Vida was present, the question of authority became moot. Shortly before we finally finished, Milo called back and demanded to speak to me.

"Are you okay?" he asked in an anxious voice.

"Yes, yes, I'm fine." I found myself smiling. "I was shaken up and pretty scared, but now I'm all right."

"Jeez." Milo's relief flowed through the phone lines. "I had a hell of a time figuring out where Vida was staying. It's taken me this long to run you guys down."

"I may not be home today," I said, twisting around on the sofa so that I couldn't be easily overheard. "Could you call the office to tell them? In fact," I went on, lowering my voice to a whisper, "the guy who hit me is the husband of the deceased."

"The guy who . . . ? What?" Milo sounded confused.

"Didn't Vida give you the background?"

"Yeah, all twenty minutes of it. Say again?"

I did, though this time I spoke in an almost normal voice. From what I could tell, Vida was pouring out her connection to the Imhoff tragedy.

"I'll be damned," Milo said in wonder. "Talk about coincidences—I thought we had a lot of them in Alpine. But I guess Cannon Beach is even smaller."

"It is," I agreed. "Do you think you can find out anything from your vis-à-vis in Astoria?"

"I don't know the sheriff there," Milo admitted, "but he can probably fill me in to some extent. The question is why? Didn't Vida say you've got deputies with you?"

"Come on, Milo," I said in mild reproach. "You know they won't tell us what they'd tell you. If you don't dredge up something, Vida will make you pay."

"I know." Milo sighed. "You sure you're okay?"

"Yes, really. How was Bellevue?"

"The usual shit. Brandon wants to quit school and spend six months in Europe."

"Can he afford it?"

"Are you kidding? He works thirty hours a week at Jack in the Box. He wants me to lend him the money. Old Mulehide might pony up, but not Pop. That's part of the trouble with kids when you get divorced—they can play one parent against the other."

I wanted to commiserate, but the deputies and Vida were beginning to stare. Apparently, she had finished her recapitulation.

"I've got to go," I said to Milo. "Thanks in advance for any help you can give us."

"I miss you," Milo said, dropping his voice, and perhaps his guard. To my surprise, his admission didn't seem wrenched. The few tender confessions that he'd made in the past had come with all the ease of extracting an impacted wisdom tooth.

Ironically, I felt compelled to say that I missed him, too. But did I? Except for Vida's insistence on calling

Milo, I'd scarcely given him a thought since arriving in Cannon Beach.

"I'll be home very soon," I said, trying to inject a sense of intimate enthusiasm into my voice. "See you then."

We finished filling out the forms. Jeff McConnell hadn't seen the accident itself, but had arrived on the scene seconds after the impact.

"I heard it," he said, "but I was just coming around the bend and didn't see it. Does that count?"

It didn't. McConnell started to leave, but St. James and Neal wanted to ask some questions about Gordon Imhoff. Had Jeff seen Gordon since his disappearance the day after Audrey Imhoff's funeral? Did Jeff have any idea where Imhoff might have been for the past few weeks? Did he recognize the car that Imhoff was driving? Had he noticed the license plate?"

McConnell answered no to all of the questions. While he had known Gordon for several years, they had never been close. He was as shocked as the next one when Audrey was killed. And a final no: he couldn't imagine Gord hurting a fly.

Jeff was dismissed. St. James double-checked the paperwork, then asked me some of the same questions that he and Neal had posed to McConnell.

I explained that the Taurus Gordon had been driving looked very much like the car I'd rented in Portland and turned in at Seaside Sunday morning.

St. Charles looked puzzled. "You turned in one car and rented another? Didn't you like the Taurus?"

"I liked it fine," I said, and shot Vida a caustic look. "My plans changed. When I inquired if I could get the Taurus back, I was told it had already been rented by someone else. By the way, the license number is . . ." I rummaged in my purse, searching for the original rental agreement. I recited the plate for the deputies.

"Was it the same number as Imhoff's?" Neal asked, joining his partner by the fireplace.

"I don't know," I replied. "I never really noticed the plate on his car. But I have a feeling it could be. You see," I said carefully, "Gordon Imhoff was in Seaside Sunday morning. I saw him using the phone at the Shilo Inn."

Vida was as startled as the sheriff's deputies. Once again, she tried to take over the interrogation, but Neal and St. James asserted themselves. I had to state no fewer than five times that I didn't know Gordon Imhoff and that even though I had noticed the unkempt man at the Shilo Inn, his presence hadn't suggested anything to me except that he might be a drifter and that he needed to make a phone call. After the officers had finished questioning me and given instructions on how to proceed with the car-rental agency, they finally left. It was then that Vida whirled on me, her hands clenched as if she wanted to shake me silly.

"Why didn't you tell me?" she exclaimed. "Are you saying that car was the same one we saw parked at Rosalie and Walt Dobrinz's house?"

"It might have been," I answered calmly. "I didn't see the plate there, either. The car was parked too far down the drive. But I couldn't tell you about seeing Gordon in Seaside because I didn't know it was him. He looked like a bum. It was only after Jeff McConnell identified him that I realized why the man who hit me looked familiar. He'd cleaned up, but when my mind began to clear, I knew it was the same person. Isn't that what I just told the deputies about ten times?"

Apparently accepting my explanation, Vida began to pace around the small living room. "You didn't mention to the deputies that you'd seen the green car at the Dobrinz house."

"That's because I can't be sure," I responded, increasingly aware of new aches and pains. My neck hurt, my back ached, and my right arm felt as if I'd pulled something. "What good would it do? If Gordon had gone to his mother-in-law's yesterday, he wasn't there today. He was driving 101, hitting me broadside."

"It explains Rosalie's refusal to let us in the house," Vida said, pausing at the front window. "Gordon was inside. She couldn't let us see him."

"Maybe he's tired of running," I remarked. "Though he certainly didn't want to stick around for the cops."

"An awkward situation for him," Vida said, still peering out the window.

"Awkward for me, too. We're going to have to go into Seaside and get this mess straightened out with the car-rental agency." The comment didn't elicit a response from Vida; she was still at the window. "What are you looking at out there? Is Gordon crawling around in the bushes?"

Vida gave a shake of her head. "It's a white car. It's driven by twice, very slowly. A man's at the wheel. Who could it be?"

"Not Gordon," I said, removing my emergency pill bottle from my handbag. "It could be anybody. I'm going to take some Excedrin."

Vida finally turned around. "Are you sure you're not hurt? You could have internal injuries."

I shot Vida a disparaging look. "Thanks. Maybe I'll bleed to death before I can get out of Cannon Beach."

"You can't possibly drive home in your condition."

Vida's voice followed me into the kitchen. "You should rest today, and perhaps by Wednesday you'll feel well enough to start out."

"Wednesday!" I exclaimed, glugging down two Excedrin. "The paper comes out Wednesday. Or," I inquired as I returned to the living room, "have you forgotten?"

"Of course not," Vida huffed. "But I honestly believe Leo and Carla and Ginny can get the paper out in our absence. Have you no confidence in your staff?"

"You have no confidence in Carla, and mine's pretty shaky." Everything about me seemed shaky at the moment. Maybe I was suffering from delayed shock. I collapsed on the sofa just as a knock sounded at the door.

Vida rushed to answer the knock, but not before she peeked out through the front window. A tall, fair-haired man in his thirties stood in the doorway. "Ms. Lord?" he said.

I could see Vida's shoulders tense. "I'm Mrs. Runkel," she said crisply. "How may I help you?"

"I wish to see Ms. Lord," the man said with a faint Down Under accent. "Is she in?" His long, tanned face appeared over Vida's shoulder.

Vida, who didn't seem pleased to give way, grudgingly allowed that I was present. "But," she added in a warning tone, "Ms. Lord is unwell. She's been in an auto accident."

"Really." The man was unimpressed. He waited for Vida to step aside, then headed straight for me. He was wearing tennis shorts and a sweatshirt emblazoned with KANE PROPERTIES—CANNON BEACH AND LINCOLN CITY. I guessed who he was, but he introduced himself in a cool, aloof manner.

"I'm Stuart Kane. I understand you've been badgering

my wife. I must ask that you stop. Christina is very high-strung."

I held my aching head. Stina Kane was vivacious, loquacious, and effervescent, but didn't strike me as high-strung. And I certainly hadn't badgered her.

"Excuse me," I said, wishing the Excedrin would kick in, "but you must have me mixed up with one of your dissatisfied clients. I had a couple of drinks last night with your wife at the Driftwood Inn and we talked for a while. I thought we had a rather pleasant time."

"You don't understand," Stuart Kane said, and I sensed he was trying to be reasonable, though not succeeding very well. "Stina is easily upset. She cried all night."

I was flummoxed. "Why?"

"Why do you think?" Stu's arrogance came through, not only in his voice, but in the set of his prominent jaw. "A complete stranger barges into her life and asks all sorts of personal questions. I don't understand it. Neither does she."

"That makes three of us," I said, irritated. "I didn't ask her any personal questions. We were talking about Audrey and Gordon Imhoff."

Stu let out a beleaguered sigh. "I suspected you'd deny it. But that doesn't change things. I must insist that you keep away from Stina. I don't want to have to send her away again." He turned on his heel and headed for the door.

Unluckily for him, Vida was standing in it. "I cannot imagine," she said in her sternest voice, "how you expect to gain the confidence of potential clients when you impugn your wife's reputation, Mr. Kane. If someone is to be sent away, I should hope it's you. Meanwhile, don't ever bother us again." Vida moved with amazing agility, and ushered an astonished Stuart Kane out of the motel room.

"What was *that* all about?" I inquired after Vida had firmly closed the door behind our departed guest.

"He thinks his wife told you something she shouldn't have," Vida said, peeking through the window to make sure Stuart Kane had left. "I wonder what it could have been?"

Driving me into Seaside hadn't been on Vida's schedule. She wasn't particularly pleased by the prospect, but grew more affable when I reminded her that had I not been involved in an accident, we might never have known that Gordon Imhoff was alive and well in the Cannon Beach area.

We were on the road before ten. The fog had lifted, and except for some bits of glass that glistened like dew, all signs of the wreck had disappeared. The Neon was gone, presumably towed off to Seaside.

"I'm surprised you didn't call the Imhoff kids to tell them about their father," I said to Vida as we drove past another big RV camp.

"The girls are in school," Vida replied. "Derek's probably at work. I wouldn't confide in Dolores, even if she were home. She's not family."

My business at the car-rental agency was no more complicated than negotiations for the average Mid-East cease-fire. I was hampered by Gordon's defection, though the agency rep was able to tell me that on Sunday Mr. Imhoff had indeed rented the Ford Taurus I'd just turned in. I was surprised that he'd used his real name, but Vida pointed out that he'd have to present a valid Oregon state driver's license.

"Which," she noted as we left the agency, "indicates

his days of hiding were numbered. If Gordon wasn't recognized immediately at the rental agency, someone might have realized who he was later."

I only half heard Vida. I could rent another car, but since the other driver had left the scene, his coverage eventually would have to pay for the rental, no matter who was at fault. Until he was tracked down, I'd be paying for both the original rental and the replacement. There'd also be the deductible on my policy. Did I know what it was? My brain was so fuzzy that offhand I couldn't remember. I realized I should have called my agent, Brendan Shaw, earlier. I asked to use the phone and dialed the Sigurdson-Shaw number in Alpine. Brendan commiserated, but informed me that the deductible was five hundred dollars. With a sinking feeling, I thanked him and hung up. Then I told the rental rep I'd wait to get another car. I didn't feel like driving at the moment.

"Very wise," Vida stated as we started back to Cannon Beach. "You're much too nervy."

"Not anymore," I countered. "I'm stiff and sore and the headache's still there, but my nerves are under control."

"Nonsense. You could black out at any moment." Vida left the city limits, pressed down on the accelerator, and began to hum in her off-key voice. I couldn't be sure, but the tune sounded like "Poor Jud Is Dead" from *Oklahoma!* If that was it, her choice didn't make me feel any better.

"Where am I being taken as an unwilling hostage?" I finally inquired. We were winding south again, passing numerous roadside gift shops, flower stalls, eateries, and the launching pad for scenic helicopter rides.

"To call on Rett Runkel," Vida responded. "We owe it to him to let him know his son is all right."

"Rett? Oh, great. Now my stomach can get upset, too. What about telling Rosalie?"

Vida sniffed. "Why bother? Rosalie knows."

Rett was tinkering with his pickup, an old rusted-out Ford model with a broken windshield. T-Bone was lying on the sparse grass, but went into his guard-dog stance when we pulled up.

It took a while for Vida to relay the information about Gordon and his involvement in my accident. It took even longer for the news to sink in on Rett Runkel. When it did, he evinced no surprise.

"I figured Gordy was around here someplace," Rett said, wiping his dirty hands on an even dirtier rag. "Them cops aren't much good when it comes to lookin' for somebody who don't want to be found."

I could tell that Vida had expected a different sort of reaction from her brother-in-law. "Will he stop in to see you?" she asked, groping for some kind of solid information.

Rett and T-Bone both eyed Vida curiously. "Gordy? Naw, we aren't real close. I never saw that much of Audrey, to tell the truth. You raise kids, they raise hell, and then they're old enough to be on their own. That's the way it ought to be, anyhow."

"You don't see Marlin, either?" I put in, just to make sure Rett remembered that I was present.

"Marlin comes by now and then," Rett responded, leaning against the pickup. "He was here about a month ago to borrow some tools. Always borrowin' something. Says he doesn't own much 'cause he don't need much. But when he needs something, he comes to ol' Dad. 'Course he never returns anything, either." Rett's blubbery face wore a scowl. "Someday I'm goin' up to his place with this pickup and collect my stuff. I could probably fill this thing with what's mine."

"Indeed," Vida said in an undertone. She and the dog were eyeing each other with suspicion. It was T-Bone who gave up, sitting back on his haunches and scratching himself. "If Gordon should drop by," Vida said, now redirecting her attention to Rett, "would you tell him I'd be pleased to meet him? I'd hate to leave without having met Audrey's husband."

"Why's that?" Rett asked, puzzled. "You never met Audrey."

"All the more reason," Vida replied cryptically. Then, with a sweeping gesture, she indicated the shabby trailer. "Perhaps he'll want to stay with you."

"Like hell he will," Rett rumbled. "I don't need no company."

"I gathered that," Vida said, and turned on her heel. "Good day, Everett."

Rett Runkel belched at Vida's departing figure. T-Bone growled low in his throat. If not closely related to a jackal, the dog might have been part wolf.

I wasn't sure about Rett's species, either.

We didn't take the first turnoff into Cannon Beach, but drove on until we reached the RV camp and the Elk Creek Road. I presumed that we were headed for Marlin's; instead, Vida pulled into the parking lot by the RV headquarters and used a pay phone to call Rosalie Dobrinz.

"Rosalie will meet us at Mo's," Vida informed me when she returned to the car. "I promised to treat her to lunch."

"Did you tell her about Gordon?"

"No. It's better not to until she's with us in person."

Mo's was a longtime tradition on the Oregon coast. The local Mo's was part of a chain of seafood restaurants between Astoria and the California state line, all of which touted the clam chowder. While working for *The Oregonian*, I had occasion to visit almost all them, though I personally considered the french fries as their standout menu item. Not that I was any expert—it had taken me ten years to figure out that Mo was a woman, not a man. I suppose I was too busy eating.

During the tourist season, there is almost always a long line waiting to get into the restaurant. But as the year moved deeper into October there were no lines, at least not on this Monday at midday. A dozen cars bearing out-of-state license plates, mostly from Washington and California, were parked in the big lot. Since we had traveled the shorter distance, Rosalie hadn't arrived yet.

"How did you talk her into driving up from Manzanita?" I asked Vida as we waited outside in the sunshine.

"I told her I had something very important to discuss," Vida responded, adjusting the wide-brimmed straw hat she usually reserved for summer wear. "Judging from her tone, Rosalie is rarely invited to discuss anything of importance. Life must be very dull for her, don't you think?"

"I don't think having your daughter murdered is dull," I replied.

"No, certainly not." Vida watched a dark blue sedan pull into the parking lot, but it didn't belong to Rosalie. A young couple in shorts got out and headed for the restaurant. "Nor would coping with the daughter's marital breakup be dull. You must wonder—do people create crises because the rest of their lives are so unspeakably routine?"

The thought had occurred to me before, as I was sure it had to Vida. But it flirted with criticism of small-town life, or so it seemed to me. The people I had known in Seattle and in Portland hadn't seemed nearly as screwed up as my fellow Alpiners. From the start, I'd wondered if they compensated for the lack of civic and cultural distractions by actively searching for trouble.

"Audrey doesn't seem to have been the kind of person who would enjoy a rut," I pointed out. "That was her goal, to get out of here and start over."

Vida sighed. The young couple went past us and entered the restaurant. "It always comes back to that, doesn't it? Audrey, and what she wanted. I'm beginning to understand her, to become acquainted. Very headstrong, independent, restless. Yet not without some compensating qualities. We must ask Rosalie about Audrey's good deeds."

Another ten minutes lapsed before Rosalie Dobrinz arrived in an aging Chev that was almost as big as Vida's Buick. Emerging from the car, Rosalie took a last drag off of her cigarette, tossed it aside, and came huffing toward us with an air of combined apology and anticipation.

"I couldn't get away," she said in an anxious voice. "Walt needed some help with the kitchen drain. He's got a million tools, but he never seems to have the one he needs."

As we waited to be seated at one of the trestle tables, I regarded Rosalie more closely. She seemed to have developed a tic in the last twenty-four hours, and her hands shook ever so slightly. She was still short of breath when we sat down.

"So what's going on?" she asked, her small eyes glistening. "Has something happened?"

Vida appeared to be engrossed in the menu. At last she looked up. "You must know." The owlish expression was fixed on Rosalie.

"Know what?" Rosalie tried to look innocent, but she wasn't much of an actress.

"About Gordon. Where is he now?"

"Gordon!" The exclamation meant to convey surprise, but it wasn't convincing. "Now that's funny you should ask, because the sheriff's people came by asking the same thing."

"And?" In contrast to Rosalie, Vida remained calm.

Rosalie held out her pudgy hands in a helpless gesture. "How should I know?"

"Rosalie." Vida became confidential, leaning forward, with her large bust brushing the trestle table. "You and I are related by marriage. Or were," she added hastily. "That is," she went on, gathering steam, "we married brothers. We have to be honest with one another. I know perfectly well that Gordon stayed with you and Walt. I also know that he came back this morning, let's say around nine-thirty."

Rosalie was so astounded by Vida's guesswork that her jaw dropped and she gaped like a beached trout. "Oh! I . . . it wasn't . . . it's not the way you . . ." She gulped and withered under Vida's gaze. "Does the sheriff know?"

"I've no idea," Vida replied truthfully. "What did you tell the deputies today?"

"The truth," Rosalie answered so promptly that I believed her. "Gordon hadn't shown up when they stopped by. He came along not five minutes after they left."

"Was he watching for them?" I asked, keeping my voice down. We had just been joined by a family of four who were being seated about five feet away from us at the long table.

"I . . ." Rosalie hesitated, her eyes darting in the direction of the newcomers. The mother and father seemed absorbed in settling an argument between their two sons, who looked to be about eight and ten. "I guess he was. The Wilkinsons down the street both work, and they leave their garage open. Gordon knows that because he's sold things to them. He'd pulled in there to wait. He'd expected the sheriff to send someone after him. I guess he got into a wreck."

"That he did," I said, and explained my role in the search for Rosalie's son-in-law. "So where is he now?" I inquired.

Predictably, Rosalie turned cagey. "I'm not sure. He took off not long afterward. He didn't say where to."

It was safe to assume that Rosalie was lying. Gordon may very well have left the Dobrinz house, but I was sure that his mother-in-law knew his destination. I guessed that Vida felt the same way.

"Why doesn't he simply turn himself in?" she asked with a touch of impatience, perhaps for Gordon, maybe for Rosalie as well.

Rosalie let out a heavy sigh. "I don't know. He can't run forever. He's not a fugitive. I don't understand it."

Our server arrived and orders were taken. Rosalie insisted she only wanted coffee, but Vida finally coaxed her into a bowl of clam chowder.

"Was this weekend the first time you've seen him since he disappeared?" Vida asked after the server had left.

Rosalie nodded in a listless manner. "I was so worried. Gordon's like a son to me. More of a son than Audrey was a daughter, if you get right down to it. Gordon never had much of a childhood. His parents were protesters, always marching for some cause. Black people, lettuce, Vietnam—you name it, they were there with their signs and their slogans. I always felt that's why Gordon wanted to settle down and live a peaceful life. He'd been all over the place when he was growing up."

"And yet," Vida noted thoughtfully, "he's been on the run, as they say."

"Yes." Rosalie nodded twice for emphasis. "That's what I mean—it's not like him."

"Then why?" Vida let the words fall like heavy stones.

Rosalie put a hand over her eyes. "I don't know," she said softly. "I don't want to know." Her chunky shoulders began to shake. "I'm afraid to know. I hope I never have to find out."

Chapter Nine

EVENTUALLY, ROSALIE REGAINED her composure and we talked of other things. Vida asked about Audrey's alleged helpfulness toward others. For the first time her mother brightened at the mention of her daughter's name.

"Now, that's where Audrey did her share," Rosalie declared with enthusiasm. "Somehow she got involved with driving patients to doctor appointments, especially seniors. It was a volunteer thing through the chamber of commerce. Even after a lot of the other merchants dropped out, Audrey still carted folks around. There's only one doctor in Cannon Beach, you see, so if you go to somebody else, you have to drive into Seaside or all the way to Astoria."

"How very kind," Vida remarked, nibbling at her fish and chips. "I hope her efforts were appreciated."

Rosalie's enthusiasm dimmed. "Well . . . you know how people are. Some take everything for granted. But Audrey didn't complain about that, except in the beginning. In a way, I was surprised she kept at it."

"Did she have to make many trips?" I asked, deciding that the french fries definitely met my memory's muster.

"Oh . . ." Rosalie's forehead furrowed. "I'm not sure. We didn't chat much. I suppose she went a couple of times a week. At least that's how often she was taking

Rupe Pickering while he was having his cancer treatments, or whatever it was."

Vida shot me a covert glance. "That would be Ruth's husband? Doesn't Ruth drive?"

Rosalie's expression showed disdain for Ruth. "Ruth doesn't do much, if you ask me, except make those ugly metal dingbats. She won't drive on the highway, and freeways scare the pants off of her. I guess that's what happens when you marry money. You get spoiled."

I recalled the modest house where Ruth lived. "She's rich? I'm surprised."

"I don't mean she's rolling in it," Rosalie amended, "but Rupe's dad owned some beachfront property they sold way back. They made a bundle off it. And both Rupe and Ruth were what you'd call careful. Or," she added with bite, "what I'd call downright tight."

"I wondered," I said with a small smile, "how much money you could make from building kites and beating out metal sculptures."

Rosalie crumbled crackers into her chowder. "That's the other thing—they would have starved if they'd had to rely on what they made from their so-called work. Believe me, Audrey and Gordon couldn't afford to pay Ruth much when she came to work for them. I think the only reason she filled in at the Jaded Eye was to push those damned sculpture things."

Vida was gazing around the big restaurant, taking in everything from the splendid ocean view to the clusters of luncheon customers. "Lovely," she commented, more to herself than to Rosalie or me. "Though I miss the mountains. They make you feel so safe," she added, turning to Rosalie. "Protected. The ocean is more dangerous. And there's no end to it. I'm not sure I like that."

Rosalie gave a little shrug. "I've always lived on the

coast. I was raised in Astoria. That's where I met Rett. He was stationed in the coast guard there."

"He never suggested taking you to Alpine to meet the rest of his family?" I could hear the barely concealed scorn in Vida's voice.

"He'd mention it now and then," Rosalie responded, "but we never went. He thought his relatives were a bunch of stuffed shirts." Realizing too late what she had said, Rosalie put a hand to her mouth. "Sorry. That was his opinion, not mine. How could I know one way or the other?"

"You couldn't," Vida replied, tight-lipped.

"Rett had a lot of opinions," Rosalie said, obviously trying to explain away her ex-husband's attitude toward the rest of the Runkels. "I didn't agree with half of them. That's one reason we got divorced. That, and his drinking."

Vida's censorious manner fled. "Does he still drink?" she inquired in a confidential tone.

"Not like he used to. His liver got to acting up, and the doctor told him if he didn't quit, or at least cut down, he'd be dead within a year. That was in 1990. But of course we'd split up long before that."

"Hmmm." Vida finished her coleslaw, propped an elbow on the rough wood, and leaned her cheek against her hand. "Ernest was such a wonderful man. I can't help but think that Everett must have shared some of his finer qualities. Are you ever sorry you left him?"

The color rose in Rosalie's weathered face. "You bet. No man is perfect. At least Rett had a sense of humor. Walt's a sourpuss. Half the time he turns off those damned hearing aids so he doesn't have to listen to me. And I don't know what your husband was like in bed, but I'll tell you his brother was some top gun. Walt's like a limp noodle, if you'll forgive my frankness."

Having never, ever heard Vida discuss the physical side of her marriage, I was fascinated. Indeed, I expected her to take umbrage at Rosalie's candor. But Vida surprised me.

"Ernest was an excellent mate, in every sense," she declared, wrapping the statement in her own brand of dignity.

Rosalie nodded, as if the two women had suddenly bonded over the bedside manner of the Runkel brothers. "You know what they say—if a marriage is on the rocks, the rocks are in the mattress. But that wasn't the case with Rett. Except, of course, when he drank. Then he lost it. He lost everything, including me. If only his liver had pooped out on him sooner."

Vida stared at Rosalie over the rims of her glasses. "You'd still be there?"

"You bet. And we'd both be the better for it," Rosalie asserted, her eyes roaming the high ceiling as if she could envision a happier time, a better place. "He wouldn't be stuck out there in that damned trailer with that damned dog. We'd still be a family."

Vida didn't blink. "With Marlin and Audrey and Gordon and the youngsters?"

Rosalie's lower lip quivered. "Maybe Marlin wouldn't have needed all that dope. He was only fifteen when Rett and I split up. Maybe Audrey wouldn't have run off to California. Maybe," she went on, her voice breaking, "Audrey wouldn't be dead."

"My, my," Vida exclaimed as we drove back into Cannon Beach, "such a do-gooder! Who would have thought it of Audrey?"

"You sound skeptical." I had just taken two more Excedrin; my aches and pains seemed to have intensified.

"The elderly are gullible," Vida said as we slowed behind a big camper. "Think of all those pigeon-drop schemes or whatever they are. Old people fall for them constantly."

Vida's reaction intrigued me. "You think Audrey was a schemer?"

"Where else did she get all that money in the separate account?"

I kicked myself for being so slow on the uptake. "You're right. It's possible. Rupe Pickering?"

"Among others, I suspect. Take Opal Iverson." Vida glanced at me to be certain I recognized the name. "Opal has a sixth sense when it comes to people who are about to die. Dust Bucket Cooper was barely seventy, and seemed healthy as a horse when Opal started to bake him pies and offer to run errands. Three months later Pastor Purebeck was giving the funeral eulogy. Dust Bucket left her three thousand dollars. Then there was Alva Peabody, who was in her eighties, but very spry. Three trips to the Grocery Basket, and an afternoon going over dress patterns at Sew 'N Sew, and Alva was six feet under. Opal got Alva's car and fur coat, though frankly, it looked as if it had been made out of dog hair. The coat, I mean, not the car. It was a Pontiac. Just last winter, Opal started calling on Bertha May Amundson, and you know what happened to her in that big February windstorm. Whomp!" Vida slapped her hand against the dashboard, in apparent imitation of the cedar tree that had fallen on poor Bertha May. "Opal ended up with the sterling silver, a spinet piano, and two nice lamps."

Though I'd proofed the obituaries and written the windstorm fatality story myself, I hadn't known about Opal Iverson's opportunistic role as Alpine's Angel of Death. So caught up in Vida's recital was I that we were pulling up by the Imhoff house before it dawned on me that the Buick had turned off the main road.

"We're calling on the kids?" I asked in mild surprise.

"I hope not," Vida answered. "With any luck, they'll be in school or at work. Let's hurry."

"Hurry and do what?" I inquired, obediently getting out of the car.

"We need to make a search," Vida responded, walking swiftly to the back door. "Aha! As I suspected," she said, letting us in, "they didn't lock the door."

They didn't clean house, either. The clutter had multiplied, and the sink was full of dirty dishes. Soiled laundry was strewn all over the place, and a glimpse into one of the bedrooms revealed an unmade bed.

"This isn't legal," I pointed out.

"It isn't *illegal*," Vida asserted. "I'm their aunt. I want to straighten up. They could use some help."

It wasn't my place to argue. "Shall I dust?"

Vida was already going through kitchen drawers. "I've checked some of these," she said, her hands moving like a magician's. "Audrey didn't keep much of interest in here except for household bills. Really, several are past due. I must remind the children about them."

We moved on to the master bedroom. Judging from the chaos, the room was being used. I noted a rumpled waitress's uniform, an apron that looked as if it belonged to a grocery store, pink underpants, white Jockey shorts, two pairs of blue jeans, and several T-shirts. I guessed that Derek and Dolores had moved in. Their takeover struck me as unfeeling.

Vida had gone straight to the walnut bureau. "Bankbooks," she said in an expectant voice, holding up a manila envelope. Then her face fell. "Oh dear—these are for the joint accounts. Now, where would Audrey keep the other ones?"

I was looking through the dresser. "Not here. This is all cosmetic stuff and jewelry and panty hose."

"A strongbox," Vida said, heading for the closet. "Gordon and Audrey must have kept their private papers there."

"But wouldn't Audrey hide any records of her personal account?" I asked, checking under the bed where I spotted more rumpled clothes and several shoes. There was sand everywhere, and the scent of the sea permeated the house.

"Yes," Vida replied with a grunt as she wrestled with the contents of the closet. "That's why I'm going to look in this suitcase. It obviously belongs to a woman."

If the bright floral tapestry pattern didn't betray the owner's gender, the contents did. The suitcase was filled with sweaters, slacks, and shoes.

"Audrey was packed and ready to leave," Vida remarked. "Let's look at the mate to this luggage."

The smaller tapestry bag revealed blouses, shirts, and undergarments. We checked the zippered compartments of both bags, but found nothing of interest. Vida fetched two plain black cases from the closet. They appeared to be empty. The smaller of the two, however, made me pause.

"Look," I said to Vida, using a fingernail to pick up a bit of green flaky residue that clung in one corner.

Vida sniffed at my finger. "It looks like oregano, but it smells like something else."

"It *is* something else. I'm pretty sure it's marijuana."

Vida stared at me, then began scraping at the tiny flakes. "Goodness! Where did this come from?"

"I can make a guess," I responded, reaching into an inside pocket. "Ah! What's this?"

"This" was a scrap of paper, caught in the pocket's lining. "It says 'Friday P.M. Bring two thousand dollars. Do not go to Ja . . .' The rest is torn off."

Vida snatched the note out of my hand. " 'Jail,' I presume. An attempt at humor. But what about this two thousand dollars? And 'Friday P.M.'?"

"Have you ever seen Marlin's handwriting?" I asked as Vida carefully slipped the scrap of paper into the pocket of her poplin jacket.

"I've scarcely seen Marlin," she replied. "Why Marlin?"

"Because his place reeks of pot. Audrey might have been the one who brought it to him. I don't think he gets out much," I added dryly.

Vida, who was still crouched on the floor, grew thoughtful. "No, he certainly doesn't. But to whom was the two thousand dollars owed? Audrey?"

"To whoever sold Marlin his pot," I answered, then frowned. "Unless . . ."

"Unless what?" With a small grunt, Vida rose to her feet.

"Unless Marlin is actually growing pot up there in the woods. The climate's not ideal, but it can be done."

"Indeed. It has crossed my mind. Look at those young people who were raising plants up on Mount Sawyer last year. And then this spring Milo caught Darryl and Sheree Gottschalk growing marijuana at their place by Cass Pond. They argued that it was a much-needed business venture to help the local economy. The incoming community-college students would be wonderful customers. Darryl even tried to join the chamber of commerce." Vida shook her head in wonder.

Vida finished going through drawers in the matching nightstands. We found nothing of further interest, nor did we locate a strongbox. I could tell that Vida was growing frustrated as we went into the living room.

"We're fighting the clock," she declared. "We mustn't forget Jesse Damon. I'm convinced that even if he wasn't involved in Audrey's death, he knows something."

I shrugged. "The police must have questioned him. Why would he tell us anything of interest?"

"Because we're not the police." Vida fingered her chin while her eyes darted around the living room. "If you had a car, you could drive over to Salem."

"Vida," I began, irritated, "we've been through that before. I'm not going to Salem. And if I felt like driving any distance, I'd go home."

"Yes, yes, of course." Vida dismissed my protest with a wave of one hand. "I checked that desk over there earlier. Nothing. The cupboards and bookcases speak for themselves." She snapped her fingers. "The Jaded Eye! That must be where Audrey and Gordon kept their important papers. Do you think Ruth Pickering would let us in?"

For once, I was a step ahead of Vida. "Ruth can't have the only key. Have you looked here?"

"You're right." Vida gave me a big smile. "I believe there were keys in the desk. They didn't mean anything to me when I peeked in there Saturday. Let's look."

The dozen keys on the big silver ring weren't marked, but Vida was convinced that one of them must belong to the Imhoffs' shop. "Now, here's what we'll do," she said, outlining her strategy like a general going to war. "Drop me off at the Jaded Eye. You go up to see Marlin and find out what he knows about the marijuana in the suitcase. You can drive that far, can't you?"

Vida had me in a bind. If I pleaded physical disability, I wouldn't be able to head for Alpine in the morning. If I agreed to call on Marlin, I might end up driving all over Clatsop County, not to mention inland to Salem. And, if I had to be honest, my aches and pains were bearable.

"Okay," I conceded, "I'll go see Marlin."

"Excellent. Let's check the children's rooms and then we'll be on our way."

It appeared that Stacie and Molly shared a room with twin beds and a closet crammed so full that garments tumbled onto the floor. One of the beds was made, however, and in fact, one half of the room was relatively tidy. Judging from the cutout photos of younger teen idols on the wall, I guessed that Molly was the neater of the two sisters.

"Goodness," Vida said in mild dismay. "Where shall we begin?"

"You begin," I responded. "I'll check out Derek's room." It occurred to me that if he and Dolores had moved into the master bedroom, Derek's former room might be easier to tackle.

"Very well," Vida agreed a bit grimly. "Though I can't imagine we'll find much."

I was turning in to the short hallway when we heard a commotion at the back door. Glancing over my shoulder, I exchanged startled looks with Vida. We both hurried into the kitchen, where we found Stacie and Molly screaming at each other.

"It's not my fault!" Molly cried, her voice full of tears. "It's everybody's fault! Why do I always get the blame?"

"Because you whine," Stacie shouted. "You always want everything your way! Why can't you just shut up and chill?"

Sensing our presence, they turned at the same time and

saw us in the kitchen doorway. Both sisters stared, and Molly began to blush furiously.

"What are you doing here?" Stacie demanded, catching her breath.

"We came to help you clean," Vida replied, not missing a beat. "You need to pay bills, too. I don't suppose you have a checkbook?"

The routine question seemed to calm Stacie. "No. Derek and I've talked about opening an account, but we haven't gotten around to it."

"I thought you had an attorney in Seaside," Vida said, pulling out a chair from the kitchen table. "Do sit, girls. We have some important things to discuss."

Molly removed a maroon backpack from her shoulders and hugged it to her chest. "I don't want to discuss anything. I'm tired of discussing things. I'm going to my room." She stalked off into the hall.

"Bratfinger," muttered Stacie. "I just tried to tell Molly that if we're going to make it on our own, she's going to have to stop acting like a baby. She's spoiled, because she's the youngest. No matter what she gets or gets to do, it's never enough. Sometimes she made my folks crazy."

Such as it was, the admission was the first hint of sympathy I'd heard from Stacie for her parents as a unit. "Most kids are like that," I said, recalling Adam's constant badgering over the years.

From under the blonde hair that covered most of her forehead, Stacie gave me a disbelieving glance. "I'm not. I always knew there were limits, especially with Mom. And Derek—well, Derek would say okay, and then do what he wanted anyway and hope he didn't get caught. Derek's a jerk sometimes, but at least he doesn't whine like Molly. Molly acts like she's some kind of whipped puppy. 'Poor Molly,' 'poor me,' that's her line. It gets real old."

Vida was nodding sagely. "We need to talk about your future." My House & Home editor gave me a sidelong look. "My car keys are in my purse, Emma dear. Go ahead and take them. I'll be here when you get back."

The dismissal was underlined by the "Emma dear." Vida had never called me that in all the years I'd known her. With a faint sigh, I started to look for her purse. Then I remembered that she'd probably left it in the girls' bedroom.

Molly didn't respond when I first knocked. I called to her and received a belligerent "What?" Gently, I opened the door.

"Your aunt left her purse in here," I explained with a smile. "She was going to . . . ah . . . make Stacie's bed for her."

Molly was curled up on her own bed, her face turned to the wall. "Stacie's a slob."

"You're not," I said, spying Vida's purse next to the pile of clothes that had been disgorged by the jammed closet. "How was school?"

There was a pause, as if Molly was trying to decide if the question was worthy of an answer. "Okay. We got out early."

That explained the Imhoff sisters' unexpected arrival. "Nice. What's your favorite subject?"

"Math." Molly still hadn't turned to look at me.

I sidled up to the foot of the bed. "I hated math. I'm still not very good at it. I liked history best."

There was no comment. I was scarcely surprised that Molly wasn't interested in my long-ago academic pursuits. At fourteen, Adam hadn't been interested in anything that went on outside of his adolescent self-absorption.

"So," I said brightly, "you and Stacie plan to go on living here together?"

"I guess." The answer was muffled; Molly had now stuck her face in the pillow.

"What about Derek and Dolores? Will they get married and find their own place?"

"I guess."

I took a deep breath and went for it. "I saw your dad today."

Molly's chunky little body went rigid. I waited. Finally, laboriously, she rolled over and peered at me from under her hand. "My dad? You couldn't have!" The denial was a sudden shriek. Molly jerked into a sitting position and beat her fists on her thighs. "No! He went away! He's gone!"

"Hey!" I scooted between the twin beds and sat down next to her. "He's fine. In fact, we had a car wreck. That is, we hit each other. But nobody got hurt."

It took several moments for my words to sink in. "No," Molly repeated, but this time without conviction. "He left. It must have been somebody else."

"It was your dad," I asserted. "He was very kind. He wanted to make sure I wasn't injured."

Molly raised a pale, apprehensive face to me. "Where is he?" Her voice was almost inaudible.

"I think he went to see your grandmother, but I'm not sure where he is now." I attempted a reassuring smile. "You'll probably hear from him soon."

"No!" Molly's vehemence made her cough. Then the cough turned to tears, and the tears bordered on hysteria. "No, no, no! He can't! He's got to go away again!"

Her outcries had brought Vida and Stacie to the bedroom door. "What's this?" Vida exclaimed.

"See what I mean?" Stacie was angry. "Molly's a

mess. She's always a mess. Shut up, bratfinger! All you ever do is cry and whine!"

With a hand on Molly's shaking shoulders, I turned to Stacie. "She has a right to be upset. I was telling her about your father."

Stacie looked puzzled. I assumed Vida hadn't yet informed the older girl about my unconventional meeting with Gordon Imhoff.

"What about him?" Stacie asked, her tone defensive.

"He and I were in a car wreck this morning. He's okay." I kept my voice neutral. "Have you talked to him?"

Stacie's eyes rolled up like venetian blinds. Then she fainted.

Chapter Ten

"THE TROUBLE IS," Vida said, pouring hot tea into mismatched mugs that were a far cry from her own English bone china, "these children are overwrought. They're trying to carry on, and very bravely, too, but it's all been too much. They need some stability in their lives." She sighed and looked straight into my eyes. "That's why I must ask for a leave of absence. I intend to remain here until they get on their feet. Emotionally speaking, that is."

My initial reaction was a selfish one: how on earth would I put out *The Advocate* without Vida? Nightmarish visions of Carla at the Burl Creek Thimble Club and the John Knox Quilting Bee and the Daughters of Norway Lutefisk Eating Contest danced through my head with leaden feet and horrific typos.

Yet I had to acknowledge Vida's perceived responsibility, even though it didn't strike me as her problem. She hardly knew these Runkels. My only demurral, however, was to suggest that Grandma Rosalie might perform the task instead.

Vida scoffed. "Rosalie is probably a decent sort, but I don't think she's particularly competent. Besides, she smokes. That doesn't make for a good role model."

Since I had smoked off and on during my tenure at *The*

Advocate, I felt put in my place. Nor was this the time for an extended argument: Stacie had regained consciousness almost immediately and was now lying on her unmade bed. Vida picked up the mugs and took them in to the girls. Molly was sitting like a statue, staring blankly into space.

There was a small table between the twin beds. Vida set the mugs down and put a hand on Stacie's arm. "Drink this, dear. I've added milk and sugar. It'll perk you up in no time."

"I hate tea," Stacie declared. "I'd rather have coffee or a Coke."

"Tea has caffeine and is more bracing," Vida asserted. "I must insist. Please take at least a few sips." She turned to Molly. "You, too. You're looking very peaked."

Stacie grimaced, but obeyed. Molly picked up her mug and blew on it. "I like herbal tea sometimes," she allowed. "This is different. I can't smell any herbs or spices."

"It's Earl Grey," Vida said. "A great favorite of many, though I drink Red Rose. Now, Stacie," she said, regarding the older girl, "what upset you so?"

Stacie's lip was curled over the tea mug. "I thought he was dead."

"I see." Vida remained nonchalant. "So you fainted from relief."

"Relief?" Stacie seemed puzzled. "Well . . . I guess."

I was standing at the foot of Stacie's bed. "You thought your father had been killed?"

Stacie sighed and nodded. "Why not? It made sense. Somebody might have wanted to get rid of both my mother and my father."

Vida frowned. "Now, who would want to do such a thing?"

Stacie didn't have to search for an answer. "Mr. Kane."

Vida perched on the edge of Stacie's bed. "Why would Stuart Kane do such a thing?"

"Because," Stacie replied, sitting up and brushing the long hair off her face, "he was jealous. He wanted to end my dad's affair with Mrs. Kane and get her back."

"That's no reason to kill your mother," Vida pointed out.

"Yes, it is," Stacie asserted. "If they were both dead, Mr. and Mrs. Kane could get the shop."

"The shop?" Vida's frown deepened. "You mean the Jaded Eye?"

Stacie nodded, the hair falling back over her face. "The Kanes have been trying to buy the shop for the past year or so. It's a good location, right in the middle of town. Their office is on Pacific, near the beach. It's off the beaten track. Visitors don't go by it unless they have a reason."

I asked if the Kanes had made an offer to Audrey and Gordon.

"Yes," Stacie answered, "but Dad wouldn't take it. He said it was too low. Besides, he didn't want to sell. He loved the Jaded Eye."

I was skeptical. "A commercial site on Hemlock doesn't seem like a motive for murder. There must be other good locations. Besides, your father is alive."

My words seemed to calm Stacie. But Molly began to tremble. "I want him to stay away," she said in a gulping voice. "It isn't safe for him to be here. If you see him, can you tell him that?" The appeal was to me; maybe she thought I was going to take to the road and collide with him again. I didn't know what to say.

Vida did. She leaned across the narrow space between the beds and took one of Molly's quivering hands. "Tell me—do you honestly think your father killed your mother?"

Molly's eyes grew very wide and then she squeezed them shut. "Yes. Yes, I do. But it wasn't his fault."

Molly pulled her hand free and turned back to face the wall.

There wasn't much more that we could do for the Imhoff sisters at the time. Convinced that they were no longer in a combative mood, and that even the young must struggle alone with their special demons, we resurrected our original plan. I drove the Buick and dropped Vida off at the Jaded Eye, but waited until I made sure that one of the keys on the ring she'd purloined would fit the store's lock. The next to the last one she tried opened the door, and with a wave, she sent me off to Marlin's so-called pad.

When I pulled into the restricted space that served as a turnaround, there was no sign of my would-be host. I waited a few minutes, then realized that Marlin would have seen the Buick and assumed that Vida was driving. I got out of the car and went up to the shack he called home.

The smell of pot hung in the air. I knocked on the door, which may have been the sturdiest part of the house. After a long pause I heard various bolts and locks being opened.

"Emma, is it?" Marlin's eyes were dilated and he looked very mellow.

"Emma it is," I said, taking advantage of his spaced-out state and edging my way inside. "I borrowed your aunt's car."

"Why? It's a boat. You should have something more sporty, like a 'Vette."

"My real car's a Jag," I said, and wondered why I felt a need to impress Marlin Runkel. "It's old," I added, as if to make amends.

Most of Marlin's furnishings were old, too, but some of them were obvious antiques. Indeed, the interior of the house was a far cry from the exterior. If not exactly neat, there was a certain order to it, with all the usual necessities and some intriguing objets d'art. A Native American rug, a Japanese screen, a pair of African masks, and even a couple of what looked like Ruth Pickering's metal sculptures adorned the small living room, which I assumed also served as a bedroom. A door led into a tiny kitchen and, I hoped, a bathroom.

"Toke?" Marlin offered, indicating what looked like an old tin button box.

I shook my head. Even in my youth, I'd never tried marijuana. Most of my friends had, and my brother, Ben, had puffed away for several years, quitting only when he entered the seminary. But I'd always been timid about trying new things. Someone had once told me that pot could make you lose control, and that frightened me. Then I'd met Tom Cavanaugh, and lost control without the aid of any strange substances, unless you count love. I'd spent the rest of my life paying for that surrender.

"What's happening?" Marlin asked, leaning back against the faded couch that looked as if it might have dated from the Twenties.

"Not much," I replied, wondering if I could pin Marlin down in his present dreamy state. I pointed to the tin box. "You grow this stuff?"

Marlin chuckled. "You the fuzz?"

"I told you, I own a newspaper. And no, this isn't for a story. I was just curious." My manner was nonchalant; I was trying to match Marlin's mellow mood.

"I'm on to you." Marlin winked through a blue haze. "You and that battle-ax aunt of mine are playing private eye."

"Journalists always search for truth," I remarked, picking up a carved myrtlewood pear and pretending to admire it.

"So do I." Marlin swayed a little, the smoke encircling his head like a nimbus.

"Pot must be harder to grow in this climate," I said, putting the pear aside.

"Truth is supposed to set you free," Marlin said, gazing off into the distance. "Death sets you free. Audrey's free."

I wasn't sure where this conversation was going; maybe up in smoke. "Is that good?" I asked innocently.

Marlin stared at me blankly. "What?"

"Growing pot so close to the ocean," I said, switching gears. I might as well. Marlin and I weren't traveling the same highway.

"A dry climate's better. You get stronger stuff." Marlin cocked his head to one side. "How's yours?"

"My . . . ?" It didn't matter what Marlin meant. "Fine," I said. Then, because it didn't seem to matter what I asked, I inquired about Jesse Damon. "Did you know him?"

I didn't think it was possible for Marlin to look blanker, but he did. "I don't think so. Does he write?"

"No. He's someone who knew your sister. A college student."

"Oh!" Marlin's round, pallid face actually showed a spark of interest. "I don't really know the kid. He was just one of Audrey's amigos."

"They were . . . close?"

Marlin laughed, a funny little squeaking noise. "That's

cute." He pointed his thumb at me. "You're cute. It's too bad I don't screw anymore."

"Is it." My voice was flat.

"Screwing is big trouble," Marlin declared, now very serious. "Big trouble. You get some chick in trouble, and you have to marry her. Like Gord did with Audrey. Or my old man did with my old lady. It runs in the family. Anyway, you get married and you end up miserable. Honest to God, that's what happens. I know—I've seen it with my folks, I've seen it with Audrey and Gord. I don't screw, I don't get married." He took a long drag on the joint. "It's better that way. I do all right by myself. It's better that way."

I wasn't sure if the repetition was intended to convince me—or himself. "I'd better go," I said, with a sense of hopelessness. There was no way I was going to get much out of Marlin Runkel. "Thanks for your time."

"Sure." He didn't get up as I headed for the door. "Screwing killed Audrey. You can count on it."

I turned with my hand on the brass knob. "How so?"

Through the smoke, Marlin stared at an African wall hanging that appeared to depict a fertility rite. "Sex is death. Every time, you die a little. Audrey died a lot."

The trail that led behind Marlin's house was well maintained, though steep in places. It wound up the hillside, past the two sheds, and among the alder and oak trees. My aches and pains intensified as I trudged along, taking an occasional backward glance. Marlin hadn't seemed inclined to follow me as far as the door, let alone anywhere else, but once he finished his joint, he might notice that the Buick was still parked in the turnaround.

Though I probably hadn't covered more than two hundred yards, it felt as if I'd gone a mile by the time I reached Marlin's marijuana crop. It was big, a full city block, and judging by my weekend gardener's standards, the plants were thriving. I broke off a small piece and slipped it into my handbag. Then I started back down the hillside.

By the time I got to the sheds, my sense of urgency had grown. Still, I stopped to peek inside the one that was closest to the trail. Sure enough, it looked like a laboratory. Marlin must cure or process his illegal substance on the premises. Not bothering to investigate the other shed, which I assumed was used for storage, I hurried back to Vida's Buick.

It was gone.

How long had I been on the trail? Fifteen, twenty minutes? I hadn't looked at my watch when I left Marlin. The car keys were in my pocket. Whoever had moved the Buick must have hot-wired it. Anxiously, I paced the turnaround for a few moments, then considered knocking on Marlin's door.

But if he'd moved his aunt's car, there could be trouble. Marlin might have come out of his pot-induced state, discovered that the Buick was still there, and realized I was snooping. Despite his openness about smoking dope, he might not want anyone to see that he was growing it and, I assumed, selling it.

I stopped pacing and started down the Elk Creek Road. I hadn't gone more than a couple of hundred feet when I saw the Buick. It had been run into a tree, and the front end was smashed. The fender on the driver's side was clamped onto the front tire. I could tell right away that the car wasn't drivable.

Two wrecks in one day were too much. I didn't wait around to see if anyone was lurking in the woods, watching me. Ignoring the protests of my sore body, I ran all the way down to the RV park. At the halfway point, the strap came loose on my left sandal. I removed them both and kept going.

It took me several minutes to catch my breath after I reached the pay phones outside of the main building. A handful of vacationers eyed my panting, disheveled state with curiosity as they passed by on the narrow walkway. Just as I found the number for the Jaded Eye in the directory, my thoughts became less jumbled: I was only about four blocks away; I might as well walk.

They seemed like long blocks, though. Huffing and puffing, I arrived at the shop shortly after three. Vida was still inside.

"Well!" she greeted me, then took in my breathlessness and drooping figure. "Oh, good grief! What now? Can't I leave you alone for five minutes?"

I didn't try to explain until I sat down in an antique rocker. Vida grew increasingly dismayed as I related my slightly garbled tale. Then, when I got to the part about the Buick, she exploded.

"What! You've wrecked my car, too? I can't believe it!" She whipped off her glasses and began to rub furiously at her eyes.

"I didn't wreck your car, damn it," I said angrily. "I'm putting my money on your nephew. He knew I was nosing around and got pissed off."

"Watch your language!" Vida practically bared her teeth.

I bristled, but didn't defend myself. While I'm not exactly a filth-mouth, I'm usually careful about profanity or vulgarity around Vida. It occurred to me that much had changed in the past two days since I'd arrived in Cannon Beach. If our roles are occasionally interchangeable in Alpine, we both—usually—remember that I'm the boss. But two hundred and fifty miles away in this seaside town where Vida's heretofore unknown relatives resided, my House & Home editor definitely had the upper hand. I was beginning to feel like a child who had been allowed to tag along on what should have been an adults-only trip.

"Bottom line," I said, curbing my temper, "we don't have transportation."

Vida had stopped rubbing her eyes and was holding her head in her hands. "The children have a truck. We'll borrow that."

"A truck?" I vaguely recalled seeing a pickup parked on the Imhoff property. "Which of us is going to drive a truck?"

"I will," Vida responded. "Ernest had a truck for a while. I drove it now and then." She went over to the counter where the telephone was located. "I'm going to get the Buick towed. I suppose it'll have to go to Seaside. Drat. I hope it's not totaled. It's a 1985 model, you know. I've no idea what the Blue Book value is."

It took some time for Vida to make the arrangements. She also called Brendan Shaw to notify him of the accident. Brendan, a usually jovial man, indicated that his policyholders weren't having very good luck in Oregon. He informed Vida that under the circumstances she should notify the police. If someone else had moved the car without her permission, then it had officially been stolen.

While Vida made her calls, I fixed my sandal, then wandered around the crowded shop. There was a great deal of myrtlewood, seashells, rocks, glass balls, and driftwood. But the Imhoffs had acquired some intriguing collectibles, including antique dolls, a Lionel model train, a Flying A gas pump, a Pacific Tel & Tel phone booth, and what might have been a genuine Tiffany lamp with a dragonfly pattern. Inevitably, various metal sculptures by Ruth Pickering sat on tables, desks, and the floor. Most of them, as Derek had put it, were definitely butt ugly.

"There," Vida said with a sigh. "I've contacted everyone, including the police. But I didn't mention Marlin's name. We don't know he did it."

"They'll investigate," I pointed out. "They may find his marijuana plantation."

Vida looked stricken. "I didn't think of that. Oh, dear."

"It *is* illegal."

"The Runkels don't need any more scandal," Vida declared, as if she were the spokesperson for the entire tribe. Come to think of it, I suppose she was.

"What did you find here?" I changed the subject; I was getting sick of the Runkels.

Vida's wide shoulders slumped. "Nothing much. No bankbooks. No private papers. I'm beginning to think that Gordon and Audrey used a safety-deposit box, together and perhaps separately."

"Could be." I fingered one of Ruth's pieces, which looked vaguely like a two-headed symphony conductor. The edges were rough. I caught my finger and tore the skin. "Damn! Now I'm bleeding. These goofy things are dangerous."

Vida and I locked glances. "How did your friend Bill describe the weapon?" she asked, her brain obviously working in tandem with mine.

I thought back to our conversation in Astoria the previous day. It seemed like a week had passed since then. "He said it was heavy and pointed, like a harpoon. And yes, it was probably metal." Gingerly, I touched the long, thin sticklike part of the sculpture that had reminded me of a conductor's baton. "Several of Ruth's pieces have sharp points. Some of these, the ones in her yard, those I've seen at the Imhoff house. I wonder."

"So do I. But," Vida added hastily, "we don't know."

"The killer may have dumped the weapon in the ocean," I said, finding a Band-Aid in my purse and applying it to my cut.

We were silent for a few moments as the time ticked away on a slightly battered grandfather clock. "Did Marlin say anything of interest?" Vida finally asked.

"Only that Audrey died because she . . . was promiscuous." I was watching my language. "Or so he implied. Oh, he knew about Jesse Damon. He called him one of Audrey's 'amigos.' "

"We must speak with Jesse," Vida asserted. "Give me that phone number. I'm going to call him from here."

Jesse wasn't home, but another male voice answered Vida's call. Apparently, he was Jesse's roommate. He informed Vida that Jess, as he called him, would return sometime after five.

"We'll call then," Vida said, her finger tracing something taped to the counter. "This is the shuttle schedule. We can catch it southbound at three thirty-six."

According to my watch, it was now three twenty-nine. Vida locked up before we headed out onto the main street. Assuring me we could flag the shuttle down, we crossed to the other side of Hemlock and stood in front of the Cannon Beach Book Company. Sure enough, the little bus slowed when Vida waved her arms like a windmill. Five minutes later we were back at the Imhoff house.

Molly was still in her room, but Stacie was out on the front deck, trying to catch some October rays. There was no sign of Derek or Dolores, who I assumed were at work.

When Vida explained her plight with the Buick, she carefully omitted where the accident had happened or Marlin's possible involvement. Stacie listened without any expression until her great-aunt requested the use of the pickup truck.

"I don't know about that," Stacie said, pulling up the straps of her bathing suit. "If you take the pickup, all we have is Mom's Tracer. Dad took the van."

"I take it you haven't heard from your father?" Vida made the remark sound like an accusation.

Stacie shook her head. "I don't think we will. It's better that way."

"Where's the—Tracer, is it?—now?" Vida inquired.

"Derek has it," Stacie replied. "He drives it to work. Dolores has a crappy old beater."

"I must insist on borrowing your truck," Vida said, assuming a majestic stance.

Clearly, Stacie wasn't used to the royal prerogative. "How long?" she asked.

"At least until tomorrow," Vida responded.

Stacie gave in. "The keys are in the desk in the living room. I'll get them."

Aware that the keys were in her purse, Vida forestalled Stacie. "Never mind, dear. I can find them myself. You enjoy the sun. Winter's coming, after all."

We went through the motions of searching the desk. "I found them," Vida called.

There was no response. "Now, I wonder," Vida murmured, going over the big silver ring, "which ones are for the truck?"

I started to say that we'd have to try all of the ones that looked like car keys, but was interrupted by the sound of the back door. Vida and I looked up. Gordon Imhoff stood in the doorway to the kitchen.

"Gordon?" Vida gaped.

He merely glanced at her, then stared at me. "You," he breathed. "You're the one from the wreck."

I nodded. "Yes. And this is your aunt by—"

Stacie bolted into the living room before I could introduce Vida. "Dad!" she shrieked. "What are you doing here?"

Oddly, Gordon's expression was embarrassed. "I'm home."

"You'll be arrested," Stacie said in an agonized voice. "Don't stay. Please, Dad. Go away again!"

A figure had crept into the hallway. Gordon's back was turned, and he didn't see Molly, who hung back and started crying.

"Daddy!" she sobbed. "You need to leave!"

Gordon turned at the sound of her voice. "I'm not running anymore," he said simply. "I'll turn myself in."

"No!" Molly cried. "You can't!" She flung herself at her father. "Let's all run away! I hate it here!"

Gordon cradled Molly in his arms while Stacie kept aloof, her pretty face distorted with emotion. "Bratfinger's right for once. We should go away. It's been awful since . . . you left."

"Excuse me," said Vida, taking a step toward Gordon and Molly. "I'm Audrey's aunt, and I think we should sit down and talk sensibly. Would you care for some tea, Gordon?"

Gordon looked at Vida as if she'd just emerged from a spaceship. "Tea? *Tea?*"

"A cocktail, perhaps," Vida said, the suggestion sounding as if she'd offered pure poison.

"I could use a Scotch about now," Gordon admitted,

keeping Molly under his wing as he steered her to the couch. "It's been a long day. God, it's been a long month." He collapsed, with Molly beside him.

I'd seen some liquor bottles in the kitchen when Vida and I were snooping. A drink didn't sound like a bad idea to me, either. I'd also had a long, harrowing day. Leaving Vida in charge of her errant relations, I exited the living room and went off to play bartender.

Eavesdropping was easy. Vida asked Gordon where he'd been since his disappearance. He'd stayed mostly on the coast, as it turned out, living in his van, which had eventually broken down Saturday night some thirty miles down the coast, outside of Tillamook. On Sunday he'd hitchhiked into Seaside, where he rented the Ford Taurus. Then he'd headed south again, to stay with his mother-in-law in Manzanita. When he'd hit me earlier in the day, his plans were unformed. Gordon hadn't yet decided whether to come home, turn himself in, or go back to Rosalie and Walt's place to think some more.

"I considered heading for the Bay Area," he was saying as I brought him a Scotch and served sodas to Vida and the girls. There hadn't been any bourbon, so I'd made myself a screwdriver. I'd rather drink Drāno than Scotch. "But that seemed foolish," Gordon went on after taking a deep sip. "There were too many loose ends here, and I couldn't let you kids take responsibility for them." Gordon eyed both his daughters with a fond expression.

Molly had stopped crying and was curled up next to her father. "I love you, Daddy," she said.

He hugged her. "I love you, too, kitten."

"This is all very well and good," Vida said, ignoring her soda. "But we must be practical. If you turn yourself in, what will you tell the sheriff, Gordon?"

His pale blue eyes regarded Vida with bewilderment. "I'm a fugitive. What else can I say?"

"Technically, that may not be true." Vida cleared her throat. "I don't care to be indelicate, but are you also a felon?"

Gordon's mouth twisted into what might have been a smile—or a grimace. "That's pretty up-front, Vida. Or should I call you Aunt Vida?"

Gordon's concern for etiquette seemed inappropriate. Apparently, Vida thought so, too. "Vida is acceptable," she replied tersely. "You didn't answer my question."

Gordon sighed. "I can't discuss it. After all, I don't know you, do I?"

"Oh, good grief!" Vida exploded. "We're related, for heaven's sake!" She glanced at Stacie and Molly, who both looked frightened. "We can talk about it later," she added, apparently figuring that Gordon's reticence was caused by the presence of his daughters "Perhaps it's more important to decide on what you're going to do now."

"We should go away," Stacie insisted. "I can pack in ten minutes."

"Me, too," Molly put in, still clinging to her father.

Gordon scratched at his trim beard. "I don't know. . . . It doesn't seem right."

"Dad!" Stacie had gotten to her feet and was standing by the sofa. "Make up your mind for once! What's to hold us here?"

"What about Derek?" Gordon asked in a mild, un-ruffled tone.

"Derek can stay with Dolores," Stacie countered. "They're going to get married anyway. We can sell the house to whoever it was that wanted it so bad. We can sell the shop to the Kanes. We'll have enough money to start over."

Gordon grew thoughtful, but finally gave a slight shake of his head. "I never wanted to move or give up the shop. It seems kind of pointless to change my mind now."

Stacie's eyes were hard. "Does it?"

"May I put in a word?" Vida spoke from her place by the hearth.

None of the Imhoffs responded, but all gazed at her with varying degrees of curiosity.

"Gordon, you must turn yourself in to the police. Otherwise, you remain a missing person, or, as you put it, a fugitive. You can hardly conduct business of any sort if you're running from the law. Be realistic," Vida added. Like me, she apparently was beginning to comprehend that Gordon had problems facing hard, cold facts.

Taking a big gulp of Scotch, Gordon closed his eyes. "I don't know."

Molly, who had been dislodged while her father drank, grabbed his free arm and shook it. "I want to go! Let's pack!"

Gordon started to say something, apparently thought better of it, and put a hand on his younger daughter's knee. "Okay, you two get your stuff together."

Molly let out a shriek of joy while Stacie rushed from the room. Vida stared at Gordon with a damning expression.

"You're making a terrible mistake," she said.

Gordon cradled his drink in his hands. "I don't want to talk about it."

Vida continued to stare at her nephew by marriage, then shrugged. "As you will. We're borrowing your pickup, by the way."

"What?" Gordon was puzzled.

"We need a vehicle." Vida didn't explain why.

Gordon turned to look at me. "Because of this morning?"

"Partly," I responded. "Are you really selling the house and the shop?"

Gordon didn't answer. His glass was empty; he got up to head for the kitchen and, I assumed, to get a refill. "The gearshift sticks sometimes," he called from the other room, "and the left rear tire needs replacing. Otherwise, good luck."

Vida and I heard the tinkling of ice and the sound of running tap water. We gazed at each other in bewilderment, and I wondered if we also heard the sound of doom.

Chapter Eleven

TWENTY MINUTES LATER the three Imhoffs had departed. Their farewells to us were perfunctory at best, and I felt sorry for Vida. While I might criticize her for inserting herself in their midst, I knew she was basically well intentioned.

But if Vida felt rejected, she didn't complain. "You've been drinking," she said, starting for the back door. "I'll drive."

"You were going to drive anyway," I pointed out. "Besides, one drink doesn't turn me into a highway marauder."

"You're right," she agreed, stopping to take a look at the girls' empty bedroom. "You don't need to drink to drive badly. This morning's accident was proof of that."

I was standing in the kitchen door that led into the hall. "That's the first wreck I've had since I bought the Jag," I argued. "And that's saying something, considering the weird people we've got behind the wheel at home."

"Durwood Parker has had his license taken away," Vida said, referring to Alpine's most infamous driver. "Oh, I know he sneaked off in his wife's car last summer and ran into the Gay Loggers' float at the Summer Solstice parade. I also know that there were some ridiculous fools who applauded his effort. But after Milo put him in jail for three days, Durwood swore he'd never—ah! Just as I suspected! A diary." As she spoke Vida had been rummaging around in drawers. Now she turned to face me and held up a mock-leather diary with a gold clasp. "It's Molly's, of course. Girls Stacie's age don't keep diaries."

Watching Vida slip the diary into her purse made me feel uneasy. "Are you going to read it?" I asked, already knowing the answer.

"It will help me become better acquainted with Molly," she replied, going through another drawer. "Perhaps I'll learn more about the family's dynamics. I may even find a clue to Audrey's murder. You know," she said, shutting the last of the drawers and turning to leave the bedroom, "a mention of something that a fourteen-year-old might not consider important but which may actually shed light on her mother's death."

It occurred to me that stealing Molly's diary might be revenge for the family's ingratitude. "It's your grandniece," I said with a shrug. Then, after we had clambered into the pickup, which was an older Chevrolet model, I remarked that it was hard to believe that Gordon and the girls would simply take off.

"Did they leave a note for Derek?" I asked.

"I don't think so," Vida answered, struggling with the gears. Her hat, a bilious green straw, kept hitting the cab's roof.

"But won't he wonder where they went?"

"Derek doesn't know his father returned," Vida said, finally putting the truck into reverse. "Oh, he may hear about it through the grapevine. Then he might put two and two together."

"It's crazy," I muttered as we bounced along on the dirt drive that led to the main road. "Speaking of crazy, where are we going?"

"It's almost five," Vida answered, fighting both the steering wheel and the green straw hat, the crown of which had been flattened by the cab's roof. "I want to talk to Milo before he leaves work. We're going back to the motel. He may have left a message."

I doubted it, but I was wrong. Milo had called the Ecola Creek Lodge shortly after three. Vida furiously dialed his number while I left the door open and raised a window to air out our lodging. The sun still shone brightly, and the unit seemed stuffy.

Unfortunately, there was no extension that would allow me to listen in on the conversation between Vida and the sheriff. I tried to guess what Milo was saying from what I could hear on my end, but gave up after the first couple of minutes. Vida didn't take notes. She never does, no matter how complicated the interview or story. Everything is filed away in my House & Home editor's efficient brain.

I strolled outside, wandering across the street to a grassy expanse that bore a sign denoting Les Shirley Park. I watched the ocean for a few minutes and took big breaths of sea air. The setting was peaceful, beautiful, soothing. It had been a long time since I'd been to the coast. Maybe someday I could visit when I wasn't embroiled in murder and mayhem.

Vida was still talking to Milo when I went back inside, but she hung up after another minute or so had passed. I flopped into one of the easy chairs while she remained on the sofa.

"Well!" she exclaimed. "That was most enlightening. I think."

"Milo did some digging?" I asked, mildly surprised, though I don't know why. He would have paid dearly if he hadn't.

"Yes, he was very helpful, and assures me that the Clatsop County law-enforcement personnel are working very hard on the investigation. There's nothing new on the weapon. But," Vida continued, looking pleased, "Milo was able to learn some things about the people who might be considered suspects."

"Such as?" I asked.

She grimaced. "The family, of course. The children were all in bed and asleep, which really isn't an alibi, but at least they weren't awakened by any odd noises. Gordon was staying at the shop, and told the sheriff's people he was sleeping, too.

"Then we get to Marlin, who claimed he wasn't asleep, but sitting up watching some old movie on TV. I gather Marlin doesn't have ordinary sleep habits." Vida looked mildly disdainful. "Everett was questioned, but said he was asleep in his trailer home. Indeed, he stated that he had passed out that night. I don't doubt it. Rosalie and Walt were home in bed. Ruth Pickering, also. As for Stuart and Stina Kane—who were interrogated because of the allegations of an affair between Gordon and Mrs. Kane—they said they were asleep at home—together." She wiggled her eyebrows.

"This is all pretty weak stuff," I noted.

"Yes"—Vida nodded—"which is what makes it interesting."

I asked about Jesse Damon, but Vida said Milo hadn't mentioned him. "Maybe," I suggested, "that's because he was so far away at the time of the murder. I've never really figured him for the killer if only because of the distance between Cannon Beach and Salem."

Vida didn't comment. After the fact, it occurred to me that the younger generation doesn't always view long drives in the same light that we somewhat older, less flexible folks do. Adam, for example, thought nothing of making frequent two-hundred-and-fifty-mile trips between Ben's mission church in Tuba City and the Arizona State campus in Tempe.

"Others were questioned, including the neighbors, John and Marie Skelly," Vida continued. "I'd intended to talk to them myself, but they've been away for the weekend. It turns out that John Skelly has a bad back and is a very light sleeper. He stated that he heard nothing." She gave me a quizzical look.

"You mean. . . ?" At first, I wasn't sure what Vida was getting at. Then it dawned on me. "No car arriving? No shouts? No running footsteps?"

"That's right." Vida acknowledged my astuteness with a single nod. "Now, to be fair, the Skelly house is the one on the north. The house on the south side belongs to summer people. If you picture the Skellys' place, it's about a hundred feet away from the Imhoffs'. And it's a great deal further from the dock. Even if John Skelly was awake, he might not hear voices. But he'd probably hear a car."

"Which leaves us with two choices," I mused. "There was no car, or else whoever drove it left it parked by the road."

"That's credible, given the hour. There wouldn't be much traffic, and there's plenty of room to park between the road and the driveway." Vida paused, apparently thinking through the scenario. "There's also the possibility of a boat."

"True," I agreed. "John Skelly probably wouldn't hear a motor over the roar of the ocean. If the boat had a motor," I added, then thought of something else. "What about tire tracks?"

"It was too dry," Vida answered. "They couldn't get much from the drive. As for the beach, the tide was coming in. Any tracks below the waterline would have been washed away. And closer in, where the waves rarely hit, the sand is far too powderlike."

"Hunh. No wonder the local sheriff isn't getting very far. Who else did they interview?"

"Half the town," Vida responded. "Milo didn't get all the names or responses, but the gist was rather the same as what we've found out on our own—Audrey had a tarnished reputation, she suffered from wanderlust, she should never have left Cannon Beach in the first place. Gordon is a very decent man, if a bit weak, but after the initial adjustments to small-town life, he pitched in and did his share. The children are regarded as nice enough, though Derek is often sullen and drives too fast. Stacie was termed 'stuck-up' by at least two of her peers. Molly's teachers called her very bright, but having low self-esteem. In other words, they're typical teenagers." The concept somehow seemed to please Vida, maybe because it excused their personal flaws.

"You left someone out," I said, suddenly realizing that my last two Excedrin had worn off.

"Yes," Vida responded, "so I did. Dolores. Well now. She comes from an unfortunate background, with parents who drink and fight and generally have provided an unwholesome environment for her and her five siblings. She dropped out of high school midway through her senior year, though I gather she is smart enough. She and Derek have dated for over two years. Audrey was opposed to a long-term relationship—namely marriage—but Gordon took a softer stand. He and Audrey had married young, after all."

"Which may be why Audrey was against an early wedding," I pointed out. "Where was Dolores the night that Audrey was murdered?"

"At home," Vida replied promptly. "Quarreling half the night with her parents. She had been with Derek until almost midnight. Mr. and Mrs. Cerrillo didn't want him staying so late. I suspect they didn't approve of him."

"Because he's an Anglo?" My aches, pains, and head were beginning to throb again.

In Vida's Alpine world, there are few minorities. When she was growing up, the term *intermarriage* referred to a union between Catholics and Lutherans. To some extent, it still does. But in the past decade the town has seen the arrival of African-Americans, Asians, and Hispanics. Since the opening of Skykomish Community College, the minority population has increased tenfold, which puts it at about thirty. It took Vida a moment to consider Derek and Dolores's ethnic plight.

"That might be so," she allowed. "I gather such sentiments work both ways."

"So they do." I sighed. "Prejudices of every kind die hard. Look at Dr. Flake and Marilynn Lewis." The reference was to our departed Caucasian MD and his African-American nurse. Brave souls both, but when they decided to get married, they'd left Alpine and moved to a Seattle suburb. Most of us had hated to see them go, but I couldn't blame them for turning their backs on the inevitable censure they would have faced in Alpine.

"Yes," Vida said sadly. "Such a lovely girl. And Peyton Flake was so competent, if a bit eccentric. His ponytail upset a great many of the elderly patients. I do hope we get another doctor soon to help out Gerald Dewey. He's far too overworked."

The talk of the medical personnel spurred me to get up and take two more Excedrin. "What else did Milo say?" I called from the kitchen.

"Not too much," Vida answered. "He was sorry about my car. Oh, he asked about you. I mentioned that threatening note you got on your rental."

I'd almost forgotten about the note. "I think it was one of the Imhoff kids," I said, returning to the living room. "They never exactly warmed to me."

Vida shot me an ominous look. "Nonsense. They're not demonstrative."

I let the remark pass. Vida was obviously making excuses for their lack of affection toward her—as well as me.

"So what Milo found out," I said, sitting back down in the easy chair, "isn't much more than we already knew. Which means the authorities don't know much, either."

Vida made a face. "Well—yes. But it strengthens what we've learned. We're on the right track."

I uttered a derisive little laugh. "Which is taking us nowhere. Say, Vida, what about Gordon and Stina Kane? Didn't Milo mention the affair?"

Behind the big glasses, Vida's eyes grew wide. "Nooo. Only that there were rumors, and that's why the Kanes were questioned. The other extramarital venture he brought up was Audrey and Jesse Damon."

"Which was flagrant?" I suggested.

"Not precisely," Vida said, with a disapproving glance for me which indicated that Runkels would never put their sins on parade. "Audrey was frequently seen with Jesse. She had been observed with other young men during the past few years. The conclusion seemed obvious."

"I wonder." The words were barely a whisper.

"What?"

I shook my head. "Nothing. Are you hungry? It's going on six."

"I could eat a little something," Vida said. "There's that log house on Hemlock that reminds me of your place. Whatever is it called?"

"It doesn't matter," I responded. "We can't miss it." The Excedrin was working. "Let's go. I'm ravenous."

Vida, however, demurred. "I was thinking about a brief stop first. On Pacific. It can't be far from the restaurant. We ought to call on the Kanes."

"They're probably gone for the day," I said a bit impatiently. "This isn't tourist season."

"We could drive by and see," Vida said. "It wouldn't take but a minute."

"Ohhh . . ." I knew defeat when I met it. "Okay, but if they're in, let's not take forever. What could we ask them at this point?"

"I'll think of something," Vida said, opening the front door.

Gordon Imhoff was standing on the porch.

He had driven the girls into Seaside and put them on a bus to Portland. From there they would take a connecting

Greyhound to Martinez, California. Gordon had a cousin there who would let them stay for a while.

"I haven't seen Kirby in years," he said, standing uneasily in the middle of the living room. "But he's about the only relative I have who's reliable. My mother's somewhere in New Mexico and my dad died three years ago. Not that they were exactly dependable types."

It hadn't been easy to get Stacie and Molly to leave without him, Gordon admitted. But the choice was simple: either they left, or they stayed. Whatever his daughters chose, he was going to face the music. Did they want to go through what might be an ugly episode? Better to let him remain in Cannon Beach and try to get things straightened out. Maybe it wouldn't take long. Gordon had tried to paint an optimistic picture.

"My, my," Vida finally said. "I'm rather surprised. Are you going to contact the police tonight?"

Gordon shook his head. "I need a decent night's sleep. The couch at my mother-in-law's place isn't very comfortable. Besides, I want to see Derek. For all I know, he doesn't realize I'm here."

"You might as well join us for dinner," Vida said. "We were just leaving."

Gordon hesitated. "Derek may be home by now. I should talk to him."

"I understand Derek can't cook," Vida said. "Can you?"

"Actually," Gordon replied with a self-deprecating smile, "I can."

That was more than I could say for Vida. But she coaxed him into coming with us. I was pleased with the arrangement. Over dinner I could discuss the accident with Gordon. I had to find out about his coverage so that I could rent another car and head home in the morning.

We were walking under the archway to the parking lot when we saw a Cannon Beach police car pulled alongside the pickup. A young policeman and an even younger policewoman were standing not by the truck, but next to the Ford Taurus I had briefly called my own.

The policeman whirled around when he saw us. He stared, as did his companion. "Are you Gordon Imhoff?" the policeman demanded.

Gordon's shoulders slumped. "I am. You know that, Corey. Am I under arrest?"

"Well . . . ah . . . I guess so." Corey gulped. He glanced at the young woman, a pretty girl with long braids the color of winter wheat. "Or is it just for questioning, Tami?" he asked, trying to inject some authority into his voice. Fleetingly, I wondered if Corey was trying to impress us—or Tami.

"I can call the sheriff and ask," Tami offered, sounding both hopeful and excited. I suspected that except for Audrey Imhoff's murder, the local police weren't accustomed to serious crime.

Corey nodded. "Do that. We don't want to mess up."

"How did you find me?" Gordon inquired, his composure unruffled. "Was it the rental car?"

Corey frowned. "No." He glanced around the parking lot. "Oh! The Taurus! We should have seen that. But we got a call that someone had left an illegally parked pickup in the motel lot. We came to ticket it. People can't park here unless they're registered guests."

"People are very nervy," Vida remarked. And then it dawned on her that the pickup was the one we'd borrowed. "Wait! You can't ticket that truck! It's mine! I forgot to tell Madge at the desk. Oh, dear!" She raced over to the office.

A worried-looking Tami had returned from making her call. "They want us to bring you into Astoria, Mr. Imhoff. It's just for questioning. You're listed as a missing person, but under the circumstances, they'd like to talk to you. There's also something about leaving the scene of a traffic accident this morning. I'm sure you can explain all that." The young policewoman's manner was very apologetic.

"That's fine," Gordon responded, avoiding my gaze, "but I can drive myself. I'd like to see my son first, though. Could we make it around eight?"

The officers glanced at each other. "Yeah, I guess," said Corey. "Why not? We'll call Astoria and let them know."

I was amazed at the local law-enforcement officials' cavalier attitude. But they knew Gordon, they trusted him, he had an exemplary reputation in the town. Still, I doubted that Milo would have treated a witness in a homicide case so casually. Especially when that witness was the victim's spouse and had been missing for almost a month.

Gordon was talking easily to Corey while Tami returned to the phone. "You don't want to have to drive all the way into Astoria," Gordon was saying. "Who else is on duty tonight?"

"Just us," Corey replied, "but we could get some backup. Ron and Betsy are standing by."

"How's Ron?" Gordon asked. "Aren't he and Amy expecting?"

"Any day now," Corey said as both Vida and Tami approached us. I was glad to see Vida; I was feeling left out of the chummy conversation. I was also losing the opportunity of finding out about Gordon's insurance. But I was tired and hungry; maybe it was more important for Gordon to get his life squared away than for me to secure a free rental car.

"That's taken care of," Vida declared, tapping one foot. "Well?" She looked first at Gordon, then at Corey and Tami. I still felt left out.

"I'm going to Astoria later," Gordon said. "I'm afraid I'll have to skip dinner after all."

"Later?" Vida blinked. "I don't understand."

Gordon explained while Vida listened with a dubious expression. "This sounds very peculiar."

"It's okay, ma'am," Corey assured her. "It's not like Mr. Imhoff's a criminal. Sorry about the pickup. We didn't realize it belonged to a guest." He tipped his hat and left with Tami.

Vida put a hand on Gordon's arm. "You won't change your mind?"

Gordon laughed. "Of course not." Then he turned serious and finally looked at me. "I've got insurance. It's with Oregon Mutual. There's a 1-800 number in the local phone book. I'm really sorry I took off this morning. I guess I panicked."

I gave Gordon a halfhearted smile. "I'll call this evening. I assume they have twenty-four-hour service. I'd like to pick up another car and leave tomorrow morning."

Vida didn't seem worried about my dilemma. She was still eyeing Gordon, and not without a certain amount of compassion. "You'll get through this all right? It might not be as easy as you think."

"I've got to get it sorted out eventually," Gordon replied, then gave a little shrug. "It's no big deal. After Audrey's funeral, I ran away because I was upset, that's all. I needed time to think. Having your wife murdered isn't easy to deal with."

"Certainly not," Vida agreed, withdrawing her hand. "I realize all this has been very difficult. Your solitude must have helped."

"It did," Gordon said, but he didn't meet Vida's gaze. "I can cope better now."

"Insights," Vida said softly. "I'm sure you had time to come to some conclusions. About Audrey's death, I mean."

Gordon seemed startled. "Conclusions? Well . . . Not really. What's to conclude? The sheriff hasn't been able to find the killer. How could I figure it out? As terrible as it may be, I'm beginning to believe that Audrey's murder will go unsolved. It happens."

"Not as often as you think," Vida said. "Frequently the police know who did it but have no proof. Then the killer goes free but the case is solved, at least in the minds of the law-enforcement officials. Of course it's very frustrating for them."

"Yes," Gordon said slowly. "I suppose that's the way it works sometimes. Well, I'll be seeing you. You're heading home soon, I suppose?"

It occurred to me that with the girls gone and Gordon back on the scene, there was no need for Vida to stay in Cannon Beach. But I was mistaken.

"I'm taking a leave from work," Vida responded with a sharp glance in my direction. "I've not had a real vacation for some time. This area is such a pleasant place to recreate, don't you think?"

"It's ideal," Gordon said, though I thought he looked put off by Vida's words. "Just bring the pickup back when you're ready." He held out a hand.

If he'd intended to dismiss Vida from his life, Gordon

was misguided. He didn't know her the way I did. She shook his hand and gave him a friendly smile.

"I'll be seeing you," she said.

It sounded more like a threat than a promise.

Chapter Twelve

"IT'S A CRIME of the mind," Vida asserted after we were seated at Morris Fireside Restaurant. "There are no clues, motive is elusive, the list of suspects is vague. Whoever killed Audrey did it because of something up here." She tapped her temple.

"You mean it was a psychological killing?" I asked.

Vida nodded. "A mind temporarily deranged. What else?"

I gazed around the restaurant with its arched ceiling and log interior. A cheerful fire crackled in the big grate, and the polished wooden tables were almost all filled with diners. Even as I studied the handsome dining room a couple was being ushered to one of the few vacant tables, which happened to be right behind Vida.

"Hey," I said in a whisper, "the Kanes are here. Don't turn around."

Vida turned around. "Mr. Kane," she cried, sounding delighted. "How nice! Is that Mrs. Kane? We haven't met."

Stuart Kane's angular face froze. "I'm sorry, I've forgotten. . . ."

But Stina rescued the moment. "Emma? Introduce me to your friend. How are you doing? I heard you were in a wreck this morning."

It didn't surprise me that in a small town news would travel fast. I made the official introductions, though they scarcely broke any ice with Stu. He murmured greetings, then turned his back on us.

That didn't faze Stina, either. "Is it true Gordon Imhoff's back in town? Somebody said he was the one who hit you."

I assured Stina that the tale was true. "He's going to get things squared away with the sheriff this evening." It wasn't easy leaning around Vida *and* Stuart Kane to communicate with Stina.

"Great," Stina called back. "Gordon's a good guy, even if he won't sell the blasted shop." She stopped making eye contact with me to look at her husband. "Isn't that right, babe?"

Stu's answer was a growl I couldn't make out.

Vida fanned herself with the big plastic menu. "My!" she said in an undertone. "Such an obnoxious man!"

Fortunately, Stu couldn't hear Vida over the din in the busy restaurant. But something set him off. A moment later he was on his feet, shouting at Stina. Then he hurled the menu onto the floor and stalked out of the dining room.

I leaned sideways in my chair to signal to Stina. "Are you okay?"

Stina was doing her best to stay composed, but that full lower lip trembled dangerously. "Sure, I'm used to it. Stu's temperamental."

Vida had scooted around in her chair. "Come join us. We could use some company."

Stina hesitated, then stood up, grabbed her chair, and pulled it over to our small table. "Why not? I've got to eat. At times like this, food's my only friend."

"Men are so thoughtless," Vida remarked, giving Stina

a sympathetic little smile. "Sometimes my Ernest had no tact whatsoever. I don't like to speak ill of the dead, but there it is."

"Lucky you," Stina muttered, then turned to me. "Are we drinking?"

"We can be," I responded cheerfully.

"Lucky?" Vida echoed.

Stina nodded vigorously. "Yes. It sounds like Ernest is dead."

"He is." For once, Vida seemed taken aback.

"Then your troubles are over," Stina said, tight-lipped. "Most of them, anyway."

Our server arrived before she could go on. Stina ordered a martini; I opted for bourbon. Vida primly asked for a refill of her ice water.

"Sorry." Stina sighed. "Stu's a prick sometimes. Luckily, he doesn't show that side when we're dealing with clients."

"What set him off now?" I inquired. "Was it us?"

"No." Stina started to rub at her eyes, apparently remembered she was wearing eyeliner, and carefully folded her hands in her lap. "It was what I said about Gordon Imhoff. Stu can't stand him."

That figured. No doubt Stu was jealous of his wife's lover. Naturally, I kept my mouth shut, and so, surprisingly, did Vida. We waited for Stina to go on. Before she continued, however, our drinks arrived.

Stina took a big sip of her martini. "I'm tired," she said, and her shoulders sagged as if to prove the point.

"It must be very hard running your own business," Vida said, still sympathetic. "Especially in the off-season when sales must drop off."

"Oh, right," Stina agreed. "We're used to that, though. It's not that. It's . . . other things."

"Oh?" Vida's tone was encouraging.

Stina took another big drink. "You're from a small town? Then you know how people talk. They've nothing much else to do, especially after the tourists go away. Yak-yak-yak, babble-babble-babble. I hate it."

I offered a commiserating smile. "Gossip is more than a hobby, it's a lifeline."

"It's bilge," Stina asserted. "It's malicious, it's cruel, and it's destructive."

I could sense Vida bristling. To her, gossip was merely informal news. She thrived on it, she relied on it, she turned it into her daily bread.

"It's natural for people, even those who live in cities, to speculate and discuss what goes on among their friends and neighbors," she said in a remarkably quiet voice. "Would you rather have them talk about personalities they see on television instead of real people they know and care about?"

Stina stared. Clearly, she wasn't prepared for a philosophical discussion of gossip. "What I meant," she said in a heavy tone, "is that gossip shouldn't be vicious and it shouldn't spread lies. I'm sick—*and tired*—of hearing that I had an affair with Gordon Imhoff."

Vida and I both exhibited extraordinary calm. "It's not true, I take it," I said as casually as I could muster.

"Of course not." Stina uttered a contemptuous laugh. "I like Gordon, he's a nice guy, I've tried to talk him into selling the Jaded Eye, I even tried to help him through his crisis with Audrey. But there was no romance. I'd like to know who started that rumor. How could they get it so *wrong*?"

"Wrong?" Vida breathed the word.

Stina drank from her glass, nodded, and put a hand to her mouth. "Wrong. Backward. It was Stu and Audrey.

Why do you think he stormed out when I said nice things about Gordon? Stu hates him. And why not? One of them probably killed her. I wish to God I knew which."

It's amazing how people try to hoodwink other people—and themselves—with fallacious rationales for their behavior. Stuart's affairs had started out—or so he'd explained to his wife—as a marketing tool. Women, he'd told Stina, were almost always the ones who made decisions about buying property. Thus it was important to court the wife. Literally.

"It drove me nuts at first," Stina admitted over her second martini. "But we were making money. Nobody's perfect, I told myself, and this was a second marriage for both of us. I didn't want to be a two-time loser, and I guess Stu didn't, either. We came to an agreement. I could spend whatever I wanted on myself—within reason—if he could have his little flings. Well, I pampered myself for a while, but then I decided we should have a baby. That was three years ago." She made a face. "No baby. Neither of us had kids the first time around, so maybe there's something the matter. Stu insists it can't be him, and I'll be damned if I'll admit it might be me." She put her hand to her mouth in that gesture that was becoming familiar. "Why am I telling you this? I don't know you."

"That's why," Vida replied. "Your story is safe with us. We have no one to tell."

"Everybody needs to talk to somebody," I put in, having proved how companionable I was by also ordering another drink despite Vida's glare of disapproval. "If this were Alpine, I'd—" With a jarring motion, I set my glass on the table. "Good God! I forgot to call the office! Excuse me, I must get to a pay phone."

There were two phones just outside the restaurant entrance. I dialed hastily and hoped that Leo was home.

Milo answered. In my anxiety, I'd called his number by mistake. "How are you doing?" he asked, sounding relaxed.

I pictured the sheriff on his couch with his feet up, a TV dinner before him, and either the news or a sporting event on TV. It was not an unpleasant mental picture. Indeed, I envied him his repose.

"I'm beat," I said. Then, because I was unwilling to admit that I'd called him by mistake, I thanked him for contacting the Clatsop County Sheriff's Office.

"No big deal," he said. "Vida would have killed me if I hadn't. How's it going?"

"Not very well. Tell me—if you were the local authorities, what would you be looking for? Besides the killer, I mean."

"Motive. It sounds like a crime of passion. Who cared enough to bash in What'sername's head in the middle of the night?"

Vida and I'd already considered the impulsive nature of the crime. "Love? Or hate?" I asked.

"Either. Both." Milo laughed, a familiar, reassuring sound. "Hey, Emma, since when did you start giving me credit for insights into human nature?"

It wasn't that Milo lacked perceptiveness about people. Rather, it was his narrow focus, his strict adherence to going by the book. The Skykomish County sheriff relied on facts, not feelings, when conducting a criminal investigation.

"I guess you're thinking differently because this isn't your case," I responded, feeling a breeze stirring the shrubbery next to the restaurant. "You don't have to bring it into court."

"I'm glad I don't," Milo said. "It sounds like a tough one. So when are you coming home?"

I sighed. "Hopefully, tomorrow." I explained about Gordon Imhoff and his apparent willingness to take responsibility for the wreck.

"He's got to," Milo said. "No matter who's really at fault, if a driver leaves the scene, it's considered a hit-and-run. He's screwed."

Gordon had only himself to blame, so I tried not to spare him any pity. "Has anything big happened at home?" I inquired. "Anything for the paper?"

"A bunch of cows got loose from the Overholt farm and wandered onto the road by the reservoir. Then a couple got on the railroad tracks, and they had to flag down the Burlington Northern."

This sounded promising. "Did Carla get a picture?"

"I don't know," Milo replied. "Oh, Darla Puckett's gourds got stolen off her front porch last night, and who-ever did it apparently knocked the head off some kind of statue she had in the yard."

"Bo-Peep?" I recalled Vida's description of Darla's walleyed garden statuary. It occurred to me that had my House & Home editor been in town, she might be considered a suspect.

"Could be. Jack Mullins checked it out." Milo paused, and I envisioned him lighting a cigarette or taking a swig of beer or polishing off the last of his Hungry Man frozen TV entrée. "Otherwise, it's been pretty quiet now that they're getting the fire damage cleaned up."

"Fire damage?" My grip on the receiver tightened. "What fire?"

"The one at the old loading dock and the abandoned warehouse on Railroad Avenue. Didn't I tell Vida?" Milo sounded mildly surprised.

"No." The word dropped out of my mouth like a rock. If Milo had mentioned a fire, Vida certainly would have passed on the news. "When did it happen? Was anyone hurt? How did it start? What's the damage estimate?"

"Whoa!" Milo laughed, but not as wholeheartedly as usual. "We don't know yet how it started. It was during the night. The first alarm went off around three. No injuries, because the warehouse is vacant and nobody was on the loading dock. An investigative team is being brought in tomorrow. Maybe this'll be the spark—excuse the expression—to put over the bond issue for a paid fire department."

Alpine had relied on volunteer firefighters for most of its history. Part of the reason was lack of funding; another part was tradition. Most of the fires in the area occurred in the woods, and special crews were always brought in to fight the flames. In the course of any given year, there were rarely more than a dozen alarms, most of them minor. Voters couldn't see why they should spend money to pay for employees to sit around and play cards. But with the advent of the college, I'd mounted an editorial campaign to create a county-wide firefighting department. Coupled with my crusade to get the sheriff appointed instead of elected, I felt I had a large stake in the upcoming election.

"I hope Carla covered the story," I said, feeling annoyed with myself for being in Cannon Beach instead of on the scene in Alpine.

"She was there," Milo assured me. "I saw her."

"Thank goodness." I leaned against the pay-phone stall. "We should have a strong front page. I'm going to call Leo." Then, lest Milo think me self-absorbed, I asked how things were going for him off the job.

"Mulehide and I are really getting into it over this

Europe deal with Brandon," he said, sounding vexed. "She says she paid for most of Tanya's wedding, which is a damned lie, so I should cough up for Brandon's trip. I pointed out that ever since our divorce, she's had the kids almost all to herself. Those visiting rights are so much bullshit. How many times do you remember me having any of them come up here?"

While there had been some holidays and a few weeks during the summer, I had to admit that the Dodge off-spring weren't frequent visitors to Alpine.

"You're damned right," Milo said, more heatedly. "They may have grown up here, but they lost touch real quick. They made new friends in Bellevue, and then they got involved in sports and social activities and they always had excuses for not coming to see me. I'd say fine, no problem, and the truth is, I was usually tied up with the job and didn't have much spare time to spend with them. But now, when-ever the subject of money comes up, it's Old Dad who gets tapped. I'm sick of it. I haven't seen Michelle for three months, and the last time I talked to Tanya was in June right after the wedding."

"Stick to your guns," I urged, for lack of anything more helpful. "It's not like going to Europe is a necessity."

"Hell, I've never been to Europe," Milo grumbled. "The only place I've ever been except for the West Coast is Vietnam, and that was at government expense."

I couldn't blame Milo for begrudging his son a conti-nental tour. But I had to get in touch with Leo. "I'll call you when I get home," I promised, and rang off.

Luckily, Leo was at his apartment on Cedar Street, no doubt eating the same kind of TV dinner that Milo had served. I felt a pang for the sheriff and my ad manager: both were casualties of broken marriages, and in each case, their ex-wives had remarried.

"Carla got some great shots of the fire," Leo informed me. "She may not be able to write a decent story, but she's a damned good photographer."

"What about the cows?" I inquired.

"We got a break there," Leo replied. "Ellsworth Overholt took some pictures of his own, just in case the train ran over Bossy or Bessie. I talked him into dropping off the roll at Buddy Bayard's studio so it could be developed and we could use one of the shots."

"And Darla Puckett's garden statuary?"

Leo laughed. "That one intrigued Carla. She got some wild hair to juxtapose the headless Bo-Peep next to the photo of the stray cows. You know, run a cutline that said, 'Little Bo-Peep has lost her head, Overholt cows have left their shed.' Or something like that."

I gritted my teeth. "You dissuaded her, I trust?"

"Uh . . . You don't like it?" Leo sounded taken aback.

"It's dumb." I wasn't in the mood for whimsy. "How's the issue shaping up so far?"

"Good. Fine." There was a pause; I sensed that Leo was mentally redoing the page with the Bo-Peep and cow pictures. "We've got the fire with two pix, the college-related stories and photos, a three-car pileup on Highway 2, that story you did about the land exchange between Weyerhaeuser and the forest service, and whatever else comes in at the last minute. Or fits what we have left over."

The summary sounded satisfactory. "So everything's moving along okay?"

"Sure. I can ride herd over Carla, you know. So to speak. We've got cow fever, I guess." Leo laughed again.

"Leo, are you drinking?"

"What?" He sounded genuinely shocked. "No. And

what if I had been? I almost never have more than two these days."

I knew that, and was chagrined. "Sorry. I'm not exactly myself." I stopped before I started making excuses. "I should be back sometime tomorrow afternoon."

"Don't push it," Leo said, and I thought I detected a note of concern. "We're doing fine. Hell, babe, you've only missed one day. What do you expect us to do, shut the place down and party? Carla's cute, but she's not my type."

Leo was right. In terms of work, I'd only been absent today. Somehow, it seemed much longer. The past three days had stretched out in my mind, as if distance could alter time.

"Thanks for everything," I said. "Make sure you proof all of Carla's stuff. I'll see you tomorrow."

I hung up, feeling vaguely disappointed. Leo and Carla were getting along without me. And without Vida. Though it shouldn't have, the thought rankled.

Vida and Stina were halfway through their entrées by the time I returned. My panfried oysters had grown a bit cold, but they tasted good anyway. Oddly, Vida didn't inquire about *The Advocate*. She was still wrapped up in Audrey's murder.

"Stina was telling me that Audrey was moody," Vida said, giving me an arch little look. "I was wondering if she was on medication. Or something like that."

Under the influence of a third martini, Stina's own mood had grown expansive. "I heard she was always moody, even as a kid. Maybe it was her folks. They fought a lot, and he was a drinker. Look at Marlin— would you call him normal? I figure the whole family's out there in cuckooland."

"Not the *whole* family," Vida said with a hard stare. "I

was thinking more of a nervous condition. Perhaps Audrey suffered from depression. Or perhaps she was simply . . . high-strung." The stare softened, but it stayed in place.

Stina wasn't about to be lured into self-revelation. "I don't think so. I don't know much about mental instability, but in Audrey's case, it came down to selfishness. The world revolved around Audrey, in an off-the-wall kind of way."

Vida frowned. "You mean she wasn't a . . . braggart or a blowhard?"

Stina grinned. "That's right. It was as if it was her right to get her own way, to be the center of attention. She didn't work at it. She didn't have to. It just *was*. And always had been." A note of bitterness crept into her voice.

"That's very hard on children," Vida remarked. "And husbands," she added, as an afterthought.

"Gordon's too soft." Stina finished her martini. "He was a sap to marry her in the first place."

"They were very young," Vida allowed.

"She conned him." Stina removed the tiny plastic sword from her discarded olive and snapped it in two. "She told him she was pregnant."

My eyes widened. "Was she?"

Abruptly, Stina straightened her shoulders and stared at me. "I don't know. All I hear are rumors."

"Which," Vida remarked idly, "you despise."

"Yes." Stina gazed into her empty glass. "So let's talk about something else. We went to New Zealand last winter to visit Stu's family. It was my first trip Down Under. I loved it. His family was something else." She made a puckish little face. "What about you two? Any kids, grandkids?"

While usually delighted to talk about her grandchildren, Vida exhibited mild reluctance. But we both realized that Stina wasn't going to say any more about Audrey Imhoff. The dinner wound down, after I'd flashed a photo of Adam, and Vida had shown off her three daughters, their husbands, and the grandchildren, which included the reprehensible Roger. If ever there was an indication that bad blood ran in the Runkel family, Roger was it. Now entering his teens, he suffered from the Three S's: spoiled, surly, and selfish. Worse yet, Vida doted on him.

Stina expressed what appeared to be genuine interest in our progeny, but may have been part of her professional bag of tricks. Still, I thought I detected a slight wistfulness in her expression when she looked at Adam's baby picture.

Vida offered to give Stina a ride home, but then realized that only two could fit into the pickup's cab. That was all right with Stina—she could walk. The Kanes lived by Whale Park, only a couple of blocks away.

We wondered what kind of reception she would get from her husband. "I'm guessing that Stuart blows hot and cold," Vida said as we climbed into the pickup.

"Short fuse, quick recovery?" I replied. "Maybe. Did you believe Stina when she said it was Stu who was having the affair with Audrey?"

"I don't know." Vida was having trouble with the gears again. "She's candid, but not necessarily truthful. If you know what I mean."

I did, sort of. We finally pulled away from the curb, and it occurred to me that we weren't heading back to the motel. "Now where?" I sighed.

Vida didn't answer directly. "Such a nuisance, not having two cars. Really, you must get another rental tomorrow."

"I am. I'm taking it to Alpine."

Vida ignored my statement. "I want to make sure the Buick's been towed. You can show me where the car went into the tree."

I started to repeat my intentions to leave in the morning, but a sudden thought struck my brain. "How old was Audrey?"

Vida paused, apparently calculating. "Forty-three. I believe she had a June birthday."

"And Derek, the eldest child, is what—nineteen, twenty?"

Vida nodded. "He'll be twenty in November or December. I don't recall which."

"Which means," I went on as Vida drove out of town toward Elk Creek Road, "Audrey was twenty-three when she had Derek. Either she wasn't pregnant at the time of the wedding, or else they weren't as young as everyone says they were when they got married." In small towns, especially two decades ago, a twenty-three-year-old single girl would have been considered a virtual old maid.

"You're right," Vida said. "How strange that I hadn't figured that out for myself. But that's Rett and Rosalie's fault for not keeping up with the rest of the family."

I didn't bother to correct Vida's attempt at self-defense. "Who told us they married young in the first place? Stacie?"

"I think so, yes." As Vida turned onto the road that led to Marlin's place, she grew thoughtful. "Of course Stacie was repeating what she'd heard from her parents. At least from her mother. Frankly, I don't recall the precise context."

I didn't either, yet the apparent discrepancy bothered me. There wasn't time to discuss it further, however: we were approaching the tree that had sent Vida's car off to the body shop. Night had fallen, and it was difficult to see.

"There," I said, pointing to the left side of the road. "I'm sure that's it, where the ferns and underbrush are beaten down. The Buick's gone."

"Good. I'll call the repairmen tomorrow to see if they're getting started on the job. I suppose they'll have to wait until they get a check from Brendan Shaw." Vida had braked by the tree and was peering up the road. "Goodness, where do I turn around?"

I grimaced. "There really isn't a place until you get to Marlin's."

The pickup moved ahead after another struggle with the gears. A couple of minutes later we could see the lights in Marlin's house through the trees.

Then we saw Marlin. He was standing in the doorway of his so-called pad, with the bow and arrow aimed at Randy Neal and Charles St. James.

Chapter Thirteen

THE DEPUTIES WERE trying to talk Marlin into dropping his weapon. St. James stood behind a tree, halfway between his patrol car and the house, while Neal held back in the refuge of the squad car.

Vida started to get out of the pickup, but I grabbed her arm. "Don't," I urged as all three men turned to look in our direction. "We have to take cover, just like the deputies. Douse the lights. I doubt if they can see who's inside the cab." Marlin certainly wouldn't expect his aunt to show up in a truck.

Marlin's glance in our direction had been too brief to allow either deputy to make a move on him. But Randy Neal had gotten out of the squad car and was coming toward us. As the deputy crept carefully between the vehicles his over-the-shoulder glance stayed on Marlin.

"You think I'm kidding?" Marlin shouted. "You think I can't shoot straight?"

"I think it would be foolhardy," St. James replied in a calm voice. "If you put an arrow through me, my partner will nail you before you can shoot again. All we want to do is talk."

"I know who squealed," Marlin shouted. "It was that bitch who hangs out with my so-called aunt."

I was rubbing my forehead in annoyance when Neal

reached the pickup. He stayed flat against the passenger side, and I quickly rolled the window all the way down.

"Ms. Lord? And Ms. . . ." Neal's startled voice trailed off.

"Runkel," Vida snapped, leaning across me. "The so-called aunt."

Neal cleared his throat. "Yes, I mean . . . yes, Ms. Runkel. You'd better leave. We have police business here."

Vida pounced. "Is it about Audrey?"

"Ah . . . no." Consternation showed on Neal's fine features.

"My car?" Vida queried.

"Your car?" Neal sounded puzzled.

"Never mind." Vida looked peeved, then seemed to be making up her mind about something. "Let me talk to that ridiculous nephew of mine."

Her ridiculous nephew still held the bow and arrow at the ready, and was conducting a one-sided argument with Charles St. James. "This is private property," Marlin shouted. "Didn't you see the sign back there? I've already told you everything I know about my sister. Go away, leave me alone."

St. James stepped out from the shelter of the tree trunk and held his hands up in front of him. "I'm not going for my gun," he said, still calm. Then he reached inside his regulation jacket. "We have a search warrant."

"I don't give a shit if you've got a judge and a jury. Get the hell off my property!" A note of hysteria had crept into Marlin's voice as the bow and arrow wavered slightly.

At the side of the pickup, Neal was telling Vida that she shouldn't try to talk to her nephew. Vida was arguing. Neal seemed to vacillate. It was all the leeway Vida needed. She opened the door and got down from the cab with amazing alacrity.

"Yoo-hoo! Marlin!" she called, the battered green straw askew. "Stop making a fool of yourself! Do you want to end up in prison?"

Marlin took one look at Vida, turned tail, and ran inside the house. The door slammed behind him.

"Oh, good grief!" Vida exclaimed.

"That wasn't smart," Neal muttered.

"Marlin's not smart," Vida retorted. "Did I hear the other deputy say he had a search warrant? For what?"

"I'm sorry, I can't say," Neal replied stiffly. "But we're going ahead with our business. Would you . . . ah . . . mind?"

Vida was blocking Neal's path. "Mind? Mind what? I'm not stopping you. But tell me how you plan to get inside. Tear gas?" There was a derisive note in her voice.

"Ma'am," Randy Neal said in a pleading tone, "it'd be better if you left. We can't have civilians on site while we do a search." The deputy awkwardly managed to sidestep Vida, who was blocking his path.

I had also gotten out of the truck and wandered over to stand behind Vida. Up ahead, St. James was using a big flashlight to scour the area just beyond Marlin's house. He stopped and signaled to his partner.

"Over here, Randy."

Vida seemed exasperated. "Well! They don't want to search the house after all. Oh, dear!" She suddenly turned on me. "You didn't!"

"Of course not," I said indignantly. "Marlin was off base. So are you. I wouldn't rat on him. I'm surprised the authorities didn't know about the marijuana farm before this."

"True." Vida's demeanor changed, the signs of reproach evaporating. "Then who did?"

I sighed. "Who knows? Maybe it's a follow-up, going back to when they originally questioned Marlin about his sister's death. They might have had suspicions then. After all, his place reeks of pot and they could see the sheds for themselves."

Vida tapped her chin. "Perhaps. It might have taken them some time to get a search warrant issued. Still, I wonder. . . ."

We were silent for a few moments, standing in the dark turnaround. The deputies had disappeared, either in back of one of the sheds or up the trail. The only sound was the wind in the trees and a croaking frog. A mile from the ocean, we could no longer hear the surf.

The lights remained on inside Marlin's house. I imagined him barricaded behind the door, bow and arrow at the ready. Or, now that I was beginning to know Marlin better, maybe he'd sought comfort in his illegal harvest.

"Are we calling on Mr. Runkel?" I finally asked, somewhat facetiously.

Vida stared at the ramshackle dwelling. "I don't know. Marlin doesn't seem receptive to visitors."

"Especially not to me," I noted. "He thinks I turned him in."

Vida didn't respond directly, but turned around and got into the pickup. I followed suit.

"Where now?" I inquired as she fought the gears and tried to reverse the truck in the narrow space. It was almost eight o'clock and my battered body was crying for rest.

"I'm not sure. Will they arrest Marlin on the spot? I've no idea how it works with . . . people who grow marijuana.

Is that illegal in and of itself? Or does he have to be caught selling it? Dear, dear."

"It's illegal to grow it. At least it is in Washington. I'm not sure about Oregon," I admitted. "It's been a while since I lived here, and laws can change."

The grinding gears set my teeth on edge; one of the rear tires hit a rut and jarred us. Vida wasn't having much luck turning the truck around; the old Camaro was parked dangerously close. "That suitcase," she said, huffing a bit. "The one with the marijuana in it—do you suppose Stacie and Molly took it with them to California?"

"I don't know," I replied, wincing as the back wheels spun in yet another hole. "Did you notice if they had luggage of their own?"

"I saw a type of duffel bag," Vida said, finally getting the pickup to move forward without hitting the Camaro. "And backpacks. Young people use backpacks more than luggage these days, I believe. I bought Roger a very handsome model for his birthday. He carries all his text-books and studies in it."

And grenades and handguns and extremely sharp knives, I thought with the particular brand of venom I reserved for my House & Home editor's grandson. The pickup had executed a half turn; at least Vida was making some progress, though her green straw hat had fallen off. *Maybe a cake and a pie and a gallon of ice cream to stuff into his fat little face.* She reversed again, almost hitting a tree. *Copies of* Hustler *and X-rated videos and dirty post-cards.* Locked in combat with the gears and the steering wheel, Vida finally had us going in the right direction.

"Can we go home?" I asked in my most plaintive voice. "I'm exhausted and I hurt all over. Tomorrow I'll be stiff as a board."

"Of course you will," Vida said in an annoyingly

cheerful voice. "Yes, I suppose we could go back to the motel. It wouldn't do any good to forewarn Everett."

I sat back against the worn passenger seat, immensely relieved that our evening inquiries appeared to be over. "About what?"

"Marlin's possible arrest. I shouldn't like to bother Rosalie. She's got troubles enough with Gordon."

"But Gordon was going to turn himself in," I said.

"Mmmm. Perhaps."

I didn't blame Vida for being skeptical. However, there was nothing we could do about Gordon Imhoff's propensity for self-destruction. As we wound down the Elk Creek Road I concluded that the Oregon branch of the Runkel family had a penchant for disaster that was remarkable. Though the Alpine contingent had gotten into some scrapes over the years, to my knowledge none of them had ever faced criminal charges or been murdered. They all appeared to be ordinary folks—flawed, even eccentric, but not outrageous. Unless you counted Ernest and his fatal accident. Or Roger.

Vida took 101 back into town, driving very carefully at the turn where I'd had my accident. A moment later we were in the motel parking lot. A smallish sedan had pulled in just ahead of us; the driver got out and staggered slightly when he saw the pickup. I recognized Derek Imhoff at once.

So, of course, did Vida. "Derek?" she called, opening the cab door. "Yoo-hoo! What is it?"

"I didn't think you were here," he said, hurrying to the truck. "Have you seen Dolly?"

We both got down from the truck. "No," Vida replied, putting the truck's keys into her purse. "Should we have?"

In the light that illuminated the parking area, Derek's

face looked very young and very miserable. "She's run away. I thought . . . she might be here."

"I see." Vida grew quite serious, then put a hand under Derek's elbow and steered him toward the archway that led to our unit. "Come inside. I'll make some tea."

Derek shook her off. "No, I can't. I need to keep looking. Maybe she's on the beach." He gestured in the direction of the ocean.

Vida reclaimed Derek's elbow, this time with a firmer grip. "We'll help. But first, you must tell us what happened. Come along."

To my surprise, Derek obeyed. A moment later we were in the living room, the lights were turned on and the drapes drawn. "I'll put the kettle on," Vida said. "You sit down and catch your breath."

Derek didn't sit, but began pacing the small room, stopping once to peer between the drapes. "She's never done this before," he murmured, more to himself than to me. "God, she can get mad! I never saw her so mad!"

My mind flew back to similar laments from Adam. At about the same age as Derek, he had dated a girl called Storm whose name definitely described her temperament. She screamed, she hit, she threw things, she drove my son crazy. In between eruptions, she was quiet, thoughtful, and kind; literally, the calm before the storm. Adam didn't know what to make of her, and after two months he made her his ex-girlfriend. Naturally, I was relieved.

"What set her off?" I kept my voice matter-of-fact.

"Dad," Derek answered, and then looked at me in surprise. I had the feeling that he hadn't really intended to answer the question. "I mean, Dad came home, and—" He stopped, swinging a fist at the air.

"Upset the balance?" I suggested.

"What?"

"You know—the status quo." I gave Derek an encouraging smile. "Your dad likes Dolores, though. Didn't she want to give up the master bedroom?"

Derek flushed. "No. I mean, maybe. I don't know. She just went off like a freaking rocket."

"She's not at her folks' place?"

Derek looked at me as if I were daft. "She wouldn't go back there. Anyway, I already checked. She's not there, none of her girlfriends have seen her, nobody from work, either. I thought maybe, since Dolly's met Aunt Vida, she might have come here to hang out."

The image of Vida and Dolores hanging out didn't play for me, but I made no comment. "Does she have a car?" I asked as Vida came back into the living room.

Derek shook his head. "She used to, but it broke down and she sold it for junk a couple of weeks ago. It was an 'eighty-one Citation."

"Tea will be ready in five minutes," Vida announced, standing in front of the fireplace with her arms folded across her bosom. "How long has Dolores been gone?"

Derek regarded his great-aunt warily. "Since about six-thirty."

Vida adjusted her glasses. "Not so long, then. Where's your father?"

Derek seemed taken aback by the question. "Home? I don't know. He was there when I left."

"You left right after Dolores?" Vida inquired.

"No. Not right away." Derek avoided Vida's gaze, then flopped down in one of the armchairs. "I was steamed. I didn't take off after her until about seven. I thought she'd come back." There was despair in his voice.

Vida gave a brief nod. "One might assume as much.

But she didn't. Have you looked along the beach by your house?"

Derek's head jerked up and down several times. "That's the first place I went. Like I said, she spends a lot of time on the beach, especially when she wants to think."

Glancing at her watch, Vida gave Derek a tight little smile. "She's been gone less than two hours. There's a great deal of beach to walk. She may still be there."

Derek swiveled around in the chair, eyeing the front window. "That's why I wanted to look at this end. Hey, I'm going now. I don't like tea much anyway." He jumped out of the chair and headed for the door.

Vida took a step forward as if to detain him, then stopped. "Good luck," she called.

He didn't quite close the door behind him. Vida marched across the room, peeked outside, then shut the door and shook her head. "Young people. They're so excitable."

I yawned. "Dolores didn't like Gordon's intrusion. Playing house must have suited her." I yawned again.

Vida nodded. "Yes. Her own home life sounds quite dreadful. Living with Derek and without adult supervision—or perhaps I should say interference—no doubt brought a note of normality to her life."

The teakettle whistled, and Vida went into the kitchen. Dimly, I heard her rattling crockery; my eyes were closing, my head dropping onto my chest.

It was the ringing of the phone that yanked me out of my somnolent state. Assuming it was for Vida, I waited to see if she'd rush out to answer it. But she didn't, so I leaned over on the sofa and picked up the receiver. It was Madge, from the motel office. She asked for me, and said there was a message from Mr. Redd.

"I don't know a Mr. Redd," I replied, searching my memory for anyone we'd encountered in Cannon Beach or Seaside by that name.

"You don't?" Madge sounded vaguely alarmed. "He said it was very important. Here's his number, just in case. . . ."

I recognized the number at once. It was Ed Bronsky's. "Oh—Mr. *Ed*," I croaked. "Oh, oh. Yes, I'll call him. Thanks."

Vida bustled into the living room, carrying Melmac cups and saucers. "Ed? Did you say Ed?" She sounded as if she wished otherwise.

So did I. "It's about the book," I said dolefully. "He left his name as Mr. Ed."

"My, my." Vida shook her head. "You'll have to call him, I suppose."

I sighed. "Do I? Must I? Will I?"

"He'll keep calling until you do," Vida said, heading back into the kitchen. "You know what he's like."

With leaden fingers, I dialed Ed's number. His wife, Shirley, answered from somewhere in the vast and vulgar villa they'd built above the railroad tracks.

"How are you, Emma?" Shirley said in her girlish, jarring voice. "I was just saying to Ed today that we still haven't had you over to dinner since we got settled in. Of course we're planning the Christmas gala. Do you think it should be formal or costume?"

Shirley didn't want to know what I really thought, which was that hosting a gala in Alpine smacked of the absurd. "Do whatever you feel comfortable with," I said in a dull voice, and then, because I was tired and sore and borderline cranky, I added, "make it a Dickens theme. Vida and I can come as Ignorance and Want."

"What?" Shirley sounded nonplussed.

"It was just a thought." I caught Vida's bemused gaze as she set sugar and milk on the coffee table in front of me. "Where's Ed? He called me here in Cannon Beach."

"Oh!" Shirley squeaked. "That's right! I keep forgetting, you're not here, you're . . . there. Just a minute, I'll page him. I think he's in the billiard room."

"Why not?" I said under my breath.

It took a while. When Ed finally got to the phone, he was huffing and puffing. "Sorry. Fuzzy Baugh and I were shooting a few rounds. Having a few, too. Haha!"

Knowing Mayor Baugh, I was sure that the drinks had flowed like . . . drinks. Just hearing Ed's overhearty voice turned my brain to mush. "What's going on, Ed?" I asked, in desperate need of cutting to the chase.

"I've got great news," Ed replied, and I could imagine his chins quivering with excitement. "I've got a publisher!"

My jaw dropped. Vida, who was now sitting in one of the armchairs sipping her tea, stared at me. I mouthed *the book*, but she continued to look puzzled.

"You found a publisher?" I echoed for Vida's enlightenment. "Wonderful, Ed. Who is it?"

"Vane Press," Ed answered. "That's V-A-N-E, out of Redmond, over on Seattle's east side. They're top-notch, and they really like *Mr. Ed*. They say it's got legs."

"It does, huh? That's really . . . grand."

" 'Down-to-earth'—that's what Skip called it," Ed continued, his stomach no doubt expanding along with his voice. " 'Gritty realism' is how Irving put it. Remember the part when I was in first grade, and some of the fourth graders locked me in the paint 'n paste room with the skunk?"

"Uh . . . yes, I remember that." Milo had been one of

the malefactors. The sheriff had told me the tale first, and somehow his version had been much funnier than Ed's.

"Skip said every reader could relate to that incident," Ed asserted.

I'd never been locked in a supply room with a skunk, but I wasn't arguing with Ed. "Who's Skip? And Irving?"

"The publishers. Skip O'Shea and Irving Blomberg. Now the fact is," Ed went on, lowering his voice, "they're real entrepreneurs, and just getting this venture off the ground. I'd talked to Kip MacDuff, and to be frank, he didn't sound like he knew what he was doing when it came to publishing a book of this magnitude. Nothing against Kip, he's a good kid, but he's young, and let's face it, Emma, this is *Alpine*. Vane Press is located right in Redmond, practically next door to Microsoft. They're talking movie deals, TV, maybe even letting Bill Gates have a crack at something on-line. Then there's that production company Gates is tied into, DreamWorks, and once that guy gets his teeth into . . ."

I let Ed bluster on. Vida was drinking her tea and flipping through the pages of the local chamber-of-commerce guide. She looked as bored as I felt.

"So," Ed finally said, winding down, "all I need is to put in the thirty grand and we're off to press. *Mr. Ed* should come out in time for Christmas."

"I see." I saw that Vane Press should have been spelled V-A-I-N, as in vanity press. The book would get published in a limited edition, and all costs would be absorbed by Ed. At least that was how I understood vanity presses to operate. I saw a rush print job that couldn't possibly offer any kind of quality—not that there was much to begin with in Ed's manuscript. I saw limited, if any, distribution, and no advertising budget. Most of all I saw Ed's money going down a long, dark drain in Redmond. "Have you signed a contract?" I asked.

"You bet," Ed responded. "How could I pass up a chance like this? Skip and Irving say I'll have my money back in six weeks. After that, it's all gravy."

"Did you have anyone look at the contract? A lawyer, like Marisa Foxx from the parish?"

"What do I need a lawyer for?" Ed scoffed. "What does Marisa know about publishing?"

It was hopeless. "Good luck, Ed."

"Thanks. Will you be back in time to write the story?"

I held my head. "I should be." It *was* news. No one else in Alpine had published a book, by a vanity press or otherwise, since Grace Grundle sold two of her gopher poems to an anthology put out by her alma mater, a small teachers' college in Kansas. "If not, Carla can handle it."

"Carla!" Now Ed's voice was full of scorn. "I wouldn't trust her with this big a deal! She'd probably give me two inches on page four."

That sounded just about right. "We'll see what the paper looks like when I get home," I said, hoping not to convey my irritation. "Congratulations, Ed. I'll talk to you later."

Of course Vida had to hear all about "that ninny," as she called him. She was less horrified by his folly than I, however.

"It may teach Ed a lesson," she declared. "Though if he keeps on spending at this rate, I can't help but think that eventually their inheritance will run out. That ridiculous house cost almost two million dollars."

I was aware of the price tag on Ed and Shirley's boon-doggle. While Ed had bragged endlessly about his inherited wealth, he'd always been a bit reticent when it came to the exact amount. I'd guessed it to be in the four-to-five-million range, but I really didn't know. The estate had been filed in Iowa, which meant that Vida hadn't been able to get at the records.

"Don't talk about the Bronskys going broke," I groaned. "That would mean Ed might try to get back on the paper."

"He couldn't," Vida retorted. "You have Leo." She grimaced slightly; Vida and Leo weren't always the best of chums.

Since we were on the subject of *The Advocate*, I started to tell Vida about the late-breaking news in Alpine. But before I could get the words out of my mouth, she picked up her coat from where she had set it down on the arm of the sofa.

"I know you're tired," she said with what sounded like real sympathy, "so I won't impose. But I must meet Ruth Pickering. Now tell me exactly how to get there."

"Shouldn't you call first?" I asked.

"I think a surprise visit is wise," Vida responded. "Didn't you mention that she rarely goes out?"

I suppose I had. "It's easy to find," I said. "Just keep going past downtown, then follow Hemlock as it curves, and when you get to the straight part, look for the Blue Gull and the Sand Trap inns. Her place is just a few doors down on your left. Even in the dark, you can't miss all the metal sculptures."

"Goodness," Vida said with a worried expression, "I don't believe I've noticed the Sea Gull and the Sand Castle inns. Are they this side of Tolovana?"

"Blue Gull and Sand Trap," I repeated. "You must have seen them. They're smallish, cozy-looking places."

"My night vision is getting so poor." Vida sighed. "It's no wonder I had such trouble turning around up at Marlin's. I wonder what's happened to him?"

"He's probably busted," I said with a certain amount of satisfaction. I knew what Vida was angling for, but I wasn't going after the bait.

"I hope not. It's all so upsetting. No wonder my mind is so fragmented." Vida was looking uncharacteristically vague. "What is Ruth's house number?"

"I don't remember. Check the phone book."

"Alas, I can't read those tiny numbers." Her full face assumed a pitiful mien. "As I said, my eyes have gotten very bad lately."

"As in the last five minutes?" I snapped. "Look, Vida, do you really want me to come along?"

"It'd be a comfort." Vida sighed again, clasping her hands.

"Okay, okay," I grumbled. "I'll go. But make it quick. Ruth isn't very talkative, and she doesn't say much anyway."

There was a light on at Ruth's, indicating that she stayed up at least until nine. But after we'd identified ourselves and she'd warily opened the front door, I noted that she was wearing a bathrobe. Like the smock I had seen her in the previous day, the fabric was a crazy-quilt assortment of colors.

"Mrs. Runkel," Ruth murmured, leading us into the tiny hall but no farther. "You're Audrey's aunt?"

"That's right," Vida replied in a mournful tone. "Such a lovely young woman. And such a tragedy. Like Gordon, I was widowed young and left with three children."

That much was true. But Vida immediately began to press whatever advantage she thought she'd gained. "Your magnificent sculptures! I saw them in the yard just now. Do you have more in the living room?"

"Yes." Ruth didn't budge. "What can I do for you at this hour of the night?"

"It's about your neighbors," Vida began, throwing me—and probably Ruth—off track. "What kind of people leave threatening notes on visitors' windshields?"

"I don't know what you're talking about," Ruth responded, her thin, wrinkled face wreathed in confusion.

Vida put a hand on my shoulder. I felt as if she were the ventriloquist and I were the dummy. But then I often had that sensation when I was with her.

"Emma had such a scare yesterday when she left your house," Vida explained. "Someone had put a note on her car *while it was in your driveway*. It was worded most crudely, with vile, menacing language. Now, who could have done such a thing?"

Ruth paled a bit. "I've no idea. My neighbors are very nice people."

"Really." Disbelief dripped from the word.

"They are," Ruth insisted. "Someone else must have written the note."

"Well now." Vida scanned the small entryway. "If you say so. Then your neighbors won't object to being interrogated by the police."

Since we hadn't reported the incident, I felt that Vida might be going too far. But the ruse worked. Alarm showed in Ruth's face, and she put both hands to her breast.

"Oh, no! They've been through enough with Audrey's death!"

" 'They'?" Vida's eyes had narrowed.

"The Crenshaws have, at least," Ruth said, speaking more rapidly than usual. "The sheriff's deputies were at their house again last week."

I was tired of being the dummy. "Who are the Crenshaws?" I asked.

"Hazel and Victor," Ruth replied. "He's a retired dentist, from Portland. She was his receptionist."

"What was their connection with Audrey?" Vida inquired.

Ruth gathered the brilliantly colored bathrobe closer. "Victor had prostate cancer. Audrey drove him to his appointments in Portland. Hazel never learned to drive."

"Ah," said Vida. "Was this arrangement recent?"

"Last year." Ruth seemed to be regaining her composure. "Victor is doing very well. The doctors caught it early. But the Crenshaws were so grateful. That's why Victor gave Audrey their condominium in Portland."

I caught Vida's swift glance in my direction. "A condominium!" she exclaimed. "How generous! Was Audrey planning to live there?"

"I don't know," Ruth said. "Maybe."

"So," I interjected, "that was why the deputies questioned the Crenshaws?"

Ruth gave a brief nod. "I expect so. Hazel and Victor felt it was none of their business. They're right. What does it have to do with Audrey's death?"

"That's what we'd all like to know," said Vida.

Chapter Fourteen

ACCORDING TO RUTH, the Crenshaws lived behind her, on Spruce Street. She warned us that they were early risers, and usually went to bed around eight-thirty. Sure enough, the house was dark when we drove by a few minutes later.

"Tomorrow, first thing," Vida declared, glancing at her watch. "It's well after nine. Gordon should be in Astoria by now. Let's make sure."

I started to protest, but we were less than three minutes from the Imhoff house. And, I admitted, I was curious about Gordon, too.

"Maybe Dolores has come back," Vida said as the pickup rattled and bumped along the road to Tolovana.

But there was no sign of life at the Imhoff residence. The Tracer that Derek had been driving was gone, and so was Gordon's rented Taurus. Vida and I sat in the cab, watching the darkened house for several moments.

"I'd like to think Gordon has done the right thing," she said. "I'd also like to think that Dolores is safe."

"Safe? Why wouldn't she be safe?" Despite the doubt in my voice, I felt a small shiver of alarm.

"It would be different if we knew who killed Audrey and why," Vida said in a troubled voice. "But we don't, and until we do, how do we know who is safe and who isn't?"

"We don't," I agreed.

"What if Dolores saw something, or knows something? Or made a recent discovery?" Vida fidgeted with the steering wheel. "I don't mean that she's actively sleuthing. Perhaps she came across information that would lead to the solution of the case. Dolores might not even know what it was, but the killer would."

I found myself sinking down in the cab's passenger seat. "Why do I think Dolores doesn't care who killed Audrey?"

"Because she's young and self-absorbed," Vida responded. "She has troubles aplenty with her own family. She's all wrapped up in Derek."

"Who happens to be her escape route?" I remarked in a wry tone. "Does Dolores really care about him, or does she see him as a means of getting out of a miserable home situation?"

"I've seen too much of that in Alpine," Vida lamented. "I could tick off a dozen young people—boys and girls—in the past two years who've gotten married or moved in with someone because their home life was unbearable. Look at April Aagaard—she married a prisoner from the Monroe penitentiary just to get away from Barney and Peggy Sue. April was only fifteen, and lied about her age, and now she's married to a drug dealer who already has a wife and two children. Such a shame, but you couldn't blame her when her father and stepmother were constantly trying to kill each other with kitchen utensils. The problem is, we know very little about Dolores." Suddenly swinging into action, Vida started the truck. "Let's hope they forgot to lock the door again," she said, pulling into the spot where we had first claimed the pickup.

Both front and back doors were locked, however. I followed Vida as she strolled around the house, looking for a window through which we might enter.

"Why are we doing this?" I inquired in a tired voice. Though Vida has almost twenty years on me, her endurance never fails to amaze.

"Actually," she responded, "I wanted to see the phone book so we could find out where Dolores's parents live." Having made the full circuit, Vida gave up. "The windows all have screens. Removing them is such a bother. We'll have to find a phone booth."

There was one by the liquor store, just across the street and a few doors down from Ruth Pickering's house. I noticed that her lights were no longer on, and wondered if she was sleeping peacefully, or worrying about the Crenshaws. At almost ten o'clock on a Monday night in October, Hemlock was virtually deserted. I waited in the truck while Vida scanned the local directory.

When she climbed back in the cab, her face was set in a hard line. "I found them. There's only one Cerrillo in the book." Vida turned the ignition key, then gazed at me with a curious expression. "They live on Elk Creek Road. Shall we?"

"No!"

Vida was already guiding the truck in the direction of the turnoff to 101. "We won't stop. It's much too late. But I have to know where the house is located." She recited the number. "You watch for it. My eyes, you know. So bad these days."

I still didn't believe her, but she *was* doing the driving. It took less than three minutes to get to the Elk Creek Road. I'd remembered a scattering of houses not far from the RV park, and sure enough, the Cerrillo home was among them. The lights were on, which allowed us a fairly good view.

"Tawdry," Vida remarked. "Not unlike those disreputable places along Railroad Avenue in Alpine."

I had to agree. While the Cerrillo house wasn't nearly as dilapidated as Marlin's, it was small, in disrepair, and featured a front yard littered with car parts, rotting cardboard cartons, and rusting appliances. There was no yard: the grass, where it was allowed to grow, was tall and riddled with weeds. A broken front window had been replaced with what looked like a piece of plywood, and a downspout dangled brokenly from the patched roof. I felt a sudden pang for Dolores.

"No wonder she moved in with Derek," I murmured.

"True." Vida spoke softly, though there was no one to hear us. The closest house was at least two hundred feet away. "How far are we from Marlin's?"

I sighed. "Vida . . ."

"I'm curious, that's all. You've been here more often than I."

"A quarter of a mile? Maybe more. Your Buick crashed not too far from here."

"Hmmm." Vida fingered her chin. "I don't suppose we should check to see if the deputies have gone."

"No, we shouldn't. Please, Vida, I want to get back to the motel." My voice was so tired that it broke.

"Oh, all right. Let me find a turnaround."

She found it just about where the Buick had landed. To her credit, Vida seemed to be mastering the gears. We were about to head back down the road when the headlights of another car came around the bend behind us. Vida waited for the other vehicle to pass, but it stopped alongside the pickup. Tami of the Cannon Beach Police gazed out from the open window of the official squad car.

"Are you having a problem? Oh! Ms. . . . Gosh, I forget!" Tami looked embarrassed.

"Runkel," Vida replied. "We're fine. What's going on, Tami?"

I could see Corey behind the wheel. Tami turned to him as if for consultation. "Um . . ." she began. "Ah . . . Isn't Mr. Runkel your nephew or something?"

"He is both," Vida answered crisply. "He is my nephew. And he is something. Why do you ask?"

"Well . . ." The young woman's embarrassment deepened. "He's been arrested by the sheriff's deputies. I'm afraid they've sent him up to Astoria."

"Oh dear!" Vida's face was a mask of consternation. "On what charge?" she asked after a long pause.

Corey had leaned across the seat. "Illegal possession," he said, also looking somewhat discomfited. "He finally gave up when Mr. Imhoff talked him into riding with him."

"What?" Vida whipped off her glasses.

Tami had shrunk back against her car seat, an incongruous figure against the backdrop of gun racks and wire mesh. Corey appeared to have taken over.

"You see," he explained, very serious, "the deputies asked us to see if Mr. Imhoff could talk Mr. Runkel into giving himself up. Mr. Imhoff said he'd try, and when he told Mr. Runkel that he was giving himself up, too, then Mr. Runkel decided he might as well. Give up, that is. So they drove up to Astoria in Mr. Imhoff's car."

During the course of this narration, Vida had been rubbing madly at her eyes. She finally stopped and blinked at Corey. "Did the deputies follow them?"

"Oh, sure," Corey replied. "They left about an hour ago. We stayed around to help gather evidence."

"I see." Vida sounded grim. "Well. Thank you."

Corey touched the bill of his regulation cap. "You're welcome, Ms. Runkel. Drive safely."

"Wait!" Vida shouted just as Tami began to roll up her window. "Has a missing girl been reported this evening?"

Corey and Tami exchanged puzzled glances. "No," Tami replied. "Not that we know of. Who's missing?"

"Dolores Cerrillo," Vida replied, gesturing in the direction of the Cerrillo house down the road. "We're told she's not at home, and she's not with Derek Imhoff."

Tami giggled. "Of course she isn't. Dolores is perfectly safe. She's at police headquarters."

Before Vida could say another word, the squad car headed off down the Elk Creek Road.

I didn't care if Dolores was in a jail cell, if Marlin was in leg irons, or if Gordon was on the gallows. All I wanted to do was crawl into bed and pull the covers over my aching head. For once, Vida didn't argue. Maybe she was too astounded by the latest developments. Maybe she needed time to mull them over in her mind. Maybe she, too, had finally succumbed to fatigue.

Despite the slightly uneven mattress on the sofa bed, I slept like a rock. To my horror, I didn't wake up until a few minutes after nine. Vida was dressed and sitting in one of the armchairs, reading Molly's diary.

"My God!" I croaked in a froglike voice. "It's late! I've got to get out of here!"

"Good morning," Vida said brightly. "It's another lovely day."

I struggled with the sheet and the single blanket. Then I tried to sit up. It wasn't easy. In fact, it was almost impossible. My back had stiffened up and I felt awful. Nor did my neck respond to efforts to turn my head.

Leaning against the sofa's headboard, I took several deep breaths and tried again.

"Stiff? Sore?" Vida looked extremely sympathetic. "Just take your time. You really should have seen a doctor yesterday. Maybe," she added, unable to completely hide the smugness in her voice, "you ought to stay in bed."

I was beginning to think I had no choice. Finally I managed to sit up. After a brief wait I attempted to stand. But walking was another matter. With each tenuous step, pain rippled up and down my spine. Staggering into the bathroom, I leaned against the sink and stared at myself in the mirror.

I looked dreadful. That was hardly surprising, since I felt dreadful. Slowly, excruciatingly, I performed my morning ablutions. The hot shower helped, but only temporarily. Downing more Excedrin, I told myself I should have soaked in the tub. Maybe I'd do that later.

"Poor thing." Vida clucked as I returned to the living room bearing a mug of instant coffee. "You really must take it easy today."

I wanted to argue with Vida, to defy her, to insist that I'd feel better in an hour or so, and would be able to go home. But my body told me otherwise. I felt as if I'd be lucky to get dressed, let alone leave the motel.

"Of course I could take you to the local doctor," Vida said in a musing tone. "I believe he's located in Sandpiper Square."

It was probably a good idea. But at the moment I didn't feel like making the effort. "You go," I said in a self-pitying voice as I collapsed onto the unmade sofa bed. "I'll stay here."

"Now, now." Vida could barely contain her glee. "I have some errands to run, so you relax, and I'll be back

around noon." She stood in front of the mirror, jamming
a yellow cloche on her head. "Oh—by the way, I tried to
reach Jesse Damon again this morning. Still no luck. You
might try him later on. This is getting very frustrating."

I roused myself enough to ask Vida about Molly's
diary. "Did she reveal any deep, dark secrets?"

"Not yet," Vida answered, shrugging into her swing
coat and picking up her purse. "It goes back almost two
years, and I only got up to last fall. You might take up
where I left off—mid-November, I believe." She pointed
to the coffee table where she'd left the diary. "Most of
what Molly's written is what you'd expect—maudlin,
adolescent prattle, and some very bad poetry. However,
her handwriting is quite legible and precise."

Ten minutes after Vida left, I was soaking in the tub
and perusing the diary. Vida was right: Molly was suffering all the pangs of youth, especially insecurity about
her looks and her popularity at school. Still, I found one
of the poems rather touching. Apparently the Imhoffs had
owned a dog named Nappy that had gotten run over on
the highway.

> You almost made old age, dear friend;
>   We loved you like a brother;
> You roamed free and loved the sea;
>   Were you searching for your mother?
> But you traveled too far and got hit by a car;
>   We mourned you with words unspoken;
> There's no replacing such a dog as you;
>   Our family circle has been broken.

Nappy had been killed in January. Since I'd seen no
sign of a dog at the Imhoff house, I assumed that he had
not been replaced. I wondered if the developing prob-

lems with Audrey and Gordon had had anything to do with not acquiring another pet. Then again, maybe Molly—and her siblings—really didn't feel like getting a new dog.

I added more hot water and continued reading. There was a boy Molly liked, Cassidy, with hair "the color of sunshine" and "eyes like the sea." Cassidy talked to her in the halls; he ate lunch with her in February; he helped her with her homework in March. Then he was gone. His parents had divorced, and Cassidy had moved to Corvallis with his mother. Molly was heartbroken. There were several poems, bitter, melancholy, self-pitying. To my knowledge, Adam had never written poetry, but if he had, I was sure his teenage creations would convey the same melodramatic tone.

I'd gotten up to May by the time the bathwater had cooled again. Six months' worth of adolescent self-absorption was enough for one session. I returned the diary to the coffee table and got dressed. The hot soak had helped, but I was still semimiserable. It was clear that I wasn't returning to Alpine within the next twenty-four hours.

Reluctantly, I dialed *The Advocate*. Ginny answered in her polite, efficient voice. When I explained my predicament, she expressed sympathy, but also apprehension.

"Carla's not going to be able to stay late tonight," Ginny said in her most serious voice. In the background, I could hear the Erlandson baby fussing. "She has a really, really hot date."

"In Alpine? It can't be that hot." I sounded cross. "She'll have to cancel. Under the circumstances, I don't want Kip left alone." Ordinarily, our production manager could be relied on to put out the paper without anyone holding his hand, at least not in person. But that was because I was always on top of what was happening and was five minutes away if he should need me.

"She can't," Ginny replied simply. "She won't."

"Damn! Who is this super-stud?" I demanded.

"Hush!" I gave a little start at Ginny's tone, then realized it wasn't for me but for her small son. "Here, Brad, play with the pretty bells." Ginny cleared her throat as what sounded like small sleigh bells jingled in the distance. "Sorry, Brad's getting hungry. Anyway, Carla's going out with Ryan Talliaferro, from the college. You know," she added reasonably, "the dean of students."

I knew Ryan. He was single, late thirties, good-looking in a slightly chunky sort of way, and very intelligent. It was the latter attribute that made my mind boggle.

"What's he doing dating *Carla*?" I all but shouted.

It was the wrong thing to say. Ginny and Carla are close friends. "Why shouldn't he?" Ginny, of course, was on the defensive. "They started going out last month."

Vaguely, I recalled something about Carla meeting Ryan for coffee or lunch or a drink or maybe all three, but assumed the meetings were professional, since she was covering the college.

"I don't know," I said vaguely, trying to move my head in directions it didn't seem to want to go. "Maybe I thought he was too old for Carla. I keep forgetting she's almost thirty."

"She *is* thirty," Ginny responded. "Do you want her dating some kid like Kip? Anyway, they're going to Café Fleur, and it's their first really formal date. You can't ask her to break it. What about Leo?"

"Leo will do," I answered in a subdued voice. "Put him on."

Leo assured me that he could either stick around the back shop or stay by the phone. "Everything's shaping up just fine. Stop worrying. You must have really racked yourself up, babe."

"More than I thought," I admitted. "What about Vida's 'Scene'?"

Leo emitted what sounded like a grunt. "We still don't have much. Edna Mae Dalrymple's slip fell off on the library's steps yesterday. Pete Patricelli's pizza delivery truck had a flat tire over on Sixth Street. Roy Everson at the post office found a bagful of Christmas cards that never got delivered, but he doesn't want us to mention it. He says he's going to send them out the last week of November and nobody'll know the difference."

I winced. Roy was the local postal supervisor, and a nice guy. I didn't want to get him in trouble, but a bag of mail ten months old *was* news. "Use it," I ordered. "But make it funny. Now that Roy's found the stuff, he shouldn't sit on it. He could get in trouble."

"I don't know," Leo quibbled. "If we do run the thing, maybe it should be a news story. That way, Roy could explain how mail gets lost, and how it usually doesn't happen."

"Make excuses for himself, huh?" I shot back. "The Alpine post office isn't much bigger than my house. Where was this sack, up Roy's butt?"

"Whoa!" Leo's laugh was jagged. "You must be feeling crappy, babe. What have you got against Roy Everson?"

"Nothing," I huffed. "And don't call me *babe*."

"Okay, okay," Leo responded in what may have been a soothing tone. "I'll talk to Roy. We'll work something out."

"Anything new since we spoke yesterday?" I asked, trying to shed my irritation.

"No, not really," Leo said. "The county commissioners will be asking for bids on the new bridge by the golf course at their meeting tonight. Carla wrote that up in advance, since she saw the agenda this morning and those three stooges drone on until about midnight."

I knew how the commissioners acted at their monthly meetings, many of which I'd been forced to attend. All three were past their prime, to put it mildly, and inevitably became mired in irrelevant detail, which often led to endless personal anecdotes. No one had the power to tell them to shut up, and nobody seemed willing to run against them. Position number two was on the upcoming ballot, and as usual, there was no opposition, unless you counted Crazy Eights Neffel, our resident nut, who ran for just about everything.

"Okay, I leave this edition in your hands," I said with a sigh. "I'd like to say I'd be home tomorrow, but right now I can't be sure."

"We'll make it," Leo said, the usual breeziness returning to his voice.

"You mean I'm not indispensable?" The remark was only half-facetious.

"That's right," Leo answered glibly. "Neither is the Duchess. But don't tell her that. She'd clean my clock."

I was about to confess to Leo that *The Advocate* seemed to be the last thing on Vida's mind these days, but a knock sounded at the door. I rang off rather hastily, then dragged my pitiful body across the room.

"G'day," Stuart Kane said with the first real smile I'd seen on his face. Indeed, he looked vaguely abject. "Should I throw in my hat first?"

His hat was a sharp-looking straw with a paisley band. "No, come in," I said, mustering up a smile of my own. "Have a chair. I'm sorry the sofa bed isn't made up, but I'm not feeling very well today."

"Oh?" He looked almost sympathetic. "Sorry to hear it. Flu?"

I shook my head, but didn't want to go into the details. Besides, I assumed that in a small town like Cannon Beach, everyone would know about my accident by now. They certainly would in Alpine.

"I must apologize." Stu looked around, presumably for Vida. "Your friend isn't here?"

"No. She had errands. Would you care for coffee?" I offered.

"No, thanks." Stu sat in one of the armchairs while I unceremoniously sank down on the unmade bed. "I was extremely rude last night at the restaurant. You must forgive me. So will your friend. Ms. Runkel, isn't it? Audrey's aunt?"

I nodded. "I'll tell her. You've made up with Stina, I take it?" The frank query didn't seem inappropriate, given Stu's present mood.

"Oh, yes." He had removed his hat and was twirling it in his hands. "It turned out to be a good thing. We had quite a talk. I've been worried about my wife, you see."

He seemed sincere. But he was a salesman, and now that he was behaving well, I could sense his charm. "You mentioned that Stina was high-strung," I said. "I can't really tell."

"She hides it well," Stu replied. "She has to, working with the public."

"I suppose so." I paused, waiting for him to continue.

He hesitated until the silence began to grow awkward. Then he tossed the hat onto the coffee table and regarded me with keen blue eyes. "I was out of line when I came here the other day, too. As I mentioned, I was concerned for Stina. Ever since Audrey died, my wife has been upset. She's afraid, you see."

"Of what?" I wished Vida were present with her ency-clopedic memory. Or that I could take notes. It sounded as if Stuart Kane had something important to say, and if I omitted any details, Vida, as she'd put it, would be *wild*.

"Stina's afraid for me," Stu responded, his voice now grave. "I'm no saint, but I do love my wife. However, she can be irrational. Stina got it into her head that I was—how shall I put this?—carrying on with Audrey. That's not true."

"It's not." My voice was flat.

Stu shook his head. "Not at all. Audrey came to me sev-eral times, asking advice about selling the house, the shop, setting herself up in business in Portland. She trusted me, had faith in my judgment. There was no difference be-tween Audrey asking me for advice and Gordon seeking sympathy from Stina. In both cases, the relationships were innocent. But Stina has trouble believing that."

Since Stuart Kane appeared to have a reputation as a ladies' man, I could understand his wife's reaction. "You said you had a talk with Stina. Was it about the alleged affair? Did you convince her it never happened?"

"I hope so." Stu took a deep breath. "It's vital that she believes me. Otherwise—and this is very difficult for me to say out loud—I honestly think she may suspect that I killed Audrey."

Great, I thought. *If Stina's right, here's old Emma, practically paralyzed with pain, entertaining a homicidal maniac.*

"But you didn't," I said in a voice that begged it to be so.

"Of course not." Stu actually laughed. "I'd never hurt Audrey. I never have. We've always been the best of friends."

"Oh." I gulped. "That's . . . nice."

"It was Gordon that I didn't particularly care for," Stu went on. "He was all wrong for Audrey from the start. Too spineless, too unadventurous. I tried to talk her out of marrying him, but Audrey was always headstrong. That was one of her charms; maybe her greatest strength, too."

I gave myself a little shake. Something didn't track here. Was my brain as nonfunctional as my body? "You knew Audrey before she was married?"

Again came that laugh. "Of course. Before Audrey married Gordon, she married me."

Chapter Fifteen

I SHOULD HAVE guessed. Stina Kane had made allusions to Audrey that indicated knowledge prior to Cannon Beach. The Audrey-Stuart union also explained the references to an early marriage. I—along with Vida—had assumed the marriage was between Gordon and Audrey. But that wasn't necessarily so. We had taken too much for granted, and ignored other signals along the way.

Stu's account was quite simple, really. He'd arrived in San Francisco for what was to be only a visit. But he liked the city, and had fallen in love with America. He had not—quite—fallen in love with Audrey. Yet when his visitor's visa expired and he couldn't get a green card, Audrey had offered to marry him. For her, it was a lark; for him, it was his ticket to a new life.

"My parents were divorced," Stu explained. "I was ten, and had a younger sister. We'd lived in Christchurch on the south island, but my mother's family was in Auckland, on the north island. We moved there, but Celia and I were shunted back and forth, forth and back, to spend half the year with each parent. It was harrowing. By the time I was eighteen, I felt like two different people. It was an unpleasant divorce, with my mum and my dad fighting constantly, even though they were in different parts of the country. My sister and I grew up with a great deal of unbearable stress and a terrible sense of guilt. Celia's never married, and she's a very bitter woman. But I got away, I had to, and San Francisco was where I headed. I realized then that I could make a new start. Audrey helped me do that, and I'm eternally grateful."

"But the marriage didn't last?" I remarked, still wishing that Vida had been on hand for this revelation.

"No. We liked each other, we shared some interests, but we were too young and—frankly—we were never serious about the commitment. We split up in less than two years. I decided to leave San Francisco and enroll at the University of Oregon in Eugene. That's where I met Stina. She was helping to put her first husband through engineering school and working in the bookstore. Her marriage was already on the rocks. We didn't really start seeing each other until after her divorce and I finished my degree in business. Three years later we were married. We wanted to be sure, since we'd each had a failure behind us."

The irony of Stu's words struck me: he didn't want another broken marriage, yet he allegedly conducted affairs. His own family background was rooted in domestic discord. According to Stina, he hadn't gone back to New Zealand until their visit last winter. Family ties didn't bind Stuart Kane; nor did marriage vows keep him faithful.

Yet his story touched me somehow. However, when he had finished, I kept to factual matters. "Do people here in Cannon Beach know that you and Audrey had been married?"

"No," Stu replied, looking faintly embarrassed. "There was no need for them to know. Audrey had been estranged from her father for some time. If Rett Runkel ever knew about the marriage, he didn't pay any attention. He was heavily into alcoholism at the time. I believe she told her mother, but I never met Rosalie. I understand she lives down at Manzanita. I may have seen her, but I wouldn't recognize her."

"And Marlin?" I asked, wondering if he was locked in a cell in Astoria this morning.

"Marlin!" Stu made a slashing motion with his hand. "Who can say? The man's completely disassociated from reality."

"So you and Audrey and Stina and Gordon all managed to keep the marriage your little secret?" I was incredulous.

"That's right." Stu's long, lean face was very earnest. "It wasn't that hard, really. Audrey had been gone for several years, and when she returned with a husband and children, there was no reason to ask embarrassing questions. Stina and I'd been living here for a while by the time the Imhoffs arrived. I had to tell Stina, of course. It wouldn't have been fair not to. And I must admit, my wife was jealous from the start. But she had no reason." Stuart Kane gave a dismissive shrug, as if his innocence was never at stake.

"Why are you telling me this now?" I asked, and realized that my manner was openly suspicious.

Again, Stu gave me that charming smile with just a hint of self-deprecation. "When Stina and I had our talk last night, it occurred to both of us that the authorities must know by now that Audrey and I were once married. They haven't come round to question me again, but I'm sure they will. The secret will be out. Besides, I was unspeakably rude to you, to your friend, and to my wife. Maybe it's a peace offering. After all, while Audrey and I were husband and wife, Ms. Runkel was my aunt."

I couldn't help it; I burst out laughing. It hurt, so I tried to stop and ended up choking and coughing. "Sorry," I gasped. "It's just that Vida—Ms. Runkel—has so many relatives. I think half the world is related to her somehow."

"Well, it is, you know," Stu said, still looking earnest. "Six degrees of separation and all that."

"It's different with Vida." I got a Kleenex out of my shoulder bag and blew my nose. "It's more like two degrees of separation. Someday I'm going to find out that she's tenth in line to the English throne."

Stu appeared somewhat puzzled, and I couldn't blame him. "I hope to apologize to her in person before she leaves," he said. "Do you know how long she plans to stay in Cannon Beach?"

Was I imagining that Stu seemed anxious to have Vida depart? Several people appeared to wish her on her way. But at least she hadn't gotten a threatening note.

I shook my head. "I've no idea."

Standing up, Stu reached into the pocket of his safari shirt and took out a business card. "Please give her this. I'll be in touch." He flashed me another smile.

By the time Stu left a minute later, it was almost eleven. My aches and pains had been slightly alleviated by the combination of movement and Excedrin. Since there was nothing to eat except bread and a few packaged cookies, I decided to walk into town and have breakfast. Leaving Vida a note, I headed out into the sunshine.

It was a golden morning, one of those perfect autumn days with diamonds dancing on the waves. I went slowly, carefully, crossing the bridge over Ecola Creek, and down Third Street to Hemlock, where I saw a sign for Whale Park. I knew the Kanes lived close by; Stu had probably walked from their home to the motel.

I paused outside of Bruce's Candy Kitchen, dreaming of chocolate-covered raisins and honey-filled sea foam and, appropriately enough in Cannon Beach, huge haystack clusters. I'm not much for sweets as a rule, but ocean-resort candy stores turn me into a chocolate hog.

Willing myself to keep going, I started past Osburn's Grocery Store. The combination deli, ice creamery, and grocer's was one of the oldest buildings in town, with an old-fashioned front porch that ran the width of the wood-frame structure. I had almost gone by when it dawned on me that this was where Derek worked. I retraced my steps and went inside.

A middle-aged woman with rhinestone-studded glasses and a warm smile informed me that Derek had the day off. "He's sick, I guess," she said from behind the check-out counter. The store was fairly quiet, with only a handful of customers browsing the aisles. "No wonder. Those kids have been through the wringer. I'm Bea. Are you a relative from out of town?"

"I'm Emma." We shook hands, then I explained my connection to the Imhoffs via Vida.

Bea laughed. "The one with the hat? She was here about an hour ago, looking for Derek. She had his girlfriend with her. Is it true they're getting married?"

So Vida had somehow rounded up Dolores. I wasn't surprised, but I was distracted. "What? Oh—I don't know. They've got some kind of plans, I think."

Bea nodded sagely. "They shouldn't rush it, not with all that's happened. They're still kids."

A redheaded woman about my age wheeled a half-filled cart up behind me. I thanked Bea and left, wondering if Vida and Dolores had gone to the Imhoff house.

Crossing Second Street, I passed Sandpiper Square,

which was set off from Hemlock and featured several shops and boutiques I wouldn't have minded exploring if I'd felt better. The large shake-covered building also contained offices, one of which Vida had said belonged to the resident doctor. I hesitated, then kept on going. Any diagnosis more sophisticated than my own would require X rays, which I assumed would have to be taken in Seaside. In any event, I was sure that there wasn't anything seriously wrong with me. I was simply banged up and would get over it in time.

Unfortunately, I didn't want to spend more time recovering. I could take a bus, but that would mean several transfers. The train would be equally complicated. A plane was out of the question. Even if I could fly out of Seaside, it would probably be an expensive charter into Portland, and I'd still have to get from Seattle to Alpine. I was stuck in Cannon Beach until I could drive myself home.

In my musings, I'd walked too far, passing two of the restaurants that I knew served a breakfast menu. I found myself in front of the Cannon Beach Book Company with its wide veranda and mellow wood exterior.

We had no real bookstore at home, only a tiny second-hand shop tucked into the second floor of the Alpine Building and a combination outlet on Front Street that featured greeting cards, wrapping paper, novelties, and the current best-sellers, mostly in paperback. Fending off my hunger pangs, I wandered inside to stand transfixed in front of tables with enticing covers. Recalling the crammed bookcase in the Imhoff house, I went up to the woman who stood behind the main desk and introduced myself.

"You were in the wreck with Gordon," she said,

shaking my hand. "I'm Valerie Bryan. I own the store."
She gave me a big smile.

"You know Gordon?" I said.

"Honey, I know everybody. This is Cannon Beach."
She was still smiling. The bookstore proprietor was a
pretty woman with a deep tan and short, smartly cut gray
hair. Her brown eyes crinkled at the corners. "Aren't you
from a small town, too?" she asked. "Somewhere up
toward Stevens Pass?"

"Right, Alpine." I glanced around to make sure I
wasn't holding up any of Valerie's customers. A stoop-
shouldered man was absorbed in something near the back
of the store while two middle-aged women chattered
over the cookbook section. A mother with a toddler in a
high-tech stroller perused children's books. "Everybody
knows everybody there, too, though it's somewhat bigger
than Cannon Beach. I own the weekly newspaper."

"Ah!" Valerie's eyes sparkled. "Another female entre-
preneur. I've been involved in PR and publicity myself.
But this is better. I'll never get rich, but I love what I'm
doing."

"That's what Audrey wanted, I gather. To start her own
business." I paused, waiting for Valerie to comment.

"She had her own business, the Jaded Eye." She gave
me a hard, but not unfriendly stare. "If you ask me,
Audrey wanted to escape. Big mistake, nobody can do
that, because what you're really running away from is
yourself."

"Did you know her well?" I inquired.

"Not really," Valerie replied, toying with the cord on
which her glasses hung from her neck. "I knew Gordon
better, although they both came in occasionally. In fact,
Audrey was here the afternoon before she died."

My interest was piqued. "How did she seem?"

Valerie didn't take time to reflect. "Full of herself. She was leaving. I couldn't help but taunt her a little, because it was Friday the thirteenth. I'm not really superstitious—in fact, I was born on Friday the thirteenth, in May. But I'm a city girl, from Seattle. I've only lived in Cannon Beach for the past three years. I told her she'd be sorry. Sharks are swimming in city waters. Making it on your own is tough."

An older couple, well groomed and with the air of affluent retirement, entered the store and nodded to Valerie before moving into the art section. "How did Audrey react?" I asked.

Valerie shrugged. "Like Audrey. She didn't care what people thought. Anyway, she said she wasn't worried. She'd managed to put aside enough to make it on her own."

The man who had been at the back of the store came up to the desk with a copy of Jon Hassler's *North of Hope*. I stepped aside while Valerie waited on him and exchanged brief chitchat.

"Valerie," I said, lowering my voice after the man had left, "I can't save ten cents. Can you?"

Valerie erupted into a derisive laugh. "Are you kidding? I'm still putting a kid through college."

"So am I. In a way," I added almost in a whisper. There was no need to get sidetracked with Adam's change of career choice and what that might entail now that he had finally gotten his degree from Arizona State. Still, I felt a growing sense of kinship with Valerie Bryan. "So how did Audrey do it?"

Apparently, Valerie was feeling equally chummy. "Chicanery. But *nice* chicanery." The bookstore owner leaned closer. "Audrey played Ms. Good Works, hauling oldsters to doctor appointments and physical therapy and wherever else they needed a ride. She bestowed her charity on men only, and they were very grateful."

I gave Valerie a knowing, conspiratorial look. "Men like Rupe Pickering and Victor Crenshaw?"

Valerie nodded slowly. "Among others. Rupe left her a fair-sized chunk of money in his will and I hear Dr. Crenshaw and his wife flat out gave her their condo in Portland. But there was more to it than just the old coots. I've heard that . . ." Straightening up, Valerie addressed the middle-aged couple.

The well-kept pair of seniors needed help selecting a fiftieth-wedding-anniversary gift. While gracious and polite, their manner conveyed that when they needed something, they expected to get it. Immediately. Valerie came out from behind the front desk.

I sensed that Valerie's customers might take up quite a bit of her time. Apparently, the store owner knew as much. In a businesslike tone, she turned back to me.

"You might want to check with the young man who's attending law school at Willamette University. His last name is Damon, I believe." She gave me another brilliant smile before leading her charges into the gardening and landscape section.

I made up my mind to try Jesse Damon again as soon as I had breakfast. However, it was almost noon. I might as well have lunch. I approached the Lazy Susan Café with my stomach growling, but discovered that the restaurant was closed on Tuesdays. Luckily, the other eatery I'd selected from the chamber-of-commerce guidebook was virtually next door. I went into the Lemon Tree Inn and was seated in a small booth.

Vida arrived just before my BLT did. "Goodness," she

exclaimed, slipping into the seat across from me, "I was shocked to find you'd left the motel. Thank heavens you told me where you were headed. However did you manage to walk so far?"

"It's only about five blocks," I said dryly. "Short ones. Besides, I think the exercise loosened me up."

"Foolish," Vida remarked as the waitress brought my order and offered another menu. "No, no, I'll have only hot tea. And a green salad, with ranch dressing. Ah . . . what type of soup do you have today? No, not soup—a turkey sandwich. That sounds very nice. On white. Do skimp on the mayonnaise. I'm watching my figure."

Vida always was, and it never changed, not one way or the other. "The lovers are reunited," she announced after the waitress had gone back to the kitchen. "Though I may take credit for it, I'm not pleased."

"Why is that?" I asked, biting into my BLT.

Vida sighed, then glanced around to make sure no one could hear. While the restaurant was filling up, the booths offered privacy. "I'm very upset with Dolores. She's not a suitable girl for Derek, and that has nothing to do with the fact that she's Hispanic. She could be a Finn, and I wouldn't approve. Dolores is a born troublemaker."

I asked why. Vida told me. The quarrel had erupted with Gordon's return. Dolores resented his intrusion into what had become a settled, comparatively quiet routine. Gordon had tried to calm her, but Dolores refused to listen to reason. It wasn't an approach she was accustomed to when it came to family disputes.

"Then Gordon decided to keep out of it," Vida explained, "but the argument between Derek and Dolores escalated in the usual manner. They each began to criticize whatever real or imagined faults the other possesses.

Finally, Dolores left, just as Derek told us. She did in fact walk the beach for a while, but then she began to consider retaliation. She was angry with Derek, with Gordon, with the entire family. So she went into town and to the police station to tell them about Marlin's marijuana farm." Vida now looked angry, too. "It was a terrible thing for her to do."

I suppose I couldn't blame Vida for being mad at Dolores. After all, Marlin was Vida's nephew. But he was breaking the law, and I was somewhat surprised by my House & Home editor's attitude.

"How," I inquired, after sifting through Vida's recital, "did Dolores know about the pot farm?"

"Because her parents got marijuana from Marlin. They not only drink, but they smoke that silly stuff as well." Vida looked much put out. "In a sense, Dolores was getting back at her family, as well as Derek's."

"But they've reconciled?"

"For the time being." Vida's mouth turned down.

"And Gordon?"

"He's back home. The authorities questioned him until very late last night in Astoria, but released him." Vida managed a smile for the waitress, who had brought the salad and hot tea. "I'm rather surprised."

"Why?" I asked after the waitress had left. "He can't have had anything new to add since he was questioned a month ago."

Vida lowered her eyes. "But he did. He admits to having been at the house that night."

I stared. "My God! When?"

"Around midnight." Vida had turned grim. "Before Audrey went swimming. He said he wanted to see her one last time before she went to Portland. He thought he might be able to talk her out of it. But he lost his nerve.

Or realized he couldn't change her mind. Gordon vacillates so much that it's hard to tell what he means, even after the fact."

"No one saw him at the house?" I asked as food began to fuel my body. Maybe I could get through the day after all.

"Well . . . that depends." Vida sprinkled extra salt and pepper on her salad. "Gordon saw someone, so maybe that someone saw him."

"What?" I'd raised my voice, causing the young couple in the booth across from us to stare. Giving them a phony little smile, I turned back to Vida. "Who did he see?" I whispered. "Why didn't he tell the sheriff before now?"

"It was a man, but Gordon didn't recognize him," Vida replied. "He was on the beach, just standing there, watching the waves. That's not unusual, so Gordon didn't think anything of it."

"Until now. Why did he change his mind?"

"Because the man was there so long," Vida answered, swishing a piece of lettuce in the ranch dressing. "It seems that Gordon dithered for quite a while, pacing around outside of the house, trying to make up his mind. When he finally did, and decided to leave, the man was still there. In retrospect, Gordon thought it odd."

"Could Gordon describe him?"

"Average height and weight. Jacket and pants. Hair. Anywhere between twenty-five and sixty." The turkey sandwich arrived, along with pickles. Vida took a big bite before continuing. "It's all very vague."

I tried to think of anyone we knew of who might fit Gordon's sketchy description. Stuart Kane was too tall; Jesse Damon was too young; Rett Runkel and Walt Dobrinz were too old. Surely Gordon would recognize his father-in-law and his mother-in-law's husband. He'd also know his brother-in-law, Marlin.

"Would a killer wait that long on the beach?" I mused. "If it was a stranger, how could he know that Audrey would go swimming in the middle of the night?"

"It's all very unsatisfactory," Vida declared. "On a more precise note, I called on the Crenshaws. Yes, they gave Audrey their condo. So sweet, so kind, so helpful, blah-blah. They're childless, and why shouldn't such a lovely person have something in return for all her time and effort on their behalf? Really, I think they're a pair of ninnies."

"I heard about the Crenshaws, too," I said. And then I launched into my encounter with Valerie Bryan at the bookstore. Vida wasn't surprised about Rupe Pickering—she'd already guessed as much. But she wondered anew about Jesse Damon.

"We must drive over to Salem this afternoon," she proclaimed, eating the last of her pickles. "It should be a nice outing."

"Vida—" I began, then stopped. "You haven't heard about my visit from Stuart Kane." I'd saved the best for last.

Vida was practically choking on her tea by the time I finished. "He told *you*! Not me! Oh, good grief! How could he! I'm glad I never knew him as a nephew-in-law! He would have tried my patience!"

"Maybe so," I remarked absently. "He does want to apologize in person."

Vida harrumphed. "He'd better. Oh, dear—this changes everything."

"How?"

"What if he's telling the truth about not having an

affair with Audrey? What if Stina's telling the truth about not carrying on with Gordon? There's no jealousy motive. I can't believe there was anything ... physical between Audrey and those older men she was carting around to medical appointments. They were all ill. So we have nothing left from the romantic angle except that silly, elusive boy, Jesse Damon."

"There were supposed to be other young men," I reminded Vida. "Jesse was only the most recent."

"But that's the point. The others were probably temporary, too. Summer help, lifeguards, whatever." Vida was looking very vexed.

"Young men don't murder their older mistresses," I said. "Think about it. A kid like Jesse comes here for tourist season and finds an attractive woman twice his age who's some kind of thrill seeker. For him, it's just carefree sex. For her, too, I suspect. There's no emotional attachment. Audrey wasn't moving to Salem, she was going to Portland. They had a fling. So what?"

Vida had her bill in hand and had risen to her feet. "Even casual lovers tell each other things. Jesse must know something. I really feel that he's the missing link. Let's go. If we hurry, we can be in Salem by three o'clock."

We were there by ten to three. I'd briefly succumbed to a fantasy in which Vida took off on the long inland drive and I remained in Cannon Beach, strolling through the shops, the galleries, the boutiques. But of course it was impossible to say no. I took two more Excedrin before leaving the Lemon Tree Inn and climbing into the pickup.

The trip was reasonably pleasant as we left the coast and drove toward the rich, flat farmland of the Willamette

Valley. I hadn't been in Salem for over ten years, so naturally I noticed changes, particularly around the state-
capital grounds. Vida, however, didn't seem interested in
my sightseeing efforts.

"Do try to figure out where this apartment or rooming
house is," she urged as we sailed along Twelfth Street
with the white marble capitol in the near distance.

Willamette University was on our left, adjacent to the
government buildings. It was a small but handsome
campus, built mostly of red brick, with touches of Colo-
nial architecture. I saw a new seven- or eight-story high-
rise, which I guessed was a dormitory. A few blocks
farther I spotted the street where Jesse Damon lived.

The neighborhood was modest, with many small
stucco bungalows. According to the address, Jesse lived
in the second house from the corner. It had red trim and
the street dead-ended by the railroad tracks.

The doorbell apparently didn't work. Vida thumped
the screen door back and forth. A minute later a pale,
handsome young man with a shaved head and a small
gold earring opened the door.

"We're here to see Jesse Damon," Vida announced in a
voice that brooked no argument. "He'd better be home."

The young man was taken aback. "Are you his
mother? Or his grandmother? I'm Jeremy."

"Is he here?" Vida tapped a foot.

"Yes!" Still uneasy, Jeremy then stepped aside. "Come
in, please. Jess is in the kitchen. He just got back from
class."

The interior of the house was well maintained, though
the furnishings were old. Books and file folders lay
everywhere, yet there was a basic order and neatness to
the living room. Jeremy offered us each a chair, but first
removed three thick tomes from one of them.

"I'll get Jess," he said, starting out of the room.

But Jess, who couldn't have been more than fifteen feet away, came in from the kitchen. He was average height, with a muscular build, wavy dark hair, and clean-cut, attractive features.

"It's your . . ." Jeremy started to say, but when he saw the puzzled look on his roommate's face, he changed gears. "It's somebody to see you," he finished in an uncertain voice.

Vida marched straight up to Jesse and wrung his hand. "Vida Runkel, Audrey Imhoff's aunt. This is Emma Lord, my dear friend and business associate. We're here to discuss Audrey's will."

That was news to me. It was no wonder that Jesse looked startled.

"Ms. Imhoff?" he said. "What are you talking about? Does she need advice? I'm not taking probate until next semester."

Vida shot me a perplexed glance. "Ms. Imhoff is dead. Surely you knew that, Jesse?"

Despite the scattering of file folders, Jesse sank onto the small sofa. "Oh my God!"

"Jess!" Jeremy hurried to his roommate. "Hey, what's happening?"

Jesse had his hands over his face. Slowly, he removed them and stared at Vida. "Is it true? When? How?"

Vida didn't attempt tact. "She was brutally murdered. Didn't the sheriff question you? Don't you read the papers?"

Jesse sat up straight, his eyes unfocused. "No. No. I mean, I didn't know. Who has time to read the papers or watch TV when you're in law school? What's this about the sheriff?"

Vida finally seated herself in a chair by the sofa. "I told you, she was murdered. Weren't you interrogated?"

"No." At last, Jesse looked at Vida. His sea-green eyes were wary. "Why should I be?"

"You knew her," Vida said simply. "You were friends. Close friends." The insinuation was clear to me, if not to Jesse, who remained mystified.

"When did this happen?" he asked, obviously trying to pull himself together. "Who did it?"

Vida explained. Jesse continued to look bewildered. "I wondered," he muttered.

"You wondered what?" Vida asked in a sharp tone.

The wary expression was back on Jesse's face. Before he could reply, Jeremy intervened with an offer of coffee. "The pot's always on," he said in a rather ingenuous manner. "It has to be, or we'd pass out over our books."

I accepted, though Vida asked for ice water. Jeremy seemed loath to leave Jesse alone but finally went into the kitchen. Vida hadn't forgotten her question.

"I meant," Jesse began, "I wondered why I hadn't heard from Ms. Imhoff. She said she'd check to see how I was doing this semester."

"You were fond of her?" Vida asked, her voice more pleasant.

A flicker of something I couldn't define passed across Jesse's face. "Fond? I liked her. She was a nice woman." His casual attitude seemed forced.

I had remained standing next to a big stereo unit. "When did you last see Ms. Imhoff?" I inquired.

Jesse's forehead creased. "Let me think. . . . A couple of days before I left Cannon Beach."

"Which was when?" I pressed.

Jesse took a deep breath. "I got back here before Labor Day, so it must have been at the end of August. The twenty-eighth, twenty-ninth, I guess. What did you say about her will?"

Vida sat up very straight and folded her hands in her lap. "Did you expect Ms. Imhoff to mention you?"

"What?" Jesse seemed completely dumbfounded. "I didn't know she had a will. I didn't know she was dead. Why would I expect *anything*? I hardly knew her, except for . . . well, you know, seeing her around town."

"Seeing her often enough that she intended to follow your college career," Vida pointed out. "You must have been rather . . . intimate."

Jeremy entered with coffee mugs and a glass of ice water, which he balanced with aplomb. I couldn't help but wonder if he was working his way through college as a waiter.

"Look," Jesse said, accepting a mug from his roommate, "Ms. Imhoff was the friendly type. She had kids about my age, maybe a little younger. She talked about how she wanted her son—I think he was the oldest—to go to college. She'd never gotten a degree, and she was sorry. So when I'd see her around town, she'd ask me about school, and how I decided to go into law and all that kind of stuff. It was no big deal. I liked her, and I'm sorry she got killed, but we weren't all that tight."

He sounded sincere, yet his eyes kept veering away from Vida—and me. Apparently noticing the evasion, Vida didn't give up.

"That's not what we hear in Cannon Beach. You were rumored to be more than friends with Audrey Imhoff."

Jesse shot Jeremy a quick, furtive glance, then took a deep breath. "Okay." He sighed. "I don't need people spreading false rumors about me. Is it all right?" He looked again at Jeremy, who nodded. "I wasn't the least bit interested in Ms. Imhoff as a woman. Jeremy and I are gay, and we're very happy with the way things are. Go ahead, go back to Cannon Beach and shout the news down Hemlock. We don't give a damn."

Chapter Sixteen

"REALLY," VIDA SAID after we were in the pickup and figuring out how to get back to I-5, "I hadn't expected *that*.
Why are you laughing?"

I couldn't help it, even though it hurt. "Because it's
funny, that's why. It shows how wrong people can be. All
the tales of Audrey's extramarital affairs have come to
naught."

"I don't think so," Vida said doggedly. "Her mother,
her father, both alluded to her promiscuity."

"Rett's a drunk," I asserted as we finally found a sign
for the interstate. "Besides, he was speaking mostly
about her wild youth in San Francisco. And Rosalie may
really be talking about her daughter's ability to attract
men, which doesn't mean Audrey slept with them. For all
we know, Rosalie was jealous. Rett Runkel and Walt
Dobrinz weren't exactly Oregon's Most Eligible Bache-
lors. Sometimes mothers envy their daughters' youth and
good looks."

"Silly, if they do," Vida declared, guiding the pickup
along the on-ramp to the freeway. "I can't imagine being
jealous of Amy, Meg, or Beth."

Since Vida's three daughters were all plain as
pikestaffs, I could understand their mother's feelings.
But of course Vida thought they were quite beautiful,

which was both natural and admirable. My son, who closely resembled his father, was just plain handsome. I was already worried about how he would fend off the unholy advances made by his future female parishioners.

"He's lying," Vida said, jerking me out of my reverie.

"Who?" I asked, trying to get comfortable as we hurtled along toward the exit to the coast.

"Jesse. Oh, I don't mean about not having an affair with Audrey or about being gay. Those things are true," Vida went on. "But he wouldn't look me in the eye. And that was rubbish about expecting Audrey to keep in touch regarding his studies."

"I'd better check in with Valerie Bryan," I murmured. "She wouldn't have mentioned Jesse unless she knew something."

"The bookstore woman?" Vida slowed as we left I-5 and headed west. "She sounds interesting. I'll talk to her myself."

"I wonder why Jesse was never questioned by the sheriff," I said. "They heard the same rumors we did."

"Maybe they were able to check into Jesse's lifestyle before they went to the trouble of interrogating him," Vida suggested. "Or else they discounted him because he was so far away."

"Maybe." I tried to relax as we crossed the green-and-gold farmland. Many of the fields had already been harvested, and the dark, rich earth had been turned for the fall planting. Somehow Oregon always seemed more orderly than Washington. While the two states share much of the same rugged beauty, the Columbia River flows like a parent between two similar, yet disparate children. Oregon is tidy, more domesticated, proud and aloof; for all its rampant growth—or maybe in some ways because of it—Washington still seems untamed, often harsh, even careless in the facade it presents to the wider world.

"You're daydreaming," Vida reprimanded as we began to wind through the coast range.

"Sort of," I admitted. I thought back to the exchange in the small living room in Salem. "You never did explain what we were doing there."

"They never asked," Vida responded. "Which in itself is strange. Why? Was it because they were relieved?"

"About what?"

"Not having to answer other, more difficult questions."

"Such as?"

"I wish I knew."

After another hour had passed, we reached Highway 101 and headed north to Cannon Beach. It was only then that I realized I could have hopped a bus in Salem and gone home.

The Bistro was a small European-style restaurant surrounded by late-blooming flowers and trailing vines. Vida had balked at first, saying it might be "too pricey." But I prevailed. If I'd been dumb enough not to pack up my things and get out of town permanently, then I intended to enjoy what I could of Cannon Beach.

"Kip should be putting the paper to bed about now," I remarked, glancing at my watch. It was going on seven, and we had arrived back at the motel in time to change for dinner.

"Yes," Vida agreed in a vague voice. "I wonder how late the bookstore is open?"

"Fairly late, I think. I don't remember exactly." It seemed to me that Vida had forgotten about *The Advocate*, maybe even put Alpine out of her mind. Solving the mystery of her niece's death seemed to consume her. I tried to tell myself that she needed my help, but I'm not sure I believed it. Maybe she only needed me as a prop, or a sounding board.

We discussed Molly's diary over excellent pasta and prawns. Vida intended to read the last four-plus months after dinner. I admitted I'd found nothing so far that was of interest.

"As of May, Molly hadn't mentioned any problems between her parents," I noted. "That seems odd, since I recall the kids saying that the trouble started around the holidays last year."

"Self-absorption," Vida responded. "From what I read, Molly was primarily concerned with her weight and her hair and her friends at school. She rarely mentioned Stacie and Derek, and when she did, it was usually because they'd criticized her or made her feel rejected."

"Poor Molly." I sighed. "She's at an awful age to lose her mother. It's never easy, but fourteen is really rough with girls."

"Indeed. All three of our girls were grown by the time Ernest died." Vida gazed into the glass of red wine I'd persuaded her to order. "If they'd been younger, I might have considered remarrying."

"How's Buck?" I asked, wondering if Vida had forgotten him, too.

"He's fine," she retorted, looking at me over the rims of her glasses. "Your implication is amiss. Buck and I have no plans to marry. We enjoy our lives the way they are."

I didn't apologize for the hint. "He's settled into his new home?"

Vida nodded. "It was basically in good repair. And such a steal. He's thinking of leaving the handicapped access as it is. None of us is getting any younger, you know."

Vida referred to the house at Startup that Buck Bardeen had purchased a few months earlier from Milo's ex-girlfriend, Honoria Whitman. It had been on the market for over a year following Honoria's return to California. She had been partially paralyzed, and had converted what had once been a summer cabin into a charming residence, complete with ramps and other items to meet her special needs.

Noting that Vida still had room in her mind—and maybe her heart—for Buck, I was about to recount some of the events that had taken place in Alpine during our absence. But before I could begin, Gordon Imhoff entered the restaurant with his mother-in-law on his arm. He saw us and stopped, grinning sheepishly.

"Mama Rosie and I are celebrating my return to public life," he said. "I'm treating her because she got stuck covering for me the last few days." Gordon gave Rosalie's shoulder a squeeze.

"How nice," Vida said with enthusiasm. Then she wagged a finger at Rosalie. "I have a bone to pick with you. We'll discuss it some other time. Do enjoy your meal."

Rosalie was taken aback. "What is it? What'd I do?"

"Never mind." Vida assumed a coy look.

By chance, Gordon and Rosalie were seated across from us, at a matching table for two. Out of the corner of my eye, I could tell that Rosalie was casting equally sur-reptitious glances at Vida. But the Imhoff party was so close that I couldn't ask Vida any questions about her alleged pique with Rosalie. Nor, as it turned out, could we discuss Audrey's murder.

Thus I started to deliver the Alpine news. Vida listened

attentively, especially to the account of the fire. But it was Darla Puckett's misfortune that aroused the most interest.

"Darla must be wild!" Vida exclaimed. "Not that I thought much of all that claptrap in her yard, but such wantonness! Youngsters, I suppose."

"Undoubtedly. By the way, Carla is dating Ryan Talliaferro." I waited for what I assumed would be Vida's explosive reaction.

It didn't come. "Well now. I've only met Dr. Talliaferro once or twice, but he seems like a nice man. It's about time Carla found someone. She hasn't really had a boyfriend since Peyton Flake. And goodness knows, they were never suited as a couple. Marilynn Lewis is much better for him. And vice versa. I wonder how they're getting along in North Bend?"

Dr. Flake had bought a thriving practice from a general practitioner who was retiring. The wedding was set for November, and they were building a house outside of town. Like Alpine, North Bend is in the Cascade foothills, the last major stop before ascending into the mountains. Unlike Alpine, its proximity to Seattle gives residents a more cosmopolitan attitude. Alpine's isolation feeds on itself, breeding ignorance and prejudice.

"Marilynn told me she'd work for Flake only until he got established," I said as Vida perused the dessert menu. "She's afraid that too much togetherness could cause trouble."

"Indeed," Vida concurred. "Very few couples can survive—"

A commotion next to us cut Vida short. Rosalie Dobrinz had fallen out of her chair and was writhing on the floor, clutching her chest. A horrified Gordon Imhoff was standing over his mother-in-law, shouting for help.

Vida also got to her feet. "CPR! Who knows CPR? Quickly!"

The older couple I'd seen in the bookstore emerged from the other end of the long, narrow restaurant. "I'm a surgeon," the silver-haired man announced. "Step aside, please."

Vida, along with one of the servers and two other customers, moved back. As soon as the doctor reached Rosalie, Gordon also withdrew a couple of steps, standing so close to my chair that he just missed bumping into me.

"What happened?" I asked in an urgent voice.

Gordon was holding his head. "I'm such a fool . . . How could I know Rosie would—" He stopped, his eyes riveted on his mother-in-law.

"Call 911," the doctor commanded. "Hurry!"

Apparently, someone already had. I could hear a siren in the distance; the sound was becoming a leitmotiv for my stay in Cannon Beach. Vaguely, I remembered seeing the fire station on my dash from Marlin's house. I assumed that was where the emergency vehicles waited on call.

"Dear me," Vida murmured, leaning as close to the doctor and patient as she dared.

"She's responsive," said the woman I assumed was the doctor's wife. "That's good."

"Thank God!" It was Gordon, on a tortured sigh.

The dimly lighted restaurant exploded with controlled activity. A quartet of emergency personnel arrived, two of whom I recognized from my accident the previous day. I got up and hurriedly helped Vida move our table and chairs out of the way. By now, other diners had gathered nearby. I would have gone outside to make room, but I knew Vida wouldn't dream of budging.

She was, in fact, trying to pump Gordon, but getting

nowhere. It wasn't that he consciously ignored her; rather, he was fixated on Rosalie, his entire being drained by concern.

The doctor and the emergency personnel now formed such a tight circle that I could no longer see Rosalie, but I heard her voice. She was answering questions in a weak, but coherent manner. Finally, the woman medic I remembered as Mary Jean Pratt turned to Gordon.

"We're not sure if she's had a heart attack, but we're taking her to Providence Hospital in Seaside," Mary Jean said. "Do you want to follow us in your own car or ride in the ambulance?"

Dazed, Gordon took a moment to respond. "I'd better take my car. Rosie's car, I mean. Otherwise, I couldn't get back. Unless," he added, with a glance in my direction, "I rented that Taurus again." Gordon began to laugh, a semihysterical sound. Mary Jean put a firm hand on his arm, steering him toward the door. Another pair of medics arrived with a gurney. Moments later Rosalie was whisked away. We heard the siren fade as we were replacing our table and chairs.

"I believe I'll skip dessert," Vida said with a trace of reluctance. "We must tell Derek what's happened. And Walt Dobrinz, I suppose."

"Gordon can do that after he gets to the hospital," I said.

"He won't remember. Oh!" She gave herself a shake. "Rett! He ought to be informed. We should do that in person. Ugh."

I couldn't think why Vida wanted to call on her brother-in-law, unless it was to observe his reaction. Maybe she hoped he'd be shocked or saddened. Maybe she wanted to gloat.

In any event, after we'd paid our bill, we headed to 101

and Rett Runkel's trailer home. He was sitting out front, a beer can in one hand, a copy of *Guns & Ammo* in the other. An old-fashioned Coleman lantern sat on an up-ended peach crate. T-Bone looked up from his place next to Rett's chair and snarled at us.

"Yoo . . . hoo," Vida began, her usual greeting dampened by the baring of the dog's teeth. "It's me, your sister-in-law. And Emma."

"Yeah, so I see," Rett replied without much interest. "What now? You here to give me a bad time about Marlin?"

Vida approached Rett and the dog carefully. "No. Rosalie's been taken to the hospital. She may have had a heart attack."

"I didn't know she had a heart." Rett took a swig from his beer can.

"Rett!" Vida tapped her foot, causing T-Bone to sit up and growl again. "That's very cruel, especially under the circumstances. How can you sit here while your daughter is dead and your son is in prison and your former wife may be mortally ill?"

Rett regarded Vida over the top of the beer can. "How would gettin' off my ass help any of that? I never could help 'em even when I did. Or so Rosie always told me. 'You're no help,' she'd say. 'You're worthless.' "

"I see her point." Vida paused, her chin up. "You could change that now."

Rett sneered. "How?"

"By going to see Rosalie in the hospital. By doing what you can to get Marlin out of this mess. By being there for your grandchildren. When was the last time you saw any of them?"

"I already posted Marlin's bail. He got out this afternoon. Hey, Marlin!" Rett turned in his camp chair. A moment later Marlin Runkel appeared in the door to the trailer.

"Marlin!" Vida cried.

Marlin just looked at his aunt. So did the dog.

Rett gestured with his beer can at Marlin. "He's stayin' with me for a couple of days. It seems the sheriff don't want him back on the farm. If you know what I mean." Rett winked not at us, but at T-Bone.

Vida turned her attention to Marlin. "Your mother may have had a heart attack. Gordon has gone with her and the ambulance to the hospital in Seaside."

"Oh?" Marlin was unmoved. "Hey, Pa, you got any orange juice? I could drink about a gallon."

"Orange juice?" Rett scowled at his son. "What do I need orange juice for? I got this." He waggled the beer can.

"I'm going to the mini-mart up the highway," Marlin said. "Toss me your keys."

"They're on that hook by the door. You got a driver's license?"

"No. I haven't had one in eight years." Marlin disappeared briefly, then came out of the trailer, walked right past us, and headed for Rett's battered truck. "You need anything?"

"Nope. Yeah, some smokes. Camels, the real stuff."

In a trail of thick exhaust, Marlin left. Vida squared her shoulders, gave T-Bone a wary look, and marched up to Rett. "See here," she said in as angry a voice as I'd ever heard her use. "I don't care if you drink and smoke yourself to death. I don't care if you rot in this horrible trailer you call a home. I don't care anything about you—but you *are* a Runkel. I expect better. Ernest must be turning in his grave to think that he has a brother who is so shiftless. What have you ever done in your entire life to make the world a better place?"

"I put my ass on the line in Korea to save that big butt of yours, lady," Rett retorted. "I got shot at, damned near blown up, practically froze my balls off, and watched a bunch of my buddies get torn in two by the Chink commies. Don't tell me you've forgotten about Pork Chop Hill and Pusan and all those other places where we fought to keep things nice and cozy for dumb-shits like you?"

"In the coast guard?" Vida all but hooted. "You sailed around in a nice little boat. I suspect the most danger you got into was if you spilled gravy down your swim trunks!"

Rett leaped out of the chair, knocking it over behind him. "Bitch! You don't know dick about the coast guard! It's not like that! We saw plenty of action!"

T-Bone's teeth were bared again and I honestly thought he was ready to go for Vida. Moving quickly, I grabbed him by the scruff of the neck and spoke softly.

"Nice doggie. Good doggie. Emma thinks you're cute."

"Action, my foot! And what if you did?" Vida shot back. "That was almost fifty years ago! I suspect your grandchildren don't even know when the Korean War took place!"

T-Bone continued to growl, but he didn't move. I kept jabbering away, wishing he had a chain or a leash or, better yet, no teeth.

"You talk about those grandchildren," Rett shouted, spitting as he spoke. "When was the last time *they* came to see *me*? I ain't seen those girls since they were little kids, but they go by here on that friggin' school bus every day! I seen Derek two, three times at the grocery store.

He acted like I was some kind of crud. He wouldna talked to me if I hadna talked to him first, the little bastard!"

"It's no wonder." Vida had dropped her voice, though she still tapped her foot. "They've lost their mother. They need you, Rett. They need family. You've never been there for them. You've never been there for anyone but yourself."

"I was there for Marlin this morning, with two grand," Rett retorted. "That's more than that hump Rosie would do for him. Now whaddya think?"

"I think that's good," Vida said after a long pause, during which T-Bone stopped growling. "You see? You *can* change."

"Bullshit," Rett muttered. "Who wants to?"

"Try," Vida said softly. Then, to my astonishment, she put both hands on Rett's shoulders. "In the end, all we have is family." Apparently, she noticed the glower on Rett's face. "I don't mean me, or even the other Runkels back in Alpine. After so many years they're all strangers to you. I'm talking about your kinfolk here. This side of the Runkel family has been fragmented and estranged for too long."

Rett ducked his head. "Rosalie probably blamed it on the booze."

"Blame is easy," Vida said. "Don't stay chained to the past." She patted Rett's shoulders. "You have Ernest's eyes. They were ever so kind and intelligent. I can't believe you've drowned all that in liquor."

Rett, who had recoiled at first from Vida's touch, now stared at her. "They don't want me. None of 'em do."

"Don't be so sure." Vida stepped back. "We all make mistakes. But eventually, we have to make things better. Goodbye, Rett."

She turned and trudged off to the pickup. I followed. Rett and the dog didn't move.

Traffic was light going into Seaside. Although we had no idea where Providence Hospital was located, we were able to follow the big "H" symbols. We found the hospital on a small hill above the town. It was a relatively new one-story complex that looked as if it had been added onto recently.

After inquiring at the desk, we were sent to the emergency waiting room. Before we got there, we passed one of the receiving rooms, where we saw staff members huddled around Rosie. Gordon leaned against the door jamb with a haggard expression on his face.

Vida poked him; he jumped. "They're still not sure if she had a heart attack," Gordon said in reply to Vida's query. "I feel terrible. This was supposed to be a happy evening."

"Come," Vida said, taking his elbow and steering him to the waiting room at the end of the corridor. "You need to sit."

Gordon was docile. "Rosie's going to be okay," he said, more to himself than to us. "One of the doctors told me too many things have happened to her all at once, and she's tried to take on too much responsibility. I never should have gone away."

"She seemed chipper when she came into the Bistro," Vida remarked. "Of course I shouldn't have teased her. That wasn't very nice of me."

"What set her off?" I asked.

Gordon winced. "Well ... I had to tell her about Marlin. It upset her."

"Does she know he's out on bail?" I inquired.

Gordon looked surprised. "No. I didn't have that kind of money at hand. Who posted bail for him?"

"Your father-in-law," Vida said in a pained voice. "I suspect he has a nest egg, probably hatching under his mattress. He's certainly not spending it on housing."

"That could be," Gordon allowed. "Rett lives ... simply."

Vida mentioned that we'd stopped by to inform Rett—and Marlin—of Rosalie's possible heart attack. Gordon said he'd called Walt Dobrinz, who should be arriving soon from Manzanita. Derek hadn't answered at the Imhoff house, so Gordon assumed he didn't know what had happened to his grandmother unless he'd picked up the news on the grapevine.

"This is all such a mess," Gordon declared, getting out of the chair where he'd been twisting and twitching. "How's it going to end? Or will it just keep going on and on until we're all crazy? Or dead?"

Vida made a sharp, jerky motion with one hand. "Gordon! What kind of defeatist talk is that? Where's your spunk?"

"Spunk?" Gordon looked as if he'd never heard of the word.

Vida had also gotten to her feet. "See here, I have no intention of giving up. I never do. I'm not leaving until I get to the bottom of this."

Gordon hung his head. "It's got nothing to do with you," he mumbled.

"It does so," Vida countered. "You're Runkels. You're family."

"*I'm* not a Runkel." Surprisingly, Gordon's tone was almost savage.

"But your children are," Vida said, a bit smug.

"Whatever." With a huge sigh, Gordon wheeled out of the waiting room and returned to the emergency area.

Vida was striding up and down, seemingly lost in thought. "It doesn't make sense," she murmured. "So much of it doesn't."

"Such as?" I asked in a mild voice.

"Ooooh . . . Most of it." Vida pulled up short, standing by a table that held several current magazines, including recent copies of *Catholic Digest*. Out in the corridor, I heard voices, one of which sounded vaguely familiar. "Why kill Audrey in the first place?" Vida spoke under her breath. "What was the point?"

Walt Dobrinz was standing in the doorway. "Are you the ladies I met in Manzanita?"

Vida marched over to him and shook his hand. "We are indeed. Have you seen Rosalie yet?"

"I peeked in," Walt said, looking more confused than worried. "She seems okay. But doctors never tell you much. I guess that's because they won't admit they don't know."

"That's often the case," Vida agreed, now at her most friendly. "Do sit, Walter. I believe there's coffee over on the counter at the end of the room."

"Not for me," Walt replied, though he did join us. "I wonder if they'll send her home tonight. I hope I didn't drive all the way from Manzanita on a wild-goose chase."

Vida's friendliness took on a hint of frost. "I'm sure Rosalie is glad you're here."

Walt uttered a sound that might have been a snort. Then he pushed his thick glasses with the hearing aids up on his nose and leaned down to look at the magazines on the table. "What's this stuff? Propaganda from the

Pope?" He batted at the cover of a magazine put out by
the Franciscans.

"My brother's a priest," I said with a tight little smile.
"His church burned down last year. He had an article
about it in one of the *Digest*s." I leaned over in my chair
and randomly pointed. "I don't think that issue is here.
The piece came out in June."

Walt had no comment, but at least he stopped making
cracks about the Church. The silence hadn't grown completely awkward before Vida spoke again.

"Emma and I were trying to figure out why anyone
would want to kill Audrey. I don't suppose you have any
ideas on the subject?" It was a question we'd both asked
so often. But not, I realized, of Walt Dobrinz.

"It's the way," Walt responded without taking time to
mull. "You get mad at somebody these days, shoot him.
You want to get even, grab a knife. You get pissed off
about life in general, take it out on the guy standing next
to you. Hell, you go into Portland, you can't honk at anybody. They'll get out of the car and do you in right there
on the Hawthorne Bridge."

"Yes," Vida said in an odd voice. "That's so. Thank
you, Walter, for the insight."

Behind the thick lenses, Walt blinked at Vida.
"Insight? That's no insight. Like I said, it's the way it is."

"That's what I mean," Vida responded. She gave Walt
a big, bogus smile that left me as baffled as he looked.

Vida kept mum. On the way back to Cannon Beach,
she refused to explain herself. She could only tell me that
it was a feeling she had, a sense of the crime itself. All
along, it had been there, sitting at the back of her mind,
niggling away. There were certain things, apparently
harmless things, that kept reinforcing her train of thought.

While admitting she wasn't sure who had killed Audrey, she was beginning to understand the why of it.

"The least you can do is tell me that part," I chided after we were back at the motel.

"I can't," Vida protested. "When I know *why*, I'll know *who*."

"But you told me . . ." Lost in Vida's mental labyrinth, I surrendered. It was going on ten, and once again, exhaustion was overtaking me. "I'm going to bed."

Vida thought she'd stay up for a while and finish Molly's diary. She could read it in the bedroom so that I could turn off the living-room light. We hadn't stayed on at the hospital much longer. While the doctors didn't seem to think that Rosalie had actually suffered a heart attack, they wanted to keep her overnight for observation. Walt had been annoyed, but Gordon had offered to buy his stepfather-in-law a beer. Mollified, Walt had gone off in a better mood.

"What were you going to say to Rosalie?" I asked while getting undressed.

"What?" Vida had started reading the diary, though she hadn't yet retreated to the bedroom. "Oh—*that*. I've come to agree with you about Audrey's alleged affairs. I intended to tell Rosalie in no uncertain terms that she wasn't doing her daughter's reputation any favors by spreading such stories, or even suggesting that Audrey was promiscuous."

"Good idea. Maybe it's easier for Rosalie to deal with Audrey's death by thinking bad things about her." I put on my robe and started for the bathroom.

"That's possible," Vida said. "People do some very strange things to help themselves cope. They weren't close, remember. Perhaps Rosalie always thought the worst of Audrey, simply because they weren't real friends.

A mother must feel like a failure when that happens. Thus she may want to blame the daughter. Usually, they're both at fault."

A moment later I was in the bathroom when Vida announced she'd left her billfold in the pickup. "It must have slipped out of my purse," she called to me through the closed door. "I so hate being careless."

I was soaking in the tub when she returned. "Are you decent?" she shouted in what sounded like an irate voice.

"No," I called back. "What is it?"

"It's this."

Puzzled, I frowned at the closed door. "What?"

Then I saw a piece of white paper being shoved under the slit between the door and the tile. Big block letters, much like the ones I'd found on the Neon, read GET OUT BEFORE IT'S TOO LATE.

Hurriedly, I pulled the plug and stepped out of the tub. "Hang on," I called to Vida. "I'll be right there."

Vida wore a grim expression when I opened the door. "I found that note on the windshield of the truck when I went to get my billfold."

The piece of paper with its menacing message was in my hand. It was roughly the size of a steno tablet, though unlined, and looked as if an inch or so at the bottom had been torn off. "We've got to call the cops," I declared. "Two of these is too many."

"I agree. Though . . ." Vida hesitated. "Let me see that again."

I handed her the paper. Vida took it over to the lamp that sat on the end table by the sofa bed. "It's marker pen," she noted. "The sheet has been torn off a tablet at the top, and then torn again at the bottom. It's decent quality, more like typing or drawing paper than notebook paper."

I felt the texture. "It's too heavy for typing paper. And it's not really white, it's almost gray."

"But it's not stationery." Vida pulled at her lower lip. "Where did it come from?"

I held the sheet up under the light. "Ah! I thought so. It's got a watermark—'Vitagen.' "

Vida looked startled. "What on earth is that? A paper company?"

I shook my head. "No, there's also a symbol. See here?" I tapped the paper. "It's a combination of the male and female symbols. I suspect this came off a tablet that was a pharmaceutical freebie and that the inch at the bottom contained the company's name and logo. Haven't you noticed all the notepads and such at the Alpine Medical Clinic? Most of them have the name of some drug outfit."

Vida, however, seemed dejected by my discovery. "Oh, dear." Her wide shoulders slumped. "I was afraid of that."

"You were?"

She nodded. "I was afraid . . . well, I'd hoped it was one of the children. So like a youngster to write silly messages. But all along, I've wondered. Now I know."

Chapter Seventeen

IF VIDA THOUGHT she was going to stall me this time, she was wrong. I'd figured it out, too. "Gordon Imhoff," I said flatly. "He wrote both the notes."

"Yes. I'm afraid he did." Vida sighed and sat down in the armchair. "This one was done at the hospital. Obviously, he tore off a sheet from one of their notepads. He removed the pharmaceutical firm's name in a vain attempt to disguise where the paper came from. How foolish to write these notes!"

"He rented my Taurus in Seaside," I reminded Vida. "Someone at the rental agency must have told him it had been turned in by a woman who had given her local address at this motel in Cannon Beach. Chitchat, I suppose. He probably saw the Neon on the lot, then spotted it again in Ruth's driveway. But how did he know it was me?"

"He didn't," Vida said. "He thought it was me."

"What?" I collapsed onto the sofabed.

"That's right." Vida pursed her lips. "We'd just come from visiting Rosalie. The Taurus was parked there, and no doubt Gordon was inside the house. As soon as Rosalie returned with Walt from the café, she undoubtedly told Gordon about our visit. He probably didn't see the Buick, and Rosalie may not have known what make of car it was—only that it was white. As I recall, your

rental had Washington plates. Rosalie may have mentioned that since we were making the rounds, we'd
probably visit Ruth Pickering. Gordon drove by while
you were there, saw a car he didn't recognize—I suspect
Ruth doesn't entertain much—and noticed that it was
white, with a Washington license. There you have it."

The rationale made sense. But Gordon's actions didn't.
"Why would he do such a thing? In person, he seems
quite pleasant. Why does he want us to leave?"

Vida's glance was shrewd. "Isn't it obvious? He
doesn't want us to find out who killed Audrey."

Now that we knew—or thought we knew—who had
posted the signs on our vehicles, it seemed pointless to
notify the police. Yet Gordon's behavior was more than
annoying; it was frightening.

Or so I told Vida, who didn't disagree. "The police
wouldn't do anything, except warn him," she pointed
out. "We must simply be on our guard."

That was not the most comforting thought to take to
bed, but I did it anyway. I didn't sleep as soundly as I had
the night before, though I felt better when I woke up in
the morning. Vida was already making instant coffee, but
as soon as I joined her in the kitchen, I noticed that she
was unusually silent.

"What's the matter?" I asked. "Did you hear some bad
news about Rosalie?" It was going on nine, and for all I
knew, Vida had been out and about on this fresh, crisp
fall morning.

"No, though I should call the hospital now that you're
up." She poured us each a mug of coffee that was almost
as vile as the sludge Milo made at the sheriff's headquarters. "It's Molly's diary. I finished it last night."

"And?" I braced myself for the second sip of coffee.

"The last entry is Friday, September thirteenth." Vida cleared her throat. "Molly obviously was unable to deal with her mother's death. I find that very sad. It would be more natural, more therapeutic, for her to write, write, write, to let it all out in that dreadful maudlin teenage fashion. But she didn't."

"I agree it might have been helpful," I said, "but I understand how she feels." Though I had been much older when my parents had died, it had been a long time before I could discuss their fatal accident with anybody except Ben.

"There's another thing," Vida went on, putting so much creamer into her coffee that it was almost white, "which is that Molly never does allude to her parents' marital problems. She doesn't mention Audrey's desire to leave or Gordon moving out. During the summer months she dwells on horses. Apparently, she had a part-time job at that place right by here that rents horses."

I'd noticed both the sign and the stables, just across the Ecola Creek Bridge. During the course of our stay I'd also seen people riding horseback along the beach. I assumed the mounts had come from the nearby horse ranch.

"There was one horse of which she was particularly fond," Vida continued. "His name was—is—Commander, but she called him Fudge. She wrote a poem about him. It was rather silly."

"Girls at that age are often nuts about horses," I pointed out.

"I know that. Sometimes they never grow out of it. Look at the Dithers sisters."

I had, often. Connie and Judy Dithers were single, middle-aged, and lived off the Icicle Creek Road, where they kept horses. The two women were so devoted to their pets—there was no other word for it—that they had once led two of them into the Grocery Basket to pick out special treats from the produce section. Jake O'Toole, the store owner, had practically had a stroke. His reaction didn't faze the Dithers sisters, though they had seemed perplexed when their pets appeared to select ice cream and beer.

"The point is," Vida declared, "that she talks about the horses and some of her friends to the exclusion of family matters. It doesn't seem right."

I thought back to the adolescent years with Adam, yet I couldn't make comparisons. There hadn't been any marital strife, because I'd never been married. It struck me anew how little I knew about the institution of matrimony. I'd never had a husband, never even lived with a man. My liaison with Milo was as close as I'd come to being a couple.

Adam had grown up without a father. When had he begun to ask serious questions? Much earlier, I thought, perhaps when he was four or five. I'd put him off, saying that his father had a wife and other children. He lived someplace else, though at the time I didn't know where. I didn't want to know. Adam and I were both better off in ignorance.

At fifteen, Adam had wanted to learn about himself. He'd begun to discover girls, which scared the hell out of me. He'd talked of becoming an airline pilot or working on an oil rig or joining the Peace Corps. He'd talked mainly of himself, and I'd listened. Most of the time.

"It's her age," I said, referring to Molly. "She's in her own little world."

"Perhaps." Vida retained a worried expression. "What on earth are she and Stacie doing in Martinez, California? Are they in school? Is Gordon's cousin Kirby a decent man? Is he married? Does he have children of his own?"

Vida got up and went into the living room. I followed her. She was calling directory assistance for the Bay Area, asking for Kirby Imhoff's number. It occurred to me that Kirby's last name might not be Imhoff. But it was. Before I could interrupt, she had someone on the line in Martinez.

"Kirby's at work? I see. This is Vida Runkel, a distant relation of Gordon's." Very distant, I thought. "Oh, yes, Kathy, is it? How are my nieces, Kathy? I'm very concerned about them."

I gathered up my clothes and started for the bathroom to get dressed. Kathy, I assumed, was Kirby's wife. Or maybe his girlfriend. For all I knew, she could be his parole officer. I dressed, combed my hair, applied a minimum of makeup, and returned to the living room.

Vida had just hung up, and I didn't much like the look on her face. "They're gone," she said in a hollow voice. "Stacie and Molly ran away during the night."

The girls had arrived the previous afternoon in Martinez, which is located on Suisun Bay northwest of Oakland. According to Kathy, who apparently was indeed Kirby's wife, they had seemed nervous but resigned to the move. The California Imhoffs had two teenagers of their own, a boy thirteen and a girl sixteen. They had only met their cousins once before, but appeared to be making the newcomers feel at home. Yet when Kathy had gone to check on Stacie and Molly around eight in the morning, there was no sign of them or their belongings. Kirby had already left for work. Kathy had called him, but Kirby was employed by one of the local refineries and was unavailable because he was helping load a supertanker.

"I told her not to notify the police," Vida said grimly. "Not yet, even though they're runaways. If I were a wagering sort, which I am not, I'd bet that they're headed back here."

"I wonder."

"Why do you say that?" Vida sounded vexed, though I knew it wasn't with me.

"I don't know." I wandered over to the front window, gazing out at the park across the street and the ocean beyond. The tide was going out, with big breakers catching the sun. "Stacie and Molly would have to agree on running away and, I assume, on where they were going. I haven't noticed that they were in the habit of agreeing on much of anything."

"It's the two of them against the world now," Vida pointed out. That's different."

I didn't argue. Maybe Vida was right. "Had the California Imhoffs called Gordon?"

"Not yet. I told Kathy I'd try to reach him," Vida said, going over to the phone. "Let's hope he hasn't gone up to the hospital in Seaside."

It was Derek who answered. His father was walking the beach. Vida didn't say anything about Stacie and Molly, but told Derek to make sure that Gordon called her as soon as possible.

"Derek's leaving for work," Vida fretted. "I hope he has the sense to leave Gordon a message."

Exhibiting unusual agitation, Vida prowled around the motel suite, going from the living room to the kitchen to the bedroom and back again. Finally, she dialed Providence Hospital to ask after Rosalie. Mrs. Dobrinz had had a restful night, according to the nurse, but no decision

would be made about her release until after the doctor
had made his rounds.

"I feel better," I announced. I might be able to drive.
But this was Wednesday, the one day of the week when
the pressure was off at work. I'd see how I felt by the
afternoon. "I said, I feel—"

"Yes, yes," Vida broke in. "I heard you. Good. That's
nice. Why doesn't Gordon call back?"

"Maybe he's still on the beach. There's plenty of it."

Vida grabbed her swing coat and her purse. "What are
we waiting for? Let's go see him."

"We haven't had breakfast," I protested.

"Then I'll drop you off in town," Vida replied, already
out the door. "Hurry."

I almost took Vida up on her offer, but as we drove
along Hemlock I saw the stricken look on her face. I'd
come this far; I couldn't abandon her for ham and eggs.

The Tracer was gone, indicating that Derek had left for
work. It was Dolores who came to the door. She was
wearing a black T-shirt and tattered blue jeans. I assessed
her welcome as tepid at best.

"I work late today," she said, as if in need of an explanation for her casual attire.

"Has Gordon returned?" Vida asked, marching past
Dolores and going straight for the living room.

"No." Dolores followed us, though I had the feeling
that she was playing watchdog rather than hostess.

Vida glanced at the phone. "Has anyone called here in
the last hour? Besides me, of course."

Dolores shook her head, the long black hair swinging
at her shoulders. "I don't think so."

Vida was at the window, scanning the beach. The
breakers were crashing far up onto the sand. Vaguely, I
wondered if this had been an exceptionally high tide.

Haystack Rock and its surrounding crags looked more isolated than usual. When the tide was at low ebb, beach-combers could walk around the outcroppings, exploring pools and crevices that sheltered sealife and birds. Now the smaller rocks had disappeared, and Haystack itself was partially submerged.

"How long has Gordon been gone?" Vida asked without turning around.

Dolores had assumed her post on the arm of the sofa. "Um . . . an hour? I'm not sure. Maybe longer. I didn't get up until eight-thirty."

Vida swiveled around to pinion the girl with sharp gray eyes. "Was he gone then?"

"I think so." Dolores flinched under that hard gaze. "Yes. Derek said his dad had gone out, so it was okay to use the shower. It's stupid to have to ask permission," she added with a pout. "This isn't a detention place, it's a house."

But not a home, I thought, wondering at Dolores's choice of words. Maybe she didn't understand the con-cept of *home.* Despite her belligerent manner, I felt sorry for the kid.

"It's going on ten," Vida said, glancing at a captain's clock on the mantel. "Gordon should be back by now." She prowled around the room, pausing occasionally to study some of the accumulated objets d'art and just plain junk, which included Ruth Pickering's metal sculptures.

Dolores continued keeping watch. She kept silent as well, until I asked if she liked her job. Giving a little shrug, she said it was all right. The other employees were nice enough, and the restaurant served good food. Some-times, especially during tourist season, she got good tips. The information came not all at once, but only after a series of questions on my part. Vida kept prowling.

"The tide's so far in, how can you walk on the beach?" she demanded. *"Where is he?"*

"I think there's always some dry sand," I said. "You can't see it from here because of the dunes and the grasses."

Vida went out through the front door. "I'm going down there," she called over her shoulder.

I started after her, then thought better of it. I still wasn't entirely comfortable walking for very long. "Dolores," I said, giving the girl my most motherly smile, "would you mind if I got myself a bowl of cereal?"

She didn't mind, but she followed me into the kitchen. "Go ahead and do whatever you were doing," I said, still smiling. I didn't feel like having her watch me slurp up cornflakes.

"That's okay," she said, pulling herself up onto the counter. "I'm just kicking it this morning."

I felt like telling her that she might try housecleaning. The Imhoff residence was becoming more cluttered and less tidy by the day. Through the door to the living room I could see one of Ruth's metal sculptures, which—maybe—depicted a spear-carrying hunter. A pair of Jockey shorts was dangling from the spear.

"Did you know Mrs. Imhoff very well?" I asked. As long as I was stuck with Dolores, I might as well try pumping her.

"Kind of." Dolores toyed with the long strands of hair, then picked up a headband and put it on.

I began eating my corn flakes. "Did you like her?"

"She was okay."

That hadn't been the question. "Did you spend much time here before . . . while Mrs. Imhoff was alive?" I amended.

"Some." Dolores's dark eyes sparked for just a fleeting second. "You're treating me like a criminal. How come?"

"I'm a journalist." The job covers a multitude of sins. "Prying is my business." I tried to resurrect my smile.

"Derek's mom usually wasn't around when I came here," Dolores said, removing the headband and shaking out her hair. "She was at the shop or on the beach or hauling some old person around. If you want to know the truth, Mrs. Imhoff didn't like me. She thought I wasn't good enough for her son."

"I heard she thought you were too young to get married. That's not the same thing," I noted.

"Whatever." Dolores rolled her eyes. "She wanted Derek to go to college. She thought I'd stand in his way. I wouldn't, and I won't. But he doesn't want to go. Not now, anyway."

"There's no point in him going if he hasn't decided on a career," I said, finishing the cereal. "I don't imagine he wants to work in a grocery store forever, though."

"He can do lots of things," Dolores said airily, "without going to college. My oldest brother's an auto mechanic. He makes real good money."

It was pointless to argue with Dolores, nor did I feel as if I should. If she wanted to spend the rest of her life hustling tips while Derek carried out sacks of potatoes and chicken parts, that was up to them. I'd seen enough of that borderline lifestyle in Alpine

I was about to change the subject to something less controversial, like the abortion issue or gay rights, when Vida came staggering into the living room. I could see her from the kitchen, and rushed to meet her.

"What's wrong?" I demanded as she collapsed against a high-backed chair and gasped for breath.

"Call the police!" She was drained, her head down, her body limp.

"What?" It was a stupid thing to say. I raced to the phone and dialed 911. Dolores had come into the living room, too, and was staring at Vida. The operator answered. Panicked, I turned away from the phone. "What do I tell them?"

Vida took a deep breath and raised her head. "Gordon's dead." She stopped, then pressed a hand against her bosom. "His body's washed up on the beach."

Trembling, I relayed the information. "Tell them to hurry," Vida gasped, "or the outgoing tide might carry him off." She fumbled with the chair and finally dropped onto the cane seat.

Dolores was transfixed, her hands covering her mouth. A muffled "No!" erupted, followed by a piercing shriek. I hung up the phone, then looked to see who needed me most. Vida was struggling to regain her composure; Dolores had slipped onto the floor.

I rushed to the girl's side, but she hadn't fainted. Putting my arm around her slim shoulders, I felt her shudder convulsively. No tears fell, however, just a dry, heaving sound.

"Some other people found him first," Vida said, her voice somewhat stronger. "It was about a hundred yards south of here. I arrived while they were trying to figure out what to do. I think they're tourists."

I only half heard Vida, but sensed that she needed to talk. Dolores was leaning on me, still making those strange noises that were a cross between a groan and a sob.

Vida had stood up. She came toward us and leaned down. "Dolores—where was Gordon staying? Which room?"

Dolores's hands fell away from her ashen face.

"What? I ... Oh!" She swallowed hard. "He slept in Derek's old room. Mr. Imhoff let us keep the big bedroom." The query seemed to restore her. She sat back on her haunches and closed her eyes.

I rose, but didn't follow Vida out of the living room. "What happened?" I called to her. "Did anybody see anything?"

"No, not that I know of," Vida answered, her voice carrying from the bedroom down the hall. "But then I didn't get a chance to ... Ah! I thought so!" She rushed out of the room, waving a piece of paper. "It's a suicide note! Oh, good Lord! I feel sick!"

The last thing I needed was for Vida to succumb to any sort of weakness. "I'll make tea," I said, craning to look at the note.

"Here." Vida thrust the paper at me, then raced into the bathroom.

It didn't take long to read Gordon's last message: *I killed Audrey. I'm sorry. Take care of each other. I love you all.*

I was still leaning against the wall, waiting for Vida, when the sirens sounded on the highway. "Are you okay?" I called through the door.

"Yes. Yes. I'll be right out. I hear someone coming. Go to the back door, please."

The familiar figures of Randy Neal and Charles St. James were the first to arrive. Right behind them came the fire department, an ambulance, the Medex unit, and a Cannon Beach patrol car with two officers I didn't recognize. I was trying to explain where Gordon had been found when Vida joined me at the door.

"I'll show you," she said, looking drawn and upset. "Can you drive down to the beach?"

There was a road just beyond the vacant house next

door. Vida left with the deputies, and the other emergency vehicles followed. I remained behind with Dolores.

"What's that?" she asked, pointing to Gordon's note, which I still had clutched in my hand.

I didn't want to show it to her. "Let's make some tea," I said, taking her arm. "How do you feel?"

"Awful." She kept close to me as I put on the kettle and searched for tea bags. "Did somebody kill Mr. Imhoff?"

"I don't think so," I said, avoiding her big-eyed gaze.

"Did he drown?"

"I'm not sure."

"I thought he was a good swimmer. How could he drown?" Her voice sounded lost, as if it had fallen into a deep, dark hole and couldn't get out.

"We'll have to wait for the police to tell us what happened." I felt inept, helpless. "Should we go out on the front porch and get some air? It'll take a minute for the tea water to boil."

Dolores followed me like a lonely kitten. Outside, we could see the line of emergency vehicles moving toward the beach. "Who lives in that brown house on the other side of the summer place?" I asked.

"I don't know," Dolores replied. "They have little kids, I think."

I hoped the little kids weren't around. "Listen for the teakettle," I said, leaving the porch. "I'll be right back."

But Dolores followed me down the stepping-stones that led to the beach. The dozen or so cement rounds ended where the bank dipped until it reached the level sand. A well-trod path wound through the grasses and thistles and clover, ending at an accumulation of driftwood. I spotted the remnants of several beach fires, a single tennis shoe, a dirty towel, and assorted beer cans.

To my left, Vida and the deputies were getting out of the Clatsop County patrol car. Directly in front of them was a cluster of people, who, even from a distance, seemed uneasy as they milled around near the outgoing tide.

"Hold it," I said, putting out a hand to detain Dolores. I had just caught sight of what I assumed was Gordon's body. It lay about twenty feet from the small crowd, and looked like a pile of old clothes. "Let's stay here," I urged. "We'll only get in the way."

"I saw a dead person once," Dolores said in an awestruck voice. "He'd been hit by a car on 101, down by Arch Cape."

I, too, had seen dead bodies during the course of my career, but I didn't feel like reminiscing. The deputies, along with the local police officers, were moving the onlookers farther down the beach. Meanwhile the medical personnel had gathered around Gordon's body.

"Let's go back," I said, putting an arm around Dolores.

Somewhat to my surprise, she didn't seem to mind my protective gestures. Until Vida's announcement, I hadn't felt any rapport between Dolores and me. I still didn't, but I sensed a kind of mutual dependency.

Or did, until we got to the stepping stones. Suddenly she stopped and pulled away. Her gaze was on the front of the house, with its wide porch and picture windows.

"It's Derek's now, isn't it?" Dolores breathed. "He owns the house. He owns everything." She clasped her hands and let out a little squeal of elation. "It's mine, too! I finally have a home!"

I didn't know whether to slap her or hug her. Instead, I did nothing.

* * *

St. James and Neal had taken over the investigation.
Half an hour later they returned to the house with Vida.
She looked weary but more composed. Naturally, she
was grateful for the hot tea.

Dolores, whose euphoria had faded, was now outside,
waiting for Derek to return from Osburn's. As a result of
my prodding, I had insisted that she call to inform her
boyfriend of his father's death. I'd also advised her to tell
him that it was an accident. Derek didn't need to know
all the gruesome details at once.

"You mentioned a note," St. James said to Vida after
she was seated at the kitchen table with her tea. "May we
see it?"

Vida looked at me. "Where is it?" Her voice was
toneless.

I produced the slip of paper, which I'd left under a can-
ister on the counter. "Here," I said, giving the note to the
deputy.

St. James grimaced. "It would have been better if no
one had touched this," he said, with reproachful looks for
Vida and me. When we said nothing in our defense, he
scanned the words, then handed the paper over to Randy
Neal. "I guess that settles it. We'll be taking the note
with us."

"Of course." I gave both deputies a feeble smile.
"What did Gordon do? Walk into the ocean?"

Neal gave a slight nod. "So it seems. It's not uncommon
around here. You just keep wading out until a wave over-
takes you. Maybe it won't be the first one, or even the
second, but eventually . . ." His voice trailed away.

A silence fell over the kitchen. Above the ocean's roar,
I could hear the captain's clock, ticking away the hours in
the empty living room. I listened for the sirens that would

signal the emergency vehicles' departure, then realized there was no need for haste. It didn't matter when Gordon Imhoff got wherever they were taking him. He was already gone.

"It's rubbish, of course."

The three of us turned to look at Vida, who was sitting alone at the table.

St. James coughed softly. "Pardon, ma'am?"

Adjusting her glasses, Vida looked at each of us in turn. "The note. It's rubbish." She gave a nod at Neal, who still held the slip of paper in his hand. "Gordon didn't kill Audrey. I know that now. If I'd known it sooner, Gordon might still be alive." With a mighty effort, she got to her feet, threw back her shoulders, and lifted her chin. "As it turns out, I killed Gordon."

Chapter Eighteen

NEAL AND ST. JAMES didn't know Vida, which explained their stupefaction. But I understood what she meant, and hastened to clarify the statement.

"Mrs. Runkel feels guilty," I said in a rush, "because she's been trying to find out who killed her niece. Her efforts disturbed Gordon to the point that he took his life. But that's hardly her fault." I shot Vida a sharp look. "It's not, you know. Gordon had choices."

"He was in an impossible situation," Vida asserted, maintaining her imperial stance. Then her jaw dropped and she gaped at me. "You *know*?"

"I do now," I said. "I didn't believe that note, either."

Derek tore into the house, going straight for the deputies. "How could my dad drown? This is crazy!"

Still flustered by Vida's earlier pronouncement, St. James put an unsteady hand on Derek's arm. "Sit down, son. This is a rough one."

Surprisingly, Derek sat. Dolores came inside, too, moving to stand behind Derek's chair. I decided I might as well sit; the morning's events and my aches and pains were catching up with me.

There was no way to deliver the news easily, yet St. James tried. At first, Derek seemed uncomprehending. Then he jumped out of the chair and began beating his fists against the kitchen cabinets. "No! This is bullshit! It's a trick!" He whirled around, accusing eyes on the deputies. "Dad wouldn't do that! You're lying!"

"It's true," Vida said quietly. "Your father was under tremendous pressure. Do you know why?"

Derek shot Vida a look that was short of malicious. "It can't be true," he muttered. "It's too crazy."

Putting a tentative hand on Derek's arm, Dolores spoke softly: "People do crazy things all the time. Your dad's been through a lot."

The sympathetic remark surprised me. But it seemed to have a calming effect on Derek. He turned again to Vida, his expression now more confused than hostile. "What did you say? What am I supposed to know?"

Vida made a brief dismissive gesture with her hand. "It doesn't matter." She glanced at me, and I could barely see the slight shake of her head. But I knew what she meant: Derek didn't know why his father had killed himself.

Under Dolores's soothing touch, the young man began to collect himself. Both deputies made tactful, consoling comments, but evaded Derek's specific questions. "Take some time to work with this," Neal said. "We'll leave you two alone."

Vida and I caught the signal. We followed Neal and St. James through the living room and onto the front porch, where we couldn't be heard by Derek and Dolores.

Neal turned to Vida. "Can you give us a fuller explanation of what you think happened with Mr. Imhoff?"

"Certainly." Vida still wore her unsettled expression, but spoke in her normal, brisk tones. "Very soon after the murder was committed, I believe that Gordon realized who had killed Audrey. That's why he ran away in the first place—he's a vacillating sort, and flight was the only way he could deal with what he felt was an impossible situation."

"But he came back," St. James pointed out, "and offered a new piece of evidence."

"A new piece of flimflam," Vida retorted. "Surely you people didn't believe that silly story?"

St. James and Neal exchanged glances. "It was impossible to prove one way or the other," Neal said.

"Naturally." Vida stood at the edge of the porch, the breeze ruffling her blue-and-yellow print dress. "Gordon was desperately trying to find another suspect, even if he had to invent one. Frankly, it would have been better for everyone if he'd never come back at all."

"He'd have been found eventually," I remarked, leaning on a wicker chair. "It's rare that a person can disappear permanently."

"It can happen, though," St. James said in an aside.

"Gordon had a conscience," Vida stated. "Which is why I believe he returned to the area. That, and the fact that he was terribly worried about his children. He believed that they were all in danger. Yet after Gordon got back, he realized he couldn't face the future. His world had been devastated, and life had become unbearable." Vida's gray eyes turned to Randy Neal. "You're right about people walking into the ocean. The sea has a mighty pull, and Gordon wasn't strong enough to resist it."

Two county detectives, a big, fair-haired woman and a chubby, balding man, came out onto the porch. Before conferring with their colleagues, they introduced themselves to Vida and me as Anya Kuraskova and Rick Di Palma. Originally assigned to the Imhoff case, they had come to question witnesses and collect evidence.

Having filled in Kuraskova and Di Palma, St. James and Neal turned their attention back to us.

"Could we get to the point?" Neal inquired, trying not to show his impatience.

"In due time," Vida said with a reproachful look. "This is a complicated task, and one which I don't believe your agency has been able to bring to a conclusion."

Again, Neal and St. James exchanged hasty glances. I assumed they thought Vida was nuts. I knew better, and waited.

"What pushed Gordon to the breaking point," Vida continued, "was my involvement. And Emma's." She shot me a quick look. "It was clear from his manner, as well as certain actions, that he wanted us to leave. He was terrified that we might actually discover the truth.

"Ironically, we weren't the ones who realized the killer's identity. It was Rosalie Dobrinz who stumbled— for lack of a better word—on who killed her daughter. Comprehension dawned on her last night at the Bistro. That's why she collapsed. It was simply too much for her to bear."

The deputies knew nothing about Rosalie's trip to the hospital. Vida was enlightening them when the phone rang. I glanced inside to see if Derek or Dolores had picked up the receiver, but they weren't in sight. I assumed they were with the detectives.

I grabbed the phone on the seventh ring. The voice at the other end was female, but so agitated that I couldn't recognize it.

"Who's this? What number is it?" the semihysterical voice demanded.

"It's the Imhoff residence," I said. Giving my name might further confuse the party at the other end.

"Where's my dad? I've got to talk to him!"

I finally realized it was Stacie. With a hand to my head,

I took a deep breath. "He's not here. Where are you, Stacie? This is Emma Lord, your aunt Vida's friend."

The silence at the other end went on for so long that I thought Stacie had hung up. "I'm in Ashland," she finally said. "Just north of the California state line."

I knew Ashland and its Shakespeare Festival well, having covered it three times while working for *The Oregonian*. "Are you coming home?" I inquired, trying to sound calm.

"No. I mean, I don't know. Where's Dad?" Stacie sounded miserable.

I countered with a question of my own. If I had to deliver the bad news, I didn't want to do it twice. "Where's Molly?"

"That's the problem," Stacie wailed. "She's gone."

"Gone? Gone from Ashland?"

"Yes." Another pause. I envisioned Stacie at a pay phone, trying to collect herself. "We were on the bus, coming back to Oregon, and we had a stop here. Molly went to get some M&M's and never came back. The bus left without us."

"Call the police," I said. "She can't have gone far. Has another bus come through since you got there?"

"No. At least I don't think so." Tears choked Stacie's voice. "Do you think she was kidnapped?"

I didn't know what to think; I didn't know what to do. "Are you still at the depot?"

"Yes." The single word was very uncertain.

"Stay there. Give me the number of the pay phone. If it's the kind you can't call in on, then we'll phone the station and have them page you. But don't leave, not even if Molly shows up."

"Okay." Stacie's voice was calmer. Maybe having someone think for her brought relief.

Apparently, Vida had wound up her recital. Both deputies were looking very grave when I returned to the porch with the most recent alarming news.

"We'll notify the Ashland police and the Jackson County sheriff," St. James said, dashing off the porch and heading around the house to his patrol car.

"Such a bollix!" Vida exclaimed under her breath. "It's like a snowball, with the initial tragedy rolling downhill and collecting yet more sorrow."

"You mean Audrey's death?" I said, leaning wearily against a porch post.

Vida shook her head. "No. I mean the divorce. Or what would have been a divorce, had Audrey lived. Why can't people use *sense*?"

Neal, who may or may not have still thought Vida was nuts, wore a sympathetic expression. "For some people, divorce is the only answer," he said mildly.

"For some, yes," Vida agreed. "But for many, it's just the easy way. Marriage is hard work, and don't I know it! Ernest was no angel. And . . ." She winced, then her voice dropped a notch. ". . . I have a few faults of my own. You have to work at being married. Too many couples come up against the first whiff of boredom or some silly flaw in their spouse's behavior, and the next thing you know, they want a divorce. They think it will be easier the next time. It won't, it's themselves they want to discard, and they'll always be discontented. Meanwhile, the children suffer. And don't tell me they don't!" She pointed an accusing finger at Neal, who looked startled.

"I'm not even married, ma'am."

"That's another thing," Vida went on, gaining steam. "Too many people enter into marriage without giving it serious thought. Don't make that mistake, young man. You can't train for marriage, not even by living together. You can't study for it, research it, or get free samples. You have to *do* it, every minute of every day for the rest of your lives."

"Yes, ma'am," Neal replied in a meek voice. "I think I'd better go check up on Charles and see what's happening." The deputy hurried from the front porch.

"Now what?" demanded Vida.

"Ashland is three or four times the size of Alpine," I said, conjuring up the picturesque town set on a hillside above lush farmland. "There's not much else around there. By the time you get to Ashland, you're heading up through the Siskiyous and into California."

"In other words," Vida remarked dryly, "Molly can't have gone far. Unless someone snatched her."

"I don't think that's what happened, do you?"

"No." Vida was still standing, her gaze on the ocean where Haystack Rock was beginning to rise out of the waves. "On the other hand, I don't think she's coming back."

"Probably not. What about Stacie?"

"I hope the sheriff or the police in Ashland have the good sense to escort her to Cannon Beach," Vida said, then turned around and started for the living room. "I must call Kathy Imhoff and let her know what's happened."

Vida also phoned Providence Hospital in Seaside. Rosalie had been released, the nurse said, but so far her son-in-law hadn't come to take her home. Was he on his way?

"Not exactly," Vida replied. "I'll notify Rosalie's husband, Walter." Then she swiftly changed her mind. "No," she told the nurse, "I'll come get her myself."

Rosalie couldn't endure more bad news that would

be delivered in what Vida perceived as Walt's "ham-handed" manner. Thus we must drive to Seaside. I argued briefly, but there was nothing more that we could do at the Imhoff house.

Or so I thought. But as Vida hung up the phone she espied the underwear hanging from Ruth Pickering's metal statuary. "I can't stand looking at that another minute," she declared, yanking the shorts off the spearlike device. "It's disgusting."

I didn't know if she referred to the underwear or the sculpture. I caught myself almost smiling for the first time in what seemed like eons. "I think there's a laundry hamper in the bathroom," I said.

But even as Vida held the waistband of the shorts by her thumb and forefinger, she seemed transfixed. "Remember the Jaded Eye?" she said in a hushed voice. "Do you recall our speculation?"

Vaguely, I did. We had studied some of Ruth's creations, noting that many of them had sharp, lethal points. Like the one that sat on a low shelf in front of the picture window and had been used as a receptacle for dirty clothes. "Do you think that's the weapon?"

"I wonder." She stomped off toward the hall. "Yoo-hoo! Detectives! Where are you?"

Rick Di Palma came out of Molly and Stacie's room. He was carrying the suitcase in which Vida and I had discovered the marijuana residue. "What is it?" he asked, his brown eyes watchful.

Vida explained. Di Palma listened carefully, then went into the living room. "It's a possibility," he agreed. "We'll take it into Astoria. Anya?"

The female detective came in from the direction of the master bedroom. After listening to Vida's conjecture,

Anya went outside, presumably to get a bag big enough to hold the sculpture.

Vida pointed to the floral-patterned suitcase. "That's marijuana, isn't it?"

Di Palma started to nod, then became noncommittal. "We'll have the lab check the contents. How did you know about the . . . flakes?"

Vida didn't respond immediately. From the conflicting emotions that crossed her face, I realized that she was making a decision. "Oh, what difference does it make now? We found the suitcase while we were looking for clues to the murder. If you do your homework, you'll find that my niece—Audrey—used that piece of luggage to transport marijuana from my nephew Marlin's place to college students working in Cannon Beach." Vida shot me a quick glance. "Why should I protect Marlin when he damaged my poor car?"

"Vice is working on the marijuana angle," Di Palma responded. "Do the names Jesse Damon and Jeremy Carlisle mean anything to you?"

Vida nodded. "I've met them, though I don't believe Jeremy gave his last name. There are others, though, some of whom probably worked here the past three or four summers."

We left after that exchange. On the way up to Seaside, I congratulated Vida on her detective work.

"It was simple," she averred modestly. "If Audrey wasn't sleeping with those boys, what was the connection? It had to be the marijuana. Remember that scrap of note paper we found in the suitcase? It said to bring two thousand dollars, which, I assume, was Marlin's wholesale price. Then it mentioned something about 'do not go to ja . . .' which we thought meant jail, but I now suspect was the Jaded Eye. I don't understand the reference, but that's not as important as the tie-in with Audrey and the shop."

"Maybe Marlin was being paranoid and thought Gordon was getting suspicious. Do you still have that note?" I inquired, recalling that Vida had pocketed it.

"Well . . . yes." She seemed a trifle sheepish. "I'll hand it over, if necessary. But I believe the police can figure it out. They must have looked into Audrey's bank accounts. Where else could she get that hundred thousand dollars? It couldn't all have come from those silly old men. And how did Marlin support himself? Not that he lives a lavish lifestyle, but he must eat. I suspect that like Rett, he has money stashed all over that disreputable house of his. I don't know much about drugs, thank goodness, but I'm aware that when marijuana is sold directly from the grower, it commands quite a high price."

We spent the rest of the short drive discussing various other aspects of the case. We did not, however, talk about the murder itself or how we would give Rosalie the news about Gordon. Yet I knew the latter weighed heavily on Vida's mind. Her step had slowed after we reached the hospital parking lot. Indeed, when we came through the main entrance and saw Rosalie sitting in a wheelchair, Vida actually stopped in her tracks.

"We'll do this here," she whispered. "I want a doctor close by."

I didn't know if she meant the remark literally or figuratively. In any event, Vida greeted Rosalie with a constricted smile, then suggested we move to a far corner for privacy.

Rosalie sensed at once that something was wrong. "Don't tell me," she said in a breathless voice. "Is it . . . ?"

"No," Vida replied, pushing the wheelchair past the comfortable sofas and easy chairs provided for visitors.

"It's Gordon." Vida knelt next to Rosalie and took her hands. "This morning, Gordon—" She stopped, unable to go on.

"He's dead." Rosalie closed her eyes and seemed to shrink inside herself.

Vida said nothing. She lowered her head and squeezed Rosalie's hands.

"I was afraid of that," Rosalie said after a long silence. "It's my fault."

Vida's head jerked up. "Never! It's mine!"

"It's nobody's," I intervened.

Rosalie gave a little start, staring at me as if she'd forgotten I was present. She probably had. "No, no. Last night at the restaurant I tried to make Gordon tell me why he'd spent so much time on the run. He had all these excuses, but they didn't amount to much. I watched his eyes and I knew in my heart that something was very, very wrong. I think I always knew it. I spent quite a while with the children after Audrey died, you see. I'd begun to guess then." Putting a hand to her bosom, Rosalie paused for breath.

"He told us you were stunned by the news about Marlin," I said, to fill the gap. "But you couldn't have been. Rett indicated you already knew when he said Marlin couldn't get his bail money from you."

Rosalie gave a faint nod. "I didn't have it, at least not that I could get at right away. I'm glad Rett could do it for Marlin. It's about time he did something for somebody else. Why are people so selfish?" She began to cry.

"Selfishness was what got Audrey killed," I blurted. "She thought only of herself, and not of her family."

"I'm afraid so," said Vida, still on her knees, now patting Rosalie gently. "But it's selfish to kill, too. Then again, children learn from their parents." She lowered her voice to a whisper. "Molly's run away."

Clutching a tissue she'd dug out of her pocket, Rosalie stared at Vida. "I hope they never find her. It's better that way. Granddaughter or not, I don't know that I could face her. Not after Molly killed Audrey."

The Jackson County sheriff's deputies found Molly later that day in a barn about a mile from Ashland. She was curled up peacefully in a horse stall, and at first they had thought she was asleep. When they realized that Molly was dead, they could find no external cause. It was only after the autopsy that the authorities determined she had taken some kind of lethal medication used to put down animals. Her body was brought back to Cannon Beach, where a joint service was held for her and her father. Gordon and Molly were buried next to Audrey in the local cemetery, which overlooks the sea. Three members of the Imhoff family were united in death, instead of being torn asunder in life. I suppose it was what Molly would have wanted.

Vida stayed on for the funeral, but I went home that Thursday morning. I felt much improved, at least physically, but the Imhoff tragedy would leave a scar to last a lifetime.

I had stopped off in Portland to call Mavis. I'd meant to contact her while I was in Cannon Beach, but somehow I'd never gotten around to it. Maybe I'd been as caught up in Audrey's murder as Vida.

A brief, cryptic story about Gordon's apparent suicide and Molly's unexplained death had appeared in *The Oregonian*. Mavis hadn't made the connection with Vida or me, but when I told her about it, she was agog.

"Are you going to use it in *The Advocate*?" Mavis

asked, the excitement in her voice evoking our professional life together in Portland. "I would. It's one hell of a story."

I knew Mavis would have attacked the Imhoff catastrophe like a tiger going after raw meat. But she was made of sterner stuff. "No," I replied from the phone booth that was just off I-205 near the Columbia River. "The only native Alpiner directly involved is Rett Runkel, and he's still alive and well, living in a wretched trailer with his dog, T-Bone." I didn't add that the story might embarrass Vida and the rest of the Runkels. Mavis was a City Girl, and wouldn't understand small town ways.

Or maybe she did. "Sap," Mavis said, and then laughed. "Call me next week and let me know if you're still in business. And next time, stick around longer. We never did finish raking Tom Cavanaugh over the coals."

We hadn't, in fact. Maybe we shouldn't. The coals had gone out long ago, along with the sparks and embers.

I got back into my latest rental car and crossed the Columbia River into Washington.

"It was horrible," I told Milo that night after I arrived home in Alpine. We were sitting in my living room, each with our drink of choice. "I feel sorry for Vida. She's always set such store by family."

Milo chuckled. "Half her family's as nuts as everybody else's. She didn't even know this Oregon bunch. Vida'll get over it."

I didn't think so, and said as much. "I won't either," I asserted. "It breaks my heart to think that a kid like Molly would go so far to prevent her parents from splitting up. She simply couldn't face the idea of divorce. She never wrote about it in her diary, and I doubt that she ever talked to anyone about it."

Milo shrugged. "She was kind of like Vida. It wasn't the actual concept of family that meant so much to her, but what other people thought. That's a big deal with teenagers. You know—acceptance, peer-group pressure, all that."

"No," I said, recalling Molly's heartfelt poem about losing the dog. *The family circle has been broken.* "It wasn't just that. It was the idea of a broken home, of a family destroyed. Molly had seen what had happened after her grandparents divorced. The family had come apart, in three generations. She realized that her mother and her grandmother were virtual strangers, and that frightened her. Then there were the other kids she knew who'd been through a divorce. She'd watched them being pulled back and forth between parents, uprooted and moved away, made to feel as if they were to blame, used as pawns, and, I suspect, in some cases, not really wanted by either the mother or the father. Everybody talks about child abuse these days, but one of the biggest ways that kids are abused is by divorce. Sure, I know that in some instances, it's the only solution. You can't stay with a drunk or a drug addict or someone who's violent. But that's not what we're talking about here—Audrey wanted to move on, maybe with her family, maybe without them. Gordon didn't want to go anywhere. He could hardly make up his mind about getting out of bed, if you ask me. But neither would change or compromise or make accommodations, which is what marriage is all about."

Milo rubbed at his temple. "Did she plan it? That's kind of scary, but it happens."

"We'll never know," I replied, sipping at my bourbon. "Personally, I think she was overcome with a terrible rage. Her mother was leaving in a day or two, she was already packed. I suspect Molly had begged her mother to stay—and Audrey had dismissed the request. I can imagine Molly lying in bed that night, and suddenly feeling that there was only one way to stop her mother. Violence—as Walt Dobrinz mentioned to Vida—is a contemporary solution to problems. Molly got up, went into the living room, and grabbed the first lethal-looking thing she saw, which was a metal sculpture with a sharp point. Maybe after she got to the dock, she made one last attempt to persuade Audrey to stay. I doubt that Audrey would have been afraid of Molly, let alone moved by her daughter's pleas. Molly reacted by stopping her mother in the only way she knew how. And then she returned to the house, replaced the metal sculpture, and went to bed."

Milo looked grim. "The poor kid must have been nuts. Or driven to it. The same goes for the dad. I suppose he couldn't face living with the fact that his daughter had killed his wife. That could send even a stable guy around the bend."

I agreed. "And Gordon wasn't the most stable sort. But he understood his kids, and he knew intuitively that Molly had committed the murder. I suspect he left after the funeral because he thought the cops would figure it out and he couldn't stand seeing Molly arrested. Then, when the crime wasn't solved after a month, he decided to come back. But that solved nothing, because he still had to live with the knowledge of what his daughter had done."

Milo stroked his long chin. "I can see that. It'd tear you apart. It's no wonder he sent the girls away, but that didn't help. Imhoff was wrestling with himself." He paused. "I take it the weapon checked out?" As ever, the sheriff wanted evidence, even when it wasn't his case.

"Yes. Vida learned from my old friend Bill Wigert that there were traces of hair and skin and blood on the sharp metal point." I grimaced at the thought. "Most killers would have dropped the damned thing into the ocean. But Molly was tidy by nature. She put the sculpture back where it belonged."

"Hiding in plain sight," Milo mused. "It's not the first time that law-enforcement types have missed the obvious. I've done it myself."

"It's pitiful," I said, still thinking of Molly. "I have to wonder if the Imhoff marriage was ever what you might call a successful union. I doubt that it's possible for a husband and wife to be happy when each of them has such different goals and needs, and no apparent understanding of the other. The long-term toll on the kids must be very heavy."

Milo laughed and put his arm around me. "How would *you* know? You've never been married."

"Maybe that's why I've stayed single," I said, surprising myself. "I'm not able to do all those things." I twisted out of his half embrace and turned to face him. "Why did you and Tricia get divorced? You've never really told me."

"Oh, well . . ." He put his hands behind his head and stretched out his long legs. "We got so we fought over every damned little thing. She kept leaving the emergency brake on in the car. She could never get dinner on the table until I'd been home at least half an hour. She left her stupid hair curlers all over the bathroom floor. She read in bed at night when I was dead tired. It was a bunch of stuff, and it just kept building until we both wanted out."

I gave a nod. "So what did you do that made her crazy?" I put up a hand. "Don't tell me. I know. You got stuck at work and didn't come home when you said you would. You zoned out in front of the TV after dinner and never talked. You dumped your dirty clothes wherever you took them off. You had a dishwasher, but you never, never put so much as a teaspoon in it. You left everything in the living room, the dining nook, or—if Tricia got *really* lucky—on the kitchen counter."

Milo's hazel eyes widened. "Shit! Do I still do all that stuff?"

"You sure do," I declared, again ducking away from him. "I shrug it off. I shouldn't, though, or you'll never improve. You'll spend the rest of your life driving some woman to distraction—or divorce."

Milo looked chagrined. "I can't help what goes on with the job. Mulehide never understood that part."

"She didn't want to. She was selfish. That's what's at the heart of most failed relationships." It was the first time I'd criticized Milo's ex.

"You bet," the sheriff agreed. "Everything had to be her way. The house, the yard, the kids. I felt like a cipher."

I was neither inclined nor qualified to act as marriage counselor. "You wouldn't talk to her," I said flatly, and picked up my bourbon glass.

"It was always the same old crap," Milo asserted, then eyed me speculatively. "So you think I'm crummy husband material, huh?"

"Not crummy. Just hauling around a lot of bad habits and an inflexible attitude."

He reached over and held my chin between his thumb and forefinger. "Are you saying you wouldn't take a chance on me?"

My jaw couldn't drop because Milo was holding it. "No. Yes. What do you mean?"

His hand fell away. "Well ... I've been thinking. I really missed you while you were gone. We've been going together for what? A year?"

I sighed. Men are so rotten at details, as Vida often reminded me. "Over a year and a half. Twenty months, to be exact."

"That's a long time," Milo said. "Anyway," he went on, shifting awkwardly on the sofa, "it dawned on me that maybe we should think about getting married. Or wouldn't your church allow it?"

It wasn't a question of what the Catholic Church allowed. "I don't think so," I said, giving Milo a sad little smile. "I just told you, I don't think I'm marriage material."

"You don't know. You've never tried it." Milo looked bewildered.

"That's not a very good argument for getting married," I pointed out.

"Is it because I flunked the first time?"

I shook my head. "Not really." I hesitated, then covered his big hand with mine. "It's me, Milo. I don't think I'm the marrying kind."

He sat back on the sofa, gazing up at the beamed ceiling. "So you're satisfied with going along the way things are?"

I was hoping he wouldn't ask. And yet he had to, or else the burden of truth would fall on me.

I kept my hand on his. "I think we need a break."

I felt him tense. "As in breakup?"

My attempt at a smile was dismal. "That sounds like teenage stuff. We're friends, aren't we? I don't ever want to lose that."

He was silent for quite some time. "Is it all that dumb

stuff you mentioned? The dishes and the TV and the dirty clothes?"

"No. If that really bothered me, I *would* have said something. It's me. I feel . . ." I didn't know how to say it. I wasn't even sure what I wanted to say. "I just feel uncertain. It's not fair to string you along because I like your company and the intimacy and the sex and the companionship."

"You don't love me." It wasn't a question.

"I do. But not the way you mean, or want me to." The confusion on his long face was disturbing, more so than I'd expected. "Do you love me? You've never said so."

Milo slipped his hand out from under mine and fingered his chin. "I think so. Like you said, we're not teenagers. What the hell *is* love, anyway?"

"I don't know." But I did. I remembered it vividly, wonderfully, painfully.

"Okay." He took a last sip of Scotch, then stood up. "I'll pass on dinner. You haven't put the steaks on yet, I take it?"

I shook my head. "I haven't even thawed them." Maybe I'd known all along it would come to this.

"Okay," he repeated, then picked his jacket up from the back of the sofa, ruffled my hair, and started for the door. "See you around, Emma."

"Sure."

Milo left.

Vida was holding forth in the news office, excoriating everyone on the staff, including me. It was Wednesday, October 23, and she had just returned from Cannon Beach the previous night. This week's edition of *The Advocate*, which I had been able to supervise, had just come off the press.

"Carla, I fail to see how you could cover the pudding-off at the Congregational church without taking a picture of the winning pudding!"

"Jeez, Duchess," Leo murmured, "it's a *pudding*, for chrissakes!"

"Hush, Leo, and mind your mouth." Vida was giving Carla her most intimidating look. "Well?"

Carla tossed her long black hair over her shoulders. "That's because Violet Hollenberg dropped it. She was holding it up with the blue ribbon on it, and Ione Erdahl bumped into her. All that was left was glop."

"Ooooh!" Vida yanked off her glasses and rubbed her eyes. "What good is a pudding-off with no pudding?"

"You've still got a picture of the winners," Carla pointed out.

"Violet's not looking at the camera, Lorena Clay has her eyes closed, and Ione's smile is much too artificial," Vida fumed. "Was Ione third? I suspect she ran into Violet on purpose."

Carla said nothing. Since my return, her usual vivacious manner had been replaced by a detached, otherworldly demeanor that suggested she might be in love. Or on drugs.

"Ginny," Vida was saying to our office manager, "you might reconsider bringing your baby to work. He threw up on three days' worth of my mail."

"It was only one day," Ginny countered. "And it was just handouts you'd never use."

"Ginny can bring Brad if she wants to," I declared, annoyed at Vida's preemption of my authority.

Vida ignored me. "I cannot think," she said, putting her glasses back on and turning to Leo, "how you could possibly run the Skykomish County Planned Parenthood ad next to the birth announcements on my page! Did you bother to read the copy?"

"Sure," Leo replied cheerfully. "I wrote it."

"It's unbelievably tasteless," Vida declared. " 'Unwanted pregnancy' and 'Don't rush into motherhood' indeed! We'll have calls from parents, grandparents, uncles, and cousins."

Leo appeared unperturbed. I, however, was next.

"I understand you inserted that equally indecent item in 'Scene' about Wilbur Hinshaw losing his dicky."

"He did. It was at the Moose Lodge. They were dressed up for some kind of ceremony. Ed told me about it." I was trying to keep a straight face. Certainly it wasn't any worse than one of Vida's recent 'Scene' observations wherein she'd noted that, *After a very hectic summer season, Park Ranger Wes Amundson's wife Annagreta was glad that her husband's business was falling off.*

Leo had erupted into laughter. "Hey, I just got a great idea! Maybe we should start calling it '*Ob*scene Around Town.' How do you like that, Duchess?"

The black look that Vida gave Leo would have withered most people down to their socks. But our ad manager kept laughing. Vida got up from her chair and stomped out of the office.

Ginny picked up Brad, who had been rolling around on the floor, and went into the front office. Leo started to say something to me, but his phone rang, and he merely winked. I hadn't asked him about his get-together with Tom Cavanaugh. I didn't intend to. There was always the possibility Leo might mention their meeting at some point. If so, I'd listen. Politely.

Carla was staring off into space, humming. My reporter was definitely living in another world these days. Eventually, she'd tell me why. I'd listen to her, too. Listening was part of my job.

I decided to follow Vida. I didn't like having her, as she would phrase it, "on the peck."

My House & Home editor had reached the corner, by the Venison Inn. "Hey," I called, "wait up!" I virtually ran past Cascade Dry Cleaners and the restaurant. "Where are you going?"

With a nod, she indicated farther along Front Street. "The GM dealership. I brought the Buick in this morning to make sure everything was all right after the body shop finished with it in Seaside."

"How are they?" I asked, not having had a chance to inquire during what had turned out to be an unusually busy Wednesday morning.

"The Imhoffs? Or what's left of them?" Vida's tone was thorny, though her anger with me seemed to have run its course. "Derek and Dolores are staying on at the house. At present, Stacie is moving in with a family in Seaside. The daughter is a close friend. What she'll do after she graduates from high school, I don't know. I'm glad nothing terrible happened to Derek and Stacie. I was so afraid that Molly . . . might not be able to stop herself." Vida's voice dropped, then resumed its normal tone. "Marlin is trying to plea-bargain. The marijuana crop was burned by the authorities over the weekend. Rett wants to sue Clatsop County."

We were passing the local TV repair shop and AlpNet, the computer store. Unlike Cannon Beach, there was no bright fall sunshine. Alpine was overcast, and it had been raining off and on all week.

"And Rosalie?" I asked.

"She's coping. What else can she do? As it turns out, she likes Dolores. If Derek marries her, maybe she and Rosalie can become close. Dolores needs family and Rosalie needs a friend. Walt's no use and Rett's impossible."

"Rosalie seems like a nice woman, really," I remarked as we waited for a UPS truck to cross Sixth Street. "Will you keep in touch?"

To my surprise, Vida shook her head. "I think not. What's the point? We have very little in common."

"But you and Rosalie both married Runkels," I pointed out.

Vida was marching toward the side entrance that led to the service department. "We're not related. As for the youngsters, they never took to me. Derek and Stacie are still strangers. Blood isn't always thicker than water. Things aren't the way they used to be," she continued, looking wistful. "Family doesn't seem to mean what it used to. I suppose some of it can be blamed on all the divorces. It's a terrible thing, but the ties that bind no longer do."

Vida's reaction surprised me. She had invested so much of herself in the Imhoff tragedy. Had she been a lesser being, I would have suspected Vida of turning her back on the remaining Runkels because they were tainted. But my House & Home editor wouldn't do that. She was being realistic, shunning self-delusion, and, as she would put it, using *sense*.

Vida greeted Trout Nordby, who, with his brother, Skunk, owned the local GM dealership. Vaguely recalling that the Nordbys' real names were John and Robert, I whiled away the short wait by wondering how they'd gotten their nicknames. I'd probably heard at some point; certainly Vida would know. Meanwhile, I tried to screen out the shop's noise and ignore the various smells of grease and gasoline.

"I told them to go ahead and do a tune-up," Vida announced. "Otherwise, everything seems fine."

We went back out onto Sixth Street, where it had started to drizzle again. "Say, Vida," I said, trying to sound abject, "I'm sorry about the Wilbur Hinshaw item. I didn't intend to embarrass him—or you."

"I'm sure you didn't," Vida responded rather absently. "People have such naughty minds." At the corner, she poked me. "See that? Francine Wells just went into her apparel shop wearing a cape! Did you notice Trout Nordby's bandage on his left wrist? He hurt it trying to get a stump out of his backyard. Ah!" She stopped, right in the middle of crossing Sixth. "The car that just went by—that was Ethel Pike with her grandson, Bickford, wearing a jester's cap on his head. He'll be two next week, just before Halloween."

Down Front Street we went, with Vida's head swiveling like a searchlight. Autumn leaves—real ones—filling Harvey's Hardware's display window; a cutout of Tom Hanks in *That Thing You Do!* outside the Whistling Marmot Theatre; County Commissioner George Engebretsen greeting potential voters on the courthouse steps; Donna Wickstrom leading her day-care charges in a train of colorful plastic cars.

At the door to *The Advocate*, I gave Vida's arm a squeeze. "What's that for?" she asked.

"I'm glad you're back," I said.

Vida offered me a small smile. "So am I."

I, too, was glad to be back. The ocean was fascinating, the coastline beautiful. But I preferred the mountains and the forests. Sunshine was pleasant, but after a while I yearned for rain. If I had to live in a small town, I'd rather be in Alpine.

By chance—or maybe design—I hadn't seen Milo all day. For the first time it dawned on me that he wouldn't call or come by. The thought made me sad.

But that was my choice. I gathered up my belongings and walked through the empty newsroom. It was just after five, and the rest of my staff had already left. Outside, my beloved, aging Jag waited in its accustomed parking space. The rain was coming down harder, and it was almost dark.

I glanced down the street, past the hobby shop and Parker's Pharmacy, to the sheriff's headquarters. Milo's Cherokee Chief was still there.

I could picture him at his cluttered desk or behind the curving counter in the front office. He would be going over paperwork or getting reports from his deputies or listening to a call from somewhere in the damp, dark corners of Skykomish County. His wide mouth would turn down. The hazel eyes would be wary. He'd take off his regulation hat and brush back the graying sandy hair.

I knew him so well.

He knew me not at all.

I went home alone.

In Alpine, murder always seems to occur in alphabetical order—and you can be sure Emma Lord, editor and publisher of *The Alpine Advocate,* is there to report every detail.

Don't miss any of
the Emma Lord mysteries,
beginning with

THE ALPINE
ADVOCATE

As editor-publisher of *The Alpine Advocate*, Emma Lord is always in search of a good story. But when Mark Doukas—heir to the richest old man in town—is murdered, Emma gets more than she bargained for.

THE ALPINE
BETRAYAL

Dani Marsh—former Alpine resident, now Hollywood star—returns to Alpine for some location shooting in the Cascade Mountains only to become embroiled in the murder of her ex-husband. Once again, Emma Lord has to do some heavy investigating to get to the bottom of the story.

THE ALPINE
CHRISTMAS

It's Christmastime in Alpine, and that means snow, carolers, Christmas trees . . . and murder. The discovery of one woman's leg and another woman's nude, half-frozen body in the lake leads Emma Lord and her House & Home editor, Vida, into a deadly holiday.

THE ALPINE
DECOY

The arrival of a young African-American nurse in Alpine is news enough in this predominantly white community. When a second newcomer—a young black man—is found dead, Emma Lord suspects that something sinister is afoot.

THE ALPINE
ESCAPE

When Emma Lord decides to take a few days off, she expects some time alone to do some soul-searching. Instead, she is caught up in a century-old mystery: Her friends have found the skeleton of an unknown young woman in their basement. . . .

THE ALPINE
FURY

The Bank of Alpine has been a fixture in Alpine for generations, but suddenly something fishy seems to be going on. Emma Lord decides to investigate—and finds the bank's sexy blonde bookkeeper strangled to death at a local motel.

THE ALPINE
GAMBLE

The year's biggest news story is the development of a luxury spa around Alpine's mineral springs—and the controversy surrounding it. But even those who predicted that the spa would bring sleaze and "Californicators" didn't expect to be confronted with murder.

THE ALPINE
HERO

In the facial room of Stella's Styling Salon,
Emma Lord stumbles across the body of a
woman, anonymous under a mud pack,
throat slashed. As rumors begin to fly,
shady strangers turn up in town, and a
young woman disappears—making Emma
more determined than ever to scoop this
story.

THE ALPINE
ICON

Glamorous Ursula Randall returns to
Alpine to marry her third husband—only
to be murdered, her body dumped facedown in the river. As Emma Lord hunts for
a stop-press story, a snake-in-the-grass
killer, unappeased by one murder, slithers
unnoticed through the shadows. . . .

by Mary Daheim

Published by Ballantine Books.
Available at your local bookstore.

MARY

DAHEIM

Available in your local bookstore.
Published by Ballantine Books.